The Passion
Sins of Our Sons

Little Vinnie Calabra—Sent from Sicily to kill his half brother, Mickey Boy, he has been secretly anointed as the next don of the Family. . . .

Freddie Falcone—Mickey Boy's underboss, he is a pillar of loyalty in a sea of treachery, and his antic sense of humor helps keep Mickey Boy sane. . . .

Rosalie DeStefano—Beautiful, driven, and raised in the ways of the mob, she's torn between burning desire and intense hatred for Mickey Boy. . . .

Joe Augusta—Grief has charted his purpose in life: to exact bloodthirsty revenge against all those closest to Mickey Boy. . . .

Praise for Sonny Girard's Debut
Blood of Our Fathers

"Sonny Girard's impressive debut novel is written in tight, clean prose, and will provide its readers with an insider's gutsy look at wiseguys and wannabes, their enemies and their friends."
—John Westerman, author of *Sweet Deals*

"A hard-hitting sex-and-violence tale that cries out to be made into a movie. . . ."
—*Toronto Sun*

"Girard gives us more. We get the kind of detail that's often missing in other novels of this ilk. Loyalty, intimacy, and a networld of chilling betrayals by husbands and wives make this a different kind of Mafia book."
—*The Province* (Vancouver)

Books by Sonny Girard

Blood of Our Fathers
Sins of Our Sons

Published by POCKET BOOKS

SINS OF OUR SONS

SONNY GIRARD

POCKET **STAR** BOOKS

New York   London   Toronto   Sydney   Tokyo   Singapore

An *Original* Publication of POCKET BOOKS

A Pocket Star Book published by
POCKET BOOKS, a division of Simon & Schuster Inc.
1230 Avenue of the Americas, New York, NY 10020

ISBN: 0-671-74515-8

First Pocket Books printing January 1995

10 9 8 7 6 5 4 3 2 1

POCKET STAR BOOKS and colophon are registered trademarks of Simon & Schuster Inc.

Stepback art by Diane Sivavec

Printed in the U.S.A.

"You're So Right For What's Wrong In My Life," Copyright 1973 Razzle Dazzle Music, Inc., assigned Aldor Music.

SINS OF OUR SONS

Prologue

IN A DANK, DREARY WINE CELLAR, TWO MEN SAT FACING EACH other across a wooden table fashioned from an upended barrel. In the center of the table a single candle flickered, illuminating the items around it: a seedy, brown leather Bible with half its pages torn out; a Moorish dagger; a large, clumsy, automatic pistol.

"These, *figlio mio,* are your destiny . . ." the small, bald man whispered in Sicilian dialect while waving his hand over the crude tabletop, ". . . if you can overcome what stands in your way."

He opened the Bible and laid his hand on the first remaining page, yellowed with age and curling at the edges.

"This is the page that will burn in your palm," he continued in Sicilian; his voice remained low and conspiratorial.

Turning his attention to the knife, the old man said, "This dagger has been in my family for centuries, and has drawn the blood from generations of mafiosi hands; a symbol of Sicilian blood that was shed to drive the invaders away." He looked at the pistol and shrugged. "Just a gun, probably

1

lifted from one of Il Duce's puppet clowns, but a symbol of how we live and die."

Across from the old man, Little Vinnie Calabra sat silently, watching the old man's shadow dance eerily on the stone wall behind him. Little Vinnie's heart thumped with a mixture of excitement and contained rage. His fists clenched into tight balls and his mouth felt sour and dry.

The old man, Don Genco Salso, Mafia boss of Acireale and all of Catania Province, gathered up the three items into a piece of black velvet cloth. "But until you solve the problem with your half brother," he said, "there is nothing I or any of us in *la cosa nostra* can do for you. We are honor bound to respect his word and wishes, as he was designated heir by my dear friend, your father, Don Vincenze, before being taken from us, may he rest in peace."

Don Genco grabbed Little Vinnie's hand and held it tightly in his, the strength of his grip surprising the younger man.

"I've told you that the only way I could bring you into our thing is with his permission. What I did not tell you, and will deny ever letting pass my lips, is that if he should pass away, his wishes will be buried with him. *Finito! Tu capisce?*"

Little Vinnie nodded. Mickey Boy had to die!

1

December 12: Todt Hill, Staten Island

MICKEY BOY MESSINA SLIPPED ONE HAND UNDERNEATH LAUREL'S breast to cradle its bare flesh. Each tiny sucking motion seemed to vibrate through his hand, connecting him with the lifeblood of both Laurel and their four-month-old daughter, Hope, who, eyes closed, fed steadily from her mother's erect nipple. So overcome with passion for these two females in his life was Mickey, that he wished he could draw the milk from his wife's body himself and deposit it directly into their baby's little mouth. Instead he squeezed gently on Laurel's breast, his regulation of Hope's diet through the increased stream of fluid serving as a small substitute.

It amazed him how much life could turn around in such a short time. Just one year before, he'd been a miserable emotional wreck, having lost Laurel, who'd fled to Florida because she'd been disgusted with his mob lifestyle. One year ago he'd been lonely, filled with a bitterness and pain that had led to periodic violent explosions.

In between those ventings, the ruggedly handsome Mick-

ey Boy had been depressed and introspective. He'd questioned years of dictums drilled into his head by neighborhood mobsters, surrogates for the father he never knew.
Already past thirty, he'd wondered what he really had to
show for his years. A jail term for something he hadn't
done? A few lousy dollars? Some respect among street guys
who were fast losing the understanding of what honor and
respect really meant?

But Laurel had returned, and life had improved. At least
that part of his life: the personal part, having nothing to do
with mobs or mobsters, with danger or responsibility for
almost everyone he came in contact with. Even now, while
permeated with affection, Mickey was still a miserable
wreck, feeling trapped by the very lifestyle he'd almost lost
Laurel over. He had realized only too late that his shiny
vision of the underworld had been tarnished from the first.
Thank God Freddie Falcone, his reliable pal and consigliere,
had promised to find a way to get him out—eventually.

"Gotta go," Mickey Boy finally said, with a sigh. He bent
and kissed Laurel's breast, stretched taut and swollen with
mother's milk, then planted a kiss on Hope's head. The
smell of baby lotion in her reddish hair, twisted into a single
curl, made him smile. He nuzzled his lips along Hope's
scalp, feeling the fontanelle, that fissure of membrane in her
soft skull that would soon heal shut. Knowing how vulnerable the infant was both frightened him and flooded him with
a fierce, protective love. "I wish I didn't have to," he said,
then shrugged, adding, "but . . ."

Laurel placed one hand behind his neck and drew him to
her for a kiss. Her tongue licked a circle around his lips.

"You know, I really believe that," she said. "And it makes
me feel good."

When their eyes met, it sealed once more unspoken
understandings; a sort of telepathic communication they'd
developed in their eight-month-old marriage, which contin-
uously sealed an agreement to always be together. Now,
nothing would keep them apart.

Gone were Frank Sinatra's songs of lost love, like "Only
the Lonely" and "Guess I'll Hang My Tears Out to Dry,"
that had seemed to have been specifically targeted at him.
Now, in Mickey's mind, Old Blue Eyes gently crooned

4

"You're So Right." Yes, Laurel was right for what was wrong in his life, and did fill every void.

Mickey propped the white eyelet pillows behind Laurel—the whole room was like a cloud: white furniture and fluff, white carpet—kissed her again; breathed in the clean fragrance of her dusty blond waves; drew warmth from her. He soaked in the motherly look of her, wishing he had a camera to capture that perfect moment forever.

"What about Christmas Eve?" he asked. "Did my mother say she'd come for sure?"

"Yes . . ." Connie Messina had said she would take a break from caring for Alley and his family, in Boston, and spend a few days. ". . . and my parents, and the Buster family, and half of New York City. The only one who won't come is your brother," Laurel said with a smirk.

Just as well, Mickey Boy thought. Though he and Alley had come to a truce over his having married Laurel, it was a cold truce that made everyone concerned uncomfortable.

"And we got plenty of food?" he asked, brushing back his thick dark hair, which had already begun to turn silvery at the temples.

"Enough for the other half of the city that wasn't invited," Laurel teased. "Just in case they decide to drop by. And, before you ask, the decorations will all be in today—mechanical Santa, Rudolph with the nose that lights up, singing elves—the whole works."

"You know, I really wish I could stay; make sure they do it right. Or better yet, do it myself." He sighed. "Wait for me to get time, though, an' Christmas might go out of style by then."

Laurel moved Hope to suckle the other breast. "Get out of here," she said, smiling. "Just make sure you're around on Friday, like you promised, to go shopping uptown . . . and dinner at Rockefeller Center."

"How about we lock in for the day instead? I'll cook, you take it easy."

"Mickey!" Laurel said, her voice moving up an octave. "My whole life is taking it easy. I want to get out."

"Well then, how about we take a room at the Plaza or the Waldorf . . . don't tell nobody where we are. Dinner by candlelight, the works."

"Mickey!"

"Just kidding," Mickey Boy said, accepting the fact that he couldn't win this one. "Rockefeller Center . . . I already made the reservation." Another thing he'd have to remind Freddie Falcone to take care of.

Mickey Boy Messina started toward the shower, truly annoyed at having to leave his wife and child and the comfort of his home. He stopped before entering the bathroom and slipped a Chipmunks Christmas tape into the bedroom's stereo.

"She knows," Mickey said, turning back to face Laurel and Hope as Alvin's voice squeaked out "Jingle Bells." "She knows it's for her. You know, they say that whatever you play for a kid when they're little, they come back to it later, after they go through the rock and roll stage." Smiling, he headed for the shower again.

"Great," Laurel called from behind. "One day we'll have a thirty-year-old woman addicted to chipmunks the way you are to Sinatra. I can't wait."

"Hey, don't talk about Old Blue Eyes today. It's his birthday!"

Despite not wanting to leave the house, Mickey Boy showered with a smile on his face. Yes, life had turned around pretty good, he told himself—especially for someone who was home from jail less than twenty-four months. Instead of bitching about the bad parts, he thought, from now on he would be more thankful for the good.

Warm water ran over his face and into his mouth as he sang, "You're so right . . . for what's wrong . . . with my life . . ."

2

December 12: Laurentian Mountains, Canada

KNEE-HIGH IN SNOW, JOE AUGUSTA LOOKED WITH SATISFACTION at the glowing wreath in the window of the chalet he'd rented in St. Sauveur des Monts. His eyes moved upward to the smoke drifting out of the stone chimney. Nothing in the world could give a warmer feeling than those cottony white streamers against a chilling gray-blue sky. Too bad Chrissy couldn't see it, he thought, his face frozen in a taut smile beneath his beard—full and black and streaked white with suffering. *Poor, darling Chrissy. First Christmas in Heaven.*

Joe lifted the collar of his red plaid mackinaw against the wind and bent to shovel a little closer to the home-built brick barbecue that peeked out of one of last night's drifts. Steaks would taste a hell of lot better grilled in the open air now than in the summer, he told himself, trying to shake the image of the once lively sixteen-year-old he'd finally buried on a slope overlooking the lake.

Yes, those steaks would certainly taste good, Joe thought, tossing another shovelful of snow to his left.

But much as the former director of the Shore Haven Funeral Home and ex-underboss of the Calabra Crime Family tried to focus his thoughts elsewhere, the knowledge that Christmas was near forced him back to think of Chrissy. Chrissy, his poor innocent child, the life blasted from her before she'd had a chance to live. He, as much to blame as the others.

"Where's *Don* Vincenze now?" he asked his dead daughter, seeing her virginal glowing face and ebony curls as clearly as if she were perched on the barbecue before him.

7

"Gone Vincenze is more like it." Chuckling, he said, "Get it, Chrissy? Get it? *Gone* Vincenze?"

Joe smiled, remembering himself up on the roof, watching the front of the church across the street, feeling his heart beat fast when the doors opened and Don Vincenze Calabra stepped into the sunlight. He could see the don as clearly as if he were still alive, taking his last breath in the crosshairs of his Weatherbee .270; could see the don's head rock back from the bullet's impact; could see the red splatter all over the fancy doors; could see him die once again.

But killing that bastard, Vincenze, hadn't settled the score. Nor excused Joe himself. No, there was still Richie DeLuca, awaiting trial for Chrissy's murder in Brooklyn's House of Detention . . . and whoever else was involved in the shooting . . . and, yes, that other bastard . . . all to be taken care of. Only then would he be able to end his own purgatory and join Chrissy in Heaven. Only then.

Once more foregoing the snowblower that sat inside the wooden shed, Joe committed himself to more punishing work with the shovel.

Good woman, your mother. Joe spoke silently to Chrissy when, having cleared the path required to manage dinner, he entered the main room of the chalet.

Marie Augusta sat curled around their nine-year-old daughter, Elizabeth, in a corner of the brown tweed sofa, reading to her from a book of Robert Frost's poetry:

"... They cannot scare me with their empty spaces
Between stars—on stars where no human race is."

Never complains once, he thought. Just does what she's gotta do.

Still talking silently to Chrissy, Joe went about his before-dinner chores. He dragged kindling from beneath the wooden porch, then carried it up and stacked it near the fireplace. He tasted the venison he'd been curing in his makeshift smokehouse. He checked his guns.

With some time still left, Joe Augusta plodded down the winding path he'd cleared to the mailbox on the main road. Not that he got mail that often. Outside of one person back home, in Brooklyn, no one he knew had any idea that the name Leone scratched on the black box referred to either him, Marie, or Lizzie. Only a monthly rent statement from the property's French-Canadian owner, an occasional advertisement from a local business, or the daily newspapers from Montreal and New York, ever brought the inside of the cold metal container to life.

Once again the *Gazette* and the *Times* were the only occupants of the mailbox. Maybe tomorrow the letter he was waiting for would come. Maybe the next day. Maybe never.

Given a choice, he wouldn't trust anyone. But with both the authorities and every half-assed mob guy in New York looking for him, it was either have faith in someone else or remain totally out of touch. Faith was the answer. Faith. Faith that Chrissy would help him accomplish his mission.

Joe had just retrieved the papers and tucked them under his arm when he heard a sound coming from around the curve of white-capped firs behind him. Moving quickly, he dug into his mackinaw for the .45 automatic which was as much a part of him as his flesh, and, having nothing to dive behind for cover, he rolled around to the back side of the mailbox post, hoping it would deflect a bullet if need be.

"Ça va!" yelled the old man, André, who lived in the castle at the top of the mountain. Dressed in a navy peacoat and a knit longshoreman's cap, André was being dragged along the winding road by his Labrador, DeGaulle.

"Ça va bien," Joe called back. His voice trailed off to a whisper, *"Ça va bien."* Suddenly, his insides seemed to collapse. Couldn't go on like this too much longer, he told Chrissy. Had to take care of business soon. Had to get his satisfaction—their satisfaction—from Richie DeLuca; from Buster Alcamo and that kid, Butch something-or-other; and most of all, from Don Vincenze's blood—from his son, Little Vinnie, and from his other bastard offspring . . . from Mickey Boy.

3

December 12: Todt Hill, Staten Island

MICKEY BOY'S CONSIGLIERE—OR ADVISOR—FREDDIE FALcone, waved a piece of paper as Mickey Boy entered his car. Freddie's tightly drawn lips and set jaw belied his normally humorous nature.

"Taxes! Fuckin' taxes!" Freddie yelled. "Hard-ons wanna indict me on a misdemeanor for not filing in the last quarter, before I sold the restaurant."

"Did you file?"

"No. But that's not the goddamn point. If it was John Shpeeliabeep, they wouldn't even bother, but 'cause it's me, they wanna make a fuckin' federal case."

"Yeah, but you ain't John whatever-you-said. You're a big-time gangster now," Mickey Boy teased, enjoying the bright pink flush of Freddie's face against his silver hair. "You're an important catch."

"Important, my cock! If they knew all I did was hold your little prick when you pee, they'd laugh me off the FBI blotter." Laughing himself, Freddie crumpled up the paper and tossed it over his shoulder onto the backseat of his Mercedes. "Fuck 'em. I like being a gangster."

Despite his mood having soured once again at having to leave his home, Mickey Boy laughed along. Freddie had always been able to do that—make him laugh. Freddie's hopes to be a stand-up comic had been squashed early on by old-time neighborhood mafiosi, who had looked on entertainers as degenerates. Young, and in awe of those whose values shaped much of his area's youth, Freddie had let himself be steered to other paths, some legal, some not. As a result, he had been the funniest bartender, the funniest restaurateur, and the funniest mob associate Mickey Boy had ever known. Even now, as consigliere, though he'd toned down his humor and taken to wearing tinted glasses that made him look more dignified, the gray fox could tickle Mickey Boy's laugh mechanism at will.

None of that humor, however, took away from Freddie's wisdom and insight into mob life or his seriousness about handling Calabra Family business. More important, Mickey Boy believed, was Freddie's unswerving loyalty to him, not only as his superior, but as a human being—one with extraordinary problems.

"You know," Freddie said, "come to think of it, the only thing the government ain't taxed yet is my prick. An' that's probably because ninety-five percent of the time it's out of work, three percent of the time it just hangs around, and two percent of the time it's in a hole. Besides," he added, laughing at his own joke, "it's got two dependants, an' they're both nuts!"

As usual, Mickey Boy laughed more at Freddie's comically distorted faces and wild hand flourishes than at the joke, which, also as usual, he'd heard many times before.

When his laughing had subsided, Mickey Boy slipped one of Sinatra's "Capitol Years" albums into the tape player, raised the volume to interfere with any listening devices that might have been planted in Freddie's car, and turned to matters at hand.

"What does the old bastard want now?" he asked, referring to Don Peppino Palermo, the seventy-nine-year-old boss of the only clan comparable in size and wealth to the Calabra Family, which Mickey Boy now headed.

"Who knows?" Freddie replied.

"Maybe he's got some money to cut up from that office building we're doin' together on Broadway?"

"Sure," Freddie answered with a smirk. "Know how he cuts up money? He throws it all up in the air. Whatever sticks to the fuckin' ceiling is yours, whatever comes down is his."

"Love that old man."

A half hour later Mickey Boy and Freddie entered Don Peppino's musty, overstuffed den: red-on-red flocked wallpaper; antique-style gaslights; oil paintings of Sicily.

Typical greaseball, Mickey Boy thought, while shuddering inside.

Don Peppino, frail as a dry wishbone, greeted both men effusively, hugging and kissing first Mickey Boy, then Freddie. Though age clearly showed on the don—translucent, wrinkled skin; hunched back; wispy white hair—his eyes remained penetratingly dark and alert. And mean.

"Sette ca," Don Peppino said, waving toward two red armchairs. He shuffled to his desk, where he opened a black leather attaché case that had been sitting on top. Inside: state-of-the-art electronic equipment to detect government listening devices.

"Sit, sit," the don said again, pointing to the two provincial chairs that looked as if they had more memories than everyone in the room combined. The air stank of years of DeNobili cigars poisoning it.

Mickey Boy wondered how many times his father, Don Vincenze, had sat in that room; how he'd felt about the smell; what he'd thought of the withered old sonofabitch who looked as out of place checking the modern electronic equipment, twisting dials and reading meters, as a horse riding a man. What went on inside that seventy-nine-year-old's head? Could it leave Laurel a widow and Hope an orphan? If only his father had prepared him for all this, Mickey Boy thought, instead of remaining in the shadows of his life, never letting him find out he was his father until it was too late; until after the don's brains had been splattered over the church steps and Connie's lap by one of Joe Augusta's rifle shells.

The shot came out of nowhere, just as we stepped out of the church. Could still feel it whizzing past my ear. Heard the screams . . . death screams, from behind me. Screams that made my balls shrivel up into my body.

Dropped the crutch and fell over Laurel . . . dragged her down and covered her . . . tried to protect her from other bullets while yelling for everybody to move back into the church.

. . . No more bullets came.

And I saw it.

12

*Fuckin' blood everywhere . . . from the back of his head
. . . all over my mother's dress; the cream-colored dress with
lace by the chest. The dress she bought for what she called the
happiest day of her life: my wedding. His blood soaked
through the lace onto her skin. Even on her face . . . around
her mouth.*

*. . . And her screaming at me. "Help him, Mickey! Help
him, please . . . he's your father!"*

He's your father . . .
He's your father . . .
He's my father.

Returning from the lapse into his memory, Mickey Boy
unconsciously rubbed his leg, the one he'd hurt stopping Joe
Augusta's first attempt on Don Vincenze's life—before he'd
known it was his own father he was diving in front of. He
shook his head once to clear it. Freddie shot him a quizzical
look. Don Peppino had been too involved in his detection
equipment to notice.

Seemingly satisfied they would not be overheard, Don
Peppino poured hot espresso into three tiny cups, then
seated himself in the recliner, taking his own cup with him
but not serving Mickey Boy or Freddie.

"So, how you been?" Don Peppino asked, a smile on his
lips but not in his eyes.

"You know I'm still on parole. They could give me a
problem for being here."

"Don't worry," Don Peppino replied, chuckling. "I got no
record. The *dizgraziata* in charge of you might yell a little,
but his teeth can't bite . . . at least not for this." The don
sipped his coffee, then pointed at the other cups. "Go, take,
take."

Mickey Boy was about to get a little dig in at the old man
by declining the coffee when he caught Freddie's eyes
motioning no.

Freddie took one cup and served the other to Mickey Boy.

"You know, it musta been a year, no, maybe more, that *a
buon oumo* your father, sat here with me in this room," Don
Peppino began. "We made plans then, me an' him—a lot of
plans; plans for you; plans for *la cosa nostra.*"

Mickey Boy's foot tapped impatiently on the red floral

13

carpet. He hated the greaseball way of talking, beating around the bush before trying to stick it in your ass.

"Unfortunately, for all of us, he passed away before we could put those plans to work." Don Peppino swept one hand in front of him as if brushing crumbs off an invisible table. "But that was yesterday," he said coldly. Seeming to realize he'd triggered anger in Mickey Boy, he returned to a more sympathetic tone, saying, "After he died, I didn't want to put too many things on your head—you know I always been behind you one hundred percent." Dragging out his words in an almost singsong manner, he continued, "But now you're all settled in, an' it's time to do what we gotta do."

"An' that is?"

Don Peppino went on to explain to Mickey Boy and Freddie that both he and Don Vincenze had been convinced that five mob families in New York were just too many; that there was not enough manpower being groomed to support the setup they'd maintained since the Lucky Luciano days; that at least two of the families would have to be dissolved.

"Just like that?" Mickey Boy asked, snapping his fingers. "Who's gonna give up their crew without a fight?"

"My goombah, Giacomo . . ." Don Peppino said, referring to his close friend, Giacomo "Jack the Wop" LoPresti. The Wop, who was nearly as old as Don Peppino and had come to America from the same hometown in Sicily, had become leader of the old DiGiovanni Family after his two previous bosses had been murdered within eight months of each other. Mickey Boy had later found out that both murders had been carried out at Don Peppino's and Don Vincenze's shared behest.

". . . he wants to go with me," the old don continued about Jack the Wop. "He'll be my consigliere. Your father knew about it."

If he thought he could get away with it, Mickey Boy would have spit in the old man's face. What did Don Peppino think, that just because he was young, he could make a fool of him?

"My father was just gonna give you a whole crew, an' take nothing?" Mickey Boy asked. Though he'd overcome his initial difficulty in saying the word "father" in connection with the man he'd barely known, an internal strangeness persisted; his mind would snap to every time the double syllable passed his lips; a chill continued to attack his spine. "Sounds like a helluva guy—just not like him."

There was a lot Mickey Boy didn't know about Don Vincenze, Don Peppino said, his soft, condescending tone cutting sharply. Then he cackled, as if at some private joke. "No, no," he said. "But don't worry, your father gave nothing away; he gave *ghiaccio l'inverno* . . . ice in the winter."

The deal, as Don Peppino explained it, was that Rock Santoro was to bring his group in line with Mickey Boy, and be given a top position—underboss or consigliere—within the newly combined clan.

The last family, leaderless while its previous chieftain was being held without bail on enough RICO counts to sentence him well into the twenty-fifth century, would be split equally between the two remaining crews—Don Peppino's and Mickey Boy's.

"But he's dead, right?" Mickey Boy asked when Don Peppino had finished speaking.

"Chi?"

"My father," Mickey Boy answered. "And that means all bets are off?"

A cold stare hardened Don Peppino's hawklike features. "Agreements in our life go beyond anybody's living or dying," he said. "It's just too easy to die . . . if you know what I mean?"

"I know," Mickey Boy replied, struggling to keep from exploding over the veiled threat. "That's why I gotta feel good about whatever we do, right?"

"Naturalmente . . . of course."

"So why don't you give me a little while to think about this; time to talk to Freddie, some of my other men," Mickey Boy said. He'd already made up his mind to reject the don's proposal.

"Mah, sure. Take your time," Don Peppino replied. He leaned forward and in a hard, determined voice, added, "But hurry up. Good leaders make decisions, they don't just sit still an' hope things take care of themselves. They got balls . . . an' if they're wrong, they pay the price."

If there was one thing Mickey Boy was sure of, it was that he wasn't wrong; about Don Peppino; about anything. There was no way he'd take a turncoat like Rock Santoro, who had reportedly risen to power after murdering his last boss, into his confidence. Mickey Boy might "pay the price," as Don Peppino had threatened, but if he did, it certainly wouldn't be for stupidity.

Calling on all the patience and control he could muster to remain gracious, Mickey Boy spent another half hour with Don Peppino. They discussed the negative influence of black ghetto life on white youth, the prospects of an unusually warm winter, the right-wing bent of the Supreme Court. They purposely avoided any mention of issues that could bring them into direct confrontation: a freeze on making new members, common legitimate business interests, the previously mentioned melding of the five families into two.

Before leaving, Mickey Boy kissed Don Peppino on both cheeks.

"Statte buona, Miguito," the old don said. "Take good care of yourself."

"Yeah, you too. Stay well," Mickey Boy replied, while thinking, Fuck you, you old prick.

Don Peppino remained in his den after Mickey Boy and Freddie Falcone had left. He closed his eyes, lay his head back against his leather La-Z-Boy and thought. He mulled over the entire conversation, word for word, nuance for nuance, and facial expression for facial expression. He reviewed the talk until he felt a reaction to what had happened, rather than coming to an intellectually formulated point of view. Then he decided: this bastard son of Don Vincenze Calabra was no better than his father. It was time to do what he would have had to do anyway if Don Vincenze had lived, but with a better tool than he could ever have hoped for under those past circumstances. Times had changed. There was no longer room for even two families in New York. There would only be one to survive beyond his lifetime—his.

Dragging himself from his chair, Don Peppino went to his

desk, pulled out a fresh sheet of parchment-type stationery, and penned a sentence in Italian: *Get ready to come home— soon!* When he was done, he posted it to a Charles Leone in a suburb of Montreal.

4

December 15: Downtown Brooklyn

"HALF A CARTON FOR SIX MURDERBURGERS."

"You know I don't fuck with that shit. How about some dirty bird for tomorrow?"

"Man, the brothers'll hang me if I don't bring them joints around; givin' 'em to a European instead."

"Two packs apiece."

"Shee-it, man."

"Marboros. No generics."

"Two joints for a carton."

"Five."

"Four."

"You got it," Richie DeLuca said, sealing a bargain for his next day's meal: four "dirty birds"—quarters of greasy pint-sized chicken, stuffed into an empty plastic bread bag and dropped through the bars of his cell when the inmate cook came up from work.

"Sure you don't want none of these here murderburgers?" the cook asked, waving a bag of rock-hard meat. "Two for a pack."

"C'mon, Blood, man," Richie answered. "Get that foul shit away from my house. Smells like somebody died in that bag."

"How 'bout three?"

"C'mon, get that shit outta here."

17

"Four?"

"Blood!"

"Okay, how about a pack up front? For tomorrow, man. You know we cool."

"Take my money, you better bring my chicken, Blood. Can't run no games on this white boy. You know that, right?"

Everyone on the unit knew not to fuck with the white "Mafia boy" who'd set one black inmate's hair on fire in a dispute over a book of stamps, and who'd stabbed another in the groin over use of the phone. As one of only two white inmates on the floor, Richie's choices were to either be a monster or a perpetual victim, like the other white youth, a drug dealer from Ocean Parkway who turned over all his commissary to the butch-boys and was rumored to be giving them head too. Monster suited Richie just fine.

Richie laid back on his cot—three lumpy, plastic excuses for mattresses, which piled together were not as thick as a second-rate one outside—and stared up at the gray metal walls covered with jailhouse graffiti: a stick-figure woman with huge tits and cunt; a seductively realistic drawing of a gorgeous black woman's face; Death to Pigs; Fuck the Warden; Heavy '81; Li'l Poncho '91; Sex Machine the Homo. More than a goddamned year spent either cuffed to a hospital bed or stuck in this six-by-ten breadbin, shitting on an toilet with no seat, which doubled as a cooler for his milk and soda; staring at those Neanderthal scribblings as if they were top-rated television shows.

It was tiring. And depressing. And mind-numbing to think that if his forthcoming trial went the wrong way, he'd never see the streets again; be destined to spend the next thirty or forty years shut off from the real world. Stuck with Li'l Poncho and Sex Machine the Homo for the rest of his life.

Shit!

He wondered where Little Vinnie was. And what that half-a-hump was doing while he wasted away in a stinking cell that sweated the energy out of him in the summer and made his bones shrink in the winter. Probably having a good time, that goddamn scumbag.

Richie could picture the events that had put him in that

cell as if they'd happened the day before, rather than thirteen months earlier—and he did: day after day after unchanging day. He'd gone over every bit of conversation in his mind, repeating it in every conceivable way to imagine how it might have turned out better.

He hadn't even wanted to participate in the proposed murder of Skinny Malone that day. What did he give a shit about some petty snub, or whatever, that had prompted Buster to put a hit on Skinny? But an order was an order, and Mickey Boy was sitting in jail on a parole violation, unable to help get him out of the assignment. To make matters worse, Little Vinnie Calabra had not only attached himself to the job, without Buster knowing, but had taken over and become boss.

What if he'd refused to allow Little Vinnie to bully him and Butch Scicli into accepting him as leader that day? Why hadn't he had the balls to tell Little Vinnie, "Fuck you, you don't even belong here!" and reported him to Buster? Because Little Vinnie was the don's son, that's why, and one insult like that could keep him in the shithouse for years—if it didn't get him killed.

What if he'd stopped Little Vinnie when he realized that it wasn't Skinny Malone sitting in the car with a hat pulled over his eyes, but Chrissy Augusta? he'd asked himself over and over. Could he have stopped him? He'd tried screaming, yelling at Little Vinnie to stop, not to shoot. Could he have done more? Jumped over the Corvette? Distracted Little Vinnie? Shot the bastard instead?

But he hadn't, and Chrissy had died, her brains splattered on the Corvette's dashboard. Maybe he deserved to spend the rest of his life suffering in prison just for having witnessed the crime. Or maybe not. After all, he hadn't even fired a shot; hadn't killed anyone that day or any other. Guys that he knew were stone killers were out eating, drinking, and getting laid, while he laid there, preserved physically by the absence of distractions like liquor, girls, and hustling, but rotting inside. Wasn't there any goddamned justice in life? Obviously not.

"DeLuca, attorney visit!" came the guard's scream. "DeLuca, move your ass!"

"Coming, boss!" Richie yelled back while hurriedly

throwing on a clean set of tans—didn't need underwear since they were going to strip him naked and check up his ass anyway. Also no need for legal papers. That was what he—or more precisely, Mickey Boy, God bless him—paid a lawyer for. If Ira Golden didn't know what was going on, he certainly wouldn't.

A few minutes later, Richie plopped himself down on a plastic chair in front of the heavily girthed attorney. The room, though small, spare, and open to a guard's view through a window, at least was private enough for conversation.

"Since you didn't tell me what you wanted last time," Ira Golden said, "I used my own discretion. Thought you'd enjoy these." He held up a small paper bag. "Fried shrimps from Queen, down the block."

"Good choice. You sure this room ain't bugged?"

"I've been feeding you for more than a year, and you ask the same question each time. Yes, it probably is bugged, but no, they can't let us know that they've violated client-attorney privilege. Now, if you don't want the shrimp . . . ?"

"Are you crazy?" Richie answered. "Turn 'em over. I just don't want to get hit with a RICO one day, for eating illegally . . . four counts of shrimp, two cannolis, an' the big one: the dirty water hot dogs." He carefully opened the bag, unwrapped the shrimps, keeping them hidden so that the guard wouldn't spot them, then stuffed one into his mouth. "Mmmm. This is like I died an' went to Heaven." Still chewing, he cursed the other inmates, who would rather get drugs than a steak, or even fresh air.

"They'll live with no food and rats crawling on them, as long as they could get some shit to smoke or shoot in their fuckin' arms."

Richie went on to say that there should be two distinct types of jails. "One for those druggie hard-ons, where they juice 'em up an' let 'em sleep it off on a dirt floor, and one for normal guys, where you could live like a human being an' get whatever you want—lobsters, filet mignons, the whole bit."

"Well, jail may not be your problem for much longer," Ira Golden said, smiling. "We caught a great Christmas present last night, and your friend thought I should come personally and tell you."

Thank God he had one friend like Mickey Boy, Richie thought. Mickey Boy, having served six years in prison, knew the frustration of being locked up, and made sure Richie never felt cut off from the outside world. Having Ira Golden visit at least once every couple of weeks, and make additional visits to inform Richie of any new event in his case, did more for Richie's morale than anything short of freedom. Must be costing a pretty penny too, Richie mused. Fat lawyers like Golden didn't work cheap.

"What'd Santa bring?" Richie asked. "A pardon from the Pope?"

Ira Golden smiled, his cherubic cheeks turning a bright pink. "Not quite, but close. Judge Leonard had a heart attack."

New York State Supreme Court Justice Samuel B. Leonard had been assigned the case of *People* v. *DeLuca* as soon as an indictment had been handed up, and from the first day of his assignment he made no bones about the fact that he intended to see to it that Richie spent as much of his natural life behind bars as could possibly be arranged, and no matter how it had to be arranged—just as long as the law wouldn't be bent to a point where Richie would be given grounds for a reversal on appeal. He'd arbitrarily knocked down every one of the thirteen motions Ira Golden had submitted, often shaking his head and mouthing the word "Denied" while Golden was still speaking. In private he'd told Golden that he was going to crucify Richie DeLuca.

But Ira Golden and Mickey Boy had been smarter. Most defendants being held with no bail would rush to trial; take their shot at freedom quickly, or lose and be sent to a regular prison where conditions were better than in a detention facility. Richie would have done that too. Anything to get out of that stinking hellhole.

Mickey Boy, however, through Ira J. Golden, had advised Richie to play it cool, as if he were out on bail and had all the time in the world. Stall. Stall. Stall. Time could only heal, he said; take the case out of the limelight; let the public anger and thirst for vengeance subside. Besides, time could not help the State's case one bit; all it could do was weaken it.

Stall—and sit.

Stall—and rot.

Stall—and feel like you're losing your mind.

Now, it seemed, that strategy had paid off . . . in a way Richie never would have imagined. A heart attack . . . a goddamn sky-opening, light-at-the-end-of-the-tunnel heart attack. Yes, he thought, there is a God.

"What if the new judge we draw is just as bad?" Richie asked.

"Can't be any worse than Leonard would have been," Golden replied. "With any luck, we'll draw someone I'm intimately familiar with . . . at the very least, someone who will just treat us fairly. We might even get you bail." He shook his head. "Who would have ever believed Leonard would turn out that bad? After all, he was a Carter Democrat."

Later, after lights out, Richie lay awake on his three grungy mattresses, staring up at the stick figure's cunt and Li'l Poncho, still visible in the catwalk light that shone through the bars. He tried to feel optimistic about the possibility of bail and of a fair trial, but was afraid. Small hopes, he'd found in the last year, were only temporary, and made the loss of them that more painful.

Instead he replayed the events of that last night of freedom, that nightmare evening—all in slow motion.

Why was I even there? Never killed nobody, and never wanted to kill nobody.

Buster . . . that's why.

And Little Vinnie.

Followed that motherless bastard toward Georgie's Vette . . . hand so wet and slippery . . . thought I'd drop the .32 Buster gave me onto the ground.

My fuckin' hand shoulda fell off that night.

. . . Fuckin' eyes shoulda gone blind.

Saw the Irishman's blue cap . . . saw the curly black hair. Couldn't wait to get back to Butch Scicli, in our car.

. . . Saw the goddamned girl's legs sticking out of that blue and gray Catholic school skirt.

God, how I tried!

Calling that piece of shit, Little Vinnie, "No, no, don't shoot!"

His gun already in the air.

". . . Vinnie, don't shoot!"

"Vinnie, please don't shoot," Richie moaned as he envisioned Chrissy Augusta's brains splatter on the dashboard. The pain in his shoulder and chest, where he'd been shot by the off-duty cop who had happened upon the scene (and the pain in his hand as Butch had driven the getaway car over as the gunshots felled Richie), were nothing compared to the burning in his heart when he thought of poor Chrissy Augusta—and he cried.

5

December 23: Todt Hill, Staten Island

FRANK SINATRA CROONED FROM THE SPEAKERS IN FREDDIE Falcone's Mercedes. The lyrics reached inside Mickey Boy, who sat in the front passenger seat, and saddened him even more than he'd been throughout the holiday season.

Sure, it wasn't nearly as bad as last year, when he'd been pining over having lost Laurel, but it was bad enough, what with Don Vincenze having died.

At that moment, however, it was the memory of prison, and those who remained behind, that made him most melancholy. For them there would be no snow, mistletoe, nor presents on any tree.

Prison was supposed to harden men, Mickey Boy thought, not make them soft. But six years of vulnerability, of being psychologically naked—having someone check your asshole and under your balls after visits, watch you when you take a shit, and know everything about your family, background, and behavorial patterns—had sensitized him.

And Christmas was worst of all.

He could picture those who wouldn't be home for this Christmas, or many more, or any, ever again. He'd sent money to some of them; Christmas cards to many more. Little bits to make them know they weren't forgotten.

Was it near four o'clock? He checked his gold Piaget. Only one-thirty. Four o'clock would be count time; prisoners in facilities all over the country standing by their beds, while teams of correctional officers passed by—glancing sideways, staring without seeing; the less brilliant of them bobbing their forefingers to keep track—counting the warm bodies to make sure no one escaped, or as the inside joke went, to make sure no one broke in for the fine food the prisons offered.

Today the stand-up count would be for a bag of candy too. Or a gift box of sausage and cheese. Sausage or peppermints to take the place of a mother, son, or daughter.

Richie too.

Through the speakers Sinatra vowed to be home for Christmas, if only in his dreams.

No dreams, pal, Mickey Boy thought. I'll get you home.

"Talk about juggling hot coals," Freddie said, interrupting Mickey Boy's joyless reflections. "First this asshole P.O. of yours, then, when you get him outta the way, you got a bunch of *capodecimes,* that half of 'em are probably trying to figure out how they could get your spot, while they're kissing you on the cheek an' brown-nosing you—'A hundred years, you gotta live . . . Anything I could do? . . . My life is your life'—all that bullshit. Phony bastards!"

"They could have it," Mickey Boy replied. "Nobody's gotta ask twice for me to step down."

"Pazienza, pazienza. All things in good time. Today, worry more about why your parole officer would call you down on the day before Christmas Eve. It ain't to give you a fruitcake . . . though I think he may be. The way he looked at me that time I came up with you . . . like he was undressing me with his eyes," Freddie joked.

"Nah, he ain't a fag . . . maybe a little drunk most of the time," Mickey Boy replied. A lot drunk was more like it. What he needed was a gin patch instead of the nicotine patch he wore behind his ear.

"But that don't make him a bad guy," Mickey Boy went on. "He's certainly better now than when he used to live just to break my balls."

". . . I'll be home for Christmas," Sinatra repeated. ". . . If only in my dreams."

Poor Richie.

"He still gives me the creeps," Freddie continued on about the parole officer. He zipped through the toll section and onto the Verrazano Bridge toward Brooklyn, cursing the driver of a black Jeep Wrangler that cut in front of him.

Mickey Boy's spirits lifted slightly when Sinatra ended "I'll Be Home for Christmas" and began singing the happier "Christmas Waltz."

Freddie waited in the car while Mickey Boy went up to the fourth-floor office of the Eastern District's Federal Parole Department at 75 Clinton Street, in downtown Brooklyn. Mickey Boy signed in at the window, then took a seat to wait to be called by his parole officer, Anthony Steven Spositoro.

Why the fuck did Spositoro want to bother him today? Mickey Boy wondered, echoing Freddie's earlier sentiments. Sure, Spositoro had been a ball buster at first, had even violated Mickey Boy a little more than a year ago. And he'd become even worse for a time, after Buster Alcamo had arranged for some girl, Rosalie, to lie at the hearing and get him off the hook. That had really fired Spositoro's ass.

But all that had changed the night the blotchy-faced P.O. had run into Don Vincenze, who, with the help of two of his bodyguards, had brutally set Spositoro straight. No more harassment—or else.

Since that time, Spositoro had been almost meek, doing his job with a personal detachment that seemed painful to him but let Mickey Boy relax—at least that was one pressure off his back. Now, all he had to do was sign in once a month, and keep from being pinched on some new charge before his parole was up. Not too hard, considering how insulated he kept himself, and how little he left his home.

That was why Mickey Boy found Spositoro's call on the day before Christmas Eve so unnerving.

Mickey Boy lifted his arm to check the time, but couldn't. He'd left his tie and all his jewelry with Freddie. Didn't want to look too good. Why wave a gold flag in front of any government bull? Even one who was under control.

"Does Mr. Spositoro know I'm here?" Mickey Boy asked, guessing he had waited for about fifteen minutes.

The woman behind the window answered without looking at him. "Just relax," she said. "Someone will be with you shortly."

After another ten or so interminable minutes the front door opened and a chill wind seemed to enter the room in the form of a block of a man, about five feet seven inches tall, a couple of feet wide, and all gray: hair, coat, scarf, attitude.

"Mr. Messina," the gray block of ice said as he opened an interior door leading to one of the private offices. "Come with me."

Mickey Boy slowly stood. What the fuck was going on? he wondered as he stepped past the man, who shut the door behind them.

The man hung his hat on a rack, then, still wearing his coat and scarf, sat behind the desk and spread open a folder he'd been carrying. Without looking at Mickey Boy, he said, "My name is Mr. Halloran, and I'm your new parole officer."

"What happened to Spositoro?"

"Mister Spositoro, and it's really none of your concern. I'm here now, and I see we've got a couple of problems."

Mickey held his breath; his heart quickened; his palms felt wet. Was this going to be like last year, when Spositoro had cuffed him just before Thanksgiving and led him off to MCC to wait for a parole violation hearing to be set?

Not for fuckin' Christmas, he thought. *Please, God, not now.*

"I see you claim to be an outside salesman for—"

"I don't claim nothing," Mickey Boy interrupted. "I am."

Halloran continued as though Mickey Boy hadn't spoken. ". . . for Viva L'Italia Provisions. A Mr. Vizzini covers you while you meander all over the city, and we never know where you are." He looked up from the folder. "No more. Viva L'Italia's out. Get yourself a new job, Mr. Messina, one where I can visit you at least eight hours a day, or go back to jail."

Mickey Boy tried to be calm, despite feeling he would explode. "Wait a minute, my job's been okayed by—"

"Past tense. I am your keeper now, and it is my job to see that you stay out of harm's way . . . one way or another."

No sense arguing with this asshole, Mickey Boy told himself. The best thing was just to agree, then get Ira Golden on the case as quickly as possible.

"Okay," Mickey Boy said. "I'll start looking right after the holidays."

"You will have acceptable employment within seven days or your holiday will finish in a federal institution. If you cannot find a job, and need help, let me know now. I can get you to work by tomorrow morning."

"Thanks, but no thanks," Mickey Boy snapped. "Anything you could do, I, or my lawyer, could do better."

Halloran smiled. "Lawyers do not frighten me. And they do not extend your deadline one minute. Now, fill out this monthly report." He slid a form across the desk to Mickey Boy. "On second thought, I'll be moved into this office next week. You can bring the form with you when you come in to tell me where you'll be working. If you do not, this report will not mean a thing."

Mickey Boy found the parole officer's quiet confidence unnerving and infuriating. He angrily snatched up the form and stuffed it, crumpled, into his pocket.

"You done with me?"

Halloran stood and, ignoring Mickey Boy, went to the rack for his hat. He turned as he adjusted the brim, then picked up the folder and went to the door. Holding it open for Mickey Boy, he finally spoke. "See you on the job, Mr. Messina."

"That dirty cunt-faced puke!" Mickey Boy screamed. "Fuckin' hard-on Irish bastard! His fuckin' father shoulda flushed the load that made him down the fuckin' toilet!"

Freddie drove without replying. Though humor was a constant with him, it was obvious this was not the time for it. With Mickey Boy still ranting, Freddie paid the toll at the entrance of the Brooklyn Battery Tunnel. When he was in Manhattan, Mickey Boy was still cursing and screaming. A couple of minutes later Freddie pulled into a parking lot on the Chinatown side of Mulberry Street.

"What the fuck are you doing?!" Mickey Boy screamed. They were supposed to be at Buster's club, in Little Italy, for his annual Christmas party—administrative brass and captains of the Calabra Family required to appear; open invitation to any other made member of their crew. Another thing that thrilled him as much as a heart attack.

"I figured we'd stop by one of the Chinamen, down here. Give you a chance to cool off and think things out before we go to the club."

The burning blood in Mickey Boy's face made the outside temperature seem even colder than its thirty-eight degrees as he and Freddie walked around the corner toward Mott Street. They stopped into a Chinese bakery on Bayard Street and ordered coffee and lemon cakes.

"You okay now?" Freddie asked when they had eaten half the pastries.

"Yeah, thanks," Mickey Boy replied. "But you hadda see this guy. He was just like a piece of stone; didn't wanna know a fuckin' thing. An' quiet . . . scary quiet. Never raised his voice even this much," he said, pinching his thumb and forefinger close together. "Believe me, this guy's no Spositoro. I could feel big problems with him."

"Fuck him," Freddie said. "Turn it over to Golden. He'll know how to rip this Irishman a new ass. Just tell Golden he hates Jews . . . and, of course, lay some extra cash on him. Lawyers are like that." Leaning forward, he asked, "Did you hear about the three guys who went to a funeral: a businessman, a mob guy, and a lawyer?"

"No jokes now, please."

"Okay," Freddie said, throwing his hands up in surrender. "I'll save it. Unfortunately, we're gonna have a whole lifetime to complain about these bloodsuckers."

While eating a second helping of the light, spongy Chinese cakes, Mickey Boy and Freddie kicked around ideas about how to get Mickey Boy out of being stuck in one place all day for Halloran to find him.

"Maybe if this guy really gets on my back, I'll be no good for nobody, an' they'll pick somebody else to run things," Mickey Boy said.

"You know better than that," Freddie replied. "First they'd choose up sides, like, who hates who, then the both sides would put you an' me in a squeeze—one of those 'either you're with us or against us' kinda shit. Then would come the bodies dropping . . . all the guys we love, on both sides . . . and the wakes. Then the vultures: first that old fuck, Peppino, looking to glom everything we got that's worth more than a ceci bean, then the feds, to wipe up who's ever left. Sound pretty? Think that's what your old man had in mind for the future? Is that what you wanna leave?"

"An' what am I gonna leave if this Irish asshole sends me to jail? Will that make them happy? Will that make them hold together?"

"Maybe," Freddie said. "Especially since you only owe a year an' a half. Knowing you're in the can might be like kids being good while their mother's sick."

"I don't believe this shit!"

"What?"

"That going to jail is better for everybody than me being out."

"I only said maybe. But if you're talking about staying out and not taking control, like by going to meetings," Freddie added, "then the answer is yes, going to jail would be the lesser of two evils."

The trouble with him, Freddie said, making sure to inject that his criticism was that of someone who loved Mickey Boy like a brother, was that he was too idealistic, he didn't see the world, their world, for what it really was. Freddie understood that Mickey Boy had leapt to the top in one unintentional stroke, after Don Vincenze had been murdered, without having the benefit of uncovering the myths of their life one by one, as he would have had he progressed up the ladder a rung at a time.

"You gotta get over thinking about the way things should be, and live your life by the way they are," Freddie said. "Otherwise, my dear friend, you're gonna make us both be part of a pinochle game with your old man, wherever he is. An' I play like shit with those heavy wings on my back."

"Now who's not in reality? A fuckin' red tail an' horns are more like what we'll be wearing."

"Speak for yourself," Freddie said with an understanding

smile. The truth was, he said, that if he could, he would take over and release Mickey to live in peace somewhere with Laurel and Hope. But he, even as consigliere, didn't have enough of a track record to inspire confidence among the soldiers; and Buster, who'd been Don Vincenze's underboss, and remained in that position under Mickey Boy's rule, didn't have enough brains. "Everybody knows that he was nothing more than your old man's rottweiler."

Knowing Freddie was right didn't make Mickey Boy feel any better, or any more secure. He'd had enough of prison, and didn't relish taking a chance of going back because his father had been too conniving to spread power around.

"Come on," Freddie said. "Have another cake from these little yellow bastards that overran our neighborhood, then take a deep breath and be heroic—fat and heroic. Go out there an' make these fuckin' mental midgets we got around us know who's boss."

Freddie reached across the table and grabbed Mickey's wrist. Squeezing it affectionately, he said, "I promise you again, as soon as I see that either me or some other decent guy could take the reins and hold 'em, I'll find a way out for you. I swear on my dead mother."

Mickey sat without saying a word. All his life, from when he was a kid finding a sense of family in the streets, he'd dreamed about moving to the top; of being a wiseguy; of being a wiseguy's boss. From now on, he told himself, he'd be more careful of what he wished for.

Suddenly Mickey felt as though he needed air, as though he was being strangled from the inside.

Had to break it.

"No, fuck the Chinaman's cake," Mickey Boy finally said. "Let's go to what little bit of territory we got left and have some real goodies."

A queasiness welled up in Mickey Boy's stomach as they approached Buster's club, the Lower Manhattan Fishing Association, on the Little Italy side of Mulberry Street. Lost on him were the Italian reds, whites, and greens that mingled with glittery holiday decorations to welcome visitors. Lights and garlands stretched overhead from one side of the street to the other. Neapolitan Christmas songs decorated the air. Puffs of breath, like lively clouds of transparent cotton, danced to the music in front of cheery red faces.

Mickey Boy looked first to Buster's club, then at the Focacceria Villarosa, the Sicilian restaurant next door.

Thank God, nobody around, he thought. He rolled his window all the way up. "Keep moving," he ordered Freddie. "Don't slow down; just keep moving."

Freddie shot him a quizzical glance, but kept rolling slowly in the bumper-to-bumper traffic. He turned at Broome Street.

"Think anybody saw us?" Mickey Boy asked.

"Yeah, two zeppoles and a sfogliatelle," Freddie replied. "What the hell's going on? You okay?"

"No. I don't wanna go in."

"But we just went over that," Freddie replied.

"I don't know, I just don't feel right. Maybe we could set up meetings somewhere else?"

"Too late. These guys are already here," Freddie said. "Besides, they already been complaining that they don't see you enough."

"I'll see them. I just don't wanna do it stupid."

"Okay. How about if we go upstairs at the Villarosa?" Freddie asked. "We could have everybody slip upstairs there. At least it would make you look like you're trying to outfox your P.O., instead of looking like you got Kool-Aid running through your veins."

"Yeah, that's great . . ." Mickey Boy replied angrily, ". . . as long as nobody there goes bad within the next fifteen years."

"Statute of limitation is only five."

"Plus ten if they RICO you. Fifteen."

What had once been unthinkable—upper-level hoods, like Sammy "The Bull" Gravano and "Little Al" D'Arco agreeing to testify for the government—had become all too commonplace. Mickey Boy wasn't the only one to feel paranoid about meeting too many mob guys, or discussing anything even marginally incriminating. It had especially shaken up lower-level hoods, who had not only been obligated to put everything they did "on record," but were happy to. Every success was a boast, each one another step up the mob ladder. Now they were refusing to report. Either that, or activities in the street had ground to a hundred percent halt—which, of course, they hadn't.

The part that angered Mickey was that he was just plain scared. He felt weakened inside. Like caring about Laurel and Hope had made him vulnerable. And he hated it.

"Look, pal," Freddie said, "if you're worried about who's gonna become a rat in the future, it's too late." He smiled. Not the normally jovial, excitedly contagious Freddie Falcone smile, but a sympathetic one. "You just gotta do this."

6

December 23: Little Italy, Manhattan

FUCK YOU, YOU SONOFABITCH! ROSALIE DESTEFANO THOUGHT, as she threw on her new lynx jacket and stormed out the front door of the Focacceria Villarosa. She looked back over her shoulder at the upstairs office that Mickey Boy's asshole buddy, Freddie Falcone, had commandeered for some kind of a Christmas meeting. *Assholes!*

With her teeth tightly gritted, Rosalie pulled her jacket closed in the front, swung her dark curls away from the building, and continued marching toward her black Pontiac TransAm.

Smug bastard!

Mickey Boy Messina really thought he was hot shit, didn't he? So nice. So polite and smiling, while really laughing at her. "Hi, how've you been?" he would ask.

Like you really fuckin' care!

He hadn't been so nonchalant when she'd waltzed into his parole hearing last year. No, then he'd been all eyes and ears—and quite a bit more. That stiff dick poking her in the stomach when she hugged him wasn't saying, "You're not for me." No, that thing was standing at attention for her; for her tits, which made Laurel's look like apples in a melon patch; for her legs sticking out of the minidress; for her.

Then she'd been good enough to save his ass, but not good enough to go to dinner with, or take to a movie, or fuck.

Let's see how long his classy bitch of a wife will stick around when shit really happens, Rosalie told herself. Then, maybe, he'd realize what a gem he'd really lost; that she was more suited for him than any schoolteacher; that he was just as common as she was. She couldn't wait.

Rosalie slammed the door of her car and twisted the ignition key till the engine cried out in pain. She felt like slamming into the blue Thunderbird in front of her, then totally smashing the white Miata in back. Instead she worked her way out of the spot inch by inch, cursing the moving traffic that refused to open up and let her get away.

Fuck you, Mr. Mickey Boy Messina, big-shot cocksucker!

7

December 24: Maspeth, Queens

MICKEY BOY PULLED UP BEHIND THE BLACK SEVILLE AND stopped, waiting for the line of cars to crawl forward. It wasn't often that he got to be alone these days, especially in a car. Either he had Freddie chauffeuring him wherever, or used the other time he had left to satisfy some desire of Laurel's. This, however, was one time he'd insisted on being alone. Freddie'd argued, but he'd won. What could Freddie do for him anyway, if someone was out to do him harm? What good did Tommy Bilotti do for Paul Castellano that night in front of Spark's?

The line moved a few feet, then stopped dead. It seemed like everybody in the world had picked that day to visit. Mickey Boy respectfully cut Frank Sinatra's Christmas tape off, then dropped his front windows an inch or two, to let some cool air circulate through the interior. Suddenly, the automobiles took off through the hilly landscape as if nothing had been holding them up from the first.

Mickey Boy spotted the tall obelisk shape he'd been looking for, darkened by the brilliance of white clouds behind it, then turned left. When he hit the perimeter, he turned right, searching again for a landmark that would tell him where to make his next turn.

Ugly black thing, make another right.

Halfway down the hill.

Stop by the crossed American and Italian flags, which always seemed to be replaced and new.

Mickey reached into the backseat and dragged out the huge wreath he'd just bought from the vendor across the street, careful not to let the wire or long spikes scratch his leather interior. Then, careful not to slip on any muddy slicks, he made his way across dead grass and leaves to the headstones marked CALABRA.

ANNA MARIE CALABRA
b. February 20, 1921
d. March 22, 1979
BELOVED WIFE AND MOTHER

Mickey Boy stiffened. Despite his discomfort, his eyes remained riveted to the dates. Only fifty-eight years old. A young woman. Probably a nice woman. No nicer than his own mother, but lucky enough to be a wife.

He walked slightly to the right, aware of the stiffness beginning in his right leg, and stopped at the foot of the adjacent grave. He stared at the gray marble headstone, so hard and cold, just like the body buried beneath. And, like the person it represented, it was neither black or white, but a combined gray.

SINS OF OUR SONS

VINCENZO MICHAEL CALABRA
b. January 14, 1920
d. March 25, 1989
RESTING IN HEAVEN

Marge and Linda, the don's daughters, had chosen the inscription. Obviously, Mickey had thought when he'd first seen it, they were pissed enough at finding out they had an illegitimate brother, him, to disown the old man as a husband and father. Threw him right the hell out of the club for all time. They had, however, softened in time, as evidenced by two wreaths identical to the one he'd bought, stuck firmly into the winter-hardened earth. They had the same collection of shiny ornaments, pinecones, and red plastic berries; even had the same wide red ribbon, which read, FIRST CHRISTMAS IN HEAVEN. The only difference was the second ribbon on each, announcing, FATHER. Two more of the same wreaths, except with "Mother" ribbons, blocked the lower part of Anna's headstone.

Mickey Boy looked down at the wreath in his hands and laughed. Even though his half sisters hadn't met him until after their father's death, and didn't talk to him now, they still shared at least one trait of the old man: they bought only the most expensive. By contrast, the one lone rose, wrapped in an unmarked cellophane cone filled with baby's breath, and stuck to the right of the two "Father" wreaths, stood out for its good taste and quality. It was not the most expensive, but it was by far the best. It was, no doubt, Connie's.

Mickey Boy moved around to the right side, near the single rose his mother had left, and touched the headstone. Maybe there was some way he could connect with the man who had made him believe his father had died. Maybe now the real father, who had died without ever calling him son, would offer him some guidance, some direction out of the mess he'd dumped in his son's lap.

Standing there in the cold, staring down at the lifeless marble, Mickey Boy felt no sorrow for the murdered body beneath. Instead he felt sorry for himself. Just like his fir wreath, which was left no room near his father's headstone, he carried the same blood as four other siblings, yet had no one: Alley, who shared his mother's blood, lived a different

life, one in upper-crust Boston, and carried a bitter resent-
ment toward him for marrying Laurel, who had been Alley's
girlfriend through his teens; Marge and Linda, sisters on
Don Vincenze's side, who refused to acknowledge him as
their father's son; and that scummy piece of shit, Little
Vinnie, Vincenze and Anna's son, who Mickey Boy had
beaten silly at the don's wake, then chased out of the
country. Alone in a crowd of brothers and sisters. Not an
uncle or aunt in the bunch for Hope. What a fuckin' joke,
Mickey Boy thought. Like starving in the Four Seasons
restaurant.

December's chill reached past Mickey Boy's topcoat and
turtleneck sweater to pinch his chest and shoulder blades.
The leg that he'd been shot in felt stiff and ached. What was
worse, there were no answers. No revelations from the spirit
of his father, either above or below. When he left the
cemetery, it would be back to the same old bullshit; trapped
in a life he'd vowed to exit only dead.

"Thanks for nothing, Pop," Mickey Boy muttered with a
sad chuckle. Defiantly, he plunged the wreath's spikes into
the hard earth, between and in front of the other two.

"Merry Christmas."

On his way home, Mickey Boy stopped by Ferrara's pastry
shop on Grand Street, ordered two huge baskets of candy,
cakes, and fruits in wine, then gave a busboy two hundred
dollars to deliver one to his half sister, Marge, and her
family, in Huntington, and the other to Linda, her husband
Gus, and their brood, in Massapequa. Maybe they would
come around in time.

Though he felt Alley was a lost cause, due to his past
relationship with Laurel, he'd send him a Christmas tele-
gram, in London. Maybe time would heal all his wounds.

As for Little Vinnie—fuck him!

8

December 24: Todt Hill, Staten Island

FRANK SINATRA CROONED THE WORDS TO "I'LL BE HOME
For Christmas" from the speakers in Freddie Falcone's
Mercedes.

On another level of Mickey's consciousness, he and
Laurel swirled around overhead, waltzing in circles past the
top of the seven-foot Christmas tree, swooping down to
brush the gathering of her relatives on one side of the room,
then up again to look down on Freddie Falcone and Buster.

". . . Merry Christmas, and may all your dreams come
true . . ."

Mickey's mother, Connie, entered below them, carrying a
huge pyramid-shaped stroofela: tiny balls of fried dough
covered with honey, then smattered with pieces of dried
fruit and multicolored confettini. Connie had made the trip
from Boston, where she'd spent the last three weeks with
Alley, her son with the deceased Al Messina, who had also
legally adopted Mickey Boy. Before Mickey married Laurel,
Connie had lived exclusively with Alley and his family.
After the marriage, she visited Mickey and Laurel often.
Since Hope had been born, however, she'd more or less split
her time between her sons. Alley, a successful architect, who
saw his ex-girlfriend's marriage to Mickey Boy as a personal
attack for having dumped her, had invited his mother to
spend Christmas and New Year's with him in London.
Connie, however, had preferred to come to New York. To
her, holidays should always be spent at home.

Behind Connie, Buster's wife, Nettie, carried a platter of
Italian pastries: cannolis, sfogliatelle, pasticciota.

Mickey shifted on the couch, his stomach moving a bit

slower than the rest of his body. He felt as though he would burst. How would he ever fit a piece of cake on top of the food he'd already consumed? he asked himself, coming back from his waltz with Laurel. It had gone on all night. Food, food, and more food. First a salad of mixed seafood—scungillis, shrimps, and octopus; then linguini with clams; then fried shrimps and scallops; then lobsters. Mickey groaned as he pictured it all. But it was a satisfied groan.

Mickey looked over at Laurel's side of the family—her father, manager of a Chandler's shoe store; her cousin Anthony, a computer specialist working for some Wall Street brokerage with more names than he could remember; another cousin, Terri, a production assistant at a music video company; yet another female cousin, Tammy, a doctor at Mt. Sinai Hospital.

From them, he looked toward the sixty-five-year-old Buster, seemingly ten years older than just last Christmas, his former burly build and robust complexion replaced by a thinner frame and a color near that of his steely gray hair. Next to him sat Freddie, sharp for his mid-fifties. Freddie's carefully coiffed silver hair seemed too formal for the times, his blue Italian knit shirt and sharkskin slacks too gangster chic, his pinky ring too gaudy for the nineties.

Mickey tried to see himself from outside his body: a guy in his mid-thirties, who was beginning to gray at the temples and develop wrinkles around his eyes from the pressures of a life he'd found himself stuck in. Even a potbelly, he thought, embracing his distended stomach with both hands.

He looked back to the more modern side of his new family, then back at his men. It just wasn't right . . .

Laurel startled Mickey by grabbing his hand.

"Come on," she said, "let's get you some dessert."

Mickey wanted to pull her to him, wrap himself around her and smell her hair, kiss her neck. No way, however, to do that with everyone watching. After all, he told himself, he had to conduct himself with respect—do the right thing.

"All right," he said, allowing Laurel to help him up. Then, still troubled by the contrasts he'd absorbed, he went to fill himself some more with chocolate and ricotta cream.

9

December 24: Little Italy, Manhattan

ROSALIE FIDGETED IN THE CORNER, WATCHING THE CLOCK AS IT approached twelve. She couldn't wait till they put the goddamned little Jesus in the manger of the huge Nativity set that took up an entire corner of the room. Then, at least, her parents would be satisfied that she'd stayed around for Christmas Eve. Then she could take off and finally be alone.

It wasn't the festivities and the food that annoyed her, so much as seeing everyone else paired up and happy. Not that she begrudged them. It's just that every pot, even her ugly cousin Nancy's, had a cover. Every pot, that is, except hers.

She'd had plenty of offers, of course, being only twenty, and having long ebony curls that hung over a body that could, and on occasion did, stop traffic. But what did she get? Wannabe gangsters who floated into the focacceria downstairs? Make-believe tough guys who could be manipulated with a feel of her tit or a sniff down below? Guys looking for a quick hump, then out the door? Fuck them. They could ride out in the flashy Eldorados that brought them.

The only one she'd met that really attracted her, made her really feel like she wanted to lie down on a railroad track for him, was Mickey Boy Messina. There was a real man, no make-believe tough guy. And he obviously knew how to treat a girl—always with Laurel up his ass before he even married her. Now, with a ring and baby, Laurel really had him hooked. Yes, he would have really been good for her, and she would have turned herself inside out to make him happy as all hell.

Only, Mickey Boy had rejected her as if she was nothing

39

more than a rag. She'd lied for him, perjured herself to give him an alibi to beat last year's parole violation, said she was fucking him when he was really at Buster's crap game two floors below, and what had he done to show his appreciation? A lousy box of candy and a bouquet of flowers. Rosalie was sure Laurel got a hell of a lot more thoughtfulness than that.

Fuck Laurel!

Across the room, Rosalie caught her second cousin's husband, Rico, an Italian immigrant who tried too hard to play American cool, giving her the eye again. Baldy-headed dog, she thought, amused at how obvious he'd behaved all night—even with his wife around. These greaseballs were all the same.

"I'm going to go downstairs, bring up more ice," Rosalie told her father, loud enough for Rico to hear.

"Hey, I'll go along," Rico chimed in with his heavy accent. ". . . Carry the ice for you."

Laughing to herself, Rosalie led the way down the dark staircase of the turn-of-the-century building and into the main room of the Focacceria Villarosa. Garlic and tomato smells lingered in the air, overpowering stale wood and tobacco. Light from the restaurant's neon sign flickered in through the café curtains in front. The floor creaked under each step.

She could feel Rico closing the gap between them as she stepped behind the bar. At the far end she deliberately bent from the waist, rummaging for a bucket to fill with ice, allowing Rico to come up flush against her. She felt his erection press against her backside, made believe she didn't, and wriggled a little as she retrieved what she had been looking for and filled it from the adjacent ice bin.

Rico grabbed her as soon as she stood and turned around. He jammed his tongue into her mouth and mashed her breasts with one hand. He ground his hips into hers.

Rosalie placed both hands on Rico's chest and shoved him back about three feet. "Whoa," she said. "Take it easy, stud. Don't you get enough at home?"

"Sei molto bella," he whispered. You are so beautiful. *"Baciami."* Kiss me.

Rosalie could feel Rico's panting breath as he moved in

again. This time she let him kiss her neck, her collarbone, lift her breast out of her sweater.

"Il tuo seno e come dei meloni," he said. Your breasts are like melons. *"Bellisima."*

She clutched his hair with both hands as he licked and sucked her nipple.

"Stop," she moaned, pushing his head away.

Rico dropped to his knees in an instant. He lifted her skirt and ripped at her panties like a starving animal digging for food. Rosalie wanted to force him back, but instead opened her legs to accommodate his face burrowing between them. It had just been too long.

Rico's tongue slid up into Rosalie. He lapped at her vagina as frantically as he'd torn her underwear off, giving her some sexual sensation, but not even coming close to real pleasure.

"Slower," Rosalie said. She pulled back on his hair, trying to get him to lick more near her clitoris than inside.

Rico, taking that for a different kind of message, stood up and bared his penis.

Rosalie pushed him back a second time. "Fuck off, Rico," she said, straightening her skirt. "If I wanted to make it with an animal, I'd go to the goddamn zoo."

"But, I'm sorry," Rico pleaded in broken English. "It's just that you're so beautiful, so hot . . ." He began toward her again.

Rosalie laughed inside. *Asshole!* To Rico, she said, "Come here, sit on the bar, let me make you enjoy yourself." When Rico jumped up to sit on the bar, Rosalie grabbed the bucket of ice and dumped it in his lap.

Rico jumped and howled at the same time. "What, the fuck! You *putana* bastard!" he screamed.

Rosalie snatched the empty bucket and ran to the kitchen to get ice from the other machine. "Shh, Mr. Napoli Cool," she said, laughing. "Want everybody to come down? Wanna you wife here?"

10

December 24: Laurentian Mountains, Canada

THE WIND BIT DEEPLY INTO JOE AUGUSTA'S CHEST AND BACK. ON the snow around him lay his jacket, vest, and insulated undershirt. All over his torso, scratches and cuts bled from a branch he'd beat and scraped himself with.

Already on his knees, he forced his arms open to a Christlike pose and threw himself, face forward, into the snow. Hot tears melted tiny veins into the pure white. His blood made tiny pink spots.

"Chrissy, my baby, I'm sorry . . . I'm so sorry," he moaned. The words became more difficult to enunciate as his body shook and his jaw tightened. "Please, baby, please forgive me. I didn't know you would be hurt. Not you, my baby . . ."

By the time Joe rose, his extremities were numb and his flesh burned. He could barely struggle into his clothes. His teeth would not stop chattering.

Joe made his way through the wooded area, back toward the chalet. In spite of the penance he'd done, he still felt his heart torn in two. Tears continued to stream down his face.

"Merry Christmas, my baby," he sobbed. "Merry Christmas in Heaven."

He stopped short of the inviting light from the chalet's window and leaned against the stucco wall of the house, waiting for the tears to stop, waiting to look decent for his wife and Elizabeth.

Finally, Joe regained control over his tears, though his shaking hadn't stopped. That was okay, he could cover that up. Shaking would give no clue to the torture he'd put himself through; a torture he would continue until he could kill Richie DeLuca, Buster Alcamo, Little Vinnie Calabra, Mickey Boy Messina, and himself.

Satisfied that he'd reinforced his resolve to settle scores for Chrissy's death, he stepped into the room—a room devoid of any hint of a joyous season—to wait for Christmas to pass.

11

December 25: Todt Hill, Staten Island

IT WAS TWO A.M. when the last guest finally left. Mickey sat by himself, in a corner, watching Connie gather up the tablecloth from the eighteen-foot-long table they'd dined on, but not seeing her. From early in the evening, he'd been in a sort of dreamworld, preoccupied with the bubbling of an idea that he just couldn't put his hands on.

"Leave it," Laurel said. "We can clean up in the morning." She grabbed Mickey by the arm and whispered, "Right now, I've got a special Christmas present for you . . . upstairs."

Still lost in his thoughts, Mickey kissed his mother, then followed Laurel upstairs. As if in a dream, he went to Hope's room, stopping by her crib to pat her head while Laurel went into their room to change. He bent into the crib to kiss the baby, then shuffled off down the hall.

When he reached his bedroom, Laurel was still in the bathroom. He undressed and lay down on his side of the king-sized bed, on top of the satin spread, looking down at his small potbelly, wondering exactly what it was that bothered him so.

Laurel stepped suddenly from the bathroom, into the light that shone through the open door. On her head she wore a

Santa Claus hat; on her body, a sheer red nightie with white maribou trim around the collar and cuffs; on her feet, red high heels with furry white pom-poms.

Mickey shook his head to make sure this wasn't part of his evening's dreamlike state. The fact that it wasn't made him want to laugh out loud. If it wasn't a sex book, which she accumulated like baseball cards or beer mugs, it was some absurd outfit that was supposed to get him excited, or some sex aid, like a cock ring or French tickler, that she'd picked up at an X-rated sales party that her old girlfriend, Shari, had thrown. Tonight was the absurd outfit.

To Mickey, having been brought up with the ideals of old Italian mobsters, sex had definite limitations, and ramifications that went beyond the act itself: Any girl who takes a prick in her mouth is no fuckin' good . . . Cunt-lappers can't be trusted, they oughtta be shot . . . If my wife ever acted like a *putana* bastard, I'd break her skull . . .

But Laurel had defied all that. She'd become as skilled as a surgeon when it came to sex, by absorbing manual after manual, trying each and every technique on him to see which satisfied him, and her, the most. He'd gone along with just about everything—except, of course, letting her tie him up, or playing with her vibrator too close to his ass—because he loved her enough to battle the demons of his past teachings; because there was nothing he wouldn't do for her.

Laurel swayed as she walked, letting the nightie open to reveal sheer matching panties. She slowly put one knee on the bed, then slinked across the satin toward him.

Despite the humor he found in the situation, Mickey found himself hard and ready to go. He reached for her panties.

"No need," Laurel said, lifting one leg. "They're crotchless." With that, she climbed on top of him and impaled herself on his erection through the opening in the garment.

"Come here," Mickey said, grabbing her shoulders. All he wanted was to hold her tight, cling to her inside and out.

"No, lie still," she whispered. She bent backward, away from him, undulated a few times, then sat upright and rotated on his penis till she was facing away. A couple of humps later she swung around again. Perspiration beaded up on her forehead, neck, and chest. Laurel groaned. She shucked the nightie, so all she had on were the open-crotched panties.

"Like this?" she asked throatily. "It's called . . ."

Laurel slept, but Mickey stayed awake. He sat by the window, staring out over the treetops at the starry sky. Laurel had worn him out, once again working him out from directions of sex books she'd read. He didn't have to be a genius, he told himself, to know that there was something wrong when someone had to try that hard. Sad.

As he had all night, he tried to sort out things, tried to get a grip on what was on his mind. Was it Buster? he wondered. Or Freddie? Or both? Or, more likely, all of them, including himself? The last seemed to hit home. Yes, it was all of them, and the way they lived. They were the past, not the future. No longer were they the romantic figures he remembered from his youth. There were no more neighborhoods where everyone depended on them for fairness and justice.

Mickey thought back to that last night at Nicolo Fonte's. How he'd loved working after school for the *avvocato* . . . loved seeing him handle the legal problems of those less fortunate in a neighborhood just struggling to survive. To him, Fonte had been a white knight, a savior put down in South Brooklyn. How he had wanted to be like him, to help people, to do good.

That last night, however, Fonte had suddenly turned on him for no reason. Called him an idiot. Said he could never be a lawyer if he lived twice. Told him to get the hell out and stay out.

How he had hated Fonte after that—and even now.

But he'd found another way, Mickey Boy told himself. Another way to be a knight, to help others with less strength and will than he: *la cosa nostra.* Theirs was a line that went back to the thirteenth century, of Sicilians running their own underworld government; men of honor, who gave the native Sicilians the only justice they could get in the face of Bourbon, Turk, and Moorish rulers.

In this country, early twentieth-century mafiosi adhered

to the same tradition for their immigrant, foreign-speaking brothers, who were treated like dogs by the ruling Irish. Theirs was a government of the people. Mickey had heard the stories of how mobsters had kept neighborhood people in food and clothing—mostly stolen, to be sure, but didn't Robin Hood do the same thing? He'd heard how they offered their hand to all in need, and it had filled his own need for a positive, romantic self-image.

Yes, they had taxed. Didn't every government do that? he'd always asked himself. Without the ability to legitimately tax, they taxed by theft, extortion, and providing services, like gambling and booze, that people wanted. That had been his justification. *La cosa nostra* had been necessary.

Necessary, that was it! Mickey Boy suddenly realized. Times had changed, and with it they'd become unnecessary. In fact, not only weren't they needed anymore; as each day dawned, with each new indictment, they were becoming despised by the very people they were supposed to defend: average people.

No, his future wasn't to get himself out, as he'd hoped, Mickey Boy now told himself—it was to get everyone out.

12

December 25: Acireale, Sicily

GENTLE VOICES, SINGING THE AVE MARIA, ECHOED OFF THE BAroque marble and stucco carvings of the fourteenth century church. The chanting filled the cavernous hall from its slate floor to its huge cathedral ceiling so thoroughly that it seemed to permeate every part of Little Vinnie's body, then got lost. Warmth from the bodies of the congregation, which had chased away the dampness on other winter days, was gone.

Music, food, yes, even religious ceremonies, had given him the greatest pleasures of his life, up until recently—till that bastard of a half brother of his had unwittingly reached across the Atlantic to fuck up his life again. Now, everyone looked at him like a leper, laughing that he couldn't be made here, in goddamn Sicily, until he'd avenged Mickey Boy's insult in beating and banishing him. Each day that went by, that he didn't set a definite date to go back to America, made them laugh at him more. He could goddamn feel it.

Even Ninfa, Don Genco's lovely, yellow-haired, virginal grandaughter, who he knew was crazy about him, was laughing inside. Ninfa, who had the same vivacious smile and perky mannerisms that Chrissy Augusta had possessed, would never be allowed to date, let alone marry, him until he'd taken care of business. Life in this beautiful land of his choice would be unbearable until he'd proved what kind of man he was.

When the Christmas Mass ended, Little Vinnie approached Don Genco, whom he'd accompanied to church along with almost thirty members of the don's family. He hooked one arm inside the old man's, helping him negotiate the couple of steps that led out to the piazza.

"Padrone, per piacere," Little Vinnie said. He continued carefully, in the don's local dialect. "Please, walk with me for a moment."

Don Genco excused himself from the rest of his churchgoing family, then continued along with Little Vinnie. They walked past the don's waiting blue Mercedes and across the street, where trees and bushes formed an oasis from the gray stone all around. Don Genco looked up at the sun, sniffed the air, seemed to glory in the fifty-two-degree temperature. *"Fa bel tempo,"* he said, smiling, then added, in English, "Beautiful day for December, eh?"

Fuck the weather, Little Vinnie thought, while he mumbled agreement. The way he felt, he didn't care if it was hailing hand grenades.

Little Vinnie's throat knotted up and his palms turned clammy. He held fast to the fabric of the don's jacket, hoping his hand would not slip and touch the old man's; not give away how anxiety-filled he really was.

The old man let out a little cackle of laughter. *"Ma che vuole?"* he asked. Tell me, what is it you want?

"I'm ready to go to America," Little Vinnie blurted. "I was hoping you would help me to get there without notice."

Don Genco smiled his impish smile, gold teeth glinting. "You know that to me you are like a son," he responded in Sicilian. "There is nothing I would not do for you. You gotta remember, though, that there is a certain respect I must show to your brother, Don Miguito. If I give you any help, it must be with, how you say . . . for good judgment?"

"Discretion."

"Si, si, discrezione," the don repeated. "It must be done with discretion. *Capisce?"*

Of course, Little Vinnie responded. He would sooner die than ever divulge a word of Don Genco's participation in his mission to murder Mickey Boy.

The don did not respond to that, did not threaten that death would surely follow if he did. Little Vinnie believed he actually liked him too much to do that. Besides, it was understood anyway.

Don Genco did promise to procure a phony passport, a ticket to the United States via Naples, enough cash to keep him going, and an introduction to the one man who would know of his mission and extend discreet help to him there.

"I will make all the arrangements for you soon. Meanwhile, enjoy yourself, maybe ask my son-in-law's permission to court his daughter, Ninfa. She is very beautiful, huh?"

Little Vinnie tried to answer, but stammered something unintelligible. Was the old man joking with him? Would he insult the don if he responded too quickly, or too enthusiastically? Was it a trap?

"Don't worry," Don Genco said, as if he had read Little Vinnie's mind. "Ask her father. He will approve. And when you have completed your task in America, you may find that you would like to have her join you, as your wife. Or, if you choose to return here and inherit all I have . . ." He waved his hand in a small circle.

"Yes, yes," Little Vinnie said, "Here is where I want to be. And Ninfa is the one I would be honored to have for my wife."

Don Genco turned to face Little Vinnie. He pulled him down a bit by his shoulders and kissed him on both cheeks.

"Dio ti benedica, figlio mio," he said. God bless you, my son.

13

December 28: Downtown Brooklyn

SNOW FLURRIES SWIRLED AROUND MICKEY BOY AS HE, FREDDIE Falcone, and Ira J. Golden approached the Federal Courthouse for the Eastern District of New York, at Cadman Plaza.

"We lawyers used to be able to go around this," Golden said, preparing to go through the metal detector inside. "Now the judges and prosecutors don't even trust us not to want to kill them." He emptied his pockets of change and keys, and sent his briefcase through on the conveyor belt to be X-rayed.

"I don't blame'em," Freddie said. "Even their own mothers woulda drowned them if they knew how they was gonna turn out." As he stepped up and dumped the contents of his pockets into a small tray, he asked the squat black female guard, "What about the plate in my skull? Want me to send my head through separately?"

"Come on, there's people behind you," she replied, without cracking so much as a smile.

Mickey Boy felt the same way.

When Freddie walked through the six-foot-high rectangular detector, the buzzer went off.

"What else you got?" the guard asked.

Freddie removed his belt and cuff links, then bent toward the guard. "Here, take my teeth," he said, reaching into his mouth.

Grimacing, the guard backed up a step.

Mickey Boy couldn't help but laugh, despite the jitters he felt. Appearing in court was like going in for surgery; it never got easier. This was the building that he'd been mistakenly found guilty in; this was where he'd been handed a ten-year prison sentence; this place made him feel like he wanted to throw up. He stopped by the newsstand and bought a roll of sour candies; something tart to cut the foul coating on his tongue.

On the elevator ride to the third floor, Mickey Boy wished he had Laurel to hold onto, but was glad he'd argued with her to stay home. This was the part of his life he never wanted her to experience, ever.

When he saw that Judge Palmer was busy, clearing his calendar of cases where the defendants were incarcerated, and that Halloran had not yet arrived, Mickey Boy chose to wait in the hall. Freddie, of course, stayed with him. Ira Golden went inside.

"How does it feel to be here?" Freddie asked.

Mickey Boy shrugged.

"Let me guess. Like you're gonna get an enema with battery acid?"

"No. More like I already got it, and could still feel it burning."

"Makes sense," Freddie said. He gave Mickey Boy an exaggerated hug around the shoulders. "That's why you're not full of shit, like most everybody else."

Just then Mickey Boy spotted his parole officer, sour-faced and once again dressed all in gray, and a gangly, pinch-faced man who didn't look old enough to shave, walking their way. Judging by the leather briefcase the tall man carried, Mickey Boy figured he was the U.S. Attorney assigned to the show-cause order that Golden had filed.

Halloran acknowledged Mickey Boy with a nonsmiling nod and a terse, "Mr. Messina." Still moving, he turned toward Freddie. "Mr. Falcone," he said, drawing out the silent vowel at the end of the name to sound like "Falconee."

"Assholee," Freddie said as the two government men disappeared into the courtroom.

"That's Mister Assholee," Mickey Boy corrected. "C'mon, let's go inside."

A few minutes later the court clerk announced the case of Michael Antonio Messina versus the Federal Parole Department of the Eastern District of New York, and, specifically, Parole Officer Francis K. Halloran.

Judge Palmer, a cherubic man in his forties or fifties, seemed as amiable in character as in appearance. "I'm more familiar with this type of procedure than I would like to be," he said. He smiled at Mickey Boy. "Not that I don't like seeing you gentlemen every now and then, just to see how you are."

Somehow, the judge's flip manner scared Mickey Boy more than if he'd been serious. To his way of thinking, life's blows hurt more when your guard was down than when you were prepared.

Ira Golden and the U.S. Attorney, Murray Katzburg, exchanged arguments about the motion Golden had filed, pressing the Government to show cause why Michael Messina's job had suddenly become unsatisfactory to the Parole Department.

Katzburg took the position that employment of a parolee was exclusively at the discretion of the parole officer in charge.

Golden argued that since Michael Messina's job with L'Italia Provisions had been previously approved by the Parole Department and Michael Messina had always filed satisfactory work reports, and since no incident had come up to change any of that, the Parole Department would be violating its own guidelines. To back up his claim, he cited a section of the "Rules and Regulations for Federal Probation Officers," presenting both the judge and U.S. Attorney with photocopies of the pages involved.

"Where did you get that?" Frank Halloran snapped. "That doesn't get distributed around. One of your clients steal a copy?"

Golden smiled broadly. "Nothing like that. One of your guys happened to forget it on the table after discussing a client over lunch. I just copied some pages before returning it."

"How convenient," Katzburg said with a laugh.

The only one in the entire courtroom who seemed serious about the proceedings was Halloran. "What was his name?" he asked Golden.

"Should I refuse to answer until I consult with an attorney?" Golden asked. "Or just lie, and tell you I forgot?"

"None of your fuckin' business would be more like it," Freddie whispered to Mickey Boy.

Judge Palmer broke up the discourse between Halloran and Golden. "Realistically," he said, "I cannot stop the Parole Department from violating their own guidelines . . ."

Mickey Boy's heart sank.

". . . however, I want the Parole Department to be aware that if Mr. Messina should bring suit based on those charges, he will be guaranteed victory, and, probably, a substantial cash award." He dismissed the motion, then, standing, said, "Are we off the record?"

The stenographer nodded, and began packing her papers.

"Good." Judge Palmer turned toward Halloran and the U.S. Attorney. "Work this out among yourselves," he said. "You don't want to make this guy any richer than he already is."

The bright pink of Frank Halloran's flushed face, contrasting sharply with his otherwise total gray, pleased Mickey Boy, yet sobered him too. This would be one pissed-off guy after him now.

14

December 28: Todt Hill, Staten Island

TWINGES OF ELECTRIC SENSATION SHOT THROUGH LAUREL'S NIP-
ple and her breast, traveling from there up to her collarbone
and down to her vagina. For a moment she closed her eyes,
luxuriating in the sensation, imagining that it was Mickey's
lips pursed tightly on the tip of her breast . . .

Then she opened them quickly, forcing herself away from
the fantasy to the reality of Hope drawing life's milk from
her.

When Hope, sleepy as a cat, refused to suck anymore,
Laurel started to push her nipple back in the baby's mouth,
then stopped, feeling guilty, as though she might be doing it
more for her own pleasure than Hope's benefit.

"I must be going crazy," Laurel muttered to herself as she
cleaned and covered herself. "Too much time alone." She
carried Hope up to the nursery, laid her gently in her crib,
and turned the key on the mobile above. Pink and white
satin stars with faces circled to the chimes of "Twinkle,
Twinkle."

Laurel shuffled off to the bathroom, still feeling unsettled
by the excitement she'd just felt and edgy at the thought of
Mickey Boy in court. She wouldn't be so goddamn nervous,
she told herself as she stripped off her clothes, if he would
have let her accompany him. But no, he had his asshole
buddy Freddie, and that fat lawyer, Golden, to keep him
company. The boys' club. They'd be there to boost his
morale. He'd know what the hell was going on as it
happened, and was probably even less nervous about his
fate than she was.

Standing sideways, Laurel was pleased at the reflection in the mirror. Though she knew that would end, her tits were still a hell of a lot bigger than before she'd become pregnant with Hope, and they seemed not to have begun to sag—and the couple of nipple hairs that had sprouted during her pregnancy had, thankfully, disappeared. She tensed the muscles around her breasts and released them a few times, trying for an isometric antidote to gravity.

The small bulge below her navel remained troubling. It had subsided a lot with exercise, but hadn't totally disappeared. All in all, not bad, she told herself as she turned to face the mirror face-to-face. Her eyes wandered down again to her underbelly, this time surveying the light stretch marks there. God, how she wished she could pull her pubic hair up to cover them. She wondered if they bothered Mickey as much as they did her. Could that be why his sexual interest in her seemed to lessen each day?

On the other hand, Laurel thought, her body was still a hell of a lot better than most. Her thighs were not fully down to size, but smooth and taut, without cellulite bumps and craters; her hips femininely wide without looking fat; the junction at the bottom of her pubic mound, despite her thigh problem, still open and inviting—what more than one of the guys she'd slept with, before Mickey, had happily called a "gap." She was sure there were still plenty of men who would jump through hoops just to bury their faces there.

"I really do have to get out more," she told herself. "I really do . . ."

Laurel jumped when the phone outside the shower door rang. "Hello," she said quickly, her heart dropping when she heard her mother's voice.

"No. No, I haven't heard from him yet," Laurel replied to her mother's question. "In fact I thought this might have been him now."

"What are you doing?" her mother asked.

"Going crazy." With the phone at her ear, Laurel continued to survey her naked body in the mirror. She stretched up on her toes, satisfied that her legs would still look shapely and sexy in a spiked heel, if she ever had the occasion to wear them again. Even New Year's Eve would be spent in the house; another party for her and the cleaning girl to spend the following two days putting the place in order.

"That's nothing new with you lately. Besides that, what are you doing today?"

"What I do every day," Laurel said. As she went through the list of feeding Hope, watching "All My Children," and doing some laundry, a tear rolled down her cheek.

15

January 8: Todt Hill, Staten Island

"I WANT TO GO OUT."

"Okay, go to the mall, buy something," Mickey Boy said, while using the remote control to flip television channels, from soap opera to soap opera, till he landed on a channel broadcasting "The Beverly Hillbillies." Boy, it felt great to be home in the daytime. He'd begged off an appointment with two feuding union officials, claiming to have come down with the flu, and had even called in sick to L'Italia, just in case Halloran tried to track him down on the job.

Laurel's voice rose an octave, to an irritating pitch. "I don't want to go to the goddamn mall!" she said. "I don't want to buy anything!"

Mickey Boy dropped his feet from the coffee table and reached into the basket of fruit and candy that one of the union men had sent over—like that would do him any good in a decision—and pulled out a can of mixed nuts.

"Mickey! You're dropping that shredded stuff all over the rug!"

Mickey Boy smiled while popping the can's flange top. "That's why they make vacuums." He wondered why they couldn't have put a larger can of nuts in the basket.

"And who's going to vacuum it up?"

"Don't the cleaning girl come soon?"

"Tomorrow."

"Good, then she'll do it."

He was amazed that Laurel's voice could go up higher, but it did as she carried on about not living like a pig even for one day. Talk about exaggeration. Too happy at being able to stay home not to find humor in the situation, he waited for Laurel to go for the vacuum cleaner, then called, "Hon, do me a favor, while you're there, get me a cream soda?"

Laurel walked in front of the TV and turned it off.

"Aw, come on, hon," Mickey Boy said. "I was just teasing you. Come on, put on the TV, like a good wifesome."

Laurel crossed the room and sat down on the sofa next to Mickey. "I am a good wife, and a good mother," she said, "but I need more. There's more to life than just this."

"What's this?" Mickey Boy asked. "A house like a mansion, in the best neighborhood in the city? A Mercedes? A beautiful baby girl an' a husband that's crazy about you? How many husbands could take off from work just to stay with their wives, like I did?"

"No," Laurel said. "You took off to stay with Buddy Ebsen. I just happen to be here."

"Come on, you know that ain't true. Okay, I won't watch TV. Wanna talk?" Mickey Boy winked at Laurel. "Wanna go upstairs an' play around, before the baby wakes up?"

Laurel sighed. "Yes, I would like to do both those things, but that isn't what this conversation is about. I want to get out. I want to do something with my life, besides being penned up in this lovely prison. I want to go back to work."

"No, c'mon, we already settled that."

"No, you settled that . . . or rather, just put it off. Well, the put-off time is here. I want to go back and teach, even part-time, to start."

No way, Mickey Boy argued. Regardless of all the bullshit those degenerates that controlled the media tried to feed people today, a wife, and more importantly, a mother, had an exalted place in the home. Working mothers were why so many kids were fucked up. Who would be there for Hope when she came home from school?

"Mickey! Hope's life can be measured in weeks, not even years yet. You're worrying about school now?"

"Why, it ain't gonna come to that? What would you do then, quit? Is that part of the deal?"

"No. But arrangements can be made, for Christ's sake. My mother, your mother—"

"My mother's in Boston, with Alley."

"But maybe she'll stay with us by then. Who knows? And it wouldn't be the worst thing if we hire a live-in; let her stay with Hope for the little time till I get home."

Why didn't he just go to his appointment? Mickey Boy wondered. He was sure he was being punished for shirking his duty to stay home and relax.

"Look," Mickey Boy said. "For a lot of reasons, I don't want my wife working . . ." He put up a hand to stop her trying to interrupt. "Some is because it doesn't look good for a guy in my position, some is I would worry about your being safe if there was ever a problem, and some is because I just don't fuckin' like the idea. Okay?"

"What is this, a goddamn royal decree, from the Middle Ages?"

Mickey Boy's head began to pound. Control it or lose it, he told himself. "I don't mean it to sound that way," he said, "but it just don't sit well with me."

"And how about me? Or don't women count in this macho male world of yours?"

"No, you count very much, because I love you. Everything I do is for you and the baby. And I do understand how you feel, that you need to get out and do something with your brain," Mickey Boy said. "Tell you what. How about you work with me?"

Laurel's eyes narrowed.

"No, I'm not making fun of you," he said. "I mean it."

"Mickey, don't be ridiculous."

"I'm serious. You know how I keep wanting to find a way for everybody around me to go legit," he said. "How about we really start trying to move on that . . . you an' me. I ain't got too good a head for business anyway."

"You really do mean it," Laurel said.

Mickey smiled. Yes, he did, though he wouldn't have done anything about it so soon, he thought. But anything was better than hearing her fucking voice get any higher. The pounding in his head began to subside. Taking Laurel's hand in his, he explained what he wanted her to do.

"Now can I put on the TV?" he asked once he'd finished giving Laurel her marching orders.

Laurel pulled him to his feet. "No," she said, with a devilish smile. "Now we're going upstairs to make good on your earlier offer."

16

December 25: Cobble Hill, Brooklyn

NICOLO FONTE LEFT HIS BROTHER'S SOUTH BROOKLYN BROWNstone, on First Place, and walked over to Court Street. Boy, it felt good to see the old neighborhood after more than twenty years. To him, it hadn't changed a bit. Yes, store names had surely changed, and the yuppies now called it Cobble Hill, but the brownstones remained, and the church, and the pizzerias, and the overall Americanized-Italian flavor he remembered. Twenty years in Naples had made him appreciate it.

He wandered over to look for Aiello's pork store. Though closed for Christmas Day, it was there, the darkly cured prosciutto and red-hot capicolla still in the window. Nicolo Fonte smiled. He smiled once more when he spotted the International Longshoreman's Association building. He turned the collar of his camel-hair topcoat against the cold and walked another block. Of course, his storefront office had been abandoned decades ago. But when he stood in front of the red brick tenement that had housed it, staring at the video store that had taken its place, he could still see the green café curtains that had hung there for years, the old-style wooden front that had been replaced by metal and glass, the gold-stenciled letters on the window that said, NICOLO FONTE, ESQ., then, proudly, one line below, AVVOCATO . . . Lawyer.

Fonte removed his glasses and wiped his eyes. No tears for the changed store, none for what had happened to his life—his exile in Italy had made him a rich man. They were for the young, idealistic lawyer who had devoted his life to helping others, with dreams for a future in politics as one more way to help those not strong enough to help themselves. A young, innocent man who would never return.

After standing silently for five or so minutes, he shrugged, to concede his acceptance of life's unfair cycle, gathered the front of his coat tighter to keep the chill out of his roly-poly girth, and began his walk back to his brother's home.

Coming here alone, to visit the ghosts of his younger days, had been a good thing. It had purified a part of him, a large part. Only one thing remained for him to do in order to cleanse the remaining ache in his heart: find Mickey Boy Messina.

17

January 20: Bayside, Queens

MICKEY BOY FELT LIKE A JERK. IT WAS NOT ONLY THE FIRST TIME since becoming head of the Calabra Family that he'd gone to any kind of business meeting without Freddie Falcone, it was also the first time he'd taken Laurel.

He decided on Christmas Eve that if he had any mission in life, it was to get all those under his influence to adapt to the impending twenty-first century. The only way to do that, he was sure, would be to phase out any criminal behavior they might be involved in, and get each and every one to earn a better than average income through legitimate enterprise. The cultural thread of his mob ancestors—honor and respect—had to be preserved. The criminal thread had to go.

To begin, Mickey Boy had met with those captains and made men of his who were already running successful businesses. What he hoped for was a consensus, some kind of support for the idea of spreading around legitimate wealth. Instead, all he found were underlying animosities between members, jealousies, fear of the more crime-oriented of their family, and a general mistrust of anyone sticking their nose into their businesses. The one thing they had all tried to cover up was the greedy part of their natures, although, he was sure, it was at the root of all their other problems.

Mickey Boy had walked away from that first round of talks disgusted, but definitely not defeated. He quickly initiated another round of meetings, this time with legitimate business people from outside the Calabra Family, or any other crime family for that matter. People who had made their mark within the framework of society, without the added advantage of the large sums of money and contacts he had at his eventual disposal.

Now, the first of those meetings would be at a private dinner with relatives of Laurel's, and she would be by his side.

He made a right from the service road of the Cross Island Parkway into the parking area of Café on the Green, a charming house-turned-restaurant overlooking the Throgs Neck Bridge. Its quaint style reminded him of New England, of the inns he'd seen on his trips to visit Alley in Boston.

Mickey Boy gave the parking attendant a ten-dollar tip to keep the car right in front—where FBI agents, or whoever else was following him, wouldn't get a chance to get inside and plant a bug—then escorted Laurel inside. The atmosphere of flowers, trees, and open views toward Long Island Sound impressed him immediately. And the smell made his mouth water. Laurel's cousin Thomas had certainly made a good choice, on the face of it. If only the food would live up to the ambience, Mickey thought, the day would be a success no matter what happened at the meeting—though, a little luck would certainly be appreciated.

Frank Sinatra's voice echoed the lyrics to "Luck Be A Lady Tonight" in Mickey Boy's brain.

"Buon giorno," greeted an elegant-looking maitre d' in full tuxedo dress. "Can I help you?"

"Yes," Laurel replied while Mickey Boy peeked into the lounge area, where a brick fireplace burned in the center of the room. "We're with the Grecco party, upstairs."

"Of course," the maitre d' replied. "Please, this way," he said, indicating a stairway with his outstretched arm.

Mickey smiled his pleasure to Laurel, then started up the stairs, she in front of him, the maitre d' bringing up the rear. She looked so great, Mickey thought, admiring the way the plum-colored silk suit and matching pumps hugged her ass and showed off her legs while still being classy enough to belong to a countess—or a businesswoman. And, thanks to his living up to the promise he'd made her, that's what she would soon be. That is, if things worked out.

Luck!

Of course, to have a woman involved in his business was completely against everything he had been taught by his mob mentors, but, he'd reasoned, Laurel was a special person, one he could implicitly trust. Besides, times were changing, weren't they? Wasn't that the whole point of his move? He prayed it all worked out.

It could kill him if it didn't.

Two flights up they entered what served as Café on the Green's corporate dining and meeting room. The other guests were already seated: Laurel's father Jack, the manager of a Chandler's shoe store; her cousin Thomas, the guy who worked for a brokerage house with four or five names in its title; Thomas's brother-in-law Jeffrey, an executive for Bank of America; and Jeffrey's father, Sam, a corporate lawyer; invited but missing was Tammy, Laurel's doctor cousin.

At least they were all related to him in some distant way, Mickey thought. He found that reassuring, considering that the door he intended to step through led him into complete darkness.

Luck!

Mickey walked around the table, shaking hands with each of his guests, noting the uncomfortable looks on their faces. He had specifically asked that they not bring their wives, or, in the attorney's case, girlfriend.

"I know I asked you all not to bring anybody with youse," he said immediately. "That's because they have nothing to do with the business I wanna discuss. Laurel does. Any problem with that?" Getting them to agree with anything would be a cinch, he knew. Asking them was just a formality, to make them feel good. Every goddamn one of them was scared shitless of him. So shitless, in fact, he wondered why the hell they had agreed to meet at all.

When no one objected, Mickey said, "Good. Now, why don't we eat first, then talk later? Okay?"

Of course.

An hour and a half later Mickey finally shoved the last plate away. He'd devoured a half order of pasta cartuccio—three kinds of pasta cooked in parchment with a variety of seafood—as an appetizer, wolfed down a swordfish steak smothered in mushrooms, tomatoes, and balsamic vinegar, tasted a bit of everyone's dish who sat near him, then washed it all down with homemade profiterols—chocolate-covered cream puffs. Bad, but not that bad, he thought, considering it was the only day he'd broken his New Year's resolution diet.

"Thomas, I gotta thank you for picking this place," Mickey said. "Food's great. I just hope it didn't make us too sluggish to think."

Everyone laughed.

Mickey hoped their laughter was genuine. Fear had to become respect, and cooperation, if he was to succeed.

"Okay," he continued. "How about we get down to business?" When no one objected, he began in earnest. "You all have an idea what the cops and FBI say about me . . . you know my reputation."

Everyone appeared uncomfortable, but nodded.

Mickey told them that he was going to be forthright with them, and that he expected them to be the same.

"I'm a guy caught out of time. I made some tough choices, coming out of a tough life. They may have been wrong. If so, I'm trying to fix 'em. That's why I'm here."

He paused, trying to gauge the reaction on each of their faces, then continued, "That's where I am. Nobody close to me is gonna get robbed, get in trouble, or get hurt in any way. You have my word."

Mickey went on to say that if, for any reason, they had any reservation about being with him or discussing business, they should not be ashamed, and excuse themselves now. No hard feelings.

No one moved.

Lady Luck!

"Okay," he said. "Now, I've got a problem. I got a real lot of people that look to me for help, sort of like a government. A lot of them are crooks. Some because they want to be, it's in their blood. The rest are crooks because they don't know what else to do. Mostly they're gamblers or bookmakers, that kind of stuff. Guys who got started when it was no big deal, then got stuck when times changed. Those are the guys I'm really interested in. The others I'll have to deal with in another way."

When everyone's eyes opened wide, Mickey Boy reassured them, "Nothing like you're thinking . . . this ain't the Roaring Twenties."

Mickey Boy went on to give his guests a brief history of the Mafia, in Sicily. He began with the legend of the Mafia's name: an acronym for a thirteenth-century liberation slogan, "Morte Alla Francia Italia Anela . . . Death to all the French is Italy's cry."

"As a bit of a historian," Sam, the attorney, interjected, "I'd like to point out the fact that there was no Italy for thirteenth-century Sicilians. It would have been 'Death to all the French is Sicily's cry' . . . or, MAFSA."

"I told you it was a legend."

Once again everyone in the room laughed.

Mickey Boy went on to more accurately describe how Sicilians always needed a people's government, and they looked the other way when crimes were committed because it was like a tax. After all, every government needed funds to be effective, didn't they?

Thomas mentioned that most governments seemed to require funds to be ineffective.

The group got another chuckle out of that.

Pleased that the group seemed relaxed, Mickey Boy continued with his train of thought about the Sicilian experience. He said that later, when the immigrants came to this country, they needed the same kind of justice system in the face of an Irish grip on the city. All through these periods, the mainstay of their existence was honor and respect, and because of that, the average people either supported them or looked the other way when they committed crimes.

"Now the times have changed. There's no way we could compete anymore. It's time to fade out. But what do we do with all the people we got? How do we help them understand that if they don't give up crime, they'll be washed away? They'll be like dinosaurs . . . gone?"

"I don't understand what that has to do with us," Thomas said.

"The only way those people, and that history of honor and respect, could survive, is to get them into legitimate businesses. All you guys are in legitimate business, and I'm sure you got some ideas of businesses you'd like to see get off the ground. I need suggestions, plans, to get some kinds of businesses going. I got access to all the cash we'll need, within reason . . . and you guys'll have a piece of whatever it is we could get off the ground."

"I'm an attorney," Sam interjected. "And at an age where I'm not looking to conquer any new worlds."

Sam was invited, Mickey Boy replied, only in his capacity as a lawyer. He said that even though he was familiar with many lawyers, most of them did criminal work; the others, he couldn't trust. If Sam was agreeable, he would represent any of the legitimate business ventures he embarked on.

"You could get paid regular fees, or you could have a piece. It's up to you," Mickey Boy said. "That is, unless you don't want to be involved with me at all?"

Sam smiled. "I take an hourly fee. We can work out a retainer toward that."

Mickey reached across the table and shook his hand.

Everyone else seemed pleased and even more at ease than they had been.

Laurel sat by silently as Mickey Boy laid out parameters for what he needed: something that could put a lot of people to work, in management, lower levels, and one or two useless positions; something that could be expanded; something that was not too complicated for his people to understand, like chemical engineering or sophisticated computer technology; something with a high profit factor; something that had ancillary businesses for them to branch out into; something that didn't require licensing, as many of his people could not obtain licenses; something he could begin quickly.

"I don't want answers tonight," Mickey Boy said. "I want you guys to really put some time into this, and we'll meet again soon. And one thing, please, when you suggest a couple of things, try to know the answers to any questions I might have. I ain't the smartest guy in the world, and if you can't answer my questions, the project ain't worth getting into."

A buzz immediately filled the room as the men spoke in bits, giving each other reminders of things they might have discussed in the past.

"One other thing," Mickey Boy interrupted. "I don't wanna hear one word about this out in the street. What goes on among us, *stays* among us." He paused, and looked at each of them. "If it doesn't, then I will get mad . . . an' I guarantee you, you don't wanna see me mad."

The entire group went downstairs for a couple of good-bye drinks in the lounge. They settled in at the corner of the bar, with Mickey Boy facing the open fireplace, the windows facing the water to one side. He scanned the room, looking for law enforcement agents who might be trying to take notes or listen in on their conversation, but found no one suspicious-looking. They were there, he knew, but were either getting too sharp to be recognized or his instincts had become dull. In either case, it was a good thing he was making a move toward total legitimacy.

"Here's to the future," Mickey Boy said with a raised glass of Sambuca. "To our future."

Instead of the *"Salutes"* and *"Cent'annis"* he would normally hear in his circle of friends, there were "Cheers" and "To the future." Yup, things were changing.

Laurel stretched his way and kissed him.

It pleased Mickey Boy that his guests felt enough enthusiasm to begin tossing out ideas, all of which, however, he knocked down for one reason or another. A chain of video stores? Too expensive to stock; not enough jobs; too much competition from major chains. An elegant restaurant, like Café on the Green? Too much specialized work; too many restaurants failed each year; too many problems with mob guys hanging around.

It went on like that for another hour.

When Mickey Boy left, he found his car as he'd left it, under the nose of the attendant. He gave him another ten dollars.

Mickey Boy sat in his car awhile, soaking in the beauty of the tiny white lights twinkling in the bushes around the restaurant, of the Throgs Neck Bridge sparkling over the water. It felt like a magical beginning for the rest of his life—at least, until tomorrow, when he had to see Ira J. Golden about his ongoing battle with the Federal Department of Parole, vis à vis *Mister* Halloran, in spite of, or especially due to, his victory in court three weeks before.

Luck be a lady tonight!

18

February 13: Laurentian Mountains, Canada

JOE AUGUSTA STEPPED OUT OF THE TORONTO DOMINION BANK into the blinding sunlight. He'd drawn money from an account that had grown more thin than made him comfortable. Either that old greaseball, Don Peppino, would have to make arrangements for him to return to New York soon, or would have to wire up more funds, which he'd repay once he had access to his cash, back in Brooklyn.

Pure white snow and mountain greenery gently nestled the woody Galleries des Monts shopping center in its lap. The cloudless sky shone the brightest blue imaginable. So beautiful, Joe thought. Too beautiful for him to deserve.

Shoulders bent, he trudged along to his black Jeep Grand Cherokee and the ride back to the chalet. As he passed in front of the Monte Verde restaurant, a voice startled him:

"Joe! Joe, that you?"

Joe's first reaction was to turn and run, get in the Cherokee and disappear into nature's cover. He pulled himself together, though, and spun to face whoever had recognized him.

"Hey, howya been?" It was Johnny Calabrese, a made member in Jack the Wop's family. Johnny stared at Joe, trying to make sure of his identification through Joe's beard, fur hat, and red plaid mackinaw. A brassy-looking redhead bundled in black fur stood next to him.

"Excusez-moi?" Joe asked. His heart pounded beneath his layers of clothing.

"Joe? Joe Augusta?" Johnny Calabrese asked again.

"Je ne parle pas anglais," Joe retorted. He waved his hand

in circles, then quickly made off, grumbling in audible Quebeçois, *"Salaud! Va te faire cuire un oeuf!"*

Joe shuddered as the night's chill sliced through every part of his body that wasn't layered at least twice with garments. He shifted from right to left without moving too much of his body, and without taking his eye off room number 12 of Les Shutes du Nord, the out-of-the-way motel he'd followed Johnny Calabrese and his whore of a girlfriend to. They had been there since lunchtime, with the curtains drawn, probably fucking like dogs. Had to come up for air soon, Joe hoped; for food, at least.

When his nose felt like it would fall off, the door to the motel room opened and Johnny ushered his girl out. They started for the rented white Lincoln Town Car to their left. Johnny opened the door for his girlfriend, then walked around the front toward the driver's side.

Joe Augusta moved like a flash. He came up on the side of the car as Johnny opened his door and bent to get in. Joe pulled his silencer-outfitted .22 and fired quickly, catching Johnny behind the ear. The bullet's impact slammed Johnny's head against the roof molding, causing him to fall outside, to the parking lot floor, rather than inside the car.

"Shit!" Joe cursed as he kept moving toward the car. He fired two more bullets, one high, one lower, at the redhead, who was staring his way. The first bullet caught her in the face and splattered the passenger-side window with blood. The second hit her at the base of her throat.

Joe stopped at the car, pumped one more bullet into Johnny Calabrese's head, then dragged him into the car, stuffing him on the floor in back. He picked up the keys Johnny had dropped to the floor, jumped into the driver's seat, pushed the girl down, and started the Lincoln's engine. Despite the cold, he lowered the passenger window and pulled out of the lot.

Though Joe cursed the little things that had gone wrong—Johnny falling outside the car, the window getting fucked up—he felt relieved that it had gone as well as it had; that no one had come upon him while he did his work.

He proceeded to a deserted spot nearby, where he'd parked the Cherokee. Working quickly but methodically,

Joe wrapped the two bodies in plastic drop cloths he'd kept for just such an occasion, then transferred them to the Cherokee. He hid the Lincoln behind a copse of trees, where the Cherokee had been. He would come back for it later, when he completed his task.

Joe drove north along Boulevard Ste. Adele until he reached an uninhabited section of woods about twenty kilometers from the motel. He parked, then dragged the bodies out and about three hundred feet down a steep slope, one at a time. His third trip was for the shovel to burrow into the snow with. His heart pounded, his legs cramped, and spittle burned the corners of his mouth as it froze. He worked mercilessly, dragging the heavy bodies about, trying to arrange them in the tunnels he'd dug in the snow.

Joe would have much rather buried the two of them, but there was no way to dig in the Laurentian Mountains' frozen earth. The bodies would have to stay this way until spring thaw. Then, at least, when they were found, he would be far enough away not to care.

Covering up his tracks was the worst part—absolutely impossible. With any kind of good fortune, no one would stop there until at least the next morning's heavy snow filled in his tracks and the sloppy ruts the corpses had sculpted.

Joe sped back to Les Shutes du Nord. Using a flashlight as his only source of illumination, he emptied every belonging of the dead pair from their room. If it appeared that they had run out on their bill, there wouldn't be nearly the commotion there would if their possessions were still around. That would give him enough time to dispose of the rented car.

Joe transferred his cleaning detergents from the Cherokee into the Lincoln Town Car, then went about the problem of moving the cars. First he moved the Cherokee a half kilometer or so down the road, then jogged and walked back to the Lincoln. He drove the Town Car past the Cherokee by another half kilometer, then began the jog-walk process again. He repeated the piggybacking once more, this time hiding the Lincoln in a good spot.

Soaked with perspiration underneath his layers of insulated underwear, flannel, and wool, Joe went about cleaning out the interior of the Lincoln. He scrubbed every bit of blood visible, though he could not completely get the stains out of the rug. "Shit!" he cursed over and over as he worked.

When he felt satisfied he'd cleaned the Lincoln as well as it could be cleaned under the circumstances, he removed the license plates and scraped the Budget Rent-A-Car sticker off the back bumper. If he'd had the tools, he would have removed the tags from the car too. Anything to stall for time if things went bad. Time for him to get away.

Finally exhausted, Joe Augusta drove south in the Cherokee until he reached his chalet, in St. Sauveur des Monts.

The digital clock read 4:12 when Joe stepped into the downstairs shower stall. He turned up the water to a near scalding temperature and stood under its stream, his tears mixing with the hot water that turned his body lobster red. He'd always hated killing, fought against it every time its possibility came up, but too often found himself in a position where he had no choice, where he had to use the skills he'd honed by shooting the heads off running chickens as a youth.

Tonight was another case of having no way out. These two had been much too dangerous—to him, and to his mission for Chrissy, up in Heaven. He couldn't very well have let Johnny Calabrese go back to Brooklyn and blab. No. No way. He just prayed Johnny hadn't been gossipy enough to phone back home and mention whom he'd thought he'd seen.

No, it wasn't his fault, Joe excused himself. It just had to be done. Johnny Calabrese and that flashy cunt of his had to die.

But now there would be one more spirit to haunt him, Joe thought with anguish as he turned up the hot water. They'd already come back to take his darling Chrissy away. Now they would be stronger. Would they try for Elizabeth next?

"No, no, no," Joe wailed as he slipped down to a sitting position. His arms went around his knees, his head bent down to meet them. The scorching water beat down over him. "No . . . please, no . . ."

19

NICOLO FONTE DROVE UP THE WINDING ROAD, SLOWING BY EACH mansion, checking the addresses, until he found the one he was looking for: a large, white Georgian-style home, no more or less splendid than the others in this exclusive semisuburban enclave, set back behind a rolling lawn and sharply clipped hedges. His palms sweated on the steering wheel and his heart fluttered.

So long, he thought. So, so long.

Making a quick U-turn, with the agility of someone who had honed his skills on the Amalfi Drive, Nicolo pulled past the street that turned into a cul-de-sac a little farther up, and backed into it so he could watch the house—gain his courage to ring the bell.

Sitting alone in his car, with the windows fogged up, Fonte shook his head, feeling once again the excruciating emotional pain he had felt so long ago. Cursed himself again for being a coward, for running away—though Naples had treated him more than well. Shed yet another tear for what he had done to a young and noble boy.

Fonte reached inside his coat for a handkerchief, when his door suddenly swung open and the open end of a gun's barrel pressed against his head.

Mickey Boy shook his head to clear it of the myriad thoughts that lately kept it constantly jumbled. He heard the words of Ira J. Golden, who sat at a lazy side angle on an armchair in Mickey Boy's den, one heavy arm draped over the low back of the chair, a scotch on the rocks in his pudgy fist.

71

In one section of his mind Mickey Boy registered the fact that Golden had spoken to Halloran's superior, who had made some concessions on the job issue, allowing Mickey Boy to continue his alleged work as an outside salesman, without Halloran hounding him and people associated with L'Italia Provisions, like Guido Vizzini, who had hired him, and Mary, the bookkeeper. The problem, the superior had confided off the record, was that Halloran was a pit bull and had a powerful "rabbi" higher up in the department. Even those who worked with him were careful not to get in his way, for fear of winding up on a bureaucratic shit list.

Temporarily stalled by his boss, Halloran took a new tack. He let it be known that he was compiling a new list of people Mickey Boy was not to associate with. Generally, the rule applied to everyone was that they were not to associate with convicted felons. Mickey Boy had been as careful as possible not to violate that. In a way, in fact, it had pleased him, been the excuse for him to avoid many of the people in his organization whom he couldn't stand. The new list, however, was to contain names of nonfelons. That gave Golden the idea to submit to the courts for a ruling on its constitutionality, and to try to get a new, less prejudicial officer assigned to Mickey's Boy's case.

On another level of his thinking, Mickey Boy went over an earlier conversation with the attorney, about Richie DeLuca. Though the new judge had indicated that the case against Richie appeared extremely circumstantial, he privately let Golden know that Chrissy Augusta's murder was too high profile for him to just dump the indictment in the trash can, and denied pretrial motions for dismissal—and bail. Bringing it to a jury was the only way the judge saw to get Richie back home. A trial date was set for early the following month.

What occupied Mickey Boy's mind most was his unsuccessful search for businesses for his men. Gambling establishments, like OTB, would have been the perfect enterprise to suit his people's experience and expertise. The government, however, had taken that business over, as they could no other, and had left no room for licensees. Retail stores suggested had required too much inventory—he hated businesses where most of the money was tied up in merchandise that could either lie unsold or be stolen. Brokering consumer discount coupons, like for coffee or diapers, had intrigued him for a while. It was labor intensive, no inventory, and returned almost twenty-eight percent on face value in thirty days—it was better than shylocking. When he found out how monopolized that business was, run mostly by ex-FBI agents, and how much crime had been associated with it in the past, he tossed that idea too.

"Well, I've got to be going," Ira Golden said, standing. "Got to make a living, you know."

"Wait, I'll run a benefit for you," Mickey Boy replied. He had just given Golden another twenty thousand, in cash, toward his motion and Richie's case.

As he walked Golden to the door, Laurel passed by, carrying Hope. The baby had been so animated and alive lately. Every day was a new adventure: holding her bottle by herself, able to fully sit up, recognize him, and cry when he left her after play.

Mickey stopped to kiss the baby. She giggled and cooed, grabbed at his hair; really looked like she loved him. Laurel might not be happy staying home all the time, Mickey thought, but as far as he was concerned, it wouldn't bother him if they threw the key away and left him there, with his family, of course, forever.

When Mickey Boy opened the door to let Golden out, he scanned the street, as he normally did, looking for surveillance cars or any other unusual sign of danger. Off to his right he spotted a commotion. A group of men, who were obviously law enforcement, had another man against a brown Chrysler. All he could see of the man was his hands raised on the roof.

Under normal circumstances Mickey Boy would have stepped back inside and shut the door. He had enough problems without minding other people's business, and any contact with police or FBI presented the danger of a conflict, followed by an arrest, followed by a parole violation. Since he had Ira J. Golden with him, however, he decided to satisfy his curiosity and find out what was going on.

"Stay inside," he told Laurel, then he slipped into the moccasins he kept by the door and, with Golden lumbering behind him, started for the site.

Puffing much too heavily for his age, he thought, Mickey waited at the edge of the crowd for Ira Golden to catch up. Had to start exercising more, or wind up looking like Golden, he told himself.

When the lawyer stepped beside him, Mickey Boy pushed his way into the crowd to get a better look at who the cops had rousted. He hoped it wasn't one of his men; hoped more it wasn't someone from Don Peppino's crew.

A short, pudgy guy, with that distinct way of wearing a sweater under a suit jacket that identified him to Mickey Boy as being from Europe, probably Italy. Probably was from that scumbag, Peppino. Even had a greaseball's brush moustache.

"Caught some greaser scoping your house out," a white-haired FBI man Mickey Boy recognized said, sidling up to him. Though his manner was more teasing and sarcastic than serious, the underlying message was, as always, loud and clear. "Don't sound too good," the FBI man continued. "Why don't you take this card, just in case you need a friend."

"I got more friends than I want now."

"I could give it to your lawyer, Mr. Golden, here, if you feel uncomfortable taking it."

Mickey Boy started to laugh, but kept his eye on the Italian suspect. "Don't waste your card," he said.

Mickey Boy continued to stare at the Italian as the FBI men checked his identification. Something familiar, but . . .

Suddenly the shock of recognition surged through Mickey Boy like electricity. His mouth dried and his anger soared. His head pounded with years of pent-up hate.

"No, wait, what're youse doing?" Mickey Boy called as he pushed through to where the agents and the captured man stood. "I know this guy."

A black agent stuck an arm out to hold Mickey back. "Why doesn't that surprise us?"

"No, he's no street guy; he's a lawyer," Mickey said, thinking that the sonofabitch had done that ages ago. "His name is Fonte . . . Nicolo Fonte."

"How the fuck do you have the balls to come by my house?" Mickey Boy hissed. He paced back and forth across his living room rug in front of the bedraggled Nicolo Fonte, who sat, head bent, hat in hand, on the edge of a chair.

After having convinced the FBI that Fonte wouldn't hurt a fly, Mickey Boy had pulled Fonte into his house; had sent Ira Golden away; had chased Laurel up the stairs.

That was then. He had wanted Fonte for himself.

Now, Mickey Boy felt like strangling the huddled lump of shit; wanted to spill his blood all over the light beige rug.

"Well, you fuck, say something!" Mickey Boy demanded. "What the hell do you want? Tell me before I fuckin' strangle you here, in my house!"

"I am sorry, I should not have come," Fonte said, his head still bowed.

Mickey Boy stopped in front of him, legs spread, fists balled. His heart beat in his throat. "Cut the shit," he said. "Tell me why you came."

Nicolo Fonte looked up at Mickey Boy towering above him. Fonte's moustache turned downward and his eyes misted. "I wanted to see what kind of man you had become," he said softly. "Now I know."

"Mickey?" Laurel called, tentatively making her way down the stairs. "Mickey, please. Is everything all right?"

Mickey Boy spun, his first inclination to yell and scream, to tell her to mind her business and get the fuck upstairs. Instead he looked at her face, at the concern in her eyes, then back to Fonte's defeated figure, then back to Laurel again.

"Yeah, hon," he said. "It's okay. It'll be fine."

"Do you want me to make some coffee?"

"Yeah, thanks. That'll be great."

As Laurel hurried nervously to the kitchen, Mickey Boy plopped into the chair opposite Fonte. He stared at him for a moment, then asked, "Why did you do that to me? Was I really that dumb?"

"Dumb?" Fonte said. "No, to the contrary. The problem was that you were smart, too smart." He shook his head. "I could never understand why that bothered them, but, of course, now I know."

"Stop with the fuckin' greaseball riddles!" Mickey Boy shouted. "I hear that shit all the time."

Fonte hung his head again.

"Just say it," Mickey Boy continued. "Tell me why you

kicked me out. If it was me, don't be scared, just say it. If it was your fault, be a goddamn man an' say that too. Just fuckin' say something!"

Laurel laid out a pot of coffee and an Entenmann's crumb cake, then sat down on the sofa, staring up at him for an okay to stay.

Mickey dropped to the sofa next to her, taking comfort from having her next to him.

"I idolized you," he said to Fonte. "You knew how much I wanted to be a lawyer, just like you. How the fuck could you do that to me?"

Fonte looked up at Mickey Boy. He stared directly into his eyes. "Are you sure you really want to know?"

"Tell me."

"It was cold outside, *fa freddo* . . . so cold that the steam in my office fogged up the windows. When the knock came on the door, I had to open it to see who it was . . ." Two men, Fonte said, shoved their way inside and closed the door behind them.

"The bigger man, he pushed me back in my chair and starts choking me with my tie. 'You know who we are?' he asked me." Fonte waved his hand in small circles. "Who they are? Everybody knew. *Malandrenes* . . . hoodlums . . . thieves . . . murderers, that's who," he said.

Though he had no idea what that had to do with him, Mickey remained quiet, mesmerized by Fonte's telling.

"Then the big man said, 'The kid, Mickey Boy, he works for you?' Before I could even answer, with my tie strangling me, he says, 'Well, no more. Get rid of him.' Just like that."

When he didn't answer, Fonte said, because he could only gasp for air, the second hoodlum, who had stood by the door, ordered the bigger one to let him go. Fonte claimed that he had tried to stick up for Mickey Boy, to let them know that he could be a good lawyer one day, that he could help him. But they didn't want to hear anything about that. They wanted Mickey Boy gone.

If it were anyone else telling the story, Mickey Boy would have called him a liar and broke his jaw. This didn't make any sense.

"My heart broke, not for me, but for you," Fonte said. "I

knew how it was for you, first with no father, then losing your stepfather. I knew that now I, who was really like a father figure to you, had to go hurt you again." Tears welled in Fonte's eyes. "I just didn't have the courage to stand up to them, and to do what was right for you. I just wasn't enough of a man."

Mickey Boy felt the hurt that was so obviously sincere in Fonte.

When Fonte regained his composure, he added that the worst part was when the second man tossed a thick stack of hundred-dollar bills onto the desk. "Then he told me, *'Avvocato,* this is your moving money.' I can hear it now as clear as if he was still talking. 'This is your moving money. Make sure you relocate far enough away to make us all comfortable . . . or else my friend, here, Bastiano, will pay you a very unpleasant visit. *Capisce?'* And they left."

Mickey Boy's head filled with thunder. He felt as if he'd been smashed in the chest with a sledgehammer. How could he have done it? he wondered. How could his own father have hurt him so much? Why wasn't he alive, to feel his wrath now?

"Don Vincenze?" Mickey asked softly, not really needing confirmation.

Fonte nodded. "He wasn't called don then. He didn't need it to get what he wanted."

"And Buster?"

"Yes."

Mickey Boy would rather have hated Nicolo Fonte for the rest of his days than to have heard the truth. He would have liked it to be a lie, but knew that Fonte didn't lie. He also knew how single-minded and devious Don Vincenze had been when he'd had his mind set in some direction. The fact that the don had engineered a Machiavellian war between the families that had killed more than a dozen good men still rankled Mickey Boy. That he'd ordered the killing of a petty drug dealer, which had backfired and taken poor Chrissy Augusta's life, hurt even more. But this God-playing with his, Mickey Boy's, life was a deeper, more personal wound, one that made him begin to detest the father he'd never known, and doubt himself. What kind of disgusting, two-faced genes did he, Mickey Boy, carry inside? Would he have no choice but to eventually become a carbon copy of the old man?

If anything, all he could blame Fonte for was being weak, Mickey Boy reasoned with himself. He looked over at the shrunken figure across the table from him, nervously cutting another slice of cake. But then again, he thought, who could have really stood up to Vincenze Calabra and his own version of Luca Brasi, Buster Alcamo? Wait till he got ahold of fuckin' Buster.

Laurel reached over and took Mickey's hand. He was glad she'd heard how his life had been purposely run off a course that could have saved him tons of grief, not to mention six years of his life. Glad she could now know that there was a side of him that was always good. But the pity in her eyes now made him pity himself all the more.

Mickey Boy almost laughed, thinking of Brando's famous line, "I coulda been a contender." So many options sent down the shitter because the old man had tabbed him for his heir. Who knows, maybe he could have been more than a lawyer; maybe a politician. He couldn't do a worse job than the assholes in there now. Maybe, maybe, maybe . . .

The ringing of door chimes interrupted Mickey Boy's introspection. Laurel stood to go answer it, but Mickey Boy stopped her. Guest or no guest, he insisted they stick to his rule: only he was to answer the door. No way he would leave her on the front line to face an arresting agent or, God forbid, someone out to do him harm. Danger was for him alone; never, if he could help it, for Laurel or Hope.

Mickey Boy took his time walking to the steel-reinforced door, glancing from side to side through bulletproof windows for a glimpse of who was outside. Next would be to check the television monitor he'd had concealed behind a wall panel. When a leg was raised in front of the glass and the pants were pulled up to reveal an almost bald white leg and striped silk socks, he breathed easier.

Freddie Falcone entered, still shaking his pants leg into place. "Goddamn static," he said. "They must be sending agents in to shoot me full of electricity while I sleep. Two more weeks an' I'll probably look like a leftover in a fry basket."

"Just be happy they ain't nuking you," Mickey Boy replied. "Then they could follow you in the dark."

"Funny, funny," Freddie said, following Mickey Boy into the dining area. "I teach you a little shtick, an' now you wanna take my whole act." He paused, then added, "No, don't tell me . . . the follow-up line is, 'That's why they call me the boss.' There, I said it for you . . . still the best . . ."

Freddie quieted down as soon as he saw Fonte. Though he had no idea who he was, it wasn't hard to tell from Fonte's hound-dog expression that there was no party going on.

"Don't worry, this ain't a funeral," Mickey Boy said. "This is somebody I knew—or thought I knew—a long time ago."

"As long as he ain't your doctor."

"No, he's a lawyer."

"Shit, that could be worse." Freddie hugged and kissed Laurel, who excused herself to check on the napping Hope.

"No, not a lawyer anymore . . ." Nicolo Fonte replied seriously, not tuned in to their banter, ". . . a businessman."

The word *businessman* sparked an interest in Mickey Boy, but faded quickly, stored in the back of his head. He was in no mood to hear Fonte's life story just now.

"Freddie an' me have to go someplace," Mickey Boy said. "Just leave me a number where I could get in touch with you. Right now I don't feel like talking much."

"Ho capito," Fonte said, standing to go. "I understand." He scribbled a phone number on a piece of paper he ripped from a secretary pad. "Please call," he said, laying it on the table.

At the door, Fonte turned to Mickey Boy and stared as if looking for something—a hug, a handshake, a simple word of forgiveness?

Mickey Boy had none.

Nicolo Fonte turned his hat in his hands, then stepping out of the door, softly said, *"Mi dispiace."* I'm sorry.

20

April 1: Approaching Dulles International Airport

WAS IT SUPPOSED TO BE A GODDAMNED JOKE? LITTLE VINNIE wondered as the announcement came that they would land in about forty minutes. Sending him home on April Fool's Day? Was that the greaseballs' way of laughing at him behind his back? Did they even know what the fuck April Fool's was? Or was it just a joke of nature and timing, trying to tell him to get away as fast as he could?

But where would he go if he decided to drop the whole thing, forget that bastard half brother of his, Mickey Boy, and take off for parts unknown? What would he do? What would he have? At least in Sicily, because he was sure he didn't want to stay in New York anymore, he would have Ninfa—sweet, virginal, naturally blond Ninfa. Little Vinnie closed his eyes and tried to picture her naked. There was no doubt in his mind that her collar and cuffs matched, that there'd be a tuft of fine yellow hair waiting for him between those slender thighs.

As with all the other times Little Vinnie fantasized about the don's granddaughter, an erection formed, so strained that it actually hurt.

"Would you like a drink?" the stewardess asked, tapping him gently on the shoulder.

Little Vinnie's hands dropped to his lap. "N-No," he muttered, trying to cover his embarrassment. His eyes felt glazed, and he closed them immediately and went back to the naked Ninfa. So sweet, so fair. At first he'd been shocked to see a Sicilian with Ninfa's coloring, with eyes so light and blue. All the Sidgies he'd met in New York had been dark-haired and olive-complexioned; products of centuries of invasions by Moors, Turks, and other dark-skinned groups. In fact, others in the Italian-American community had jokingly called the Sicilians niggers. When they teased, those from Bari ate horse meat, Calabrese were thick-headed, and Sicilians were niggers. Though he hated to admit it, Little Vinnie had seen some that looked that way too. But in Sicily he'd found that many carried the blood of the North; Germanic tribes and probably Vikings. At a crossroads of sea travel, Sicily had been invaded by practically everyone who passed its way, each leaving a bit of its seed behind. Some of that beautiful northern seed had trickled its way down to make Ninfa.

Little Vinnie laughed. Would her name be "Nympha" in private? Would she be a hot little number, like the girl whose lively spirit she seemed to carry? Like the dead little tramp he'd cared about so much? Like Chrissy? As quickly as his erection disappeared, that's how fast Little Vinnie was hurled into depression. One millisecond, one goddamned moment in time that had fucked up his life forever:

They thought they were fuckin' cute, my old man and that other old fuck, Buster. They knew I had the right to be there to hit that Irish cocksucker, Skinny Malone, but like always, the old bastards would rather make me look like shit and keep me away.

They liked that Skinny beat me for money and that his scumbag partner, Georgie, embarrassed the shit out of me. What, was it their guys that Georgie pistol-whipped? No, it was my fuckin' face that got spit in.

So, when it comes time to straighten it out, who do they call? Me? No, to fuckin' rub my nose in shit, they call that half-a-hump, Richie, and that fuckin' retard, Butch Scicli. Sure, give them two a shot to make their bones, an' not me.

Cocksuckers! They jinxed the fuckin' job from the beginning . . . made me bull my way in to take over, instead of planning it right from the get-go. Made me run with those two assholes, Richie and Butch, who couldn't kill a fuckin' roach if it was under their fuckin' shoes.

"Boy, did we get lucky," me, asshole, when I seen Georgie's

black 'Vette parked by the bar. Seen the fuckin' Irishman's hat—that goddamned hat—thought I was the luckiest guy in the world.

Some fuckin' luck!

Swore I saw the Irishman sittin' in the car . . . even got a hard-on, it was so good. Meant Georgie hadda be inside the joint. Like Buster said, "If Georgie gets in the way, clip him too—this is perfect!"

Yeah, perfect as a fuckin' heart attack!

Richie sittin' in the back of the Buick. Too bad I couldn't kill him too. What a fuckin' perfect message to send to that Mickey Boy bastard . . . almost as good as the one I was gonna send later, when I was gonna fuck Laurel silly.

Laurel. Another one he'd forgotten, who he owed a special debt to.

Took me fuckin' weeks to get that bitch to meet me for a drink . . . and that night, of all nights. Woulda been perfect. After whacking that Irish cocksucker, I woulda needed a good hot fuck, like Laurel, to bring me down.

Broke my balls for that cunt, lying, telling her how we had to work something out for me and Mickey Boy to make amends for when he got out. All a fuckin' game, to make her conscience clear when she let me fuck her . . . and I played it all the way.

Maybe Mickey Boy woulda hung up when he heard I reamed his girl's cunt . . . saved me the trouble of whacking him when he got out.

Coulda killed two fuckin' birds with one hump.

Coulda been blessed twice.

Fucked twice, was more like it.

Asshole, Richie, whining in the back about trying to catch Skinny when he was alone, when Georgie couldn't come strolling out.

"Tough shit!" I yelled back. How I wished I coulda clipped him too. I knew he didn't want me along; thought who the fuck was he, like he was one step up on me or something. Besides, I wanted Georgie too. "Teach him not to hang out with fuckin' potato eaters."

Or to fuck a sweet girl like Chrissy, who should have been his; been his wife and carried his children.

"Drop us off three or four cars behind him," I told that fat fuck, Butch. "Then go up the block and make a U-turn." All the jerkoff hadda to do was drive back, making sure the power locks were open for me an' Richie to get back in, an' all the windows are open, in case we gotta dive through in a hurry. Later, with everything okay, all he woulda had to do was deep-six the swag Buick after he dropped us off.

Woulda, shoulda, coulda.

I make Richie go up on the driver's side, an' I take the other side . . . even make sure to tell the asshole not to come up past the back of the seat, so we don't hit each other.

"An' if Georgie comes out, make sure you hit him too—unless you wanna be on his side," I says. Telling him that fucks him up—I could see it—but charges me up even more. I move like a champ, between cars, heart pumped up, finger ready to squeeze away and lose that fuckin' Irishman for good.

The excitement Little Vinnie had felt that night now made his stomach sink into his scrotum. Or was it the plane dropping? The stewardess came by to push his seat upright, and check to see that his seat belt was fastened. Fuckin' cunt, he thought, then closed his eyes again.

My body was like a fuckin' machine: hand going up with the gun just when my foot steps down by the seat; my head's pounding and feels like it's gonna bust; my finger's squeezing off a round just as the gun catches the Irishman's cap straight on . . . Richie, that fuck, screaming, yelling, like in an echo chamber . . . I don't understand . . . I can't make out his words, "Don't shoot! Don't shoot!"

Too late.

My eardrums feel like busting from the noise, my nose picks up the awful burning smell . . . my finger keeps squeezing . . . two . . . three . . .

The hat flies off.

. . . four . . .

A head full of black curls smashes on the dashboard.

. . . five . . .

Blood flying.

. . . six . . .

Little Vinnie unconsciously squeezed his right fist tight, pulling the fingers that had squeezed the trigger inward as though he wanted to crush them.

I hear me screaming, "Chrissy! Chrissy!"

. . . seven . . .

Georgie coming out behind me, yelling, I turned to him.

. . . eight, nine.

Little Vinnie cursed his bad luck just as the American Super 80 hit the runway with a jolt. He cursed the pilot when the plane bounced up a bit then hit the ground a second time. Thank God he wouldn't have to go through customs; he'd done that in Chicago already when the 767 from Milan had first touched him down in the U.S. Goddamn greasers must have saved a few dollars on his flight to have him flying for nearly an entire day: Palermo to Naples, to Milan, to Chicago, to D.C. He was sure there had to be a more direct flight, at least from Naples. He felt like a goddamn bouncing ball, and his asshole hurt from sitting so long.

Coming through the gate, Little Vinnie searched for someone who looked like they might have been sent to meet him. Don Genco had promised that whoever showed up would find him. It wouldn't be as difficult as he'd thought, what with as few white faces around.

"Signor Destino?" a high-pitched voice questioned. Destino, or destiny, was the name Don Genco had chosen for his phony identification—Edoardo Destino—as a constant reminder of the mission at hand.

The man behind the high-pitched voice smiled beneath his brush moustache. About five-foot-five, and with cherubic pink cheeks and brownish-gray hair grown long on one side then combed over a bald head, Little Vinnie would have passed him by as his Sicilian-American contact. The man even dressed like he was on goddamned welfare—cheap green sweater and baggy white cotton pants—and smelled like he'd bathed in oregano.

"Yeah, I'm Destino," he said, beginning to question why he hadn't just used his own papers. Fuckin' Mickey Boy wasn't the FBI; no one sent incoming names to a computer in his house or in Buster's club. Although he might well need a quick escape route under another name after the bastard was dead. He already knew from experience that whatever could go wrong usually did.

Little Vinnie winced when the man hugged and kissed him. Now he would smell too.

"I am DoDo, *gli amici degli amici,*" the little man said,—a friend of the friends—indicating that he was a made member from Sicily. *"Andiamo."* Let's go.

Trailing behind DoDo, who had generously taken Little Vinnie's folded garment bag and now dragged it along the floor, Little Vinnie said, "I hope you got a room close by, 'cause I'm beat; need a goddamn shower too."

"No time," DoDo replied. "We gotta drive back home. I get you a room when we get to New Jersey," he said, pronouncing the last word "Jers."

Fuck New Jersey, Little Vinnie thought, all shaved and showered, and, with almost twelve hours of sleep under his belt, ready to go out and gorge himself on the first decent meal since leaving Sicily.

Even though he'd been near collapse, after having traveled on four different flights and more time zones than he knew existed, he had refused to be abandoned in the dinky Jersey City motel DoDo brought him to the night before. No way he was going to stay in a place where the streets rolled in at ten.

DoDo had argued that if he wanted privacy, which, of course, meant not to be seen by anyone who could report his whereabouts to Mickey Boy, he would have to stay there; why, he asked, did Little Vinnie think they had arranged such a circuitous route to New York in the first place? They didn't even want to chance his being seen by some local mobster traveling back from Naples or Palermo. With less mobster descendants to worry about traveling back to the U.S., Milano was a safer choice.

Still no way.

Instead he made DoDo bring him to the Holiday Inn on West Fifty-seventh Street, dependable comfort far enough away from where anyone he knew would hang out, yet close enough for him to have some fun. Besides, with his new moustache and longer hair, no one would recognize him in a million years.

Little Vinnie checked himself in the mirror, admiring how handsome the moustache made him look. That was one of the other things he loved about Sicily: moustaches were okay. Here, among American-born mobsters, who hated their counterparts from the other side, moustaches were considered taboo, said to be worn by either stool pigeons or cunt-lappers. He was no stool pigeon, anyway.

Not bad, he thought, walking out the door, a happy moustache and Ninfa to spend his life with once he got back to Acireale.

The temperature was a bit cooler than Little Vinnie had expected from a New York evening in early April. He lifted his suit jacket lapels around his neck and briskly walked toward the Broadway theater district a few blocks away. His right hand went to the back of his waistband to make sure the .38 revolver stuck there wasn't exposed. DoDo had been kind enough to provide the gun and five hundred dollars in cash. Big sport, Little Vinnie thought. A goddamn decent meal would cost ten percent of that. No problem, though. Once he could get at his own cash and bankbook, buried in the Staten Island house, he'd be okay.

Instead of turning down gaudy Broadway, Little Vinnie made a right on Eighth Avenue. It made him feel better, after he'd walked more than a half-dozen blocks, to see hookers standing on corners and in doorways, legs high as his chest, ass cheeks peeking out of tiny shorts, tits flashed from quickly opened jacket fronts. Maybe after dinner, he thought. Better yet, maybe he'd bring one back to the hotel, then call room service for food.

"Hey, white boy," one black girl called. "Want yo' thing sucked?" When he walked on, she muttered, "Faggot." Another hooker called out asking if he was a cop. Yeah, right, he wanted to yell back, if I was a cop, I'd fuckin' tell you.

A white girl, inches taller than him, with pale blond hair, sidled up to him and began keeping pace as he walked. Cleaner looking than the rest, she looked young, almost sweet. "Are you lonely?" she asked. Not if he wanted to get laid, but how he felt. That both impressed him and touched the nerve of the desolation he really felt but normally suppressed.

"Whattaya get?" he asked, walking a bit slower.

"You a cop?"

Little Vinnie used the line he had wanted to throw away before, though not as harshly.

"I have to ask that. Then if you say no and are, it's against the law."

"How you gonna prove that in court?" Little Vinnie asked, taking the girl under the arm and swinging around to go back up Eighth. "You got a tape? If not, those fuckers'll only lie to get a pinch."

The girl slipped Little Vinnie's hand under her jacket to cradle her breast. "Does that feel like a recorder?"

Little Vinnie's head and erection began to throb at the same time. It had been so goddamn long. Sicily was no joke; he'd been afraid to make a move with any female in Don Genco's circle; didn't want to make waves with any other family of mafiosi who might stop him from being made— not to mention that those zips would kill you in a heartbeat. Hookers there were safe, but he didn't have the Bank of England to draw from either. Getting a nut off once in a while had been the best he could do and one of the hardest things he'd had to get accustomed to over there.

Now, while kneading the blond hooker's breast, Little Vinnie moaned an answer. The girl bent and kissed him full on the mouth; her tongue reamed around his lips. Little Vinnie pulled back, still hot but wondering where her mouth had been last.

As they passed a recessed doorway, the girl pulled Little Vinnie in. She pulled him to her, then shoved her tongue into his mouth. Fuck where her tongue had been, Little Vinnie thought. He fondled her breast under her jacket, grabbed her ass, stuck his hand down her skirt—to feel a male sex organ—just as he also felt a strong tug on his hair from behind, yanking his head backward, and a blade pressed against his throat. Little Vinnie saw his life pass before him; he was going to die. He nearly cried out in panic.

The girl, or whatever it was, held both his hands at his sides with amazing strength; the two assailants sandwiched him so he couldn't move, his erection pressed against the girl/guy, another male organ pressed against his ass.

"Listen, motherfucker," a raspy whisper said. "Give me a hard time and I'll cut your motherfuckin' throat."

Little Vinnie nearly collapsed with relief. Just his money, thank God. He assured the thief that he wouldn't make a sound or move to impede his robbery. When the he-she slipped out from under him, he put his hands up against the door, and the other one went through his pockets. He pulled the fold of money DoDo had given Little Vinnie, snatched his wallet, felt the gun in his waistband.

"You a motherfuckin' pig," the thief said.

"No, no, I swear, man, I hate cops. Man, I'm no cop. I'm on the other side."

"Don't 'man' me, motherfucker," the thief said, lifting Little Vinnie's gun. "Make a sound an' I'll shoot you with your own motherfuckin' gun. Just stay there an' don't make no noise." The thing with balls and tits fastened Little Vinnie's right hand to the door with a set of handcuffs.

Little Vinnie jumped when he felt a little stab in the cheek of his ass, but he kept silent.

"That's just to show you I ain't fuckin' around with you, motherfucker."

When the hurrying footsteps disappeared out of hearing distance, Little Vinnie collapsed against the door. The front of his pants felt wet, as did the back, where blood from his buttock soaked the fabric.

He shook uncontrollably.

He retched.

He passed out.

21

April 1: Gravesend, Brooklyn

DON PEPPINO PALERMO SHIFTED IN HIS LEATHER LA-Z-BOY. Piles were one of the curses of old age that plagued him now, as well as a swollen prostate and a variety of aches and pains.

The don looked at the clock. Eight forty-five. He couldn't wait to put his head down on the pillow for the night, but had to wait.

Just then the front doorbell rang. Don Peppino scurried over to the window and peeked through the drawn velvet drapes. A white Paisano Pizzeria truck sat in front. Finally.

Satisfied, the don went to the door and opened it. A small man stepped in, holding a steaming pizza box that reeked of too much oregano. Don Peppino shut the door behind him.

"Buona sera, Don Peppino," the man said after placing the pizza on an empty umbrella stand and hugging the don.

"Buona sera, DoDo."

22

April 10: Court Street, Brooklyn

"THEY COULD INDICT A HAM SANDWICH IF THEY WANT TO," IRA J. Golden said. "Getting a conviction is another story."

Once again the State of New York was playing games with Richie's case; postponing it for yet another month. In a way, it was a good thing, because it illustrated how weak the prosecution team felt its case really was. Had it been strong, they would have pressed for a trial, conviction, and life sentence, then shipped him off to Attica or Dannemora before he knew what the hell was going on. Instead, they only stalled, eating up his life month by month as punishment for something they couldn't prove.

"Don't think," Golden added, "that it's a hundred-percent winner. Their case may be weak, but you never know what a jury will do. I've seen more than one defendant get convicted on circumstantial evidence."

"They don't even have that," Mickey Boy replied.

"He was there, wasn't he?"

"Yeah, but so was the baker, or the butcher, or whoever."

"But they're not indicted and waiting for trial. Richie is," Golden said. "They'll march a couple of people onto the stand who will say they saw Richie with a gun—"

"That's what I'm talking about," Mickey Boy said. "They ain't even got a gun, and they got him indicted for possession of a weapon."

"That's the ham sandwich. There was a shooting, ergo a gun. Richie was there. Someone identified him as a shooter, ergo an indictment. They present one side of a case, without any opposition, and they get their ham sandwich ready for

90

cooking. It's just up to us to prove it isn't so, and keep Richie off the grill."

Freddie chimed in with, "Bottom line is, one more month; maybe two or three, but that's it. The kid'll need the time anyway to break his engagement to some guy named Bubba. Now on to your problem with the P.O. from Hell. We got places to go, people to see . . ." He finished up by comedically singing, ". . . everything for you and me."

Golden said that was it, he could stand anything but a voice like Freddie's, and turned the subject to Mickey Boy's problems with Halloran. He said he'd file more motions, writs, habes, show-cause orders—anything to stall for time. "I'll shower them with paperwork."

But eventually, Golden told Mickey Boy, he would lose.

"This guy will keep after you, either overtly or on his own time, till he catches you off guard just once." Golden snapped his pudgy fingers. "There goes your parole."

"But I'm not even on parole," Mickey Boy argued. "I did all my time. The only time I got off was my good time, that was either given to me by law or I earned by working. How is that parole?"

"You signed a paper saying you would do it as parole time."

"They wouldn't let me out if I didn't. Ain't that extortion or something?"

"Realistically, it's coercion, but the time to fight it was before you signed, not after. There are cases still pending where parolees are fighting the jurisdiction. I can make yours one more, but I'm telling you, you'll have to stay on parole while it's in the court, and it will stay on the calendar until you finish, making it moot."

"Fuck it. Do what you can," Mickey Boy said. He was getting goddamn tired of having to fight battles on all fronts, sometimes feeling worn-out enough that checking back into jail almost seemed like a vacation. He nodded to Freddie, who dropped an envelope with another ten thousand dollars on Golden's desk. Golden shoved it into a drawer without opening it.

"Ooops," Freddie said. "I mighta given you the envelope with the coupons I save for Key Food." When Golden opened the drawer to pull the envelope, Freddie laughingly said, "Nah, don't bother. You know it's cash. Lawyers could smell money from three blocks away. If it was something else, you woulda thrown it back at me."

"Or slapped you," Golden replied, then after a pause, added, ". . . with a subpoena."

"You got me with that one," Freddie said cheerfully as he and Mickey Boy left the office. "You got me with that one." As soon as they had closed the door and were alone in the hall, Freddie's demeanor turned sour. He muttered, "Fuckin' bloodsucker."

Twenty minutes later they pulled up by Buster's brownstone house in South Brooklyn. Freddie honked twice for Buster, who was supposed to be ready and looking out for them. When no one came out, Mickey Boy and Freddie decided to go inside.

"I'm sorry, he's upstairs getting dressed," Buster's wife, Nettie, said. "He's running a little late because he don't feel so good."

Nettie poured coffee for Mickey Boy and Freddie, then set out homemade anisette sponge cake.

"You sure he's okay?" Mickey Boy asked.

Buster had been ill with a cold when Mickey Boy had come to see him over a week ago, after having talked to Nicolo Fonte. Mickey Boy had been fuming, ready to lace into Buster, but had held back when he'd seen how bad Buster looked. True, Buster was now in his sixties, but that wasn't really old, Mickey Boy had thought. He'd figured Buster might have been acting at feeling worse than he was, because he'd sensed he was in hot water.

When Mickey Boy had confronted him with Fonte's story, Buster replied that he'd never felt the don had done the right thing in that instance, but had never been one to argue with him. His job was, then and now, to follow orders, which was exactly what he'd done. He added that, right or wrong, the don had done what he'd truly felt was best. In his own way, he had loved and respected Mickey Boy more than any other of his children. He'd seen the qualities in him that he felt must be cultivated for eventual leadership and salvation of his mob family.

"What about me?" Mickey Boy had asked. "What about what I wanted?"

Buster answered that, as Don Vincenze had swore when he took his sacred vows, their "family" truly came first.

Now, Mickey Boy sat in the same position, though feeling more torn about his responsibilities than he imagined Don Vincenze ever had.

Buster entered the room looking glassy-eyed, as though he had a fever, and sneezing. His skin looked leathery and gray. His face looked bony.

"You sure you're okay to come today?" Mickey Boy asked.

Freddie chimed in that Buster should fire his embalmer and get a new one.

"Yeah, I could go," Buster replied. "No problem. Just a goddamn cold I can't get rid of—goes away, then comes back, goes away, an' I got it again."

Mickey Boy rose from his seat. With an upward swing of his head he motioned for Freddie to follow. "Never mind today," he told Buster. "It ain't that important. Go see a doctor."

Buster, the family's underboss, argued that the meeting with their captains was indeed important, that as it was, they were grumbling about the lack of direct communication between them and their leader, Mickey Boy.

"Who said I wasn't going?" Mickey Boy asked on his way to the door. "I just said you didn't have to come. Like I said, go to the doctor, see if he gives you a shot of B-12 or something; maybe pump up your blood."

"Try a vet," Freddie said. "Maybe you caught hoof an' mouth down at your club?"

He didn't need a doctor, Buster argued again. It was a cold. Rest would heal him fine.

Nettie, cleaning off the table, said to Mickey Boy, "Tell him; make him go. Big *chooch* is afraid of doctors. Go on, Mickey Boy, make him."

Mickey Boy laughed. He wondered if he and Laurel would be like Nettie and Buster someday: two old crows who loved each other dearly and bickered all the time.

"Yeah, Nettie's right," he said seriously. "Go see a doctor today. That's a direct order."

The suite at the Marriott Marquis was already occupied. Each of the eight captains of the Calabra Family whom Mickey Boy had Buster and Freddie invite were there, drinks in hand, tasting from the set-out platters of hors d'oeuvres. The other fourteen would either be spoken to at a later date, ignored, or possibly busted down and replaced.

What Mickey Boy was looking for was a solid power base of his own, built on forward-looking partners in legitimate businesses. These men he'd assembled had no criminal records. They each had a lawful business that could support them independently of any mob-related activities. They each had ten made men under them. They were all over fifty years of age, and had all been close associates of his father.

After a round of kisses, hugs, and personal small talk, Mickey Boy brought the meeting to order. He reminded his men that he had specifically had Buster and Freddie give them invitations in person, in areas they could be sure were not monitored by authorities, and insist that they mention this meeting to no one.

"I hope every word I said was followed," Mickey Boy said. "Because every word I said meant something. I just didn't say things should be done that way just because I had a mouthful of extra words that hadda come out."

Freddie, joking as ever, added, "An' I hope none of youse left your jewelry in the vault, like you were never coming back."

One of the captains, Tony Polo—short for Pologrosso, or, translated into English, big chicken—the owner of a firm that trucked fruits and vegetables to major supermarkets, held his hands out to display two gaudy diamond rings, a diamond-encrusted Piaget watch, and a gold ID bracelet with his name in diamonds. He teased back, "See, just guilty guys gotta worry about bein' set up. Guys like us got white hearts."

"Yeah," Freddie replied. "Either covered in platinum— or mold." He pointed at Bobby Rimini, an oversized executive of an office cleaning company, and added, ". . . Or fat."

Mickey Boy liked hearing the easy banter between his men—that was what family should be like—but had to cut it off to get his agenda taken care of. Either that or run so far behind for the day that he'd only get home, once again, after Laurel and Hope were asleep.

"I called you guys here because I think we need a new direction if we're gonna survive as a family," he began. "We need to make the bridge into legitimate business—"

"But we all got businesses," Patsy Luciano, a sixty-five-year-old importer of Italian food products, answered.

Yes, they did, Mickey Boy said. But what about their underlings, and those other made men who spent half their lives at sit-downs over money they'd borrowed and couldn't pay? Or those who were sneaking around trying to broker drug deals? Or those who would expose themselves to prison or death some other way? Those were the guys who had to be saved. And the men in that suite had to be the ones to do it.

"Listen," Tony Polo said. "If putting more guys on the payroll is what you're after, forget it. I break my ass each week just to get by, while those other *strombolattas* spend their time at Aqueduct or a *ziganette* game."

Patsy Luciano added, "I got two of my wife's nephews on my payroll now, an' you know what? I'd be better off with niggers from the South Bronx."

"Put yourself on for a pay," another captain, Benny Donuts, said. "I'd rather do that than start this communist shit, where we gotta give everybody a piece."

"Whoa, wait a minute," Mickey Boy said. "Relax, I ain't looking to pad up your payrolls, and I ain't," he added, pointing a finger at Benny, "trying to shake you down for myself."

Sensing Mickey Boy's anger rising, Freddie interrupted with a few joking words, then took firm control. "You were out of order," he said to Benny. "You woulda done that to his old man, and he woulda had your balls sliced up in them canapes by now."

Benny stood, embraced Mickey Boy, and apologized.

Freddie went on. "I don't wanna keep bringing the old man up, but youse all walked around with two feet in one shoe when he was alive. Whattaya wanna do, push Mickey Boy here till he goes off and becomes Attila the Hun? He could chop a ball or two off too, you know, if that's what it takes. But is that the only language you guys understand?" He paused, then opening his arms, said, "C'mon, fellas, you're the best we got."

After a brief silence, Patsy Luciano, the elder statesman of the meeting, said, "You know we always respected a *buon uomo,* Don Vincenze. An', of course, we respect you too, Mickey Boy, not only as your father's son, but as a man. You had a real good reputation even before we knew you was his blood. However," Patsy said, pausing dramatically afterward, "an' there always is a however . . . we got problems. An' before we could understand what you wanna do, I think you should understand what we're up against, an' let's clear the air."

Mickey Boy looked to Freddie for advice. After all, that's what a fuckin' consigliere was for, he thought. Should he assert himself now, and take charge? Or lay back and let the old food importer/captain in the Calabra Family have his say?

Freddie nodded almost imperceptibly.

"Go ahead," Mickey Boy said. "Whatever's on your mind, say it now."

The first thing that was on Luciano's mind was why wasn't Buster there? The others nodded their agreement with his query. They had heard that Mickey Boy had been pissed off at him a week or so ago, and wondered if he was being mistreated. After all, he was one of the most respected members of their old guard.

Just like fuckin' old women, Mickey Boy thought. They knew things they should have no way of knowing, and gossiped about them like he would expect the old hens to do at a sewing circle.

"No, Buster ain't being abused," Mickey Boy said, unable to control the annoyed edge to his voice. "He just looked like shit, an' I told him to go to the doctor instead of coming here."

With no look of disbelief, acceptance, or guilt, Luciano went on, "Now, you gotta understand, I'm not sayin' they're right, but there's a lot of beefin' by other skippers that you're out of touch with what's going on every day."

"I know everything," Mickey Boy replied. "Buster and Freddie keep me up to date."

"Yeah, but Buster an' Freddie ain't you. Not that you could do a goddamn thing more for them if you was there every day, but that's just how they are. They like to shmooze and get their chance to brown-nose the boss. Otherwise, they start to feel like second-class citizens, an' you're talking about guys with big egos, here."

"They know I got a parole problem."

"They know that, an' understand, especially guys like us. We been around, seen everything, an' to tell you the truth, seen enough to appreciate a boss that stays the fuck out of our hair. They ain't all like that, though. Some just bellyache to hear their own voices, others are like babies that want attention from their old man, and some are just jealous . . . they figure they're on the front lines every day, an' figure they should be the family's top brass."

"They could have my spot, for all I care," Mickey Boy said. "Today it's like getting the reins to a wagon that's driving over a cliff."

A laugh among all the men broke the tension slightly.

"Believe me, Mickey Boy," Luciano said, "I understand you, but some of those cocksuckers, to put it bluntly, ain't worth two goddamn cents, friends or no friends. If not for you being Don Vincenze's son, whoever would have taken over would have split this crew in fuckin' half. Those guys who ain't got two quarters to rub together would just love to take everything from everybody else. That's why you gotta be strong, and not give them any excuses."

Mickey Boy explained that what he had in mind was to create income for those members who had difficulty earning. If there weren't such a split between haves and have-nots within the family, then there would be less of a cause for jealousy, and more unity to face the other crews.

"But you're talking like these guys make sense," Tony Polo said. "What're you gonna do, give them money? If you do, they won't be worth shit. They'll blow it, then come back looking for more. You'll be like New York's fuckin' welfare system."

"I don't want to give them anything," Mickey Boy said. "I

wanna give them a shot to earn a living, so they don't have to be under pressure to do anything stupid."

"They'd shock me if they did anything smart," Luciano continued. "We got guys wouldn't get up before noon if you promised them Fort Knox. And they'd rather steal a hundred dollars than make a thousand legit. I ask you, whattaya gonna do with them?"

Mickey Boy turned to Freddie, who confirmed everything the captains had said. Yes, there was an element of theirs that would never rise above gutter level. Unfortunately, that lowest denominator kept all of them, as a whole, from moving upward and out of crime.

"For instance," Freddie said. "Say you cut loose the guys who don't wanna follow the program. What are you left with? Gentlemen. What's left against you? Animals. How do you keep the animals from trying to gobble up what you have? Whack them? After all, they're the animals, you're the gentlemen. Call the cops? Become stool pigeons? It ain't an easy thing."

"Then what's the answer?" Mickey Boy asked.

"There is none. Just gotta do the best you can. Keep some of the animals mixed in with the gentlemen, so that everything stays sort of balanced."

No, no, Mickey Boy shook his head. "No, I can't accept that. If we stay that way, we're gonna be destroyed."

"How much you gonna make these guys earn?" Luciano asked. "What about the guys who are dibbing and dabbing in *babania?* Think they're gonna be interested in going to work for what they consider nickles an' dimes?"

"I'd better not catch anybody from our family doing drugs," Mickey Boy replied.

"So we start a war?" Luciano asked. "Today we gotta look the other way with some of these kids. We could act like we don't know what's going on, but if we challenge them, the truth is, we're no match no more."

"We have to be."

Luciano shook his head. "Yeah, that sounds nice, but it don't work. We're always gonna be dragged down by the scum at the bottom. Look at what happened to those guys who thought they could lead everybody into legit business.

Frank Costello? He took a bullet in the head, then threw in the towel to Vito. Do you think Vito would have given up so easy?" When no one answered, Luciano said, "No. He woulda come after him like a fuckin' kamikaze. An' look at Big Paul . . . Castellano. A lamb trying to keep a herd of lions. Wanna wind up like him? Not me."

"So, what's the answer?" Mickey Boy asked, exhausted and disgusted by Luciano's assessment.

Freddie said, "Easy. Just keep the half-wits thinking we're tougher than they are, an' do what you gotta do a little bit at a time. No big revolutions."

The conversation kept on like that for another half hour, then they all relaxed, ate some more hors d'oeuvres, then went into the same subject again. Near eight o'clock Mickey Boy called an end to the meeting, said he had a dinner appointment he had to keep.

Mickey Boy and Freddie prepared to leave first. The rest would filter out a little bit at a time, so as not to draw attention.

At the door Mickey Boy stopped and said, "I want you all to know, I ain't giving up. If you wanna work with me, let me know. If not, no hard feelings." Before walking out, he added, "I'm gonna get this family to survive if it fuckin' kills me."

"Eighteen dollars for a dish of pasta? *Grazie a Dio!*" Good Heavens! "Do you know what pasta costs?" Nicolo Fonte shook his round, moustachioed face. "And I guarantee they give no more than a four-ounce serving for that price."

"Relax," Freddie said. "Don't look at it as money . . . think of it as dishes we'll have to wash. Just feel lucky we didn't decide to go to Le Cirque. At those prices, you'd get dishpan hands by the main course."

"What dishes, he talks about?" Nicolo asked Mickey Boy. "This one needs psychiatric help." He turned to Freddie, saying, *"Ma e pazzo?"* What are you, crazy?

Mickey Boy laughed at the sportive relationship that had immediately developed between Freddie, who was a natural comedian, and Nicolo Fonte, who had a drier, European sense of humor.

"Why don't you guys take this show on the road?" Mickey Boy asked. "Youse'll do better at that than anything you're doing now."

"Does that mean I'm fired?" Freddie asked.

"Fired, in this life, means really fired."

"Just warmed a little, then?"

"I'm serious," Fonte said. "I ship pasta all over Europe."

"What, pasta?" Freddie asked. "When I was a kid we ate macaroni. Pasta was something we stuck papers together with."

Mickey Boy laughed at the two, then stopped Freddie. He wanted to hear more about Fonte's business in Italy, just as he wanted to hear about everyone's business who came within his realm of personal conversation. He was like a sponge, wanting to soak up business knowledge, hoping to find a clue to set him on the right track for his family.

Fonte said he had built up a pasta manufacturing business that he had managed to buy when he landed in Italy. Called Pasta di Roma, the company he found was on the financial rocks, their packaging stank, and the sales force they had been using was terrible.

"I'm almost ashamed to say it," Fonte said. "But I used the money Vincenze Calabra gave me to leave America for a down payment on the factory. Then I went to work."

In the years that followed, Nicolo Fonte said, he designed a catchy package, using a gold likeness of the Basilica of St. Peter between red, white, and green stripes. The papal chefs were so impressed, he said, that they began ordering his pasta to feed the cardinals, and even the Pope himself.

"Marrone," Fonte said, clasping his hands together. "Once word got out that Il Papa ate my pasta, everybody wanted it. They'd ask for the holy pasta, like it was a communion host or something."

Fonte held up four fingers. "Four. That's how many factories I had, till I retired. And you know how many salesman I needed?"

"What is this, a test?" Freddie asked.

Ignoring Freddie, Nicolo Fonte brought his thumb and index fingers together to form a circle. "None . . . zero. All I needed was order takers. I could have used those recorded punch-in messages, if they had them then."

"How about the U.S.?" Mickey Boy asked. "Ever ship macaroni here?"

"After what I went through with Vincenze Calabra, you wanted me to come back here and have to deal with American thugs again?"

Instead of being simple criminals, with little regard to honor or principles, as Fonte said the American mobsters were, he had found the Sicilian Mafia, the Neapolitan Camorra—an even older secret society than the Mafia—and the Calabrian 'Ndrangheta to be much more in tune to the needs of the people they supposedly ruled over. Those organizations, at least in part, had a long cultural thread of weaving themselves into the major fabric of society. Some Mafia members were cabinet members or physicians as well; those in the Camorra might own real estate complexes; 'Ndrangheta people had district commissioners who were as much members of goverment as international drug lords.

"I paid them all *a pizzu* . . . a little wetting of their beak, depending on where I was selling my pasta, and everything went smooth. I always got paid; my deliveries always got where they were going; and I never got bothered by unions."

He wagged a finger at Mickey Boy, and added, "And all without one of them ever showing their faces at any of my factories or warehouses." Shaking his head, Fonte said, "No, I would have been *pazzo* . . . crazy, to deal with anyone in the United States."

"Why don't you think about it," Mickey Boy said. "I could open a lot of doors for you to ship in bulk—supermarkets; restaurant chains; distributors, like Guido Vizzini, who I'm on the books as a salesman for."

"Now it is too late," Fonte replied. "I told you, I am retired. And were I not, I still would not want the complication of dealing with American thugs—that, of course, is not meant with disrespect to you."

Meant or not, Mickey Boy felt slighted that Fonte would not trust him, would not deal with him in business.

Fonte, sensing Mickey Boy's displeasure, said, "Understand, please, that I would gladly work with you, but in the event your circumstances here should change—and you must admit, they have historically proven quite unstable—where would I be left? Who would take your place?"

Mickey Boy shrugged. Like it or not, he did understand.

The waiter brought out the pasta dishes the three men had ordered: linguini with a white seafood sauce for Mickey Boy; angel hair with porcini mushrooms and sun-dried tomatoes for Freddie, rigatoni with broccoli rabe for Fonte.

Nicolo Fonte pointed to the shallow bowls. "See, what did I tell you? Twenty-five cents a portion, if they used the best pasta. Add another few cents for the sauce."

"And another three dollars a dish for overhead," Freddie Falcone, who had owned his own uptown restaurant, added. "Today that overhead, what with the sky-high rents, could even be higher."

Fonte and Falcone continued their discussion of the restaurant business throughout their dinner. Mickey Boy listened a lot but said little.

"You know," Mickey Boy finally said to Freddie, "you should probably open another restaurant. Maybe we could build it into a small chain, all around the city. Maybe that would put at least a few of the guys to work; show everybody that they could earn legit money."

"What makes you think you'll make money?" Freddie asked. "You know how many joints open up and close every year? It's a rough world out there. I seen egg timers tick longer than some of these places stay open."

"What is it you are trying to do?" Fonte asked. "Who do you want to get a job? Maybe I can be of some service."

Mickey Boy explained that it wasn't a job he wanted to find, but a business that would be large enough to support a substantial number of his people, enough that they could divest themselves of illegal enterprises and still live decently; and a business that was simple to run.

"After all," Freddie said, adding to Mickey Boy's outline, "we ain't exactly surrounded by rocket scientists."

"I might have an idea for you," Fonte said. "But *aspetto* . . . wait. First, I must have my dessert."

Fuck dessert, Mickey Boy thought, but smiled and called the waiter. "Bring one of everything, an' hurry up," he said, then turned to Fonte, who looked disappointed in not being able to fuss and choose. "Come on, this is too important to me. If you got something, tell me—but I warn you, I got a posse of business brains working on it for weeks, and they ain't come up with one goddamn decent scheme."

"No schemes," Fonte said. "And if you are to be a true businessman, you must refrain from using hoodlum terms, like 'scheme.'"

Patience, Mickey Boy told himself. He recited an old Sicilian proverb he'd heard while growing up: With enough patience, the elephant fucked the flea. For a moment he wondered exactly where he'd heard that, then snapped to as the waiter wheeled over a cart of colorful desserts: a raspberry flan dripped over with chocolate; a glazed, web-like dome surrounding a lemon mousse tart; white chocolate layer cake, and on and on, calories on top of calories, sugar on top of sugar.

"You want the entire selection?" the waiter asked, looking at Mickey Boy as though he needed to be humored.

"Yeah, leave them . . . I'll pay for 'em all."

When the waiter left, muttering to himself, Mickey Boy turned to Nicolo Fonte. "Enjoy. Eat 'em all. Just don't worry about your manners . . . talk while you eat."

Talking while he tried to dig a tiny opening in the spiderweb dome, Fonte explained that he had been toying with the idea of opening fast food pasta take-out restaurants, much like KFC chicken outlets, where people could buy good-sized portions of pasta, in various sauces, at low prices. Each operation would be relatively simple in design —clean-cut Milanese style, in white and stainless steel, with red and green touches—and relatively inexpensive to build. Most of the business would be geared to takeout and home delivery, which would minimize the space needed for each location.

". . . Maybe twelve to fourteen hundred square feet, at the most," Fonte said. "And the profit? If we sold an entire pound in a bucket for ten dollars, we would still be multiplying our food cost by ten . . . and nowhere near three dollars per person overhead cost," he added, smiling at Freddie.

Mickey Boy did a quick assessment in his mind. For the hundred thousand a place would cost, even if it were inexpensive to construct, he would only be able to put a couple of people to work. Though, he argued with himself, Fonte had said he'd wanted a chain of outlets.

"How many of these places you figure to get off? Six? Ten? A dozen?"

"Two to three thousand."

23

April 15: Laurentian Mountains, Canada

JOE AUGUSTA PACKED THE LAST OF HIS EQUIPMENT INTO THE USED Range Rover he'd picked up to drive south with. The .38 long-barrel revolver was already underneath the compartment he'd designed in the seat, as were the two rifles and the Browning .25 automatic. He'd also stashed the identification he'd use once he was in the States: driver's license, Social Security card, voter registration certificate—all in the name of Stefano Puglisi, a young cousin who had died before his fifth birthday.

The story of Cousin Stevie was a family legend. The boy, who was born two years after Joe, in 1949, to Joe's aunt Caterina, thought he could fly after hearing a Superman story on radio. They found poor Stevie broken on the concrete, four stories below his bedroom window, with a pillowcase tied around his neck.

Later, when Joe had entered into the street life, he had checked to see if Stefano Puglisi's birth certificate had been cross-referenced with his death certificate. When he found it hadn't, he ordered a copy of the birth certificate, applied for a Social Security number, and obtained a driver's license under that name—he never knew when he would have to lose his own identity in a hurry. In fact, Joe had thought so much of the procedure that, while director of the Shore Haven Funeral Home, he'd investigated old obituaries until he'd found another young boy who had died years ago, and did the same thing under his name: Charles Leone—the name he now lived under in Montreal.

Satisfied that he'd packed everything he would need for his mission, Joe trudged up through spring's remaining snow to an embankment in the woods behind the house. He cleared away a broken branch from a well-cared-for rectangular piece of earth, then sat on a tree stump next to it.

This was the third spot Joe had moved Chrissy to after having switched coffins before her interment in a Queens cemetery. He'd absconded with her body because he'd been in the streets too long. He could almost read those feeble minds that would try to kill him, that would use Chrissy's gravesite as a trap, that would hold his baby hostage. No, he chuckled once more, with God's help he had outwitted the half-wits, and found this lovely spot. Though temporary, to be sure, it was unspoiled enough to make Chrissy happy as she watched with the angels—and waited to return home.

Joe spoke with Chrissy for a while—told her to look after her mother and sister till he returned; laughed with her over a scampering chipmunk; with tears in his eyes, sang two choruses of "Daddy's Little Girl."

Then, with his heart feeling light and expansive, and spirited by a buoyant energy that quickened his step, he set off for New York City—to murder a list of people, including Mickey Boy Messina.

24

April 19: Todt Hill, Staten Island

MICKEY BOY SANK DOWN INTO THE TUB'S SENSUOUS HEAT, OPENED his nostrils to the tart sweetness of pomegranate, closed his eyes to the undulating candle glow that turned Laurel's body a silky gold. Sitting on top of him, her rhythm slowed to a more deliberate intensity as she clasped and released his erection with her vaginal walls. Her breathing whispered off the tiled walls.

Mozart's Jupiter symphony filtered through as a background from the other room. Mickey Boy would have, of course, preferred Sinatra, but had to admit lately that some of Laurel's music did move him. Not much, to be sure— elevator music still held little meaning for him—but Tchaikovsky's 1812, Ravel's Bolero, and the Jupiter had found permanent niches among his stack of Old Blue Eyes tapes.

Laurel bent forward, grasping Mickey Boy's shoulders; her long, crimson nails digging into the soft flesh by his collarbone; her hips quickening on his, sending the perfumed water rippling upward over his chin.

At least he was home for the night, Mickey Boy thought, glad that he wouldn't have to go out in public smelling like a French whore. Last time he and Laurel had bathed together in oil, he'd met Freddie afterward carrying the scent of vanilla all around him. "New cologne?" Freddie had asked. "Or you wearing pancake batter in your shorts?"

Now Laurel bent forward even more. Heat emanated from her face, next to his. Tendrils falling from her pinned-up hair dipped into the water.

She moaned in his ear.

He sucked on her neck.

She shuddered in orgasm, the waves that racked her body sending tub water up over his face. She groaned, then whimpered.

He sighed.

Having already come, Mickey Boy was just glad he'd been able to stay hard long enough for her to reach a climax. Now he was tired; couldn't wait to sleep.

Laurel stayed in that position for a while, draped over him, with his shrinking organ still inside her. She nuzzled and kissed him, taking her time coming back down to earth.

Mickey Boy drifted off into the Jupiter and began to doze. Warm colors enveloped his mind; his tongue dried; his nostrils picked up the tingly scent of lost consciousness.

He snapped to when she bit his ear.

"You're not leaving early tomorrow, are you?" Laurel whispered throatily.

"Not till noon," Mickey Boy replied. He kissed her cheek. "We can fool around again in the morning, if you want."

Laughing, Laurel kissed him, then removed herself from the tub. She dried herself with a thick white towel, urinated while blowing him kisses, then wrapped herself in the towel. Smiling lasciviously, she flapped open the towel to expose herself, did a little wiggle and said, "Dry up. I'll be waiting."

Shit! Mickey Boy thought. There went the sleep he had wanted—no, needed—so badly. He was exhausted from the mental stress of dealing with the assholes in his crew—always bellyaching about something or other; disgusted by seeing them slowly self-destruct—another made member of his family had just been sentenced to thirty years for gambling and loan-sharking; worn out by the energy needed just to get a decent business plan put together for Fonte's idea of franchising pasta houses—details, details, details.

Tired.

Unfortunately, Laurel wasn't.

Toweling himself off, Mickey Boy thought himself fortunate that with all the stress he dealt with, he was still able to get a hard-on at all.

Laurel lay naked atop the satin sheet, her body made more pink by its stark white sheen. Her hair, tied up in a knot and ribboned in red, her pubics, trimmed to a neat bikini strip, and red furry mules on her feet, were the only dark spots from the brass headboard to the bottom of the bed. She lifted one leg, exposing her vagina, and wiggled her foot.

"Like them?" she asked. "Guys told a *Cosmo* interviewer that high heels in bed make them hot. Do they?"

Despite his exhaustion, Mickey Boy felt his erection lift the towel around his waist. He guessed she had her answer.

New soft symphonic chords, unrecognizable to Mickey Boy, but sensuously interesting, surrounded the room. The bedside lights shone soft pink. Beside Laurel, on the white enamel nightstand, a large red cosmetic travel bag lay.

That was a new one, Mickey Boy thought. She'd already filled one bag with sexual jellies, cock rings, and an assortment of French ticklers: ridges, bumps, and even feathers.

When Mickey Boy lay down alongside her, Laurel dug into the red bag. She pulled out a pair of fuzzy handcuffs and a satin blindfold and set them down next to him.

"Want to try these?" Laurel asked. She licked around his mouth and down to his chest.

"Are you fuckin' crazy? I ain't getting handcuffed."

While slowly jerking his penis, Laurel kissed her way down to his stomach. "I didn't think so," she said, coming up for a breather. "But maybe this will convince you." She slid down to take his erection in her mouth.

"Laurel."

She moved from his penis to his testicles, sucking on one of them till he felt like he would ejaculate straight up into the air.

"Goddamn, Laurel," Mickey Boy groaned.

Still, no handcuffs.

"All right," Laurel said, coming back up to face him. "Put them on me." She turned over on her back and lifted her hands toward the headboard.

Mickey Boy just stared.

"Come on, I trust you," she said. "Handcuff me."

After hesitating, Mickey Boy locked one of her hands in, swung the handcuffs behind one of the brass spokes, then fastened her other hand. He sat back to look at her.

"Happy now?" he asked.

"Come on. The blindfold too."

Laughing, Mickey Boy complied. Laurel now lay there naked, handcuffed, and blindfolded. Now what? What was the thrill she'd wanted? he wondered. Just not to see or participate in having sex?

"Well," Laurel whispered. "Do something. Do something different."

Different? Was she really fuckin' crazy? What the hell was there different about getting laid? Especially the way she was, on her back? You either see it or you put a blindfold on and don't, but it's all the same. Was that supposed to be a blind missionary position? he joked inwardly.

Trying to participate, to make Laurel happy, Mickey bent and sucked in one of her nipples, then nibbled at it with his teeth. She jumped at first contact.

"Mmmm," she whispered. "Lower."

Don't get carried away, he wanted to tell her. Her being blindfolded didn't change how he felt about oral sex, having been taught by his old-time mobster mentors that cunnilingus was filthy, that it made you less than a man. "Any guy who eats a cunt gotta be a stool pigeon," they'd said—over and over and over. The one time he'd thrown that out the window had been when he'd gotten caught up in the passion of a steamy shower with her; when he'd dropped to his knees to prove how much she meant to him; when he'd asked her to become his wife.

Never again.

Mickey Boy kissed downward to Laurel's navel, circling and dipping into it with his tongue. He slid two fingers into her vagina, then, remembering that the soaking they were getting was from his last load of semen, quickly drew them out. He looked around for a towel to wipe his fingers on, but saw none. Hers was on the floor on her side of the bed, his was in the middle of the room where he'd dropped it.

Keeping Laurel busy with his lips on her pelvis, Mickey wiped his hand on the satin sheet. He then spread her legs and prepared to mount her.

"Come on, hon," Laurel moaned. "You can do better than that. Think of something different."

"What the fuck could be different?" he shouted.

"Look in the bag."

Mickey Boy pulled a clip with tiny teeth from the bag. He squeezed it open and shut.

"You want me to put this on your tit?" he asked. "Are you nuts? This looks painful."

"It doesn't hurt much," she replied. "It's supposed to be more pleasure than pain."

Mickey Boy stared at her incredulously. *Doesn't* meant she'd tried it. He clipped the nipple clamp first onto his finger, then onto his own nipple, not releasing it fully. When he felt the first painful sensation, he drew it away.

"No, you're crazy," Mickey Boy said. He reached into the bag again, pulled the other clip and tossed it to the foot of the bed. He withdrew a narrow dildo that could only be for her ass, tossed that.

Suddenly, Mickey Boy wondered if the whole deal wasn't really the fact that she just couldn't see. Maybe Laurel hadn't wanted to put the blindfold on him at all, but had wanted it for herself from the beginning? She knew him too well to ever believe he would submit to that. Maybe it was to shut out the reality? To fantasize about sex with someone else? Maybe Alley?

Though Laurel purported to hate his half brother Alley, Mickey knew that love and hate were part of the same emotion. After all, hadn't she and Alley been lovers all through high school? Yes, she'd been hurt and furious when he'd forced her to abort a child they'd conceived, then dumped her for a girl he'd met while at college, but that was then. Time healed all wounds. Besides, women were all fucked up anyway; loved to be abused.

Mickey removed the blindfold from Laurel's eyes.

"I can't do this," he said. "I feel like a fuckin' pervert."

"What is perverted about having sex with your wife? I'm just trying to make it fun."

"Fun?"

"Yes. Don't you like fun?" she asked, as though she were talking to one of the third graders she used to teach.

"Laurel, honey, fun is things I don't get to do anymore, like playing ball in the street, or riding on a roller coaster, or—"

"And what is sex?"

"I don't know . . . pleasure? Love?" He shook his head. "Fun is not sticking a jagged clamp on your wife's nipple, or shoving a dildo up her ass . . . or blindfolding her so she could have fantasies."

"What the hell is wrong with fantasies?"

Any comedic sense of Laurel's arguing while still naked and cuffed to the headboard was lost on Mickey Boy. "I don't think of other girls when I'm with you. Why should you think of other guys? What am I, a fuckin' joke? The human dildo who helps you get your rocks off while you think of Mel Gibson or Tom Cruise?"

When Laurel tried to jump up, she seemed to realize for the first time that she was bound. "Get me out of these things!"

"No. Let the guy you dreamed about get you out."

"Idiot!" she screamed. "Fuckin' Neanderthal Sicilian moron!"

Now, this was fun.

"Call me more names, an' you'll stay like that till next Christmas."

Laurel struggled furiously for a moment, then fell back laughing. "You're such an idiot," she said when the laughing had subsided. "Want to know a fantasy?"

Mickey sat down next to her on the bed. He began to stroke the inside of her thigh. "Tell me."

"Remember when we went to see *Phantom of the Opera?*"

"He was black." His hand moved to the soft flesh on the inside of her other thigh.

"Not in my fantasy. In it, it's you with the mask half covering your face—mysterious, dangerous, vulnerable."

He toyed with her damp pubic hair. "I ain't vulnerable."

Laurel smiled. "No?" she whispered.

Mickey just stared at her, mesmerized by the sexual aura she seemed to transmit. His finger crawled slowly up and down between her vaginal lips. His erection poked his own stomach.

"In my fantasy I come to you, naked . . . you're dressed, all in a tuxedo. You turn away from me, but I don't give up. I hug you from the back, then slide around so that we're standing front to front . . ."

Mickey's breathing felt shallow. He bent and began to

suck on Laurel's breast. His finger flicked over her clitoris in a steady but gentle beat.

"Your eyes look so sad; so afraid to open up. I feel so terrible . . . how to get through?"

Mickey pulled himself alongside Laurel.

"I drop to my knees and unzip your pants. Your thing pops out all by itself, almost hitting me in the face. I take it in my—"

Mickey's tongue, forcing its way into Laurel's mouth, stifled her words as he spread her legs and entered her there too.

With Mickey pumping between the legs she'd locked behind his back, Laurel said, "No, my darling . . . *this* is fun."

25

April 22: Hell's Kitchen, Manhattan

THANK GOD THE GODDAMN RAIN STOPPED, LITTLE VINNIE thought as he steered the rented white Chevy Lumina south on Ninth Avenue. He gazed through the two half-moon shapes cleared by the windshield wipers, searching the glossy, wet sidewalks for a tall, pretty blonde with a set of balls between her legs.

Three goddamn weeks he'd been possessed by vengeance. More than the pain had been the embarrassment. Being rescued from the doorway by the police had been bad enough—he'd felt like an imbecile trying to convince them that he was a Sicilian sucker, Edoardo Destino, taken in by a female hooker and her pimp.

That someone had had the nerve to steal his shoes right off his feet while he was handcuffed to a doorknob, filthy, and unconscious, was infuriating. Getting stabbed in the ass was another thing. What if the bastards had infected him with AIDS?

Little Vinnie turned east on Forty-second Street, determined to make one more round of that area again. Dirty faggots, he thought. When he thought about it, that's what really bothered him most. He could almost vomit again thinking about having the he-she's tongue in his mouth and balls in his hand. No way those two bastards were going to get away with that.

His heart quickened when he saw a tallish blonde standing in a doorway on Eighth Avenue and Forty-fourth. He pulled close, fingering the .38 Smith & Wesson as he did.

The girl began to walk toward his car.

His finger slid back and forth across the trigger.

He rolled down the rain-dappled window.

Fuck! It isn't her.

Little Vinnie stepped down hard on the pedal, shooting northward as the rain began in earnest again.

"Mr. Destino," the night clerk called when Little Vinnie entered the hotel.

Fuck this place, Little Vinnie thought. Time to get the fuck out of here. They know me too good.

The clerk handed him a slip of paper over the desk. "A policeman stopped by and left this. He said to call, that they may have caught your muggers and they would like to see if you can identify them."

As Little Vinnie hurried toward the elevator, the clerk added, "Oh, and that man who works in the pizza place was here too."

Little Vinnie stopped and turned back. "How do you know where he works?" he asked. It wouldn't be too farfetched to believe that undercover cops, or police informants, could be anywhere. Maybe they hadn't bought the Edoardo Destino story at all. Maybe they knew who he was.

"How?" the clerk said. He pinched his nose. "Just smell. It's delicious."

Little Vinnie hurried into the new Eighteenth Precinct building, on West Fifty-fourth Street. Though he'd changed to dry clothing at the hotel, he was soaked through to the skin again.

"Detective Rebbie," Little Vinnie told the desk officer. "He called me for a lineup."

"Second floor, Detectives," the desk officer said while jotting something down, then answering a ringing phone.

Who the fuck color-coordinated this place? Little Vinnie wondered about the institutional light blue and beige paint as he took the steps two at a time. He caught himself halfway up, laughed about his rushing into a police station—he'd been brought up to think of them as enemy strongholds— then walked the rest of the way to the Detectives' room, feeling a sense of danger that bordered on sexual excitement. Imagine, walking into a police station with a gun in your belt, Little Vinnie thought. Who else but him would have that kind of balls?

Detective Rebbie, a red-faced, silver-haired Irishman, with a beard like Kenny Rogers, waved to him immediately, making Little Vinnie uncomfortable. How did he recognize him so fast?

Fuck! Why the hell did I bring that goddamn gun?

Little Vinnie walked to the detective's desk, then sat down, prepared for some unpleasant surprise.

"Think we caught your muggers," Rebbie said. "Snatched them both as they tried to pull the same thing like with you, only this time they caught a rookie undercover with backup."

A twinkle in his eye seemed to be laughing at Little Vinnie. No, there would be no surprises, no arrest or questioning about this mob thing or other, no finding the .38.

Just embarrassment.

"They made bond right away, but I pulled 'em in off the courthouse steps for you to take a look. Maybe this time we can keep 'em on ice awhile."

Fat chance, Little Vinnie thought. "Whatta we do?" he asked in the broken Italian accent he'd affected from the first time the police had spoken to him.

Detective Rebbie explained that he would be bringing him to two lineups: one for the pimp who mugged him from behind, and another for the hooker. He smiled when he said hooker.

Fuck you, cop, Little Vinnie thought.

Rebbie led Little Vinnie into a room with one-way glass, just like Vinnie had see dozens of times in the movies. A row of black men were paraded out, dressed in various weird ghetto outfits of oranges, reds, greens, and even a fuchsia.

Just like a fuckin' sideshow.

"How could I know what the guy looka like, who grab me from the back?" Little Vinnie asked using his fake accent. "I never see him." He made sure not to stand close enough to Rebbie, where a chance brush would give away the fact that he was packing.

Detective Rebbie smiled. He looked over at the men on parade, then back at Little Vinnie. Holding four fingers up in front of his chest, he said, "Look hard, I'm sure you'll recognize one of them."

Little Vinnie quickly turned away, making believe he hadn't seen the fingers. He glared at number four, a tall, wiry-looking character with dreadlocks and a goatee.

"I never see him," Little Vinnie repeated, without looking at Rebbie. He heard a frustrated huff.

"Okay, maybe we'll do better on the next crew."

When the lineup of supposed females was brought in, Little Vinnie immediately spotted the one who had set him up. This time she—or it—wore a red wig, but the shape, size, and face were unmistakable. It amazed him how a guy could possibly look so good.

"No, I no see her there," he said.

"Look at the face," the detective snapped. "Forget the hair and clothes . . . broads change that all the time. Look at the face. Is there anything you remember? A mole? A dimple? The shape of a nose?"

"No."

"Do you normally wear glasses?"

"No."

"And you're sure none of them is her?"

"No."

"No, you not sure? Or no, none of them is her?"

Little Vinnie turned to Detective Rebbie, who once again

was holding up fingers to indicate which one to choose—
two this time. His lips were pursed and his cheeks rippled
with anger.

"Sorry, they no looka familiar," Little Vinnie said.
"Could I go now?"

Thank God the goddamn rain stopped, Little Vinnie
thought for the second time that evening. This time he stood
in a doorway on West Fifty-fourth Street across from the
newly renovated Midtown North police station. His damp
clothes stuck to him, pinching under his arms and in his
crotch. The air felt thick enough to chew.

In a short while a crowd of lineup participants burst out
of the station house, scattering like shotgun pellets as they
hurried to get as far away from the law as possible.

Little Vinnie's eyes darted in all directions, finally focus-
ing on his unlikely pair of assailants. The pimp in
dreadlocks moved quicker, dragging the transvestite hooker
by the arm. She stumbled behind him on silver high heels.

When the pair was halfway to Eighth Avenue, Little
Vinnie set out after them, walking close to the tenement
buildings on the north side of the street. He skipped to catch
up when they turned southward on Eighth Avenue, then
slowed when he got them in his sights again.

"Shit!" he muttered, breaking into a run after the two got
into a cab. Luckily, he caught another cruising cab immediately. "Follow that cab at the corner!" he ordered.

The driver, an Indian or Pakistani, or something—Little
Vinnie wasn't sure—decided to question him before taking
chase.

"Here," Little Vinnie said while pushing a fifty-dollar bill
into the payment box in the bulletproof divider. "Catch
them an' there's fifty more . . . just hurry the fuck up!"

Cash being the only true international language, the
driver gunned the cab, blowing through the light on a yellow
signal, then jumping the next to turn east as it switched to
red. When he did stop for a light on Broadway, the other cab
was exactly one block ahead.

They followed the cab with the pimp and hooker into the
garment district, then through to Chelsea. The streets
shimmered with stagnant rainwater, appearing ominously

desolate. Little Vinnie had the cabbie drop back another half block to avoid suspicion.

At Twentieth Street the first cab turned. Little Vinnie had his driver stop at the corner. He peered down the street to where the cab had stopped. "Wait here, if you want the other fifty," he said, and proceeded on foot. He nervously fingered the revolver in his waistband.

Though he hurried, by the time Little Vinnie reached the door of what seemed to be an abandoned warehouse that the two had entered, it had locked shut in his face.

Fucked again!

26

April 25: Cobble Hill, Brooklyn

BUSTER HAD CANCER. ONE TRIP TO THE DOCTOR HAD ESCALATED into others, all of which determined that years of Lucky Strikes filling his lungs had given birth to at least a tumor, which, after preliminary tests, had proven malignant.

"I told youse I never shoulda gone to the doctor," Buster complained. His face appeared more ashen and drawn than it had a couple of short weeks ago. His pants, gathered by his belt, were no longer pushed to their limit by excesses of macaroni, gravy meats, and high-fat pastries.

"Every goddamn time you go to the doctor, he always finds something wrong. Cold that wouldn't go away, shit! I woulda been better off minding my own business, an' just kept blowin' my nose."

"Whattaya blamin' now, the doctor?" Freddie asked. "You think he gave it to you?"

"No, but I wouldn'ta known nothing if it wasn't for him, the sonomabitch. They're like messengers of death."

"Stop this death talk," Mickey Boy said between sips of

cold Manhattan Special coffee soda straight from the bottle. The icy drink felt refreshingly diverting. The rest of him felt like it was burning up.

Since coming home from prison two years before, Mickey Boy had come to view Buster as a sort of surrogate uncle. And while he resented Buster's part in having manipulated his life, he respected the loyalty he'd shown for Don Vincenze's wishes, and loved him for the loyalty he knew he himself could count on him for.

Now, the painful truth was, when Mickey Boy looked at Buster, he saw death. He too had no faith in modern medicine when it came to battling the Big C. For all the people he saw on TV who claimed to have won over the disease, he didn't know one. Everyone he came across with cancer died. But he wouldn't tell Buster that.

"You ain't going nowhere, and you're gonna fight . . . no, we're gonna fight. We're gonna get Laurel's cousin, the doctor, to recommend the best guy to put you right back in great shape."

"Yeah," Buster said. "Torregrossa."

"You're too ugly for Torregrossa to handle," Freddie said, straining for humor. "Even their embalming couldn't make you look good. No, Mickey Boy's right, we're gonna get you the best of the best, then get you a plastic surgeon, to make you pretty, and send you on Donahue."

Buster just shrugged.

Mickey Boy stood. "C'mon, we gotta go," he told Freddie, then went and embraced Buster. He kissed him on the cheek, and, unable to face him without showing the tears in his eyes, whispered in his ear, "Don't worry about nothing . . . money, nothing. We're gonna beat this together."

"How the fuck am I supposed to know what it could do?" Mickey Boy shouted. He threw up his hands in frustration. "If I had one going, I'd know. Otherwise, what the fuck does my guess mean? Ask me about what a line should be on a Yankee game an' I could tell you. This, no."

Nicolo Fonte and Freddie Falcone laughed. Freddie poured another glass of Corvo, then bit into his prosciutto and mozzarella sandwich. Fonte shoved a dish of marinated roasted peppers his way.

Since coming up with the idea for a chain of pasta houses, the trio had met twice, both times at Fonte's newly rented apartment on Carroll Street, a short distance from Buster's brownstone. Fonte's place gave them privacy, and a certain warmth that was lost to Mickey Boy in his well-appointed Staten Island home. Fonte's probably wasn't bugged, at least not yet. Fonte's made him feel like the kid he was, when he'd lived two blocks away, with his mother and Alley.

Today, however, on the heels of meeting with the ailing Buster, he had little patience for anything, and would not have felt better anywhere except at home, lying in bed with Hope snuggled between him and Laurel.

"You must understand that no person can guarantee any projections," Fonte said. "And no person expects them to. They are made up of intelligent analysis of what similar businesses do, plus a bit of hope, dreams, and bullshit."

"We got the hope, dreams, and bullshit down to a tee," Freddie said, his mouth stuffed with food. "It's the other one we're a little short on."

"Maybe today ain't the day," Mickey Boy said. "Let's do this some other time."

"Absolutely not!" Fonte said, banging his fist on the table. Red wine splashed over the top of Freddie's glass onto the beige Formica tabletop.

Mickey Boy and Freddie looked at Nicolo Fonte, his chubby jaw set, then at each other, then burst out laughing. When did he become a don? Mickey Boy wondered, sure that Freddie's thoughts were identical.

Fonte lapsed into the lawyer-teacher-father figure he had been for Mickey Boy as a youth. "I know how you feel," he said, referring to Buster's condition. "But you chose a noble task, and have much work ahead of you to see it through. Your going home to brood will not help your friend one bit."

When Mickey Boy began to protest, Fonte cut him off. "And as far as you being overwhelmed by the details of legitimate business, get used to them. You are totally capable of learning."

"But I can't see how I could run thousands of stores, the way you say. I could do one . . . put up the money an' get it open. But two, three thousand?"

"Do you think a Mr. Domino oversees every one of the

119

eight thousand Domino Pizza stores? Chains and franchises are like snowballs rolling down a hill. They get larger of their own accord. All you have to do is make sure that when first you release it, it is perfectly shaped so as not to veer right or left . . . into a tree."

"I think I got this," Freddie said. "We gotta make a pasta ball—maybe out of gnocci—then roll it down a hill?"

"Spoostard!" Fonte said, throwing a napkin at Freddie.

Mickey Boy held his head. He knew that Freddie, having owned restaurants before, understood everything Fonte said. But no matter how long they would work or how much would be at stake, Freddie would continue to *scooch* the ex-lawyer, would get his greatest pleasure from breaking his balls.

Fonte laid out gross sales figures he'd amassed for various fast food operations. He also handed Mickey Boy photocopies of magazine stories about the growth of fast food and take-out operations.

Mickey Boy scanned the articles quickly, not having the patience to go through them entirely. "Where the hell did you get all these?" he asked. "Were you saving this shit?"

"The library," Fonte replied. "It is a new concept in research. You might try it yourself sometime."

For two more hours they sat and fine-tuned various aspects of their proposed business. Mickey Boy felt truly amazed at the scope of its possibilities. Thousands of stores? Most of the people he knew had a hard enough time managing one establishment, let alone thousands. But then again, he wondered, shutting out Fonte and Freddie for periods while he argued with himself, maybe that was his problem. Maybe it was the people he knew.

"What do you think?" Fonte asked at the end of the session.

"I think that if I could get a quarter of the stores going that you say we could build, I could set every one of my people up for good."

"I do not think you will find ten percent of 'your people' who will want to spend the time or effort to participate."

"You're wrong!" Freddie barked. He jumped up angrily, then said, "Make that two percent."

Mickey Boy dropped his head to the table, covering it with his hands and thinking, Fuck me, if they're right.

27

April 29: Todt Hill, Staten Island

"ONE: TO GROW IN, OR AS IN, THE MANNER OF A PLANT. TWO: TO BE passive or *unthinking;* to do *nothing;* to lie on the beach and vegetate," Laurel read aloud, from an enormous Random House dictionary. "Do you know what it means, now, to vegetate? That is exactly what I am doing . . . vegetating."

Petulance made her more beautiful, Mickey Boy thought, admiring how she'd whipped her figure back into shape in their private gym. Her stomach appeared tightly trim above her black workout tights and below the matching Spandex halter.

"Stop," Mickey Boy said. "You ain't vegetating. You ain't even green yet. Look at your stomach, how white it is."

"Mickey!" Laurel shouted, and dropped the dictionary on the table with a loud thud. "You're not even listening."

"Of course I am," he said, grabbing her around from the rear. He pulled a halter strap down over one shoulder, close to exposing a breast. "C'mon, let me see if there's any green stuff down there." He slid his hand into the front of her tights. "Or down there."

Laurel pressed her body against him, twisting her neck to dart her tongue into his ear. "Why don't you look down Freddie's pants?" she whispered, then bit his lobe.

Mickey Boy yelped and let her go.

"You're with him more than me," Laurel added.

Exasperated, Mickey Boy threw himself into the dining room chair. He'd been trying to avoid an argument, but obviously had failed again.

"Okay, what are we going to fight about?" he asked. "I can only handle one at a time. Either it's me being out or you turning into a *googootz*. Which one?"

"Don't patronize me."

Mickey Boy moaned. "I'm not." He went on to explain that he was trying desperately to avoid a fight, and that if there was something on her mind, just to address it directly rather than hitting him from all sides.

Laurel shoved the dictionary across the table to him. "Read the definition of *vegetate* again," she said. "That is problem number one." Once again it was the same argument: she felt stifled being home constantly; she loved Hope dearly, and cherished the time she spent with her, but needed more; needed the conversation of adults; a change of scenery; something to stimulate her mind.

"Didn't we go over this before? Wasn't that why I made you part of what I'm doing with the business?" Mickey Boy asked. "Didn't you go to the meeting at Café on the Green with me?"

"One meeting, then you rode off into the sunset with Freddie and your newfound friend, Nicolo Fonte. When was the last time you sat down with anyone who was at the restaurant that day? Including me?"

"Guilty as charged," Mickey Boy said. "But with an explanation." He told Laurel how Fonte had had experience in the pasta business, and had come up with the idea for the fast food pasta take-out franchises.

"When he gave me the idea, it clicked in my head," Mickey Boy said. "It was something even I could understand: food."

Using his fingers to mark each point he made, Mickey Boy continued, "I could understand it; people always gotta eat; there's no big inventory that's gonna tie up a lot of cash; an' we could franchise thousands of stores, all over the country —enough to support everybody around us."

"Yeah, so now that's supposed to be why they're always up your ass."

"Tell the truth," Mickey Boy said. "If the idea came from

your father or Tammy, wouldn't I be spending all my time with them? Trying to get this plan in the best shape to go ahead with?"

"I guess now you don't need them . . . or me?"

Mickey stood and went to Laurel. He hugged and kissed her. "Nut job. More than ever, I need you guys. Now we got something for them—and you—to work with. I just don't want to go talking about it without knowing what I'm talking about. You're still gonna be the boss."

Laurel kissed him back. "Mickey," she said, "maybe I should go back to teaching . . . even part-time?"

He moaned. "Not that again. Why do you wanna do that?"

"Because I love it? After all, it is what I went to school to learn to do . . . no one twisted my arm."

"Can't you love pasta houses?"

Laurel sighed. "Yes, I could, but I'm not sure that I'm really qualified to do what you need. When it comes to teaching, I'm certain I am."

"An' I'm certain you're smart enough to run ten thousand stores, if we had them."

For the first time, Mickey felt more moved than attacked by Laurel's plea to go back to work. He paused for a moment, then said, "Tell you what. Give me the next four months to try to get the ball rolling. If it all works out, you'll stick it out with me to build the company."

"And if it doesn't?"

"Then we'll talk about it then."

Laurel groaned. "Not another stall, Mickey. I—"

Mickey put a hand up to quiet her. "No, for real. If it don't work out with the business, we'll try to work it out so that it's okay for everybody—you, me, and the baby."

"And what if I stink at business management?"

"You won't."

"But if I do?"

"Same thing. We'll talk about it then too. Okay?"

Laurel begrudgingly agreed.

"Now, if you wanna get involved now, why don't you start thinking about designing these places. Think fast food, clean, white, open, and Milanese style."

"You want me to start now?"

"Of course," Mickey said. "Why, I just hired you an' now you're quitting on me?"

"No, I just didn't think—"

"I'm definitely doing this deal," Mickey Boy said. "And the faster I get things in order, the better. I'll get Freddie to put a guy on driving you around."

"Please, Mickey, anything but that," Laurel replied. "I won't have some goon driving me around like a gangster's moll. I'm perfectly capable of chauffeuring myself."

"Yeah, but I'd feel better if—"

"Mickey, please."

Mickey Boy shrugged. "I know you're wrong, but okay."

28

May 2: Chelsea, Manhattan

LITTLE VINNIE'S HEART POUNDED AS HE WAITED IN THE DOORWAY of the adjacent warehouse. One-seventeen A.M. When the fuck would that team of homo assholes come home? Would he have to wait in this piss-stink spot all night?

This was the goddamn night. Little Vinnie had passed by this spot each night, vowing to wait and exact his revenge. But each night the flutter in his stomach had caused him to make an excuse and take off. Either there were too many people around, or the weather gave him a sinus headache, or he had something else to do.

But the laughing had finally become too much, the laughing of people he wasn't even sure knew he had held the homo's balls, then been robbed and stuck in the ass like a turkey being tested for doneness. The laughing of DoDo, when he had to bring him more cash. The laughing of that fuckin' sonofabitch of a father of his, watching from wherever—probably Hell.

When a taxi pulled up, Little Vinnie tensed. "Shit!" he muttered when the transvestite emerged alone. Bad sign. Two moves instead of one. Maybe he should leave? Try again another night. And watch DoDo laugh again tomorrow? No fuckin' way.

Little Vinnie hit the doorway just as the hooker opened the lock. He pushed her through, grabbing her by the neck—too smart to wind up with a handful of wig—and slamming her against the green plaster wall inside. He shoved the pistol in her face so there would be no mistake.

"Scream and I shoot," he said. His heart felt like it was in his mouth.

Fortunately, the hooker offered no resistance. "Okay, you fucker," she said, in a voice octaves lower than the one she'd used on him that night. "Take my money and get the fuck out."

Little Vinnie turned her around. "You look lonely," he said.

The hooker's eyes opened wide.

"What'd you think, I was still cuffed to a doorknob?"

"No, please," the hooker began to whimper. "Hale made me do it . . . I don't want to rob people . . . just give them what they want."

To Little Vinnie's chagrin, he felt an erection begin. Shit, it had to be from the power, he told himself, with more than a little embarrassment. Wasn't it the same as when he'd played electronic football as a youth and scored? He pushed the hooker toward the elevator.

"Please, take my money, and go . . . I've got a few hundred . . . I can get you more . . . Just—"

Heart pounding and hand trembling slightly, Little Vinnie pushed the hooker into the freight elevator. Its decor—veined gray mirror set in paneled walls—and cleanliness startled him.

"Okay, come upstairs, I'll give you more money," the hooker pleaded.

Like she's got a fuckin' choice.

"Just, please, leave before Hale gets here."

If Little Vinnie had been startled by the elevator, he was absolutely stunned by the loft apartment's layout. From the exposed brick walls, to the thirty or more feet of plush white sectional sofa, to the fifty-four-inch television screen, every-thing spoke of home and money.

The hooker's tone switched to a low, throaty mew. "I'll make you feel good too. No one gives better blowjobs—"

"Shut up!"

Little Vinnie ordered the hooker to lie facedown on the floor, then changed his mind. "Where's the bedroom?"

"In here," the hooker replied, scrambling to show him the way.

Mirrors everywhere. That was the bedroom. Two mir-rored walls; completely mirrored furniture, including a headboard of mirrored posts and a platform for the bed; and, of course, a rectangular mirror on the ceiling above the king-size bed. Lush green plants, a thick white pile rug, and a spread that appeared to be chinchilla, made the room worthy of a royal palace.

"Fuck me," Little Vinnie muttered.

"What?"

Realizing what he'd said, Little Vinnie snapped, "Shut up!" He then ordered, "Very slowly, take your clothes off an' let them drop to the floor."

The hooker hurried to undress, almost too quickly. Little Vinnie couldn't help staring at her breasts—full and taut, and as nice as any he'd seen on any real female.

"Stop. Leave your drawers on," Little Vinnie said. He pushed the hooker to the bed. "Lay down." When the hooker got on the bed, Little Vinnie added, "Facedown. I don't want to have to see a hard-on and tits. Too confusing." Still annoyed at himself for his own erection, Little Vinnie tied her hands behind her back, using a floral necktie that had been hanging along with a suit on a valet. Obviously the nigger's, he thought.

Explaining to the hooker that he would kill her and her pimp too, Little Vinnie stuffed a sweat sock he found into her mouth. Without letting go of the pistol, he rummaged the room, checking inside drawers and closets. Under a pile of female panties he found a banded fold of nearly three thousand dollars. Continued searching turned up another two. Fuck, this could turn into a great score, Little Vinnie thought; there might be twenty or thirty thousand hidden around. All he found, however, was the little less than five thousand dollars. There was plenty of jewelry, but he had no way of knowing if it was real or fugazy.

It was after four A.M. when Hale finally came through the front door. Little Vinnie threatened the hooker again, secured the binding and gag, then took up a position behind the bedroom door. His bowels felt like they would soon turn inside out. He bit his lip and held his breath.

It was only when Hale burst into the bedroom that Little Vinnie realized that had the black man come through slower, he would have been in trouble—standing there in full sight of the doorway, via the opposite mirrored wall. As it was, though, Hale had caught his image too late.

Pointing the gun at Hale's back with two hands to steady their quivering, and spreading his legs a bit so they'd be more firmly planted on the ground, Little Vinnie ordered the pimp to slowly clasp his hands on top of his dreadlocks. He felt a heartbeat away from just squeezing off a round and repaying in spades the humiliation he'd felt.

Instead of being frightened for himself, Hale looked over at the bed, then at Little Vinnie. "You didn't hurt her, did you?"

"Her?"

"What are you, one of the motherfuckin' Moral Majority?" Hale asked. He shouted over his shoulder at the hooker, "You all right, baby?"

A muffled sound through the sweat sock was all he got in return.

"What'd you gag her for?" he asked. "Motherfucker, you could suffocate her that way."

"I'd be careful who I motherfuckered," Little Vinnie said.

Hale burst out laughing, more heartily than Little Vinnie was sure he felt. "Man, you ain't killing a motherfucker. If you were, brother, you would have done did it already." He cautiously moved to the bed and pulled the sock from the hooker's mouth.

Little Vinnie would loved to have pegged a shot at him right then; even one right into a mirror. He believed the warehouse was otherwise unoccupied, but couldn't be sure enough to start blasting. Fuckin' nigger was smart, he thought . . . and ballsy too.

"You all right, baby?" Hale asked. The hooker whimpered and sobbed that she was fine.

Hale dropped down on the bed, leaning back against the mirror-spoked headboard and placing his hands casually behind his head. "What you want, motherfucker? Your money back?"

"Already got that," Little Vinnie replied, feeling more relaxed. He loved the pimp's cavalier attitude, especially since he believed he must be scared shitless. "Almost five grand."

Hale jumped up off the bed.

Little Vinnie cocked the revolver.

Hale sat back down.

Little Vinnie, still pointing the pistol at him, pulled out the wad of bills. "You know what?" he said. "I should kill youse both. But I like you. I like your balls." Once again, realizing their situation, he added, "Not, like, your real balls . . . don't get any ideas about me being funny."

Hale just smiled.

"You got guts. And, bein' a crook myself, I like crooks. That's why I didn't identify youse the other night."

"You a Mafia man?"

Little Vinnie smiled. "But youse embarrassed me . . . stuck me in the ass . . . took my money. What am I supposed to do?"

"You tell me," Hale said, his attitude seemingly relaxed. "You got the motherfuckin' gun."

Little Vinnie flipped off five hundred-dollar bills. "That's my five." He flipped another one. "That's my vig . . . interest for 'borrowing' my money." He flipped another one. "Make that interest too." He dropped another one for his inconvenience, and another two for the pair of shoes that had been stolen off his feet while he'd been handcuffed. "Now," he said, "what do you think I deserve for you stickin' me in the ass with that knife? Oh," he added as an afterthought, "that'll be another two bills for the pants you fucked up."

"Make it five," Hale offered.

"Done. Now, what about for stickin' me?"

"Man, take the motherfuckin' money an' stop this game."

128

Little Vinnie tossed the cash he hadn't taken for himself toward the bed. It fluttered and scattered on the rug.

"That's just to show you that you can't buy my embarrassment or honor. Understand?"

Hale smiled. "You for sure are a motherfuckin' Mafia. Man, I am sorry I fucked with you, but that's the business. You know the deal."

"Just remember, you owe me one," Little Vinnie said.

He left whistling, proud to be able to meet DoDo later that day and hand over a thousand dollars toward what he'd lent him so far. Now that the vendetta that had occupied him for these weeks was over, he'd make it up anyway, when he finally got around to going to the Staten Island house to get his own funds. Yes, he couldn't wait to see DoDo's face when he told him that he'd retrieved the money from the pair that had robbed him.

Almost as important to Little Vinnie was that he'd hooked the nigger, Hale. He wasn't exactly sure how he would use him, but it had to be an asset to have someone that no one else knew—even if he was black and looked like he wore a floor mop on his head. Somehow, Hale would help him go from fuckee to fucker.

Little Vinnie could feel it.

29

May 14: Upper East Side, Manhattan

". . . COME ON AND DO THIS . . . SHAKE THAT BODY FOR ME," pulsating loudly from speakers, surrounded and filled Laurel with a primeval rhythm. Hips shaking and bosom bouncing over the neckline of her dress, Laurel danced directly across from her doctor cousin, Tammy, in the midst of an equally gyrating crowd. Tammy, taller and less curvacious, spun and bent more gracefully than Laurel believed she herself did. But then again, Tammy didn't have to worry about the extra pounds she'd gained while munching on blackout cake while sitting home all the time, pushing a breast out, or popping a seam. Of course, Laurel could have worn something else, something looser, but her ego needed the boost, needed to see her body in a dress she'd danced in before Hope had forced her into maternities.

Both girls laughed when two yuppies in suits and ties boogied their way in between Laurel and Tammy and turned the dancing into two male-female couples. The guy dancing with Laurel looked to be in his mid-twenties, like her. He stood at least six feet tall, with chiseled features and sandy brown hair that flopped over his eyes when he danced. The fluidity of his movements surprised her. Guys usually looked like jerks to her on the dance floor. Trying to keep up with him, she swayed a little more, rolled her hips around in circles, bent forward and shook her hair loose. Even the smell of her own sweat seemed strangely exciting as the music's thumping continued.

It had been so damn long since she'd had fun like this. "Tough guys don't dance," was Mickey Boy's stock line, and because of it they rarely went anywhere that dancing took place. Occasional family parties, like this cousins' get-together, being the exception. Only this was one Mickey Boy couldn't make; tied up again with his "friends."

When the music ended, Laurel smiled at her dance partner then turned to go back to the long table that her family had reserved in the rear of the Tatou restaurant and club. Michael Bolton began to croon just as she took her first step.

"Excuse me," the young man said, gripping her upper arm gently. "Can I have this dance?"

Pastel-colored lights flashing off his face hypnotized her. Before she had a chance to answer no, Laurel found herself pressed against his body, doing a slow fox trot. She tried to inconspicuously pull her hips away from him, but his arm held her firmly around the waist. She was sure he wore Eternity.

"Mark," he said.

"Laurel . . . and I really shouldn't—"

"Married?" Mark asked jokingly.

"Very."

Instead of her answer disturbing Mark into letting her go, he just smiled.

Cute. Laurel had met so many like Mark in the time before Mickey and after Alley. She'd been hurt then, and hurt right back, teasing and using young men like this, first playing hard-to-get, then driving them wild with secrets she'd learned from the various sex manuals she collected—then dumping them. Hard and fast.

Now, however, there was no game to play. She was married and totally in love with her husband. And she felt like an old cow, flattered that a young, sharp guy wouldn't be turned off by the little bit of plump she'd accumulated as a wife and mother with too many hours in the house.

"Cheat?"

"Never."

Mark smiled. Great teeth. He moved his cheek next to hers.

Laurel turned her face away. She felt his erection rubbing against her abdomen. Mark's was the first male organ she'd touched in any way since going with Mickey. She briefly wondered how it looked—its size and shape; circumsized or not; pubic hair light, like on his head, or dark?—then felt suddenly flushed with guilt. She forced her buttocks away from him, the motion unintentially pushing her breasts harder against his chest.

Mark peeked down at Laurel's swelling cleavage and smiled. He feigned closing his eyes. "I won't peek."

"I think that's enough," Laurel said, loosing herself from his grip. "Thank you for the dance." She turned and hurried back to the extended table where about a dozen of her cousins and their spouses or dates sat.

Laurel's hand trembled as she moved it among the glasses, trying to find her white creme de menthe among the other pale drinks. Was she that terrible? she wondered. Or was she just like the fresh, lively adolescent she'd once been, excited about each new wonder of life that crossed her path? But she was no adolescent. Had time really seen her regress? Maybe it was time to talk some things out with Mickey Boy; get him to spend some more quality time with her; come to some understanding where she would be able to use her time a little better?

Rationalizing seemed to calm the flutters Laurel felt inside. She loved her husband with all her heart, and adored Hope, who was more precious to her than her own life. But there was more. There was a sense of accomplishment and self that she needed. And there was fun. She needed fun too, but seemed to get little of it. Mickey Boy was serious most of the time, pressured by his position and frustrated by the slow progress toward his goals. She understood all that, and supported him in all he was trying to accomplish. But that didn't mean she had to totally ignore her own needs, she argued with herself.

"What happened?" Tammy asked, returning to the table. "One minute you were dancing like you were auditioning to be a Fly Girl, then the next, poof."

"I didn't want to encourage Mr. Astaire," Laurel said. "After all, I am a married woman."

"Not a dead one, though," Tammy replied. "Harmless fun."

Fun.

"You've got to get out more, girl." Tammy took her hand. "Come on, walk me to the bar."

"How was your partner?" Laurel asked as they walked. Tammy was the only one of the cousins who was still unmarried and unattached.

"He seemed okay," Tammy answered. "A stock analyst. I don't think I could see myself with someone like that long-term. After being around doctors all the time, I would rather find someone in the arts . . . someone totally irresponsible and without discipline at all."

Laurel laughed. Tammy was probably the most conservative person she knew, outside of Mickey, of course. A stock analyst would probably be perfect for her, she thought.

"How about for the short term?"

"I don't think that way. Not in the era of AIDS."

Tammy elbowed her way through to the bar to order. Laurel stood back.

"Hi."

Mark.

"Hello," Laurel said coldly. She turned her head away, pretending to be absorbed by Tammy's actions at the bar.

"Are you angry at me?"

"How can I be angry, when I don't even know you?"

"Did I say something that offended you? If so, I'm sorry."

Laurel turned to face Mark, and sighed. "Really, it's not you. It's me. I'm very, very married, and shouldn't be dancing with strangers."

"I'm no stranger," Mark said, fishing out a business card from a small leather case. "Here, my card."

Laurel took it. Mark Nelson. Assistant Vice President. Legal Department. Merrill Lynch.

"I can respect how you feel about being married," Mark said. "Not too many girls feel that way anymore."

"Or guys."

"Or guys," Mark replied, laughing. "Anyway, I think that makes you even more attractive than you already are . . ."

Laurel felt flushed, flattered, and unable to respond.

"Anyway, if you ever decide to—"

"You, take it on the hop!" Laurel heard just as a heavy arm fell around her shoulders.

"Excuse me? I—"

"Take a fuckin' walk, Romeo," Mickey Boy said. "Before you need to be carried out."

Freddie Falcone slipped one arm through Mark's. Two of Mickey Boy's men moved to either side of them. "Come on, be a nice fella. You're in over your head here." He led Mark away, saying, "Let me buy you a drink an' explain to you about the birds an' the bees."

"I thought you couldn't make it," Laurel stammered.

Mickey Boy glowered. He snapped the business card out of her hand. "I thought I'd surprise you. Thought it would make you happy . . . impressive, Merrill Lynch."

"Mickey, please," Laurel said. "I am happy; happier than you can imagine, that you made the effort." She stretched to kiss him, but he backed away.

"Stop being an ass," Tammy said, returning with two drinks. She handed one to Laurel, then kissed Mickey Boy on the cheek. She and Mickey Boy had become friends, and he tolerated things from Tammy that Laurel wouldn't dare say. "Everything was innocent."

"Innocent? I find this fag stockbroker practically drooling down her tits—"

"And why not?" Tammy asked. "Look at her, she's great-looking. Would you rather have a fat old beanbag in a black dress, with a knitting needle in her hair and a wart on her chin? C'mon, you macho guinea pig, wake up and smell the coffee. We're almost in the twenty-first century."

"That don't make it good," Mickey Boy said.

Laurel turned and walked back toward her seat, silently cursing Don Vincenze Calabra for talking her into marrying into a tradition she detested and had wanted no part of.

30

May 14: Bensonhurst, Brooklyn

JOE SMELLED LIKE SHIT. HE SMILED AS HE TIGHTENED HIS NOSTRILS to ward off the odor of the seedy clothes he'd worn the last ten evenings.

When the next patron, an elderly woman in a long black coat, walked out of the Top Tomato, Joe approached her with his hand out. "Help the homeless?" To her indifference, he added, "God bless you."

Ten days of walking Bensonhurst's streets, streets that were as familiar to him as his own face.

Upon hitting the city, Joe had headed for the extreme west side of Manhattan. He drove in and out of streets bordering the theater district, looking for some flophouse hotel where he could go about his business virtually unnoticed. The thought of living in squalor filled him with a religious fervor—Christ had not lived in richness—that sanctified his mission, made it blessed by God. And, of course, by Chrissy.

The transient hotel he found suited a beggar just fine. The hallway was the best part, with old-fashioned floors of one-inch white tiles that bellied in spots, wooden banisters that had been painted light blue, and lights so dim that the walls looked a nondistinguishable dark color covered with graffiti. Half the rooms were unoccupied, used by local hookers to turn quick tricks. Joe would see them, cheap girls in Satan's outfits, leading degenerates into their lairs by the arm, sleaze oozing from their pores.

Inside, Joe's room was worse than the old Tombs. He'd only been there a short time once, waiting for bail, but could vividly compare it to the chipped beige walls, worn-out brown carpet, and ratty two-inch mattress that sunk into creaky springs. The Tombs was certainly better than this. Why anyone would come here to get laid was beyond him.

For days Joe walked the territory, among pimps and peep shows, beggars and thieves, mustering up the courage and strength to make his first foray into Brooklyn, where his destiny awaited him. Each day he became grungier and seamier looking, trying to blend into his surroundings so well that he would never be noticed. The beard, lately more gray than black, helped. His clothes began by looking too good, but after dragging them around a Tenth Avenue alley, they looked better. A can of beer, poured on them and let dry, did even more, especially for the odor.

The only problem Joe faced initially was in his eyes. Something, which he couldn't exactly put his finger on, alerted the local scum to his not being one of them, and someone to be respected and feared. Encounters with those he knew were would-be muggers, parasites waiting to take advantage of those less fit, left him standing alone. They would each back off after gazing directly into his eyes. Couldn't be the gun, he reasoned, because that was a secret between him and Chrissy, and, of course, whatever other spirits could peek into his heart.

If those scumbags could know he was a man of respect by looking in his eyes, Joe told himself, then the enemy in Brooklyn would be able to recognize him the same way.

"No, Chrissy, they're not smarter than us," he would say

to her at night, in bed, because he knew she was there with him, waiting, counting on him to truly put her to rest. "We'll outsmart them. You'll see."

So Joe took to hunching forward, so he always looked as though he were searching for coins on the ground, and squinting. Only children and midgets could look him in the eye, he thought with satisfaction. And he wasn't afraid of either of them.

Finally, Joe felt unrecognizable enough to make his first venture into the Borough of Churches; the place where his poor, sweet innocent Chrissy had died. That fuckin' hellhole of the Earth, where no one deserved to live.

He caught the BMT's R train at Times Square, riding in the subway for the first time since he was a kid. The condition of the entire subterranean experience, a gritty gloom mixed with danger and the stench of human surrender, repulsed yet reaffirmed his mission. He loved the image of coming up from inside the earth's darkness to strike.

He trudged along Bensonhurst's Eighty-sixth Street that first night, wandering aimlessly; soaking in old sights; feeling the pain of old memories; testing passersby to see if they would scream out his name as an alert.

Joe Augusta passed by Tillio Scala's club on Stillwell Avenue quickly, catching a glimpse of Frankie Maniscalco and Tony Box Cars as they heatedly discussed something or other. Joe bent his head a little farther down, catching sight of stuck chewing gum and wads of spit while he laughingly cursed the two.

When he rounded the corner, Joe stopped, leaned against the building and guffawed. "See that Chrissy, baby?" he asked. "Jerks! We got 'em good." Then, holding his .38 revolver in his pocket, Joe passed by the pair again, this time more slowly. Tony Box Cars caught a full face look at him, but went right back to his discussion. "Fuck you, fuck you, fuck you," Joe muttered while giggling.

The next six nights went about the same, with Joe shuffling past old haunts, from Avenue U all the way down to Fort Hamilton Parkway, and from Sixty-fifth Street to the water. Now he had the feel, but with little direction as to how to begin his work. Who to start with? Who could he catch at night? He needed just a bit more time to feel comfortable enough to trade the seedy streets of Manhattan's West Side for these familiar ones.

Then he saw Georgie.

Georgie "the Hammer" Randazzo . . . the piece of shit that had had the audacity to date his daughter, soul of his soul . . . the piece of shit whose car Chrissy sat in when bullets tore her eye from her head, poor baby . . . the piece of shit who had fucked his poor, virginal child before she died—the piece of shit who should have died from his wound, instead of sweet, innocent Chrissy.

Tears ran down Joe's face. The autopsy report of semen being found in sweet Chrissy stood before him as if it were just typed. His baby, his sweet, sweet baby.

Fuck you, God! screamed in Joe's mind. He spat up in the air and began cursing. People looked at him while they walked wide circles to avoid him. Joe finally threw himself against the brick side wall of a house and sunk to the ground. He stayed there until there wasn't another person on the street, then found his way back to the subway station and back to New York.

He came back again night after night, searching for what was now a familiar face, but had no luck . . .

. . . Until now.

Georgie the Hammer walked past Joe, on his way toward Eighty-sixth Street. What had once been a slick, handsome boy, now looked like an ill-kept man. His hair, which had always been shiny, black, and short, now hung straggly, past his chin. His walk, once straight and arrogant, now seemed stooped. His clothes didn't look a hell of a lot better than the rags Joe himself wore.

Joe followed, stopping to check garbage pails, with fingers black in the natural skin lines and under his nails. He wiped something wet on his jacket, then followed across the wide intersection.

The street darkened once they had walked into the strictly residential block. Old brick-front houses, most redone in newer siding and well cared for, lined both sides of the street. Garbage pails stood in twos and threes by the sidewalk's end. A few windows glowed warmly.

Joe stopped when Georgie slipped through a hole in the

fence of Lafayette High School's yard. Georgie huddled with a group of youths, dressed mostly in jeans and motorcycle jackets. A little push. A shove. Georgie argued alone against the group.

Joe Augusta hustled across the street, setting himself low between an old white Buick and a blue step van. When Georgie turned to go, Joe darted into the alley between two houses. He licked his lips gleefully. He could hear the steps of Georgie's sneakers pounding in his ears. Anticipation made his heart feel like it would burst.

As Georgie the Hammer passed the alleyway, Joe stepped out to confront him.

Georgie stopped dead.

"Georgie Porgie, pudding and pie . . ." Joe said, as he pegged two shots directly through Georgie's heart. ". . . Kissed my girl and made her cry."

31

May 14: Todt Hill, Staten Island

DRESSED ONLY IN A PAIR OF TAPERED BOXER SHORTS, MICKEY BOY slipped quietly into Hope's nursery. Laurel was already asleep, but he had not been able to have that luxury. There were too many things churning in his mind, too much energy bursting in his head for him to fall into oblivion.

That Laurel had gone to sleep angry bothered him. There weren't that many people in the world he cared about, not to be hurt by differences that cut through to the core of them.

Despite his background in the streets, Mickey Boy considered himself very moral. He'd chased girls like everyone else, but was monogamous when it concerned someone he loved. He didn't gamble, didn't smoke, didn't take drugs, didn't drink more than socially. Sex was a pleasure to him, when straightforward. Much of what went on around him seemed perverse. He was offended by what he saw on television or heard on the radio. To him, homosexuals were fags and dykes, degenerates who had brought AIDS down on society's head.

Laurel, on the other hand, was more open and liberal. To her, homosexuals were "gay," and were no more of a threat to society than redheads or blondes. She laughed at sexually suggestive television shows, and loved to hear dirty jokes. And, though she matched him when it came to not using drugs, booze, and smoking, she seemed to him to be addicted to sex. If it wasn't dirty films or nipple clamps, it was rubbers that made his dick look like a rooster's head or handcuffs and panties with no crotch.

From the very first, Mickey Boy had had to wage an internal battle between the values he'd been taught by his mob mentors and his love for Laurel. If he listened to their teachings, she was a cunt. Excuses were just that, they would say—excuses. Alley had hurt her, he'd understood that, but he couldn't fathom how she could have debased herself by going with all the guys she'd admitted to. She'd even confessed to having fucked him the first time just to get back at Alley. It amazed him that she bore no outward taint from those degrading couple of years.

Many times, like tonight, he would picture her naked with someone else, fucking and sucking herself mindless. Even now he could see her down on her knees in front of that asshole guy from Merrill Lynch. *Only a* putana, *a cunt, does things like that,* the old-timers' voices rang in his head. *No decent girl takes a prick in her mouth.*

Mickey Boy spread a quilt on the floor, then went to Hope's crib. He picked her up gently, cradling her in his arms and not moving till he was sure she wouldn't wake up. When her stirring stopped, he moved to the quilt on the floor, laying Hope down on her stomach next to him, stroking her back underneath her nightie.

Somewhere, inside Mickey Boy's being, Frank Sinatra sang, much like Hope, about her life to come, in "Dream Away."

What a wonder Hope was, he thought. Perfect little hands and feet. His color, but more of Laurel's face. He hoped and prayed she'd be a decent, morally strong girl.

Once again Mickey Boy's mind flashed an image of Laurel and that guy from Tatou. This time he had her knees pinned back by her shoulders, slamming his dick into her. Mickey Boy shook his head and sniffed at Hope's hair.

Jealousy burned deep within him; low, yet white-hot. What would she have done if he hadn't shown up? he wondered. Probably nothing. But how long would it be till she did look for someone else? He'd been preoccupied lately, really not giving her the attention she needed. It was just that the pressures were so strong from every direction. Laurel was the closest to him, and therefore he'd taken her for granted. Wasn't that what marriage was all about, though? He guessed not.

Putana! *You don't wanna marry a girl like that. She'll always keep you wondering . . . always give you grief.* The voices never completely went away, always remained close, to keep him off guard, keep him insecure enough to keep a wall around himself.

Mickey Boy kissed Hope again and settled in to go to sleep. Whatever Laurel might have done in the past, she was as pure as the Virgin Mother since they'd been together, and after all, that was what counted.

And she was the best person he knew.

And she was his closest friend.

And as his loyal, loving wife, she had given him the most wonderful gift in the world: Hope.

Dream away, child . . . let your dreams run wild . . . for the years and the tears shed might claim you.

32

May 15: Downtown Brooklyn

IT SEEMED LIKE THE MIDDLE OF THE NIGHT TO RICHIE DeLUCA AS
he splashed water from the porcelain bin onto his face. His
insides fluttered to the rhythms of farts, toilets flushing, and
grumbling. The one bulb, dimmed behind a plastic casing,
seemed especially glaring, and the rap shit that the guards
turned up full-blast seemed to punch him in the head. He
wished he could have gotten up and out before the rest of the
tier did, that he wouldn't have to be a part of them and all
their bullshit this day.

Staring into the stainless steel square that passed for a
mirror, Richie shaved his light three-day growth. He'd
wanted everything as perfect as possible for today; not even
nicks or irritated skin. He'd had his hair trimmed a week
ago by a makeshift jailhouse barber, to let it fall in right by
today. Today was the day for him to look like the all-
American boy—though his face had hardened well beyond
the boyhood stage while locked up.

Breakfast sucked, as usual. Fuckin' grits. A Coca-Cola
he'd left cooling overnight in the toilet, and yesterday's
hard-boiled eggs, which he'd bought for two packs of generic
smokes, would do.

Richie took a swig of the Coke, then realizing he was too
wound up to eat and couldn't leave such a great treat for the
roaches, spilled it into the sink and rinsed out the can. Yes,
today and the days to follow would certainly take a couple of
pounds off him.

"DeLuca, court," the hack shouted through the bars.

"Yeah, I'm almost ready," Richie replied. "Gotta give
them time to get the spikes sharpened, anyway."

141

The hack smiled, then went on to call out other inmates for either court or medical visits. Richie himself could have used a visit to sick call. Once a cold bug got into the unit, everyone got it. Now he felt his turn approaching.

Handcuffed, he was elevatored down and put into another holding tank. He shuddered from a chill that crept up his spine when he sat on the metal bench. His eyes burned from the amount of disinfectant they had mopped the floor with. He laid his head back wearily against the cinder-block wall and closed his eyes. One way or another, this shit would soon be over. Either he would be set free after the trial or be on his way to a regular prison, where at least he'd be able to walk outside each day for the rest of his life. How he wished for a hard candy to cut through the dryness.

Eternal waiting led to the property room, where Ira J. Golden had arranged for a suit and trimmings to be left for him to wear to court. It felt so goddamn good to be able to put on real clothes, to feel a clean white shirt against his skin. The administration had had a problem with shoelaces and a necktie, but Golden was able to convince them to compromise: loafers, but a dark blue silk tie. Shit, they knew him well enough, Richie had thought, to know he wasn't suicide material.

Handcuffed again, this time to another prisoner, then shoved into a smelly, cold paddy wagon. Richie sucked in a few quick deep breaths on his way into the van. Money couldn't have bought anything more refreshing, after nearly a year and a half of nothing but stale air to fill his lungs.

"You, DeLuca . . ." the guard called once Richie had left the wagon and been marched up to the bullpen behind Part VII, Superior Court of the State of New York, ". . . come with me."

The courtroom looked as though it had been carved out of a giant wooden block. The only relief from the medium brown was the clothing of the people—black-robed New York Supreme Court Justice Heather Jacobson; Ira J. Golden, in a navy-blue power suit; Assistant District Attorney Roland V. Flowers, dressed as gray as the atmosphere; a stenographer in a tan skirt and white blouse; a variety of court officers; and, of course, two flags—the red, white, and blue American, and the blue and orange representing New York. What surprised Richie was that the rows of wooden seats behind the prosecution and defense tables were totally empty. Was his trial to be held in secret? Was it easier to railroad him that way? he wondered. Or easier to cut a deal for him to go free?

Please, God.

Richie sat at the defense table by himself—except for the two officers who stood no more than twelve inches behind him. Golden and the assistant district attorney conferred with Judge Jacobson by her bench. By the look of them, none were too happy either especially the judge, who shot angry glances toward Richie.

What the fuck did I do now?

After what seemed like ages, the meeting at the bench was adjourned. Each of the attorneys went to their respective tables, obviously to await some official word from the judge.

Richie whispered to Golden, asking what was going on, but Golden shushed him with a quick elbow shot.

"In view of the circumstances we just discussed," Justice Jacobson began, "and in agreement with Assistant District Attorney Flowers and Ira Golden, representative for the defendant, Richard Anthony DeLuca, I am now putting this case over on my calendar for trial on May twenty-eighth . . ." She paused for a moment, studying her calendar, then said, "You know what, counselors, since we'll run into Memorial Day, let's say, June one. Okay?"

Both lawyers agreed.

"All right," Judge Jacobson said. "See you on the first. Court adjourned for a brief recess, then I'll hear those scheduled motions from other cases."

"What the fuck happened?" Richie finally asked.

Golden turned to him and sighed. "If it weren't for bad luck, my boy, you wouldn't have any. Your best witness was murdered last night."

33

May 15: West Side, Manhattan

"I'M SORRY, I'M SORRY, I'M SORRY . . ." JOE AUGUSTA WAILED. Saliva flowed on to the threadbare pillow along with his tears. His nose ran into the matted hair of his moustache and beard. Once again Joe flagellated himself for being cursed, for being part of things so bad.

This killing had not been like any other, had not filled him with remorse and visceral pain. This had been a triumph, a jubilation of the spirit of revenge and justice. Georgie the Hammer had been an integral step along the path to Chrissy's death. That instrument of the Devil had deflowered her and made her suffer. Lucifer's servant had died, and rightly so.

Then came the television image: a picture of Georgie the Hammer Randazzo's once handsome face; a photo of his twisted body, half covered with a sheet, his blood staining the concrete of the Bensonhurst sidewalk where Joe had left him.

Hands still trembling with excitement, Joe had stopped by the television in the shabby lobby of the hotel to see his handiwork reported; to revel in the glory of his and Chrissy's success over Evil. Joe felt as though firecrackers were exploding in his heart, showering luminous shards of joy throughout his system—until the announcer said that Georgie the Hammer was to be a star witness for Richie DeLuca, in his trial for the murder of Christina Augusta.

While the announcer went into historical background on Joe Augusta, and an added piece about him having disappeared after Chrissy's death, Joe's veins seemed to expand in his head. He felt light-headed and paralyzed. He shuffled off, even as the reporter flashed a picture of him, taken years before, when his hair was still dark and his face clean-shaven and unlined.

How could he do something so stupid? Joe tearfully asked himself. He needed Richie out of jail to kill him. Couldn't let him linger in some mountain prison, watching cable TV and munching on commissary cakes. Why had Chrissy not warned him? Why had God fuckin' let him down? *Why? Why? Why?*

Joe slammed his fist between the thin white posts of the headboard, straight into the wall. It stung his knuckles enough to make him aware that he shouldn't damage his shooting hand.

"Test me, will you!" he shouted up at the ceiling. "I'll show you. Fuck you! Fuck you!"

Joe suddenly broke into laughter. Nothing would stop him. Not man, not Spirit. Not Christ or Lucifer. Fuck them all! Even if he had to storm the courthouse wired with explosives, he would murder Richie DeLuca.

Joe fell asleep smiling and muttering, "You're the end of the rainbow, my pot of gold . . . You're daddy's little girl, to have and to hold . . ."

34

May 18: Bensonhurst, Brooklyn

A TRAIN CLATTERED AND WHISTLED ON THE TRACKS OVERHEAD AS Mickey Boy hesitantly entered the modern glass- and marble-fronted Prospero of Bensonhurst Funeral Home. Freddie Falcone flanked him on one side, Nicolo Fonte on the other. In front, two of his made men, Vito the Head and Billy Sneakers, opened the door and cleared his way.

He would have preferred going with Laurel—she had

been a supporter of Georgie and Chrissy's love affair, staying in touch with them even when he had thought better of it—but he couldn't. Protocol demanded he attend wakes and funerals surrounded by men only. Laurel would attend those types of functions only in the case of relatives or someone especially close to her. Otherwise, he would be stuck in the boy's club.

Not that Georgie Randazzo's wake would be a typical mob event. No one from any of the other families would come. In fact, by rights, Mickey Boy knew, he shouldn't be there either. Especially not in the position he was in now. Georgie had walked a tightrope by dating Chrissy in the first place; he'd gone to pieces after her death, recuperating in solitude from his gunshot wounds. Worse, he had become a drug addict. And everyone in the neighborhood knew it.

But Georgie had once been a friend. He had been part of the young kids when Mickey Boy and his crowd were tearing it up as the main crew hanging out at Spumoni Gardens. Georgie had idolized Mickey Boy in life. Visiting his coffin was the least Mickey Boy felt he could do.

Unlike the hardened faces and polished clothing he normally saw at such functions, Mickey Boy saw only people: older men dressed in black suits they'd already grown out of, their hands thick and caloused; ordinary women who would be shopping for vegetables or housewares, possibly along that very same street, early the next day; youngsters related to Georgie, their dark eyes wide, trying to understand, their skin olive-cast and dewy with innocence. They all stared at Mickey Boy and his entourage as he entered the chapel where Georgie was laid out.

Georgie's father, whom Mickey Boy knew only as Mr. Randazzo, greeted them at doorway. The tortured father looked like he had gained thirty years in the ten or so since Mickey Boy had seen him last; probably half of it, Mickey Boy thought, in the last few days. Deep folds cut under his eyes. His lower lip seemed to curl outward and down, as if it were a permanent expression of his grief.

"Thank you for coming," Mr. Randazzo said. Though he did nothing more than work at his city sewers job, like everyone in the neighborhood, he was aware of who Mickey

146

Boy was, and paid obvious homage to him. "I know my boy respected you a lot."

"I always liked Georgie," Mickey Boy replied. "He just got a little mixed up, went off the wrong way." He nodded to Freddie, who handed Mr. Randazzo an envelope. "Take that, for a *boost*," Mickey Boy said, referring to the open book where visitors' donations would be noted.

The old man felt the thickness of the envelope, then began to stammer about not being able to take so much.

Mickey Boy assured him that it was all right, that he should use it to pay for Georgie's funeral, while wishing they had chosen the Shore Haven Funeral Home instead, where he was a silent majority partner and would have had everything done on the arm—and saved five thousand dollars.

With Georgie's father leading the way, Mickey Boy then made a quick walk, with Freddie and Nicolo Fonte following, to the casket. His heart broke looking at Georgie, as he crossed himself. He remembered how he and Laurel had met Georgie and Chrissy in F.A.O. Schwarz, when both couples had first started to date, then spent the rest of the day throwing a Frisbee in Central Park and dining uptown. That was the way life should have continued. But now both Chrissy and Georgie were dead. This was the way he and Laurel could have been now, except for fortunate twists of fate.

All Mickey Boy could think of as he left the funeral parlor was one of his mother's favorite expressions: *There, but for the Grace of God, go I.*

"I want you to go over to Crazy Angelo's club, on Avenue U and West Sixth Street," Mickey Boy told Freddie. He slid into a booth at Mary's Venetian Restaurant, just a couple of blocks from Prospero's Funeral Home. Fonte slid in across from him. Billy Sneakers and Vito the Head sat apart, on either side of the front door.

"I would go there myself, but that cocksucker Halloran, he'll violate me in a minute," Mickey Boy continued, referring to the stable of ex-cons who hung out at the club and the law enforcement troops that constantly watched them—and would report his visit directly to his parole officer. "Bring Angelo here to meet me. I wanna know who wasted that kid. Even if it's junkies, he's in the neighborhood, and we gotta find out something."

"Not a smart move. Not unless you know him real good," Freddie said.

"Who?"

"Angelo."

"Not at all. Seen him around the neighborhood, years ago, but that's about it."

Freddie claimed that protocol demanded Mickey Boy, as Boss of the Calabra Family, not deal directly with lower members of other crews. "Angelo's just a made guy, and lucky to be that. If you want something from him, you gotta reach out for at least his skipper, and then only by sending me or a skipper of ours. You gotta deal on your own level."

"Fuck this nonsense!" Mickey Boy said. A boy was dead, he went on; a boy that he had cared about at one time. All he wanted was to know a reason, and if it was sanctioned by wiseguys. "What am I asking? For him to rat somebody out?"

"It ain't what you want, it's how you do it," Freddie replied. He turned to Fonte. "Ain't it the same on the other side, Nicolo? Ain't there a protocol?"

Fonte laughed. "Much more so than in America," he said. Because the Mafia, even more than either the Camorra or 'Ndrangheta, was so integrated into Sicilian and Italian society, he had come to know many members socially. "They are *gli amici* . . . the friends," he explained. "We, the legitimate businessmen who operate with their blessings, *gli amici degli amici* . . . friends of friends, though they use that same term among themselves. We honor and respect them, calling them *uomini rispetto* . . . men of respect, or *uomini qualificato* . . . qualified men."

"Here we say 'goodfellas' or 'nice guys,'" Freddie said.

But here, Fonte said, *la cosa nostra* families were sloppy and undisciplined. "Very strict in Sicily," he said. *"Soldati* there and on the mainland treat bosses as though they were almost gods, with the utmost fear and respect. They would never think of discussing business with someone beneath or even above them."

Fonte's interjection annoyed Mickey Boy. He had brought him along to further discuss their proposed pasta houses; to get all the details together to present to his new business advisory staff, consisting mainly of Laurel's relatives. He didn't need a fuckin' lecture from Fonte about greaseball mob matters. Who gave a flying fuck what some moustachioed scumbag in Palermo or Milan thought!

Mickey Boy shoved his place setting aside. "Take me home," he said, standing. "I lost my fuckin' appetite."

35

May 20: Todt Hill, Staten Island

LITTLE VINNIE SPED DOWN THE HILL, STOPPED AT THE SIGN, THEN swung the car left for a block before he doubled back. He glanced down at the *Daily News* on the seat next to him. A five-day-old story about Georgie the Hammer's murder stared back. By now it was old news, and forgotten by the media. Georgie, according to the news report, had been nothing more than a junkie, killed probably as a result of a narcotics deal gone wrong.

Fuckin' asshole shoulda died when I shot him, Little Vinnie thought.

He remembered that night. His confusion, as events moved faster than his mind could comprehend. His silent scream, "No!" when he realized it was Chrissy's brains splattered on the dashboard of Georgie's Corvette. Chrissy, poor Chrissy. The girl he'd grown up with and called Cuz—the girl he'd wanted to marry.

Fuckin' scumbag, Georgie, deserved to die.

As Little Vinnie passed by Mickey Boy's house again, his thoughts shifted to his present dilemma. How the fuck could he possibly kill Mickey Boy and get away with it?

On three different occasions so far he'd tried catching up to Mickey Boy, to clock him in order to find the best place to make the hit. Little Vinnie's conclusion was that there was no such spot.

He'd checked out Jasper's Barbershop on Avenue U, and that was horrid. Always guys around, half of them probably cops, the other half guys who would either recognize him or shoot back. Getting killed for a principle might be a greaseball tactic, but not for him. Those maniacs kept vendettas going for centuries; fuckin' wiped out whole families. What was he supposed to do, aim a fuckin' bazooka at Jasper's front window? This was Brooklyn, not Palermo.

Checking out any social clubs would have been a waste, Little Vinnie knew, because of Mickey Boy's parole situation. Instead, he'd decided to catch him either coming or going from his house. No luck again. Of the two previous occasions he'd tried passing by, he'd caught Mickey Boy coming out once. And that time, he'd been accompanied by Freddie Falcone, Billy Sneakers, and Vito the Head. How the fuck could he kill four guys and not get killed himself?

Maybe this whole greaseball setup was to have him killed instead of Mickey Boy. Little Vinnie knew how devious these old-timers could be, from hearing how his bastard of a father had manipulated half the mob guys in New York to shoot at each other. Fuck them, he thought.

Driving around the block, Little Vinnie convinced himself he was not being set up. DoDo, that oregano-stinking zip, might feed him to the lions, just for laughs, but not Don Genco. Deep down, he believed that Don Genco truly cared for him and would never do anything to hurt him.

Once more Little Vinnie followed the same route he'd gone through three or four times. Since the neighborhood was so highly residential, nothing but mini mansions and walled estates, he couldn't very well sit in one spot without drawing attention. Even driving around so much could get him in trouble. Then what? How the fuck would he go back to Sicily and marry Ninfa, then? God damn, couldn't they just have left him alone; let him live in Acireale without having to make a macho show of getting revenge? *Fuck them too!*

Little Vinnie made what he'd decided would be his last pass in front of Mickey Boy's house. He'd still have time to get back to the city before the offices sent millions of goddamn cockroaches out onto the roads to tie up traffic. Maybe he'd stop by Tempest and Hale's on the way back— keep them on the line in case he eventually needed them— then go bouncing for cunt in a few bars along the West Side.

Little Vinnie's heart quickened as the garage door of Mickey Boy's house lifted. He slowed, then turned into a perpendicular street and made a quick U-turn. As he hit the corner, a white Mercedes swung out of Mickey Boy's driveway and passed in front of him.

Laurel!

Little Vinnie drove along Hylan Boulevard with a raging hard-on pushing against his jeans. He remembered how close he'd come to fucking Laurel when Mickey Boy was in MCC on the parole violation. He'd been brilliant, and patient, baiting her into meeting him to discuss ending his and Mickey Boy's feud. She'd been willing. He goddamn well knew it as well as he'd ever known anything in his life. He could sense the sexual heat emanating from her despite how cool and noncommittal she'd tried to be.

Now Little Vinnie pounded his fist on his steering wheel. That last time, when Laurel had had a bit too much to drink, should have been the time he should have fucked her. She'd been ready, licking her lips and letting her skirt ride high as she said good-bye in his car. Instead, like an asshole, he'd let her get away.

When Laurel turned left and stopped in front of Cangiano's Pork Store, Little Vinnie pulled up across the street. Should he follow her inside? Could he? Would anybody recognize him?

He waited a couple of minutes, then drove across Hylan Boulevard and parked in front of Cangiano's. Touching his sunglasses, for security, he darted out of the car before he had a chance to change his mind.

Once inside, Little Vinnie's heart beat in his throat. His chest felt like it was strapped with a steel band. His palms perspired and his tongue felt swollen. Cautiously, he made his way through the grocery aisles toward the meat counter.

Laurel stood with her back to him, waiting, next in line at the counter. Black cowboy boots and shorts. Little blue veins at the back of her knees when she leaned forward to order. Shorts climbing into her ass.

Little Vinnie thought he would collapse. He picked two cans of something off a shelf and stepped closer. He could see the V-shaped outline of her panties. Her thighs tightened smooth and shiny. He stood close enough to smell her scent over the odors of raw pork and beef, and felt dizzy.

When Laurel took a package from the butcher and turned, Little Vinnie quickly turned away. He shuffled into an aisle and held onto a shelf for support. Light tremors filled his body. He stood there, watching Laurel in a mirror set up near the ceiling to catch shoplifters. When she went to check out, he moved.

Leaving the cans he was holding on a shelf, he walked past Laurel, on his way to the door. He purposely bumped into her, grabbing hold of her white silk-clad arms for a second as if to keep her from falling, then quickly moved on, mumbling an apology.

As Little Vinnie sat in his car, the touch of Laurel tingled on his fingers. He watched her get back into her Mercedes and leave, without following this time. It was as if all the energy had been drained from his body.

After a while Little Vinnie pulled out of the parking spot and headed for the Verrazano Bridge, filled with confidence and joy he hadn't felt for months.

Why?

Little Vinnie wasn't exactly sure, except for one thing—he knew a goddamn omen when he saw it.

36

May 25: Cobble Hill, Brooklyn

BUSTER HURT. REALLY HURT, INSIDE AT THE CORE OF HIM. It seemed like there wasn't a part of his body that didn't feel some kind of pain. Not always sharp pain, but a dull, weary sort of pain that made even lifting the spoon he sipped Nettie's homemade chicken soup with a chore. He would have shoved the bowl away, but didn't want to hear her nag about how he needed his nourishment.

Nourishment for what? Buster wondered. He was fuckin' dying. Did he have to die fully nourished? Each little bit of food or drink he was able to hold down only fed the monster that was eating him up inside. He'd rather starve the bastard out anyway.

He took another spoonful of the tasty broth mixed with pastina, tiny flakes of egg macaroni that Nettie had cooked into the soup. *Fuckin' nourishment!*

Nettie shuffled past him in the kitchen, scooping Breyer's vanilla into a glass for him. It was the same kitchen she'd fussed in for over thirty years. At least the mortgage was all paid off, Buster thought. And she'd decorated—new blond wood cabinets and white wallpaper with yellow and blue flowers—just a year ago. She would be pretty well set.

Nettie looked at him and smiled.

Brave sonomabitch. How good she was, and how much he would hate to leave her, Buster told himself. Looking back now, in a way, he was glad that the street life had consumed most of his waking hours, that he'd spent more time out of the house than in it. If nothing else, those years had made Nettie forge a life for herself, with friends, other family, and social events, like her bridge games every Wednesday. God bless her, she'd be able to go on with her life without him. She wouldn't fall apart.

On the other hand, Buster felt saddened by that same time he had spent away from her. Nettie was more than his wife, she was his best friend. He'd loved her madly when they'd first courted and married, and loved her so comfortably afterward that he knew he'd often taken her for granted. The fact that they had never been able to have children had drawn them even closer. They'd suffered the disappointment together, each worried more about how the other one felt than their own misery. That was real love, he thought. Not the bullshit love all these kids in heat thought they had today. Too bad he hadn't given her more of his time.

"Come on, 'Tiano," Nettie said. "Come eat your ice cream in the living room. I'll put on the television. 'The Simpsons' will be on soon. You like them."

"Let me take out the garbage first," Buster answered. He rose, feeling like he was creaking out loud. His breathing was difficult and hurt his chest.

"Don't worry, I'll take it out."

"Nah, lemme do it," he replied. "Don't make me like a cripple." If cancer was to take him, he thought again, it would take him as a man—whole and fighting till the end. That's why he'd refused the operation the doctors had proposed. No way he'd let them turn him into a freak, with parts missing, when he would die anyway. Fuck them and fuck the cancer. Sebastiano Antonino Alcamo would meet his Maker in one piece. At least whatever was left of him after the dirty little cells had had their fill of feasting on his insides.

Half dragging the white plastic bag, Buster stopped by the hall mirror and stared. His once burly frame had been reduced to where his shirt hung off his shoulders and his neck had room for a spare inside his collar. His belt had been tightened so much that he had to punch six new holes in it, and now the tip of it reached around near his left pocket.

He'd had a good life, Buster thought as he opened the door to go outside. For a guy who had never gone to school past the sixth grade, he'd managed to give Nettie whatever she wanted, and had been at the very center of power with Don Vincenze Calabra. He had a right to be proud.

Even hanging onto the wrought-iron railing, Buster barely negotiated the few steps leading down from his brownstone home to the street. Going back up would be the bitch. He stepped through the gate and dropped the sack on top of the two metal trash cans that had been put out for tomorrow's pickup.

"Bastiano," a low voice melodically called to him.

Buster turned. A man stepped out from the dead spot between the tree and a parked station wagon. He looked like a bum, one of those homeless that begged for coins along Court Street. *How the fuck, though, he knows my name?*

"Bastiano," the voice, which sounded vaguely familiar, said again, in a sort of singsong tone as its owner moved closer.

Buster peered in the darkness at the filthy clothes, the matted beard, the hollow, crazy eyes. Suddenly, when the bum was only two feet away, he was struck by full recognition.

"You?" Buster said.

"Yeah, me. Got an order to give out? Got anybody you wanna whack?"

Buster spat whatever mucus Nettie's chicken soup had left in his mouth into the bum's face—just as the first bullet ripped into his cancerous lung.

37

May 26: Todt Hill, Staten Island

"ARE YOUSE ALL FUCKIN' CRAZY?!" MICKEY BOY SHOUTED. "DID something happen that all of a sudden youse all lost your minds?"

Freddie Falcone and three of the Calabra Family captains sat around the kitchen table. Bobby Rimini, the 250-pound office cleaning executive, and Patsy Luciano, the sixty-five-year-old olive oil importer, indulged in coffee that Freddie had prepared. Frankie "Green Eyes" Scarpucci, a gaunt-looking thirty-year-old who ran a high-stakes *ziganette* game in Borough Park, just tapped his spoon on the cup to a hypnotic rhythm. Tony Polo, in a black and blue Fila sweat suit and a jewelry store worth of diamonds, paced back and forth behind them.

"You have to understand our point of view also," Patsy Luciano said. "We're the ones who gotta explain to our guys what happened."

"But I don't fuckin' know what happened!"

"Yeah, of course we believe you. That goes without saying," Bobby Rimini chimed in. "But we gotta make everybody else believe us."

Everyone with even half a mind who was in the streets knew that mob family members, especially those who had reached Buster's level of underboss, never got killed by outsiders. Without exception, it was always done from within their own crew, and, unless there was a factional war going on, which Mickey Boy's crew did not have, the order always came from the top. All fingers in Buster's murder pointed directly at Mickey Boy.

156

"Tell them any way you want," Mickey Boy said. "But make them know I had nothing to do with it."

Freddie tried to lighten the mood, saying, "You think they'll figure it was done by a jealous husband?" He paused to let the others smile weakly at their memory of the crusty old Buster, then said, "Nah, I guess not."

Turning serious, Freddie went on, "Patsy, how long you know me? Twenty, twenty-five years?"

"Something like that."

"An' you, Bobby, you been sending a crew in to clean my joints since I had the bar and grill on Fourth Avenue. We sat together and talked—about a lot of very private things—for hours on end, right?"

Bobby Rimini nodded his assent.

To Tony Polo, Freddie said, "An' you? Didn't I confide in you when I had problems when the Bug was my boss? An' you did the same, later, when you got jammed up with that fugazy money deal?"

"Yeah, sure, but—"

"No buts! You guys know me. Except for Frankie, here, who's younger than some of my suits."

Though straining for it, all except Mickey laughed. To him, Frankie Green Eyes was just what he was trying to eliminate from his crew: young hoodlums who tried to live in a 1930s image sixty years too late.

"No disrespect, Frankie," Freddie said. "You know I love you. And though you know me a short time, you could judge me the way you would anybody else. You're a good judge of character, right?"

"The best."

"Good. Then, when I wanna get married, I'll let you pick my wife."

They all laughed again, more relaxed than the first time.

"You guys think I would back up a move like whackin' Buster?" His quick switch from humor to serious challenge caught everyone off guard. Without waiting for them to recover and respond, he asked, "Well? You think you could find one guy out there, just one, who'll tell you, 'Yeah, that fuck Freddie, he'd whack a good guy like Buster, who's been loyal to our family, in a hot minute'?"

"It ain't like that," Tony Polo said. "It's just that we know what we know. How many underbosses you know that been whacked without the boss's orders?"

"One . . ." Freddie said, holding up his index finger in front of him. ". . . Buster."

Mickey Boy felt glad that Freddie was there to handle the flak, to run interference for him. His own patience was worn thin; he would have booted the whole fuckin' bunch of them out into the street. Let them do whatever the fuck they wanted. Imagine the goddamn nerve of them, believing that he would kill Buster? For what reason?

"Didn't you know he was fuckin' dying of cancer?" Mickey Boy finally blurted.

"Well, we heard something . . ." Patsy Luciano said, shifting uncomfortably in his seat.

"Something? He was half fuckin' dead! Maybe whoever did it should get a fuckin' medal, for putting him out of his misery!"

"You sayin' this is a mercy thing?" Tony Polo asked.

"Oh, go talk to a fuckin' case of bananas!" Mickey Boy shouted at the produce wholesaler, and stormed from the room. He could hear Freddie trying to smooth their ruffled feathers.

Mickey Boy did a quick about-face, back into the room, ready to start screaming obscenities at the whole bunch, including Freddie. He was the fuckin' boss. They had to have some goddamn trust in him, or let them get somebody else.

Just then the doorbell rang. Each of the men looked at the other.

"Who else is supposed to be here?" Mickey Boy asked.

They all shrugged.

"Nobody," Freddie said. He started for the door, then, looking out through the bulletproof window, came back. "It's that fuckin' Irish P.O. of yours."

"Shit!" Mickey Boy howled. "Eight-thirty in the fuckin' morning. Don't anybody ever sleep?"

Laurel poked her head out from the top of the landing. "Everything okay?"

"Get back inside!" Mickey Boy snapped, immediately

sorry for taking his anger out on her. "Any of youse got records?" he asked the group in the kitchen.

"I did three years in Milan, Michigan," Patsy Luciano said, ". . . in 1948."

"You drove here?" Mickey Boy asked. If Patsy's car was outside and registered in his name, it would be too late. Halloran would violate him for association with a convicted felon.

"No, I came with Bobby."

Frankie Green Eyes said, "I got a year in Riker's on a misdemeanor I pleaded out to . . . an' I drove here. But my car's registered to my cousin Sal, who's a barber."

"Okay," Mickey Boy said. "Both of youse, upstairs, quick. Hide in any room, any closet. Just hurry and stay quiet."

The bell rang again.

Mickey Boy waited, let the bell ring a third time—until the sounds of Patsy and Frankie hiding were gone—then opened the door.

Halloran walked right in. He made a beeline for the kitchen. "Well, hello, gentlemen . . . Mr. Falcone," he said, once again pronouncing it "Falcon*ee*. "My name is—"

"We know who you are," Freddie said. He took his driver's license out of his wallet and dropped it onto the tabletop. "There, that's who I am. Falcone, not Falcon*ee,*" he said, smiling. "An' we understand your job."

Halloran tossed Freddie's license back to him, but wrote down Bobby Rimini's and Tony Polo's name, address, and license number on a pad.

"I think you'll find more criminals on your staff than you'll find here," Freddie said. "Although I mighta done one night in jail for mopery." He paused, feigning deep thought. "But I can't really remember. Drunk an' outta town don't count, right? And I know Bobby here did a couple of hours community service, polishing desks or something."

"No, that's what I do for a living," Bobby said playfully.

"But you didn't learn that in jail?" Freddie asked.

"C'mon, I'm the best in the West at cleaning offices." He handed Halloran a business card. "If ever you guys need some work done."

"Yeah, you're the best in the West," Freddie jumped in. "Too bad this is the East."

Halloran turned to Mickey Boy, who had been enjoying the sport. "You didn't tell me you ran a comedian's convention here."

"Come on," Mickey Boy said. "Let's go into the den."

Once inside his den, Mickey Boy plopped down on an overstuffed white armchair. Halloran sat at the edge of the sofa, as though he would pop straight up at a moment's notice.

"Well, what's up?" Mickey Boy asked.

Halloran smiled. "Shouldn't I be asking you that? What with your underboss getting blown away last night?"

"I don't know anything about all this underboss shit," Mickey Boy said. "If you mean my friend, yes, Buster was a friend of mine."

"So?"

"So what?"

"Why did you have him hit? Power play going on? Everybody to the mattresses?"

"C'mon, Halloran," Mickey Boy said. "What are you doing, watching that Godfather shit again?"

Halloran opened a folder and began writing. "You might as well fill this monthly report out," he said.

"Isn't it a little early for that?" Mickey Boy replied. "Besides, didn't you an' my lawyer agree that him and my accountant could check them first, before I hand 'em in?"

Halloran tossed the form on the coffee table's glass top. "Okay, then, why did Alcamo get whacked?"

Mickey Boy shifted to the edge of his seat, like Halloran. "I swear to you, I don't have the goddamn faintest idea."

"What could I expect? For you to confess?"

"Halloran, I swear on my kid, I don't know who did it or why anyone would want to." He pointed to the kitchen. "Why do you think these guys are here so early? We were all friends of his, and all wondering what happened."

"Don't insult my intelligence, Mr. Messina. I know who you are, and why all your so-called friends are here. For me, this is a boon. It's a chance to flush you out of your hole so I can bust you. Got some plate numbers already."

"They'll check out legit."

"We'll see."

Mickey Boy stood. He looked toward the kitchen, nearby, then said, "C'mon, let's walk out in the back." He led Halloran out onto the terrazzo patio and sat by the table, whose umbrella was still closed.

"Halloran—"

"Mr. Halloran."

"Whatever," Mickey Boy said, trying to hold his temper. *"Mister* Halloran, you been breaking my balls ever since you got my case. Tell me what it is you want from me."

"To see you back where you belong . . . in prison."

"How could you be so sure?"

"Because I've been through the mill," Halloran said. "I have seen every kind of street punk, white-collar criminal, and sleazy mafioso. And to me, you organized guys are the worst."

"I won't admit to 'you guys,'" Mickey Boy said. "But with all kinds of druggies, muggers, and baby fuckers out there, how could you even say that?"

"Because you prey on the entire breadth and fabric of society. You kill and pervert authority, and are an affront to civilized people."

"Would it be like that if it was one of your Irish cousins on parole, instead of an Italian?"

"None of my relatives would ever be on parole," Halloran said with a smirk. "My family line has always upheld the law, not broken it."

Mickey Boy threw his hands up. This was one hardheaded Irishman, he thought. "But I still don't understand how, with all that's going—"

"If you want so much to understand me," Halloran went on, "just remember what you and your mobster friends did to Mister Spositoro."

Mickey Boy wanted to tell Halloran that Spositoro had been even a bigger scumbag than he was. The man had been obsessed with violating Mickey Boy, and had been overtly nasty about it. He'd locked Mickey Boy up once, purposely tried to cause a break between him and Laurel, and had stormed into the hospital room after Mickey Boy had been shot, to rant and rave about locking him up again. He deserved everything he got.

161

Halloran continued, "Mister Spositoro was a good man, a decent man. Now he's on extended medical leave for a job-related breakdown. Know anything about that?"

Unfortunately for Spositoro, he had run into Don Vincenze, Buster, and Eddie DaDa at the hospital, and they had bent him like a pretzel, spit in his face, and otherwise terrorized the shit out of him. If the man hadn't been able to face his shortcomings and had become a stone boozehound, as Mickey Boy had heard, then it was his own fault.

"Halloran, I—"

"Mr. Halloran."

"*Mister* Halloran, I brought you out here, away from everybody else, 'cause I wanted to talk to you in private; try to bury this ax you've got for me, and try to come to some kind of reasonable understanding."

"What is there to understand? You're a gangster—worse, a boss gangster—and do not belong on the streets. Not if I can help it, anyway."

"Let's assume for the moment that you were right." Mickey Boy held his hands up. "Now, that's just us assuming, not a confession."

Halloran sat silently.

"And we assume that if I was, I mighta found myself that way, and was stuck."

When Halloran started to speak, Mickey Boy stopped him. "Please, just listen."

Halloran nodded.

"Now, supposing I was that top kind of guy, then maybe I seen that what you said was right, that there was no place for gangsters today. And maybe I was just trying to get everybody to change, to go into legitimate businesses and not do any crimes?"

"Am I supposed to commend you for infiltrating legitimate business?"

"Who's talking about infiltrating?" Mickey Boy almost shouted. "I'm talking about investing, and running a clean business that could support families, and keep those people out of crime."

Mickey Boy went on to explain about the pasta houses he was trying to develop. He threw bits of facts and figures he had absorbed from Nicolo Fonte, and gave Halloran the backgrounds of Laurel's relatives, who would be overseeing the operation.

Through it all, Halloran sat stone-faced. When Mickey Boy was done, he asked, "Is that supposed to impress me?"

"Halloran, I—"

"Mr. Halloran."

"Mr. Whateverthefuck! I'm talking honest to you, trying to show you that I'm trying to do honorable and good things. Why don't you give me a chance? Give me a break for a while, to prove to you that everything I wanna do is legit?"

Halloran stood. "As far as I am concerned, Mr. Messina, everything you do is infiltration, and I will do everything in my power to stop you." He started for the side of the house, to leave, then turned. "Mark my words, Mr. Messina, high-priced lawyers or no high-priced lawyers, spaghetti fronts or no spaghetti fronts, I'm taking you down!"

Mickey Boy felt more disgusted than angry as he returned to the kitchen. Laurel had come down and had prepared eggs and sausages for Freddie, Bobby Rimini, and Tony Polo.

"You want something?" Laurel asked.

"Yeah, poison," Mickey Boy answered. He went to the foot of the stairs and whistled for the old man, Patsy and Frankie Green Eyes, who were still hiding. When they came down, Laurel fixed breakfast for them too, then left to care for Hope, who had begun to cry.

"Just put everything in the dishwasher," Laurel shouted while running up the stairs.

"What'd he want?" Freddie asked, referring to Halloran now that Laurel had left.

"Nothing. Same shit." Mickey Boy turned to his men. "There's really nothing for us to talk about anymore. I swear to youse, on my kid's eyes, that I had nothing to do with Buster's being whacked. If those guys of yours don't believe that, then fuck them. All I could do is try to find out what the hell happened." He began to laugh. "Between trying to find out who whacked the kid, Georgie, and now Buster, I'm beginning to feel like a fuckin' cop."

When he ushered them to the door, all the older men, with cold attitudes, said they would talk to their men. Freddie said he would talk to a few of the other captains and reassure them that Buster's killing was a mystery to him as well as Mickey Boy.

Frankie Green Eyes held back until last. At the door he hugged and kissed Mickey Boy on the cheeks. "I want you to know, pops, that whatever happened—whether you knew about Buster or you didn't—it's okay with me, an' all my guys. Don't listen too much to these old fucks. Even most of their own guys don't pay attention to them."

When Frankie had left, Mickey Boy stood with his back to the door. He stared ahead, his eyes heavy, as though they would burst into tears. His nostrils flared and his mouth tasted sour and dry. His fists pounded rhythmically on the door behind him.

How the fuck could he always come up backward? he wondered. Now he had alienated the people he was depending on to build a legitimate business, and was stuck with the scumbags he hated on his side.

No, there was just no goddamn justice in life.

38

May 26: Todt Hill, Staten Island

"FOR SALE? FOR FUCKIN' GODDAMN SALE?!" LITTLE VINNIE growled through clenched teeth as he yanked the Century 21 sign out of the lawn. He wanted to toss it up and out toward the street, but didn't want to attract undue attention. If nosy Mrs. Casselli on the left, or any of the Rothblatts, living on the other side, saw him, they'd be out to waste his goddamn time with senseless chatter, and maybe get him seen by someone else. After all, this house was no more than a half mile away from Mickey Boy's.

Little Vinnie hurried toward the driveway at the side of

the white Cape Cod and dropped the For Sale sign behind the lined up trash cans. What the hell, he told himself. Did he think they were going to hold on to the house forever?

Who'd put it up for sale, though? Who had possession? If it was his sisters, Margie and Linda, then he knew he'd get his fair share. But what if that bastard offspring of his father's had robbed them? Muscled them out? If he did, Little Vinnie told himself, that would be another reason to see Mickey Boy fuckin' dead.

Little Vinnie's heart beat in the back of his throat as he tried his key in the front door. "Fuck!" he yelled. Sons of bitches had changed the lock. He hurried around the back, hoping that they hadn't been thorough enough to change the lock on the rear door that led down to the basement.

They hadn't.

Standing in the room that still stank from his father's cigars, Little Vinnie was assaulted with memories, none of them good. This room, especially, had signaled the beginning of the end for him. He could hear that old cocksucker's gravelly voice as it had drifted up the stairs. ". . . About my son . . . my son, Mickey Boy."

A dank chill pierced Little Vinnie and made him shiver. After all, the house had not been heated all winter. Or was it the memory of his father? he wondered. Good old Don Vincenze, always there to catch every little mistake he made and use it to crush him with a lengthy, insulting reprimand, or worse, a degrading laugh.

Upstairs, Little Vinnie stopped by the kitchen. For a moment he could feel his mother there, washing his face or fixing his lunch. But once again Don Vincenze's miserable shadow overpowered Little Vinnie's warmer remembrances of his mother. Cursing, he ran upstairs to take care of business.

In his former bedroom, Little Vinnie rushed directly to his dresser, searching the top drawer for the bankbook he'd left.

Gone.

"Shit!" he screamed, pounding a fist on the dresser top. Thirty thousand dollars he'd counted on, out the fuckin' window.

Perturbed but not defeated, Little Vinnie ran to his closet.

He tossed shoes, old dirty laundry, and a stack of magazines behind him till he had a clear shot at the trap he'd had built into the rear wall's floor molding. He plucked the brad from the corner he'd stashed it in, then inserted it into the tiny hole.

Bingo! The molding sprang away from the wall.

Little Vinnie kissed the rubber-banded stack of hundred-dollar bills he pulled from the trap. Ten thousand, he was sure. The bankbook with another twenty-two grand that he'd skimmed off his father's number business was there too.

After closing the trap and throwing everything back into the closet, Little Vinnie tried the dresser again. To his disappointment, the photographs he'd had taken of him and Laurel—innocuous photos of them talking in the street, her getting into his car, or them walking into a restaurant to discuss ending his problem with Mickey Boy, who was in jail at the time—were gone. At one time he'd hoped they would be suggestive enough to drive Mickey Boy to a prison suicide. Now he would have just liked to possess them and think of what might have been.

Little Vinnie spent another hour trying on his old clothes. Most were too large—he'd lost twenty-nine pounds in Sicily, gained eight back here. He did find, however, a few shirts and sweaters that he could get away with, and brought them out with him, leaving quickly, so as not to see any more of the house than he already had.

"Fuck memories!"

What a prick that Mickey Boy really is, Little Vinnie thought. All day, after returning from his visit to his old house and seeing the TV news, he'd thought about how that scumbag had had Buster killed. Not that he himself had ever liked the old fuck. Big and virile, like a prehistoric animal, Buster had always made him feel like the result of half a load of Don Vincenze's sperm.

"Who's gonna believe he's goody-two-shoes now?" Little Vinnie muttered. All that bullshit honor and respect Mickey Boy had always spouted.

"Piece of shit, phony bastard!"

In reality, Mickey Boy was no better than their father had

been, a two-faced manipulator who didn't give a shit for anyone besides himself. For the second time that day, Little Vinnie could feel the pain again of hearing, that first time, that Mickey Boy was his bastard of a half brother. He could smell the stagnant basement air as it wafted up with the voices—Don Vincenze so smug and happy with himself; Buster congratulating him and kissing his old greaseball ass.

Tossed me out like a fuckin' old shoe.

"Fuck them all!" Little Vinnie finally said. This was his time to go out and celebrate—to unwind, to forget, and to enjoy himself. If anyone deserved it, he told himself, it was certainly him.

Little Vinnie wore the new sacklike tan blazer he'd bought at Barney's with the money he'd found at the house, over used-looking jeans that had cost him more than new ones should, and a white Calvin Klein T-shirt. He checked it out in the mirror. Not bad. With the black moustache and new, hipper look, he could probably walk on Eighteenth Avenue, right in the heart of the Bensonhurst community he used to travel, and not be noticed. And in the company of a super-hip nigger with dreadlocks and what looked like a stunning white girl, he would blend into any "in" spot.

Little Vinnie had called the pair, inviting them out socially for the first time after visiting them a couple of times in their apartment and finding them to be okay. The only other person he even spoke to socially was DoDo. No comparison.

Tempest, which was what the transvestite called him- or herself, had wanted to go to some cavelike warehouse club that specialized in "hanky spanky," but Little Vinnie had said no way, and Hale had said to pick something trendy but a little more mainstream. Laughing, Hale said they could save the whips and chains for when he and Tempest were alone.

Café Society was the night spot that Hale and Tempest had finally mentioned that Little Vinnie agreed with.

They were already there, waiting on the corner of Twenty-first and Broadway, when Little Vinnie pulled up. Hale looked like he belonged in a reggae band, in ripped jeans and a multicolored brocade vest. Tempest probably had to nail his balls up to keep them from hanging below the handkerchief-sized black leather skirt and above the spiked pumps she wore. Thinking that Tempest had the greatest legs he'd ever seen on a guy or girl, Little Vinnie gave a short honk, waved to them to wait, then drove around the corner to the nearest parking lot.

"Well, man, you ready for some heavy duty sex prowl?" Hale said when Little Vinnie approached. He greeted him with some weird combination handshake and slapping that he'd been teaching Little Vinnie during his visits to their place.

"Can I kiss you hello?" Tempest asked, batting long false lashes at him.

"Don't even try it."

"Some gratitude," Tempest said with an exaggerated huff as they started for the club. "I'm missing out on at least a dozen well-hung tricks just to try and get you some bimbo with a smelly cunt, and what do I get? Not even a peck on the cheek."

Little Vinnie blew Tempest a kiss. "There," he said. "Don't say I never gave you nothing."

"Don't blow at me unless you mean it," Tempest replied with a mock haughty air.

Little Vinnie laughed. If he wasn't ashamed, he would have given Tempest a peck on the cheek. After all, didn't mob guys kiss each other every time they met? Of course, he told himself, this was different, but it would really be harmless, and he actually liked both of his newfound friends. They were more uninhibited and honest about themselves than any of the people he'd spent his life around, either on this side of the Atlantic or in Sicily. He found himself enjoying being around them and actually having fun.

Hale repeated his complicated handshake with one of the burly doormen at the front of the club, losing a twenty-dollar bill at the same time.

The door opened for them immediately.

Inside, to Little Vinnie, wasn't much different than most of the other trendy nightclubs and discos he'd been to over the years—Xenon, Limelight, the Palladium, all the same. Of course, the decor had its own identity—black and white deco setting; tufted high-backed chairs; kinetic white lights

—and the addition of rap music, but the empty, pathetic looks on the faces of those supposed revelers, who desperately sought completion through someone else, never changed. All some of these people had to do, Little Vinnie thought, was fuckin' drool. A girl passed in front of him, wearing little more than a red miniskirt with two nipple-covering straps extending from the waistband over her shoulders. Another wore pants with the cheeks of the ass cut out. He looked at them and thought of AIDS. What a shame he couldn't be fucking Laurel somewhere, he thought.

"One Grappa." Little Vinnie ordered over the bar.

"No Grappa."

"How about Strega?"

"What is this, la dolce vita time? Sambuca okay?"

"Forget it," Little Vinnie said. This was New York, and more patrons probably got high in the bathroom than on the booze. "Stoli and tonic'll be okay." He ordered a Chivas on the rocks for Hale and a wallbanger for Tempest. Some nigger talking shit that was supposed to pass for music thumped in his head.

Been away too long for this shit. Little Vinnie suddenly longed for the tranquility of the Acireale suburbs—and Don Genco's beautiful blond granddaughter, Ninfa. He thought that he'd rather be walking with Ninfa, just holding her hand, in a dusty Sicilian piazza, than having an orgy with the oddball crew in here. Guess I'm growin' up, he thought, and smiled.

A brunette squeezed in front of him at the bar. "Sorry," she said, giving him a glancing look then turning away. She immediately turned back and stared at him.

Fuck this, Little Vinnie thought. Of all the people in the world, he had to come face-to-face with someone who could recognize him. In an instant his mind sorted out options: lie, say she had the wrong guy; speak in Sicilian dialect, making out he didn't understand a word of English; run for the nearest exit.

"Hi, Rosalie," Little Vinnie said. "Long time no see."

Rosalie DeStefano stretched into a hesitant smile. "I don't believe it," she said, raising her palm to where her breasts swelled over a black print scoop-necked dress. As always, the extra bit of fleshy padding she carried made her look sensuously inviting, like a down pillow covered with baby skin. "I thought you were gone, after . . ."

"After the problem with Mickey Boy?" he asked, trying to mask his anger. Would everyone laugh at his having taken a beating from that bastard? Well, not for long, he thought. Not for fuckin' long. "I left 'cause I wanted to. But that's one of those things that'll work itself out later on," he said. "Right now, I'm back on business that has nothing to do with him."

Rosalie, obviously uncomfortable, replied, "I'm sorry. I didn't mean to get into your personal business." She stared at him for a moment. "I like your moustache. It looks good."

Little Vinnie looked around. Hale and Tempest were on the dance floor, grinding their pelvises at each other. He turned back to Rosalie. "You with anybody?"

"Well, yes and no," Rosalie said. "I came with a couple of girlfriends, but we sort of separate in here."

Little Vinnie led Rosalie past Hale and Tempest, who winked approval, and up toward a banquette booth in the rear. Not sure how often the waitress would get around to them, he ordered backups of vodkas and tonics for him and Rosalie.

"You know, you look like him," Rosalie said, to begin their conversation.

"Like who?"

"Mickey Boy. Does that make you mad?"

Little Vinnie's hands balled up under the table. "No," he said.

"You didn't before. But with the weight you lost, and your hair a little long, like this . . ." She reached up and pushed a lock away from his forehead.

Her touch felt so good.

Little Vinnie looked directly into Rosalie's eyes: dark and fiery, but somehow strangely understanding. "Well, yeah," he said. "If you know the whole story, which I suppose you do—Mulberry Street girls knowing everything—you could guess that there's no love lost between us." He shrugged. "But I live in Sicily, and don't give a flying fart about him. I told you, I'm just here on business."

Rosalie laughed. "Secret Sidgie business? Like Sicilian Mafia stuff?" She laughed again. "Those guys over there are the only ones I ever heard use that word, Mafia. It's real over there, huh?"

Little Vinnie mumbled some inane thing. How the fuck could she ask him something like that? Especially having grown up around wiseguys all her life?

Rosalie downed her backup drink, then put her hand on his. "I'm only playing," she said.

"Those are serious games."

"Don't be so uptight," Rosalie said. "Not like your goddamn brother."

"Don't call him my brother!"

Rosalie looked startled by the reply's vehemence. "Sorry . . . I've got no love lost with him either, but I didn't think there was that much bad blood."

All Little Vinnie heard were the words, "I've got no love lost with him either." Everything else became meaningless. Here was someone who saw the real piece of shit that Mickey Boy was.

"Everybody knows, huh?"

Rosalie nodded.

He asked Rosalie why she disliked the almighty Mickey Boy Messina.

"I just don't like the fact that he thinks he's so much better than me. Like his shit don't stink." Rosalie went on to explain to Little Vinnie how she'd lied for Mickey Boy to get him released from his parole violation; how she'd lowered herself to say she was sleeping with him, when he was really two floors below at Buster's crap game.

Little Vinnie wanted to punch her in the face. The bitch had fucked up everything he'd tried to do. If she'd only minded her simple cunt business, Mickey Boy probably would have blown the hearing and gone away; saved him, Little Vinnie, all the aggravation he'd gone through for the last year and a half; left him with a chance to fuck Laurel, like he had planned.

He pushed his vodka and tonic over to Rosalie and signaled the waitress for another round. Fuckin' bitch owed him big, Little Vinnie thought as he moved closer to Rosalie.

"Believe me, I know how you feel. If you woulda stood up for me like that, I woulda kissed your ass in Macy's window."

"Sounds like fun," Rosalie replied, slurring her words slightly. Her eyes shone with sexuality. Little Vinnie could almost feel the heat.

He moved closer, until his thigh was alongside hers. "Which part?" he asked. "The window or getting your ass kissed?"

"Depends on how good a kisser you are."

Meeting the challenge, Little Vinnie slipped one arm around Rosalie's neck and pulled her close. When her lips opened for him, he shoved his tongue in, rimming around the top of her pallet, circling her tongue and skimming past the inside of her cheeks. His other hand slipped under her skirt and squeezed the inside of her thigh, just below her crotch.

Rosalie matched his ardor, sucking in on his tongue like it was life-giving. When he tried to force a finger under her panties, however, she closed her legs. "Slow down," she said, breathing heavily. "It was just a joke."

"That was no joke," Little Vinnie said, straining to laugh. He felt as though he would come right there, and downed a drink to cool himself off. Rosalie toasted them with the other vodka, and downed it in one gulp.

One more drink and Little Vinnie kissed her again. This time he moved his hand slowly up to her breast. When she didn't resist, he slid it down between her legs again. This time she opened her legs enough for him to feel the wetness of her vagina.

"Whattaya say we get outta here?" he asked, barely able to catch his breath. Rosalie nodded. "Wait here a minute. I'll be right back."

Little Vinnie struggled to walk to where Hale and Tempest stood at the bar. His erection, having no room to move in the jeans, hurt like hell. He wished he'd had the balls to unbutton his fly in the club and let it stand free.

"Do me a favor," Little Vinnie said to Hale. "Let me use the apartment to get laid. I don't wanna bring this broad to the hotel."

"Only if we can watch," Tempest said with a giggle.

"Go on, man," Hale said, while handing Little Vinnie the door keys. "Stick her one for me."

"What do you mean, for you?" Tempest asked petulantly. "Ain't I enough, you bastard?"

Twenty minutes later Little Vinnie guided Rosalie into his two friends' loft apartment. Though thoroughly drunk, Rosalie gasped at the sight of its luxury.

Little Vinnie immediately pinned Rosalie to the door, jamming his tongue in her mouth again. Her hands snaked up to the back of his head, her fingers entwined in his hair.

Without so much as coming up for air, Little Vinnie lifted her skirt and ripped her panties away. Rosalie started at his rough handling, but he shoved her back against the door and cut off her protest with his mouth. When he entered her, it was brutally, in one shot, slamming her against the wall. Rosalie cried out, but lifted a leg to accommodate him as he pounded into her like a bull.

"Shit!" Little Vinnie shouted as he ejaculated, after less than a half-dozen strokes. Rosalie kept moving, practically climbing up to his chest. Little Vinnie pulled away from her, letting a flood of semen run down her legs and onto the carpet. When she came at him again, he grabbed her hair and forced her down to her knees.

"You want it so much, bitch, then make it hard again," he growled. Fucked him so bad, he thought, by not minding her goddamned business. Had to get that Mickey Boy bastard out of jail to ruin his fuckin' life?

More than half drunk, Rosalie went right to her task, sucking and licking Little Vinnie until his erection returned.

God, she was fantastic, went through Little Vinnie's mind as he pushed her back on the carpet and pulled away her clothes. *And fuckin' beautiful too.*

But the anger that burned deep within Little Vinnie could not be assuaged by a beautiful pair of tits or a plush, inviting belly. No, the world had been fucking him over since he was small, and this Rosalie bitch had put her two cents in to hurt him too.

Little Vinnie rolled Rosalie over on her stomach, then slung his arm under her and lifted her posterior in the air. Rosalie laid her head down on the white rug, her black hair splayed out in a fan, and spread her knees open to accommodate him.

Laughing to himself, Little Vinnie entered Rosalie doggy style, pushing hard into her vagina till she groaned, then pulling back several times. When she seemed relaxed and enjoying herself, he pulled out and began forcing his soaking erection into her ass. He'd show her who the fuck was who, that he was not just some half-a-hump who shot his load at the touch of a female body; that she couldn't fuck with his life and not pay.

Little Vinnie continued forcing himself into Rosalie's rectum, even as she screamed out in pain.

39

May 26: Hell's Kitchen, Manhattan

THE CHURCH OF THE SACRED HEART HAD THE SMELL OF DEAD bodies. Not real dead bodies, but the after-presence of thousands of departed who had prayed for Eternal Life in these old, worn wooden pews since the doors had been flung open to the starving Irish underclass in 1885. Now, Joe Augusta had seen more Hispanics than anyone else entering and leaving from the bright red doors of the Gothic House of God.

Joe sat almost alone in the church; no more than three Hispanic women, spread out away from each other, bowed their heads in prayer. One old man lit a row of small votive candles.

Clenching his hands tightly in his lap, Joe stared upward through the roof and to the Heavens, where Chrissy would be watching him, alongside the Father, the Son, and the Holy Ghost. Together they would bless him, as they had last night. They had proven to him that his mission was just and holy and should be continued. He had come to Their House tonight to pay homage, and to say thank you.

Tears misted over Joe's eyes as he envisioned Chrissy, all in a white shroud, sitting on a throne next to the unformed glow of God. Why? he asked himself. He missed her so; loved her even more. Why did she have to die? Why couldn't God have been satisfied with him instead?

Why?

Why?

Why?

Full-fledged tears streamed down over Joe's cheeks onto his filthy beard. His heart opened up to flood his entire being with more tears. No amount of revenge would ever soothe them. All he could hope for was to accomplish what he had set out to do; to pay everyone back for hurting his baby, and balance the scales.

Then die himself.

That was what Joe Augusta begged for now. He would do his part, he promised, if only God would be kind enough to end his pain and let him join his darling daughter, the light of his life.

Sobbing as he stared upward, Joe began, "The Lord is my Shepherd, I shall not want. He maketh me to lie down . . ."

40

May 30: Upper East Side, Manhattan

WHAT IF YOU GAVE A PARTY AND NOBODY CAME?

Mickey Boy had heard that said a million times in his life, in relation to moments he couldn't even remember. The words themselves, however, had become a sad reality for him. He had reserved a table for eight at Sign of the Dove, and now sat in their conservatory, staring out at brick, flowers, rattan, and, of course, at Freddie, feeling like a complete ass.

Freddie looked over at him and shrugged. "I hoped this wouldn't happen," he said. "But I figured it might." He sipped his Arneis white wine between speaking.

How could Freddie even imagine that he, as boss of the Calabra Family, would send for captains of his, all of whom would not show up? Mickey Boy wondered. He knew the older captains, like Tony Polo, Bobby Rimini, and Patsy Luciano, were not too happy with him, especially after his not having shown up for Buster's wake or funeral. But deliberately slapping him in the face like this? At least if they had shown up he could have explained how he had tried to go to the funeral parlor three separate times, but had seen law enforcement surveillance keyed in on both front and back entrances. Being on parole, especially with Halloran after him, he couldn't chance getting caught with someone with a criminal record who might have stopped in for Buster's or one of the other wakes at the Shore Haven.

Freddie continued, "They'll make excuses; tell you that they had to be here or there; putting in a fuckin' pacemaker or getting their teeth cleaned . . . anything that sounds real enough to excuse them and phony enough to make you get their message. Old-timers are like that," he went on. "Everything has at least two meanings; every word they say is part of a puzzle."

"Fuck 'em! I'll bust 'em down and make new skippers. I could do that, right?"

"You're the boss. You could dance naked on Times Square if you want." Freddie paused. "Whether that's smart or not is a different story."

Mickey Boy downed his cognac with one gulp, then, holding up the glass, signaled for another. He looked over the room and wondered why he couldn't have one meal lately that wouldn't stick in his throat . . . even in a place as beautifully serene as this.

"If they want me to step down, I will," Mickey Boy said.

"It ain't gonna work like that. You either got to be boss now, and be strong, or be a victim. Not only will you split this crew in half—which I ain't so sure it ain't already—but you'd be a threat to whoever took over, without the advantage of having troops to back you up."

Freddie pointed over to the two bodyguards sitting at a table by the door, already digging into pasta dishes. Two more of his made men would be outside in a car. Since Buster's death all security, around his home and when he traveled, had been doubled . . . at least until they could figure out the whos and whys of it.

"I'll go see each one of them alone," Freddie said. "I'll talk to them like a Dutch uncle. Then we'll get a clearer picture of how far they wanna take this thing." If they tried to go to the Commission, Freddie said, asking that Mickey Boy be censured for ordering Buster's death, they'd be on thin ice. "Since they can't prove you did it. Remember, bosses stick together with bosses."

They could also, Freddie said, ask that one of them replace him, for ineffective leadership, but they wouldn't get away with that either. Everyone knew that the tougher part of the crew was the younger group, who would want one of theirs to be boss. In truth, Mickey Boy, being Don Vincenze's son and also being under forty, was the only choice for the time being, and the Commission knew that too.

"I really want out," Mickey Boy said. "But I don't want these guys murdering each other either. See if we could start finding a compromise . . ." He downed another Rémy Martin.

"You are the compromise," Freddie said, lifting his eyebrows at Mickey Boy's drinking. "How about we eat?"

"Nah, you go ahead. I'll eat at the other meeting, later, by Café on the Green. Just order me another drink."

"That's dinner. Have something now."

Mickey Boy signaled for another cognac.

Mickey Boy smiled as he walked toward the entrance of Café on the Green. He still felt a buzz from the afternoon's booze: his face felt kind of numb, and his movements felt fluid, almost like he was gliding over the parking lot pavement. The air smelled damp, from the nearby water, and refreshingly cool. The little white lights in the trees made him feel like his head was in the stars. His stomach growled.

Inside, the lights seemed especially bright, the colors of the fresh flowers especially vivid, the smell especially tempting. Since there was only one way up to the private dining room, he left his bodyguards to watch the staircase from downstairs. Only Nicolo Fonte accompanied him up.

Mickey Boy had had Fonte meet them uptown, then sent Freddie on his way to try to patch things up with the insulted captains.

On his way up the stairs he couldn't help humming Sinatra's version of "Luck Be A Lady." It had worked for him the last time he'd met with this crew. Hopefully, it would precipitate a similar success.

The lyrics to "Luck Be A Lady" rang in his head once more.

When he got into the private dining room, Mickey Boy's attention focused less on the presence of all the cousins he had invited, including the doctor, Tammy, than a particular absence.

"Who came with you?" Mickey Boy asked Laurel. "I didn't even see nobody downstairs."

"I came alone."

Ignoring everyone in the room, Mickey Boy snapped, "For Christ's sake, didn't I tell you not to do that? Didn't I say to make somebody go with you when you go out? Didn't I give you beeper numbers to call one of the guys?"

Laurel flushed red.

The room remained so silent that Mickey Boy could hear his own breathing.

"Well? What do you think I said it for, just to goddamn hear myself talk?"

"We can talk about it later," Laurel replied.

"No, we can talk about it now!"

Laurel just stared at her folded hands.

Mickey Boy suddenly realized they were not alone. He looked over at everyone sitting around the extended table. "Sorry, but I worry a lot," he said. In a lower voice he muttered, "She just don't understand."

Mickey Boy sat down alongside Laurel. Nicolo Fonte sat on Mickey Boy's other side.

When Mickey Boy tried to take Laurel's hand in his, she pulled it away, without looking at him.

Fuck her! For a goddamn schoolteacher, she ain't got no fuckin' sense at all.

Just as Mickey Boy introduced Nicolo Fonte to the group, a waiter appeared. When they had ordered, Mickey Boy took Laurel by the hand and dragged her out onto the terrace, in sight of the Throgs Neck Bridge.

"I don't think this is the time or place to discuss anything," Laurel said. "We can talk when we get home."

"No, now. When your safety is at stake, we'll discuss it in front of the Queen of England if need be."

Laurel shook her head. "No. It's not safety you're worried about. It's just your own insecurities that make you insist on bodyguards for me. I'm surprised you don't send women along."

"Are you fuckin' nuts? Buster got whacked, and I ain't got the slightest clue who did it. You think I'm worried about some jerkoff yuppies, like you met in Tatou's?"

"Now, why did you mention him?" Laurel asked. "See, it's on your mind."

Mickey Boy threw his hands up in the air. "Ah, you're full of shit!" He started for the door inside, then turned to face Laurel, who stood her ground, arms folded over her chest. "Just smarten up and do what I tell you!"

Mickey Boy's head pounded from the booze he had had earlier in the day. At least it had all worn off, leaving his thinking one hundred percent clear, he thought, before asking if anyone at the table had aspirin. Tammy, of course, handed him prescription Motrin. Once again it felt as though his food had knotted up in his chest, and, as a result, the pills hurt when they landed inside.

Desserts had already been consumed, but a second platter had been brought up for snacking. Cups of regular coffee and espresso lay scattered over the table.

"Well," Mickey Boy said, calling the meeting to order. "You guys have had enough time to think about putting together these pasta houses. Please, let me know what you think, and if you wanna be part of it or not."

Thomas, the cousin who worked for a stock brokerage,

raised his hand, then began speaking. "I took a little initiative, and accumulated some figures and articles, to show you all." He passed out stapled groups of papers from a pile he'd kept on the floor. "I got some from the National Pasta Association, and others from the New York Restaurant Association."

Thomas waited for everyone to thumb through the papers, then said, "If you'll look at page one, you'll see some lines highlighted. Notice the first item, how many stores Domino Pizza has: eight thousand. Not bad. Then look down to the box on the bottom of the page—four out of the top ten franchises in the country sell Italian food."

Sam, the attorney, wondered if that didn't indicate that the market might be saturated in that area. Thomas said definitely not. All the articles indicated that the market, especially for fast take-out food, would be the strongest in that business. Pasta was as good a bet as anything he'd seen, and if Mickey did not have all the money available for developing the chain, as he'd previously said, Thomas said he would be glad to present a packaged proposal to his bosses at the brokerage, with the intention of raising the cash through a private placement, then taking the operation public at a later date.

Mickey Boy listened to the discussion even as he stared at the pages, trying to absorb every bit of information that came to his ears and eyes.

"Operation," Tammy said. "Now you're talking my language. I'll operate on anyone who gets pasta poisoning."

Thomas ignored her and continued, citing figures and other items as the rest of the party read along. "We don't even have to overcome the issue of market testing, because there's plenty of information on chains, like Fastino's, that Pepsico owns, to prove that fast-food pasta is a viable money-maker."

"From a retail marketing level," Jack, Laurel's father said, "I can tell you that inexpensive pasta to go is a winner. And control, inventory, and cash is simple. With today's registers, everything is done together. I think it's a good idea."

Fonte interjected that he had plenty of experience with Italian food, having run distributorships of products in

Italy, and that he would help Jack, or anyone else who wanted to run the retail end.

"With the limited menu you've proposed, and recipes to work from, we don't need brain surgeons to operate these places, even on an absentee basis," Jack added.

"That's what I need to hear," Mickey Boy said. His number-one reason for getting into business at all, he said, was to provide legitimate income for all the people that he was responsible for. "I gotta get them outta the streets and into something where they don't have to worry about going away to jail."

That was precisely the problem that concerned him most, Sam, the attorney, said. He nervously adjusted his wire-rim glasses, as if unable to find the words he sought. "If, and I emphasize the word *if,* I am to be involved in this operation, in any area other than legal counsel, of course, I would be concerned about who I would be getting into bed with, so to speak."

Mickey Boy stared at him but said nothing, waiting for him to continue, to clarify his position—to possibly put his foot in his mouth.

"After all, I am an attorney of decent repute, and cannot afford to be linked to, shall we say, those of lesser moral reputation . . ."

"You mean like me?"

"Not at all," Sam snapped right back. "Let me be blunt, however. My practice is corporate. I chose that field of specialization because I did not want to be associated, on a regular basis, with a criminal element." He paused, and sipped some water. "I happen to like you, personally, and admire your noble intentions. I cannot, however, guarantee that I will feel that way about other of your associates, especially when I will, obviously, have no idea who they are until some problem surfaces. Then it will be too late."

"So you don't want to be involved?"

"As a shareholder, I can probably skirt around any possible future problems. As an attorney, I am thoroughly protected. Since financing your operation does not seem to be a problem, I prefer the latter." When Mickey Boy began to speak, Sam cut him off. "I am, however, willing to defer any fees incurred, and instead settle for a profit share. You will never have to lay out a penny, other than expenses, of course, for the corporation's legal fees."

Mickey Boy's first reaction had been defensive. He hated people that put people like him in a pocket, wouldn't give them a chance to show what they could do. On second thought, however, he realized that Sam was probably right. Who knew what could crop up later, especially with some of the harder guys he'd have to deal with? Why should the man jeopardize his license to practice law for dealing with mobsters?

"I've got a great joke about lawyers," Laurel's father said, obviously uncomfortable with the situation between Sam and Mickey Boy.

"There are only two jokes about lawyers, and I've heard them already," Mickey Boy said. He enjoyed the tension everyone else showed at that moment, waiting to see what he'd say next. "Everything else is true."

Laughter broke the mood.

"Of course I understand," Mickey Boy said. "Deal." He turned to the others. "Anyone else got a problem with who might become involved?"

"None for me," Jack said. "I've seen enough feet to last a lifetime. I'm ready to stare at customers' faces for a while."

Tammy shrugged. "Nothing for me to do . . . that is, unless it's to cut some of those lead sinkers you'll call raviolis out of customers' colons."

"I want you as a shareholder," Mickey Boy replied. "And maybe to check the information on how healthy what we serve is. I'd like to have signs with the calories, fat, protein, and so on, for all the dishes."

"You don't need me for that."

"You are in; otherwise, you get a beating." Tammy was his favorite of the cousins, and, if he did well, he wanted her to be included. Not that she needed the cash, he thought.

"I'm okay with it too," Thomas said. "I can help with financing, if you want to expand at a faster rate than you're capable of. And if you're eventually ready to go public, I'll handle that."

"I'll have plenty of financing," Mickey Boy said. "Whichever of my guys could afford it, I'll make them kick in. They'll carry the ones that can't."

Mickey Boy put an arm around both Laurel and Nicolo Fonte. "And these two are your top executives. Give them a hand."

Everyone either clapped or hit drinking glasses with eating utensils.

For Mickey Boy, the only thing he heard was Sinatra's voice, in his head, singing "Here's To The Winners."

He put both hands on Laurel's shoulders. "My wife will also be working on the design, with whatever architect we get. She'll oversee the way the joints look."

"No joints," Sam said. "Let us toast to new beginnings."

After everyone toasted their new venture, with cold coffee, the meeting broke up. Laurel quickly went downstairs, avoiding any conversation with Mickey Boy.

Tammy waited behind. "Try to understand her," she said to Mickey Boy. "It's not easy for her, adjusting to the kind of wife you would like. Laurel is intelligent, educated, and vibrant."

"I know," Mickey Boy replied. "My only worry is that she stays that way."

Tammy kissed him on the cheek. She said, "I know, and she does too. But that doesn't change the difficulty for her. And by the way," she added, "why don't you get a checkup. Between the stress you're under and the weight you're putting on, you'll be a prime candidate for a killer heart attack."

Mickey Boy just smiled. He'd be goddamn fine.

Here's to the winners that all of us can be.

41

DON PEPPINO SIPPED ESPRESSO FROM A TINY FLORAL PORCELAIN cup. He smacked his lips loudly as the bitter hot brew scalded his esophagus. Just the way he liked it.

How many more years would he enjoy simple pleasures like these? he wondered. How long before he simply vanished from the earth? Funny to think of that, him not being there, he thought, because for the span of nearly eighty years the entire world had revolved around his being.

But there were things already, signs, like the swollen prostate that had him dripping all the time, and the shortness of breath that called for a pill under his tongue now and then, and the ache in the joints of his fingers. Only one thing never conceded an inch to old age, and that was his brain. He could think, reason, and remember today as well as he had at any time of his life, he thought proudly.

In fact, Don Peppino told himself, while looking at the front page of the *Daily News,* he could think better than those *stroonzos* of today. Richie DeLuca's face stared up at him from a mug-shot photo, over an article about yet another postponement of his case, to mid-June. And these *cretini* . . . cretins, like this one in the paper, wanted to fill his shoes, take his place? If they lived twice, they could never qualify in the days when he had fought his way up from a common street thug to the boss of the most powerful family in New York. *"Son tutte stroonzi . . . they are all shits,"* he said to himself.

"Stroonzi . . . son tutte stroonzi," Don Peppino repeated. Now he would have that other *lunatico* calling him, because the *stroonzo* DeLuca's case was postponed. A once good, but

184

soft man, gone off the deep end now, he would pester him, as if he could release the boy into his clutches.

Maybe he had made a mistake? Don Peppino wondered. Maybe he should have stayed away from the *lunatico,* and found his own way to deal with his situation? The man was just too unpredictable to deal with. Of course, he could summon Don Genco's puppet, DoDo, to eliminate him, but he had another, more important job for DoDo.

In truth, Don Peppino hated to deal with the newly arrived Sicilians, but had little choice. Having been "made" in Sicily, technically they were nothing over here. They did have an agreement, however, whereby they could not enter into any illegal enterprise without the express consent of a *padrone,* like himself, a boss that had been initiated into a family in America.

But they were sneaky bastards, he thought. Could not be trusted at all. Kisses on both cheeks and flowery greetings would not erase, for Don Peppino, the memory of how they had moved on another of the families, one that controlled the Ridgewood area, which straddled both Brooklyn and Queens. They had kissed and greeted that family's boss too.

". . . No, of course not," they had answered the man, when he told them he didn't want any drugs distributed along his area's main street, Knickerbocker Avenue. "No, we respect whatever you want," they had assured him repeatedly—then murdered him.

Now one of theirs, Gaetano Cimino, here only three years from Castelvetrano, sat at the head of that entire family.

He, Don Peppino, had been smarter than that when the immigrant flood began settling in Bensonhurst, where he controlled things. After all, though he'd been "made" in America, he had immigrated here from Sicily too. He'd agreed to whatever they had wanted—but with a few of his own conditions.

For one, Don Peppino had insisted, as much as he could safely insist, that they not deal drugs through any of his men; not bring heat to people who could be associated directly with him by the authorities. To that, the newly arrived mafiosi had readily agreed, not having any respect for their American cousins anyway, and happy to keep their gold vein all to themselves.

The second was that they brought him *'u pizzu*—the proverbial Italian wetting of the beak—a small yet substantial monetary show of respect. That too meant nothing to them. With the enormous amount of money they made through their heroin pipeline, the hundred-thousand-dollar packages they delivered to him occasionally were as insignificant as a tip to a waitress for the average man.

The last request had been infrequent favors that they would do for him, like the one he would soon ask—elimination of someone he didn't feel safe sending one of his own men to do. That was an extra bonus, he believed, that they only did to worm their way into his organization for an eventual takeover.

Over his dead body, he often said to himself. In his lifetime they would only be a tool to help annoint him *capo di tutti capi* . . . Boss of All Bosses.

After he passed on, who knew? Who cared? Fuck those in the younger generation, like his nephew, who had their sights set on family leadership. If they were no match for the immigrant Sicilians, and got swallowed alive, then that was all they deserved.

Don Peppino jumped when the phone rang.

"It's me," that *lunatico,* Giuseppe Augusta, said through the receiver. As Don Peppino had predicted, he began a lament about how Richie DeLuca would not be getting out of prison soon; that he had to do something, maybe see Mickey Boy before Richie got out.

Absolutely not, Don Peppino told him. It was essential that he control his impulses. However, he said, he might have something good for him soon, and that he should call again.

"Domani sera andrebbe bene?" Joe Augusta asked, his voice jittery and impatient. Is tomorrow night good?

"Bene," Don Peppino replied. *"Alle otto allora"* About eight o'clock.

When he hung up the phone, Don Peppino rubbed his chin, thinking over the possibilities open to him. The *lunatico* was volatile, but efficient. At least he would complete whatever he set out to do. The other *stroonzo,* Little Vinnie, wasn't worth his weight in dog piss. He'd only agreed to assist the boy because of Don Genco's request.

Don Peppino laughed. That showed how brilliant Don Genco was. Probably senile by now.

Don Peppino smiled with satisfaction, then reached for the paper that contained the young Vincenze Calabra's hotel address—to give to Joe Augusta. Soon. Soon.

Vaffanculo, Don Genco, mi amico, he thought. Go and fuck yourself!

42

June 4: Little Italy, Manhattan

MICKEY BOY HATED COMING TO MULBERRY STREET. HE COULD almost feel the eyes and cameras of the law watching every move he made. Hear the notes being scratched on government pads. Feel the handcuffs clicking tighter around his wrists.

As he drove, passing bustling cafés, like La Bella Ferrara on his right and Cha Cha's In Bocca Lupo on his left, he thought about how much everything seemed to have changed, even though the buildings remained the same.

Through the car speakers, Frank Sinatra crooned his song, "There Used to Be a Ballpark," in a soft and melancholy voice.

How fitting, Mickey Boy thought . . . even though there was never a ballpark on Mulberry Street. Maybe the ballpark represented the changes in the area? Or maybe he himself was the ballpark? Torn down and reborn as something different?

. . . 'Cause the old team just isn't playing, and the new team hardly tries . . .

Mickey Boy could have burst out laughing at how true those words were. He had those old captains in his crew walking away, refusing to play ball, and the younger fucks not worth a good goddamn. That's why he loved Sinatra so, he thought. The lyrics the man sang just fit into every piece of his life. Much better than Mozart or Tchaikovsky, no matter how good or long-lasting their music was.

". . . And the sky has got so cloudy, when it used to be so clear . . ."

"Amen," Mickey Boy said.

Freddie looked over from where he sat, behind the steering wheel. "What was that?"

"Nothing," Mickey Boy said. "Just agreeing with Frank."

"I'm sure he appreciates it," Freddie said, shaking his head. "Ever talk to Caruso? Or maybe Mario Lanza?"

"I told you I should be out," Mickey Boy said. "If things keep up the way they are, I may be leading this crew from a straitjacket soon."

"Forget about it. You'll probably make more sense to them then than you do now."

Freddie pulled into the parking lot on Hester and Baxter streets. Vito the Head and another Calabra Family soldier, Gimpy Lou, whom Freddie had chosen, pulled in behind them and followed a few steps back as they turned the corner and walked north on Mulberry Street. They had left Billy Sneakers and another of Mickey Boy's men in Staten Island, to look after Laurel.

Mickey Boy waved and nodded hellos to people along the street. Some, like Benny the Bookie and Lillian Polizzoto, he knew. Others had faces he recognized but couldn't attach to a name. The remaining few were complete blanks.

"Buon giorno."

"Howaya?"

A raised eyebrow.

A wink.

"Hey."

A shake of the hand.

Mickey Boy smiled as he walked. Nodded in return. Even stopped to pinch a baby boy under the chin. He felt like the goddamn mayor, he told himself.

No . . . better. Better than any good-for-nothing politician.

To him, this was what the wiseguy life was all about. This was why he had done six years in prison, and had taken a bullet. They knew it; every one of them that pushed themselves forward to catch his eye. They knew what he'd gone through, and the power he wielded. And because of that, he would always be their court of last resort. He would be their hope for a little fairness in an unfair world. For that they respected him more than if he were a mayor, or doctor, or an Indian chief. This kind of respect was more than he could ever have hoped for in any walk of life he had thought available to him.

Mickey Boy's mood lifted. He whistled "Come Fly with Me" as he walked—until he reached the front door of the Focacceria Villarosa. His heart beat a little faster and his fingers clenched and opened repeatedly. He looked across the street, inside each of the parked cars, for cops or agents. He stared at a parked white van. Would they be photographing him from inside? He moved his eyes across the tenement windows and along the roofs.

Nothing he could see.

He could just feel it.

Freddie knocked on the side door that led to the apartment above the restaurant.

A white lace curtain was pulled aside. The door opened.

Mickey Boy and Freddie slipped inside, along with Vito the Head. Gimpy Lou remained outside. Vito and Lou both had walkie-talkies, as did Freddie. The front was definitely covered—as was the rear entrance from the shared yard with Buster's old club, the Lower Manhattan Fishing Association, next door.

Creaking and heavy thumping accompanied Mickey Boy and Freddie as they jogged up the flight of stairs.

Inside the apartment they were greeted by eighteen of the Calabra Family's twenty-three captains, either draped across the DeStefano living room furniture or munching from a buffet set up in the kitchen. The entire apartment smelled of garlic and tomatoes from the downstairs restaurant.

Freddie immediately went to a clique of the younger captains in the kitchen, many of whom had been given their rank by Mickey Boy after Don Vincenze had been killed.

Mickey Boy gravitated toward the older family brass

sitting in stuffed floral sofas and chairs. He grabbed a rolled piece of prosciutto from a plate on the coffee table, folded it and stuffed the entire salty lump into his mouth.

"You guys have any trouble getting in?" Mickey Boy asked. He craned his neck, trying to catch a glimpse of Freddie and the crew in the kitchen.

Patsy Luciano waved a hand in circles. "Mah, this joint got more secret entrances . . . it's like Houdini musta built it. The kids, in there," he said, motioning toward the kitchen with his head, "come in through a skylight in the roof. One flight of stairs was enough for me, though. I ain't climbing on no roof, so I come through inside doors from house to house." He began to laugh. "Mah, sonomabitch, I started in the house by the corner."

It felt good to see his men laughing, Mickey Boy thought. But smiling and laughing didn't mean hard feelings were gone. In most cases, smiles were far more dangerous than angry confrontations. He knew that, and kept on guard for the slightest nuance, the most insignificant change of tone or attitude, that might indicate the smiles were false.

"Well, unless they got a helicopter and spotted those guys crossing the roofs, we're okay," Mickey Boy said, reaching for a slice of wet mozzarella cheese. With the cheese in his mouth, he got down to business, saying, "I hope you guys are sure now that I didn't have Buster hit."

Patsy spread his hands in surrender. "You gotta admit how it looked. An' if you didn't okay it, then it's even more of a problem. What kind of sonomabitch hits an underboss, with no okay? What kind of balls he must have . . . and who knows what the hell he could do next?"

They all looked toward the kitchen.

What if it was one of their younger captains, getting himself in position for a move to take over the family? Who could he trust not to clip him the same way as they had Buster?

Fuck them, Mickey Boy thought. I ain't takin' out no more garbage.

When the door opened, everyone tensed. A black-haired girl with ringlets running down her back and tits full enough to feed a litter of kids entered. She smiled, asked if anyone needed anything. Any food run out? Any drinks?

The younger captains teased her, came out to hug her, patted her on the ass.

Mickey Boy watched her walk toward him and the older captains, watched her expression change to a blank, watched her tidy up and blandly ask if anything was needed. The old men ordered drinks. Mickey Boy said nothing.

When the girl left, Mickey Boy followed her into the hall. "Rosalie?" he called. "Right?"

Rosalie turned and stared at him noncommittally.

"Everything okay with you?" he asked. "You look like something could be wrong."

"What could be wrong?" she said.

"Anything . . . husband beating you . . . kids giving you a hard time . . . that time of the month?"

"And if it was, could you fix it?" Rosalie asked, beginning to smile.

Mickey Boy laughed. "Sorry, nothing I could do with leaky parts." He reached over and took Rosalie's hand. "I want you to know I really do appreciate what you did for me that time, you know, testifying at my parole hearing. It's just that I'm never really around to say thanks the right way . . . always something else to do or somewhere else to be."

Rosalie kept silent, her lips tight and her eyes confused.

Mickey Boy stood there, holding Rosalie's hand. Goddamn, she was pretty, he thought. And earthy, in a way he related to from his youth. He was acutely aware of his growing erection, but figured as long as Rosalie stared into his eyes she wouldn't notice.

"Well, anyway, thanks," he said, then bent forward to kiss Rosalie on the cheek.

Rosalie, however, turned her face, meeting his lips with hers. Their lips touched, teased, parted, touched again, and locked. The tip of Rosalie's tongue brushed Mickey Boy's teeth.

Mickey Boy nipped at her tongue, then abruptly pulled back. His head throbbed and he felt flushed.

Rosalie smiled, then wordlessly ran down the stairs, back to the focacceria.

Mickey Boy returned to the apartment in a daze. Guilt hounded him. This was the first girl he had touched since he'd married Laurel. And it had felt good. Not that he loved

Laurel any less. In fact, at that moment he had an urgent desire to run home and be with her, to assure himself that all was well between them.

What am I, nuts? he asked himself. No big fuckin' deal. Just an innocent kiss that went a little too far. What was he, a kid who had to exaggerate everything? Hadn't he kissed dozens of girls like that in his lifetime? Well . . . ? He shook his head to clear it.

"What're we gonna do?" Bobby Rimini asked. His 250-pound frame blocked Mickey Boy's way. A slew of gold and diamond charms and pendants around his neck momentarily distracted Mickey Boy. "We gonna get this meeting going?" Bobby continued.

"Yeah, sure," Mickey Boy said, his attention dangling between Rosalie and Bobby's jewelry. He tore his eyes away from the hypnotizing sparkle of gold and diamonds to look for Freddie, who seemed to be entertaining a group of the younger captains—smiles, laughs, toasts with drinks.

Mickey Boy signaled Freddie to bring everyone together in the living room, then shuffled back to where he'd been sitting. His mind drifted to Rosalie. He licked his lips where they had touched hers. He struggled to pull his mind back to the matters at hand.

"You okay?" Freddie asked.

"Yeah, just thinking."

"That's why you're the boss," Freddie said. "None of us has figured out how to do that yet."

The group, still clumped into age-based cliques, chuckled.

"Okay, time to pick a guy to fill a *buon uomo* Buster's spot," Freddie said. "Mickey Boy an' me thought about this a long time, and pretty much got every angle covered." He went on to say that Mickey Boy felt that since he was in position himself only a short while, he needed more time to get to know all his men better and to choose more wisely. Neither Mickey Boy nor he, as consigliere, wanted to bypass someone who would make the strongest, most unifying second-in-command.

"That's the most important," Freddie added. "That whoever gets the spot holds this crew together. Because, let me tell you, between the feds, stool pigeons, and other acts of nature, the other crews would like nothing better than to see us fall on our cocks. They'll be there in a hot second to fuck us in the ass for every little thing they could. Without unity, we'll be lucky to have a crew at all, let alone be alive and out of jail."

Mickey Boy could see the anticipation in the eyes of the younger captains, especially Frankie Green Eyes, and sense the fear of the elders.

"So what we decided is that I'm gonna step in, as Acting, for that spot, for a few months. By that time we could get a better picture of who'll be best for the family."

Slight disappointment from the younger group; relief from the veterans.

Freddie had been a hundred percent right, Mickey Boy thought. If he'd picked from one of the factions, at that particular time, he would have had a bloody mutiny on his hands.

"What about consigliere?" Frankie Green Eyes asked.

He certainly couldn't think he'd ever get tabbed as an advisor, Mickey Boy thought with some amusement.

"We're gonna do without one," Mickey Boy said. ". . . At least until Freddie could go back to it."

"But you should have somebody, even just as an Acting."

"If I did," Mickey Boy replied, "it would probably be Patsy here."

"Patsy?"

"Yeah, why, he ain't qualified?" Mickey Boy asked. Without waiting for a reply, he added, "But like I said, we're gonna do without it." What he really had in mind was using Nicolo Fonte as a sort of unofficial advisor. The man knew of the structure of things from his contact with the foreign mob organizations, was a great judge of human nature, and had the big business experience to help him turn his family's direction to a legitimate one.

Frankie Green Eyes seemed taken aback by Mickey Boy's attitude.

Freddie jumped in. "Hey, what'd I die?" he asked jokingly. "I'm always here to throw my two cents in. Remember, advice is my middle name."

Frankie Green Eyes smiled; coldly, without any sparkle of mirth in his eyes. "Yeah, sure. Whatever you guys say is okay with me."

"Good," Mickey Boy said, his patience thin. "We all agreed, then?" he asked.

All nodded. The older group seemed especially relieved.

"Good, then we're off to the races, with nothing changed," Freddie said. "I'll be in touch with all of youse within the next couple of weeks—hear your beefs and suggestions. Let's get this crew in tip-top shape and really together."

Everyone hugged and kissed Mickey and Freddie, and left by the secret entrances they had used to come in.

When they were gone, Mickey Boy made a beeline down the stairs. He stepped into the focacceria, looking around for Rosalie.

"Lose something?" Freddie asked, coming up behind him.

Mickey Boy shook his head, just as he spotted Rosalie bending over a table to set it up for another set of patrons. He would have liked to go over and say good-bye, maybe pat her on the ass as a parting treat, but thought better of it. Why start something he couldn't—or, more exactly, didn't want to—finish?

Freddie hooked an arm under his and led him toward the door. "You know," Freddie said, "if you wanna kill yourself, try something less painful. These fuckin' broads are only for guys who like to suffer." As they walked out, he asked, "You sure you never did nothing, maybe in another life, that you wanna torture yourself for?"

Mickey Boy smiled. His eyes darted around the area, looking for signs of surveillance, but all he really saw was Rosalie, bending over that table.

43

June 4: Little Italy, Manhattan

CROUCHED LOW TO THE GROUND, FRANK HALLORAN MOVED WITH the stealth of a feline, across the rooftop and to the edge facing Mulberry Street. He plopped down, back to the wall, and caught his breath; looked around to see if anyone could see him; wiped perspiration from his forehead with his sleeve; checked his Minolta 7000.

Doing fieldwork was not exactly Halloran's idea of what his job was supposed to be all about. But dealing with these slippery dagos had forced him to do a lot of things he didn't like. Obviously, many of them were too sharp for the FBI to catch on a parole violation. Michael "Mickey Boy" Messina was one of the best. Not good enough, though, for him, Halloran hoped.

He pulled himself up to where he could peer over the edge and focus on the front of the Focacceria Villarosa and the Lower Manhattan Fishing Association, or, in real terms, a private mob social club next door. He wished he could have set himself up directly across from the two buildings, but had to settle for something farther down the block. Without a doubt the bad guys would be scanning the rooftops from the street. As it was, he had to hope their eyes weren't keen enough to pick him up at the same distance his zoom lens could identify them by a mole on the face or a crooked nose.

No way he was going to be caught short and let Mickey Boy Messina get away, as his predecessor had. God only knew what that gang of parasites had done to drive him all the way into the bottle—not that he hadn't been well inside it before, if departmental rumors were true. Another rumor had it that Calabra Family thugs had nearly broken the parole officer's bones, and humiliated him so badly that he now doubted his own masculinity.

Those fucking dagos had better not have done anything sexual to a fellow officer, Halloran thought—he'd heard of one mobster who paid back his girlfriend's lover-for-a-night by forcing him to suck his prick. Halloran steamed. If he found out that anything even remotely like that was the case, then Mr. Mickey Boy Messina would do a lot worse than go back to prison on a violation. He, Francis Keenan Halloran, would make sure he did every day of that time in a prison hospital.

Halloran spotted Mickey Boy and his gray-haired side-kick, Freddie Falcone, walking up Mulberry Street. He snapped a picture, even though he knew Falcone had no record. He also snapped a photo of the two hoods walking a few steps in back of them.

Two hours in a blazing sun, and all he had were photos of Damon Runyonlike characters going into the restaurant and the club. He wondered if his brother officer, Clay Simon, had caught any snapshots of hoods with felony records moving between the restaurant and club through their communal back yard, from his vantage point on a building at the cross street.

Suddenly, directly across from him, the door to the roof opened. Frank Halloran managed to catch a glimpse of just one man, Frank "Green Eyes" Scarpucci, before he ducked down out of view. He shimmied across the tar roof to the fire escape ladder that came through an opening in the wall. From there he photographed at least eight known captains in the Calabra Family, most with prison records, scurrying across the roof and into the building of the Focacceria Villarosa. At least one of the men, Nick Siconolfi, was one of his parolees. Two violations for the price of one.

When the last mobster had disappeared into the restaurant building, Frank Halloran made a dash to the interior staircase of the building he spied from.

Smiling, he told himself it was not only a great day for the Irish, but a great day for New York.

44

June 4: Chelsea, Manhattan

ROSALIE SCREAMED OUT IN PAIN AS LITTLE VINNIE PLUNGED INTO
her again. "Stop, you're hurting . . . oh, God . . . please,
take it easy . . ." Her legs flailed wildly over his back.

Little Vinnie smiled. Goddamned bitches were all alike,
screaming no when what they really meant was do it more.
He'd show her what a real fuck was like, he thought, and
rammed into her again. When Rosalie dug her heels behind
his thighs, trying to contain his vicious thrusts, Little Vinnie
pulled back far enough to lift her ass off the mattress, then
slammed down hard into her again.

Rosalie screamed.

Little Vinnie covered her mouth with one hand.

She bit him.

He slapped her.

He rammed into her again, knocking the air out of her
and forcing her legs open. Then, as he began to come, he
pulled out and shot all over her.

"Jesus Christ! What the hell's wrong with you!" Rosalie
yelled, struggling out from under him. She slid off the edge
of Hale and Tempest's bed and stomped off to the completely mirrored bathroom.

Little Vinnie collapsed, laughing. What was more humorous than her standing there with semen all over her chest
and chin, was how he thought Hale and Tempest would
enjoy watching the secret video that they shot through an
inconspicuous peephole in their bedroom.

Little Vinnie got out of bed, turned off the video camera
switch, then followed Rosalie into the bathroom. "I'm
sorry," he said, chuckling at the sight of mirrored dozens of

her washing semen off their chests and faces. "I got as carried away as you did, but I'm just stronger."

"Carried away!" Rosalie said. "You should be carried away, you fucking animal!" She wrapped a towel around her. "I've had it!" she shouted as she ran past him to gather her clothes. "I don't have to be abused by you or anyone!"

Little Vinnie ran to her and grabbed her by the arm. He apologized again, telling her that he didn't want her to leave, that she was the only real friend he had. "Please," he said. "We'll be okay. I'll be gentler, I promise."

"That's what you keep saying," Rosalie replied. "You can be so nice . . . as long as we don't get laid . . . but Vinnie—"

"Yeah, I know," he said. "It's just a lot of pressure, and it just comes out sometimes."

Rosalie let him hug her.

Little Vinnie stroked her hair. "C'mon, say you forgive me."

Rosalie shrugged. "Vinnie, I'm just tired. I want to go home."

"Promise you'll see me tomorrow night," he said. "Just to make up. Just for me to show you a great evening. Deal?"

Rosalie hesitated.

Goddamned bitch had had an attitude all night, Little Vinnie thought. That's why he'd punished her, taught her not to be distant and preoccupied when it was on his time. He'd taken her to dinner at Chelsea Place, even stayed to drink and dance—taking a chance of being recognized— without even a smile in return. Who knew, he wondered to himself, if she was preoccupied thinking of some other guy she wanted to fuck?

"Well?" he asked, sweet as he could be.

"Okay, Vinnie. But no more rough stuff. Once more and I'm gone."

Lousy bitch, he thought. She was on the verge of getting the boot anyway. If he just played his cards right and found a way to approach Laurel, he knew Rosalie would be only a weak memory. There was no way she even compared to Laurel. His only problem was how to approach her.

Twice more he'd gone to Staten Island. Not with the intention of chasing Mickey Boy down and killing him, but to watch Laurel. One time she hadn't left the house. He'd had to be satisfied stopping briefly and catching a window glimpse of her through the spyglass he'd bought. The other time he'd caught her leaving, and followed her shopping again. With a life as boring as she was leading, she was probably hoping for a guy like him to bring her a little excitement. Tomorrow he'd be on the prowl again, watching, waiting for the right moment to make his move.

Thinking about Laurel made Little Vinnie's erection rise again. He lifted Rosalie up and slid her down over it, impaling her as she wrapped her legs around his waist. With Rosalie straddling him, he stumbled to the bed and fell on it, still inside her.

Little Vinnie closed his eyes as he stroked in and out of Rosalie's vagina, all the time repeating in his mind, *Laurel . . . Laurel . . . Laurel . . .*

45

June 4: Cypress Hills, Queens

"PASQUALE, PASQUALE, *AMORE MIO*, WAKE UP."

Patsy Luciano opened his eyes, glimpsing Lena Serpe through hooded lids. He smiled at her gentle, full face, framed in rust-colored curls, then turned away to face the back of the sofa and doze again.

"Pasquale," Lena insisted, shaking him. "C'mon, Patsy, you gotta get home. It's almost midnight."

Patsy rolled back over, then sat up on the edge of the couch.

Lena kissed him on the head. "Go on," she said, "before you start a *boodelle* with your wife."

That was what he loved about Lena, Patsy thought. She was so unselfish and understanding. Now, at forty-eight, she had spent fifteen years as his mistress; clinging to him from the vibrant man he was at her age, to the decaying old man of nearly sixty-five he was now. Never gave him a problem, never demanded he leave his wife, never cheated on him. He was sure of that, even now, when they rarely went anywhere, and he threw her a hump no more than once every week or so. Rosa seemed content just to cook for him, spend some time alone in her apartment—which he paid for—as if they were a real couple, and go down to the bar on Knickerbocker Avenue on Saturday nights and get loaded.

"You know what?" Patsy said as he adjusted his tie at the door mirror. "Maybe I'll tell Marie I gotta go outta town on business, an' we spend a weekend together. We could go to Vegas . . . I'll get us a junket. Whattaya say? We ain't been away for a long time."

Lena seemed excited, and that made Patsy feel good. While helping him on with his suit jacket, she jabbered about getting her hair done and wearing an outfit she had bought for something or other.

"Good," Patsy said. He needed a rest anyway, could feel the pressures building in the street to an end that he sensed could never be good. If he didn't get banged by one of the two hundred organized crime indictments that the feds were rumored to be preparing, then there would be a problem with the younger half of the crew looking to make a power grab. Everything to give him *acido*. Why, he couldn't even eat a goddamn doughnut without Rolaids having to follow it down to his stomach.

Patsy kissed Lena full on the lips. He slipped his tongue into her mouth and ran it around. Even if his *meenkya* didn't rise as often as he would like, he could always give a killer of a kiss, he thought. He held her breast as though he were weighing a melon, then said good night and left.

Patsy's steps were more buoyant going down the stairs than they'd been in a long time. He couldn't wait to land at McCarren Field, to settle into a suite at Caesar's, to roll those dice for hours on end. Just like the good old days, not giving a shit about a thing in the world.

The smell of oregano wafted up to Patsy's nose, making him hungry. Who could've gotten a pizza delivered at that time of night? he wondered. Too bad the old joints, like

Chubby's on Mott Street, that used to stay open all night, weren't around anymore. He could have gone for some sausages and pork livers, cherry peppers and brasciola.

Patsy reached the ground-floor landing still searching his mind for some place, other than a Greek diner, where he could get a few Italian tidbits. Even a pizza, the smell of which filled his nostrils.

Suddenly, a noose dropped over his head from behind. His hands reacted with the sloth of old age, reaching the rope after it tightened around his throat, rather than quickly enough for his fingers to get under it. He wanted to scream as he was being pulled backward behind the stairs, but no sound would come. His heart felt like it would burst. His bladder and bowels emptied themselves in his suit pants.

Then the lights went out.

46

June 5: Todt Hill, Staten Island

THE RINGING PHONE SEEMED TO BE AN ECHO FROM A FAR OFF place. Mickey Boy stirred, reached for the alarm clock, then realized it was the phone making all that noise and grabbed it. Lights from the TV Laurel insisted stay on all night fluttered in his eyes.

"Yeah, what?" he said.

"Me," Freddie replied. "I'm on my way over."

Click.

Laurel woke. "What was that?"

"Nothing," he replied. "Go back to sleep."

Mickey Boy got out of bed and slipped into his pants, which he'd left on the floor near his bed—easier than emptying his pockets every night.

When Laurel, visibly alarmed, questioned him further

about the call, he admitted it was Freddie, and that he had no idea why he was coming over at three A.M. It didn't take a brain surgeon, he told himself, to know it was an emergency.

Hope's crying in the nursery came through the intercom.

"Great," Laurel said, angrily trudging off to the baby.

On his way down the stairs Mickey Boy muttered, "Great . . . like I wanted to be woke up in the middle of the night."

Behind him he could hear Laurel carrying the baby into their bed.

Please let them fall asleep, he said to himself. All he needed was her harping on him while he tried to deal with whatever it was Freddie wanted.

Mickey Boy made himself a pot of coffee—no way it wouldn't be an all-night session. Between wondering what could have happened, he found himself thinking of Rosalie, feeling the sensation of their little kiss.

The thought of her had haunted him all night. Earlier, when he played with Hope, he found himself softly licking his lips and thinking Rosalie's name. The same thing happened when he cuddled with Laurel in bed. More with each stroke as he and Laurel had sex. It had filled him with guilt and excitement at the same time. The thought that Laurel would somehow sense it or read his mind had made him especially responsive during their lovemaking.

She'd gone to sleep smiling.

He'd fallen off with Rosalie's name on his mind.

Now, as he sipped his coffee and nibbled on a Yankee Doodle, he wondered if he should make a move with Rosalie. He had no doubt that she'd go with him in a hot second. Even if he looked like Quasimodo, his position alone turned women on. He loved Laurel and didn't want anything to disturb their family, he told himself, but the thought of fooling around with Rosalie did give him a rush. What he liked was that thinking about her let him divert his mind from the seriousness of whatever Freddie was coming to tell him. And under the pressure he felt, a miracle for him would be a pleasurable diversion.

Unless Rosalie would become an additional burden, which Mickey Boy expected would more likely be the case, rather than a temporary escape from his problems.

Because of his mind wandering, Mickey Boy didn't hear

Freddie pull into the driveway. The knock on the door was the first sign he had of his acting underboss's arrival.

"Patsy got whacked," Freddie said as he entered the door. He kissed Mickey Boy on both cheeks, then started for the kitchen. "Good, coffee."

"Whoa, what happened?" Mickey Boy asked, following. "Just like that . . . whacked? Who? How?"

"I dunno," Freddie said. He poured himself a cup of coffee. "Got a bagel, or anything except this adolescent shit?" he said, pointing at the box of Yankee Doodles.

Wishing he could be in bed indulging himself in harmless thoughts of Rosalie, Mickey Boy popped an English muffin in the toaster. "Don't make me nuts. Tell me what happened?"

"Dunno," Freddie replied.

"When did it happen? How'd you find out so fast?"

"Patsy's *goomarre,* Lena, called Bobby Rimini's *goomarre,* who called him on some office cleaning job he was overseeing. He called me, like I could do something the fuck about it at two o'clock in the morning. I figured if I hadda be up, you were the boss an' hadda be up too." Freddie began munching on the muffin. "Got jelly?"

"How'd Lena know?"

"Found him in her building's lobby, all croaked. I think strangled, but I ain't sure. Not that it matters, dead is dead."

That it was the younger group of captains copping sneaks didn't take a genius to figure out, Mickey Boy said. But what were he and Freddie going to do about it? he asked. How fast would the older guys look to retaliate now? How could he maintain control without taking sides and splitting the family apart?

"Nothing to do now," Freddie said. If he judged correctly, both sides would be hiding out once they got the news—the older crew because they wouldn't know who would be next, and the younger guys because they'd be worried about a quick retaliation. "I'll be able to reach them all eventually. I just hope they don't start shooting back and forth—or at us—before we could straighten it all out."

"Shit like this never gets straightened out," Mickey Boy said. "As much as you could end a beef and say let bygones be bygones, how do you forget that your best friend, or the guy who baptized your kid, got wasted by some guy you're supposed to break bread with?"

"That's what this life is all about," Freddie replied. Sure, he said, grudges were kept for ages, but they were controlled. As undisciplined as life in general was for street guys, that's how disciplined the greater picture had to be. "Guys that don't accept an agreement get themselves whacked awfully fast. There's no secrets. Always somebody to rat out how they feel. Discipline."

"Well," Mickey Boy said, "what are we supposed to do now? Sit around and look at each other all night?"

"I dunno, whattaya wanna do?" Freddie asked. "You're too tall for me to dance with . . ."

"You know what I'd like to do," Mickey Boy said. "I'd like to get dressed an' go out . . . uptown, to some dinky all-night movie, on Forty-second Street."

"A sex movie?"

"Nah, a shoot-'em-up, bust-'em-up. Steven Seagal or something. Then, maybe, breakfast at Ratner's, downtown."

"With all this shit going on?" Freddie asked.

What could possibly happen? Mickey Boy asked. No one expected him to be out at that hour. No one could be reached to accomplish anything. And with one guy already dead for the night, whoever did it would be holed up somewhere, for safety. More important, he had to get out and relax, escape the prison that seemed to encase him every day. All Freddie had to do was call Billy Sneakers and Vito the Head, and get them down early to watch Laurel and the baby.

"Let's get out before Laurel finds out," he said. "I'll leave her a note."

"You sure you wanna do this? Sit next to bums sleeping off a buzz?"

"The scroungiest."

"You buying popcorn?"

"Only if they got roaches in 'em." Mickey Boy hurried to throw on a jacket and a pair of shoes from the downstairs closet.

On his way out the door, Mickey Boy wondered where Rosalie was.

47

June 5: Downtown Brooklyn

PAUL TRANTINO STEPPED OFF THE ELEVATOR ON THE FOURTH
floor of 75 Clinton Street. A few steps later he stood in the
reception area of the United States Parole Office. Three
parolees, one a Hispanic woman, sat on the plastic sofas,
waiting to be interviewed by their officers. They looked up at
Paul, over the magazines they read, then quickly brought
their eyes away from him and back to their places on the
written page.

"Mr. Halloran, please," Trantino said to the black woman
who sat behind the window. He caught her staring questioningly at him but said nothing.

"Your name, please?" the woman asked.

Paul Trantino flipped open his leather identification folder, displaying his photo ID card and FBI badge.

"He's with someone now," she said. "But he should be
finished in a few minutes."

Paul enjoyed the discomfort the three parolees felt in his
presence, although the down side, he thought, was that they
had recognized him the minute he had come through the
doorway. His father had told him many times, "If you walk
with a crooked guy long enough, you get to limp yourself." It
was sort of like people who resemble their dogs, his father
had said. Boy, did these old-timers ever have a way of
getting their points across, Paul thought.

A few minutes later one of the private office doors opened
and Francis Halloran released a man of about fifty years old.
Even though the parolee wore chino pants and a plaid work
shirt, he carried the polished veneer of the mob.

Halloran stepped forward to shake Paul Trantino's hand,

then led him back into the office. "I handle all O.C. guys, as you can see."

"I thought you guys had disbanded the Strike Force?" Paul said.

Halloran smiled. "Officially, yes. Coincidentally, though, I seem to draw a lot of like souls—all the broken noses, if you know what I mean."

It was Paul Trantino's turn to smile. The difference was that he smiled from the sting of vinegar in his gut. He'd already read the book on Francis Keenan Halloran. Knew everything from his average record at Fordham, to his stuffed-shirt reputation at the Parole Department, to his hatred of Italian mobsters. Halloran was the type, Paul thought, who pronounced Italian "Eye-talian," and called them "dagos" off-the-record.

"Yeah, well, I had my nose broken too," Paul Trantino said. "Fighting in college and the service."

"Marines here."

"Just a simple grunt on this end."

Halloran smiled a cocky smile and shrugged. "Now, what can I do for you?"

"Saw you on a roof yesterday—well, not me personally, but my men did—on Mulberry Street. Watching the Messina meeting, I take it."

"You've got it," Halloran said. "I think I've got enough to violate him and at least one of his capos now, with my photos of the rooftop crew going in to meet him."

"No you haven't."

"I most certainly do," Halloran replied. "Whether it sticks or not is another story. I read the minutes of Messina's last violation hearing, and if that's any indication of what to expect . . . why, there were more lies told in that room than after a fishing trip."

Halloran shook his fist as though he'd snatched a fly out of the air. "But whatever happens, at least I'll have him on ice for a couple of months. And if he weasels his way out, I'll just bang him for another two, then another two after that . . . till he hasn't got any more time left that he owes."

Paul Trantino just said "No." He enjoyed remaining silent until Halloran was forced to ask for an explanation.

"Simple. We at the Bureau would rather see Mickey Boy remain on the street than be locked up. It makes our job a hell of a lot easier . . . and a hell of a lot more interesting."

Halloran's face reddened, showing off his silvery waves. "I'm sorry, but I'm violating him. Do you realize that he's the boss of the entire Calabra Family?"

"Did the ID that I showed you say I was from a foreign land?" Paul replied.

"What about the goddamn murders? He wasted another one of his old guard last night. Looks like he's solidifying his power."

"He had nothing to do with it."

"Who did?"

"Don't know. But we do know that he doesn't either."

"Bugs?"

"That's our business. Bottom line is, we've just been able to track Messina very well—made our job a lot easier—and would hate to see things splinter off between a bunch of other guys where we get lost. Especially with these bodies dropping lately." He clasped his hands. "I was hoping you would find no difficulty in cooperating with the Bureau . . . ?"

"You guys are hot shit," Halloran said. "Leaving a top mafioso out on the street, probably murdering guys every couple of days, just to make your job easier. My own opinion is that, responsible for these murders or not, every parasite we lock up, the better."

"You haven't answered me," Paul said. "Do you cooperate, and earn our eternal gratitude, or force me to go over your head, to your supervisor, or even the Parole Commission if I have to? No problem for me to get our number-one man to call the brass, in D.C."

Paul knew he had Halloran by the short hairs. The man would have to be an idiot to try to get his bosses to back his refusal to cooperate with an FBI investigation. But Halloran remained silent.

The man was an idiot.

Paul Trantino stood, extended a hand, bid Francis Keenan Halloran a cold good-bye, then set off to visit his Parole Department supervisor.

48

June 10: Upper East Side, Manhattan

WHAT A PAIN IN THE NECK, LAUREL THOUGHT WHILE WAITING FOR Billy Sneakers to get a ticket from the parking attendant. Not that he wasn't pleasant and all, but she felt stifled having someone following her everywhere. More than that, it felt eerie when that person had no understanding or interest in what she was doing.

She'd shop for groceries.

He'd watch.

She'd test foundations and lipsticks.

He'd watch.

She'd get her teeth cleaned.

He'd watch.

Never a question. Never a comment. Nothing. Just stand and watch, then graciously put her belongings into the trunk and hold the car door open for her.

Now, when they went to the Decorator and Design Building, on Third Avenue and Fifty-ninth Street, Laurel knew Billy would eerily stand facing the door, holding a pistol in his jacket pocket, while she picked out wall tiles and floor covering for Mickey Boy's pasta houses.

Even though she realized it was much too early—Mickey hadn't even looked for a location or formed a corporation—she'd had to get out of the house and off Staten Island for a change. The city had seemed like the spot, and the floor and wall decor the reasons. At least Billy would be fun to talk to over lunch. Food was a subject he always had something to say about.

* * *

"Well, that certainly didn't take long," Laurel said. She'd gone through the decorators' center in less than an hour, having quickly realized that the materials in that place were not for Mickey's operation. Perfect for an elegant restaurant, but much too pricey for fast food operations.

"What now?" Laurel wondered out loud. "How about a movie?" she asked Billy Sneakers.

Billy shuffled his two hundred pounds around as if he were an embarrassed kid. "I don't think that would be too good an idea," he said.

"Why, ashamed to be seen going into a movie with me?"

"No, no, it ain't like that," Billy replied. "Though it ain't nice to go out socially with somebody else's wife. People talk, you know."

Laurel smiled at Billy and shook her head. Cute. Tousled black hair, blue-gray eyes—no brain. Another ninety-year-old man in a thirtysomething body, she thought. What a shame.

Billy continued, "No, it's just that being in the dark, an' all, in the movie, makes it hard for me to keep an eye on everything around."

"Then it's food, I guess," Laurel said with a huff. "How about Arizona 206?"

"What's that, Mexican? I mean, it's okay no matter what it is, but I was just asking."

"Southwestern, and if you don't want to, we can go for Italian."

"No, no, I'll try it. That's okay."

When they were seated in the restaurant, Laurel said, "Order me a frozen Marguerita," then rose. "I'll just be a minute."

Billy Sneakers stood also. "I'll go with you."

Laurel argued that she didn't need any bodyguard to go to the bathroom with her. There were still some things that were private, and he would stick out too much guarding the door from the outside. What did he intend to do, search women before they entered the rest room after her?

"Don't worry," she said. "No one is going to kidnap me."

Billy reluctantly agreed.

When Laurel found the ladies' room occupied and locked,

she slipped through the interior archway to the Arizona 206 Café. Suddenly, without giving it a second thought, she darted out onto Sixtieth Street and hurried left toward Third Avenue as fast as she could on high heels. She didn't look back once, for fear of slowing herself down.

Little Vinnie leaned his head back against the wall, closed his eyes for a moment and took a deep breath. He pictured Laurel every bit as vividly as he had seen her just a couple of minutes ago: her legs hot and shapely on white and brown high heels; her cleavage, barely showing, under the short white jacket that topped a brown and white slip dress; her brownish-gold hair, swept up to reveal her creamy white neck; her lips. He tried to picture her naked—high heels, hair up, just no clothes. "Oh man," he groaned, seeing Laurel, nipples, bush, and all.

Breathing heavily and heart thumping, Little Vinnie opened his eyes and dropped his hands to cover an erection that felt like it would split open. Thankfully, passersby hurried along East Sixtieth Street as if he and his erection were invisible.

More important to Little Vinnie than the effect Laurel had on him was that he was now thoroughly convinced he'd been right all along. Laurel was hot to trot, waiting for someone like him to liberate her from the good-wife bullshit role she was playing.

Little Vinnie perked up when he saw Laurel rush out of Arizona 206 without Billy Sneakers, who was supposed to be her bodyguard, he imagined. Unless she was fucking him too? he wondered.

He crossed East Sixtieth Street diagonally, to follow close to Laurel as she quickly made her way across Third Avenue toward Bloomingdale's. He went through the door right behind her, laughing to himself at how nervous and jittery she was, looking back frantically for her keeper, while missing him, Little Vinnie, standing close enough to throw her over his shoulder or yank her dress off. The feeling of power was so amazingly sexual that it forced him to walk half bent over to camouflage the bulge in his pants.

* * *

Laurel only stopped to look behind her once she was inside Bloomingdale's, peeking out from behind a counter rack of men's neckties. Her heart beat rapidly and her joints felt tight. She tensed, waiting for Billy's heavy hand to drop out of nowhere onto her shoulder. Her eyes darted all around, scanning the men's department.

No Billy.

Thank you, God . . . thank you. Laurel hurried onto the escalator, walking up steps to hasten her rise, excusing herself to step around shoppers, who muttered as she passed.

Once off the main floor, she began to feel secure. Free, free at last, she thought, then laughed, remembering the movie *Moscow on the Hudson,* where Robin Williams escapes into Bloomingdale's. Talk about life imitating art, she thought.

Feeling light and unburdened, Laurel made her way to the lingerie department. She would have liked to go instead to a high-line sex shop, purchased something erotic and exciting to turn her and Mickey's lovemaking into an escapist fantasy. That was what sex should be about, she felt. Not only about caring and emotional giving, but play and escape from the routines and problems of everyday life.

Unfortunately, Mickey Boy didn't view sexuality in quite so modern a manner. So, instead of really going all out and throwing a little of the spice Gael Greene suggested in *Delicious Sex* into his sex life, she would content herself to buy something sheer and incredibly sexy to turn him on.

Laurel rummaged through blacks and reds, frills and almost-nothings, till she found a sheer dark blue bikini style, with black satin bows placed strategically at the nipples and crotch. She fingered it, turned it, imagined how the thong back would leave the cheeks of her ass exposed. Nice.

As Laurel turned to walk toward the register, she was jostled by a man rushing by. His hands grabbed her by the hips, from behind, to keep her from falling; his fingers slid over to press the softness at the junction of her thighs.

"Scusa, signora," the man said, hurrying past her. He mumbled other words in Italian, which she didn't understand. The voice sounded vaguely familiar.

Laurel stood there for a moment, trying to place the voice,

then quickly opened her bag to see if the man wasn't one of those pickpockets she'd seen on TV who were able to lift a wallet or jewelry in a split-second bump.

No. Everything was there.

For an instant she felt extremely vulnerable. Here she was, stuck in Manhattan with no car, and really nowhere to go. She'd tried to get her cousin Tammy to run down from the hospital to meet her earlier, but Tammy had been scheduled for surgery all day.

Laurel's thoughts turned to Billy Sneakers. The poor guy had done his job, but now would get his ass reamed because of her.

All at once she lost her enthusiasm for what could have been a frivolous, fun afternoon. She put down the negligee and started for the elevator. If she couldn't find Billy Sneakers anywhere, she'd take a cab home.

That was her big experience, she thought as she exited onto Third Avenue. Another goddamned disappointment. Another trip back to her prison.

Something had to change.

Little Vinnie laughed out loud as he bent over the down escalator's rail on his way out of Bloomingdale's, remembering how he'd totally lost control in the lingerie department and had to touch her, had to feel her flesh to bring him from dream to reality. How off balance she'd been when he bumped into her; how confused when he pressed his fingers into the soft triangle near her pelvis. He'd bet anything she had felt like coming at that moment too. He would have loved to see her face when he rushed off, mumbling in Sicilian dialect how she would one day beg to suck his prick.

Once in his car and on his way across town, Little Vinnie contemplated how he would eventually approach Laurel, without having to chance her making a scene in a crowd or running back to her bastard of a husband and report his presence in New York. He knew that if he could overcome that initial barrier of her shock at seeing him, he could convince her to remain silent—and eventually spread her legs open for him.

"Goddamn!" he yelled out, unable to contain his exuberance. Later, he thought, he'd have to call Rosalie, that douche bag, and drag her up to Hale and Tempest's apartment. Damn if tonight he wouldn't fuck her till she passed out.

"What the hell is getting into you lately!" Mickey Boy shouted. "Are you losing your fuckin' mind?!"

"Watch your language!" Laurel shot back. "Your mother's upstairs. Fool her. Make her think you're civilized."

"I'm not! And I don't give a flying fuck if the goddamn Pope's upstairs! You put yourself in danger today. Don't you goddamn realize that?"

"No, *you* are in danger. You and those gangster friends of yours who are always planning to stab one another in the back! I'm only a wife, who minds her own business and rots in the house. They don't kill wives . . . probably because they don't even realize wives are human."

Mickey Boy threw himself on the sofa, exasperated by this circular arguing. How could he convince her that the situation he found himself in was not like any other he'd ever experienced or imagined?

"Do you have any idea how scary this all is?" Mickey Boy asked.

"Give me a break," Laurel said. "What could be more frightening than our wedding? Having to set up a phony ceremony so we could sneak off and hope we didn't get killed?" She put her hands challengingly on her hips. "More frightening than seeing your father murdered in front of us?"

"That was different."

"Why? Different gun? How does the old cliché go?" she asked. "Same shit, different day?"

"You're too smart to give me stupid answers like that," Mickey Boy said. He tried to explain that the last time, the enemy and target were clearly defined. Joe Augusta had been after Don Vincenze; Joe Augusta had killed Don Vincenze.

"No one else even got hurt."

"No? What about Chrissy? Or her father? Can you imagine the pain that drove him to do what he did?"

"That's different."

"Why? Because you don't see the blood? What about the pain inside? What about the hurt you've suffered? And me?"

Leave it to Laurel to twist and change an argument so that the focus on her being wrong was diverted somewhere else, Mickey Boy thought. He could argue about not trusting friends this time, not being sure where the treachery would come from, but that wouldn't change a thing.

"I give up," Mickey Boy said. "You were right. Okay? You did the smartest thing you could have, shaking Sneakers and going off by yourself. I'm the moron, with people getting whacked all the time, worrying that you could get hurt."

"No one hurts women."

"Janice Drake wasn't a woman, then, I guess," Mickey Boy replied.

"Who?"

"Just a nightclub singer . . . that is, until she wound up in the wrong place at the wrong time, when they wanted to whack her boyfriend, Li'l Augie."

"And they killed her?"

Mickey Boy shrugged. "Yeah, but you're right . . . nobody ever whacks women."

Seeming to struggle to appear unaffected, Laurel said, "She only got killed because she was with someone she cared about . . . I, on the other hand, have nothing to worry about, since I'm not with my husband long enough or often enough to be in that kind of danger."

The danger was very different now, Mickey Boy said. By not knowing where it was coming from, he couldn't guarantee how anyone would react. Without mentioning Frankie Green Eyes or any of the other men he suspected, Mickey Boy told her that everyone he knew denied any participation in the murders of Buster or Patsy.

"They either gotta get Academy Awards or they don't know nothing about it," he said. "And the truth is, if they did know and were lying, someone would've ratted them out by now." Always someone willing to drive a coffin nail into the guy above them, ready to step up the ladder on the neck of someone else, he thought.

"That makes things even worse."

Chaos was always worse.

Suddenly, Laurel began screaming; crying hysterically and shouting about everything from staying home too much to wanting to move to Florida. Tantrums were the one thing Mickey Boy couldn't deal with. It was either rise to the occasion, and take a chance that his temper would run out of control, or wall her out and wait for it to end. He squeezed back into the corner of the couch, wishing he could disappear.

When Laurel had screamed herself out, Mickey Boy went to her, sat with her, held her close. He looked up to see his mother, Connie, peeking out from the top of the stairs, and sent her back with a small shake of his head.

"I know it's a lot of pressure," Mickey Boy finally said. "But I don't know what else to do about it right now." He assured her that his goals were legitimate and honorable, and as soon as he could, he would remove himself from any position of authority.

"If I could only get everybody on track, with legit businesses, we'll be okay. If I can't, then I promise you I'll quit, one way or another. Deal?"

Laurel sat up, sniffled a couple of times, dried her eyes. "Mickey," she said, "these are almost the same words I went through with your father, when he stopped me on my way to Florida."

Mickey Boy stiffened.

He'd always wondered what kind of deal Laurel had made with Don Vincenze, and had felt diminished by the thought of it. What could the old man have promised that was a stronger influence than his son's own love? Had the don bought him a wife, when he couldn't get his own?

This house? The Mercedes? A secret bank account somewhere?

Would Don Vincenze's manipulations control his life forever? Even with the old man in a goddamn grave?

"I only went along with his promises of legitimacy then because I really didn't want to leave," Laurel said. "All his dreams, though, are turning to nightmares. I can't keep buying those same empty dreams."

Mickey Boy wanted to ask about the house and car, and any other promises the don might have made, but he didn't.

He may not have been at his best handling women, he thought, but he was certainly savvy enough to know that this was not the best time to try to find out.

"If we can't straighten things out soon, I want to leave," Laurel continued. "Go to Florida for a while, with Hope. Try to straighten out my head."

Was that where she'd stashed a secret bank account? Mickey Boy wondered. Money she had bargained with Don Vincenze for, knowing she would want to leave him one day? Wind up with some guy in Florida who would spend all day and night ramming his cock into her? Tying her up and practicing every kind of kinky sex she'd learned from those fuckin' books?

One thing Mickey Boy had made up his mind about was that he would never forcibly hold Laurel if she really wanted to leave. He loved her too much for that; didn't want to be with her if she didn't want him anymore.

Hope was another thing.

As if it were physical, Mickey Boy felt the beginning of a wall being built around his heart, a wall to protect him from the shattering hurt he was afraid would come.

49

June 10: Hell's Kitchen, Manhattan

JOE AUGUSTA WATCHED LITTLE VINNIE CALABRA CROSS THE street. Joe shifted away from the warehouse entrance when water dripped on his nose. The rain had stopped just minutes ago, leaving everything slick and shiny; white lights and neon reflecting off asphalt and cars. The dampness made Joe's odor that much more stuffy and pungent, even in the open air, making him move just to escape himself.

Joe fell into step beside Little Vinnie, who cast him a side glance, then continued on his way. Joe thrilled at being so close to Little Vinnie, whom he'd known since the boy had been born, without being recognized.

With Joe keeping pace, Little Vinnie turned to look at him more seriously now.

"I ain't got no money for you," Little Vinnie said. "So scram."

Joe almost laughed. He could have shot Little Vinnie now, killed him cold with one bullet; but he wasn't really sure. He hadn't been since receiving the tip from Don Peppino, of where he could find the offspring of Don Vincenze, the old bastard whose order had resulted in poor Chrissy's death. At first he'd wanted to kill everyone even related to the don, but that had been hurt and anger. Not that the inner pain of his loss was not still excruciating, but the blind anger was gone. Little Vinnie had almost been like a son to him. The boy and Chrissy had called each other cousin.

When they approached a Dumpster close to Little Vinnie's hotel, Joe said, "Vinnie?" Little Vinnie, startled, stopped for a moment, long enough for Joe to grab him by his collar and whip him into the darkness behind the Dumpster. Only Little Vinnie's face was illuminated, by a streak of streetlight that angled between the bin, full of debris from the building being renovated and the building itself. He shoved his .38 under Little Vinnie's chin.

"Who are you? Whattaya want? Go on, take my money, take what you want."

This time Joe did laugh. "Vinnie, don't you recognize me?" he asked. "Did I change that much?"

Fear filled Little Vinnie's eyes. "J-Joe . . . ?"

"Yes, Vinnie . . . Joe. Surprise."

"Please, Joe, please," Little Vinnie begged. "Please don't kill me. I'm sorry about Chrissy . . ."

Joe, fully aware of his reputation for being able to shoot the heads off running chickens, was sure Little Vinnie would not attempt to run. He loosened his grip.

"I accept your condolences, Vinnie," Joe said. "I know you cared for Chrissy . . . when she was with us, that is."

Little Vinnie looked relieved but strangely confused. "Of course, Joe, you know I loved Chrissy. You know I wanted to marry her. I would never hurt her—"

"Enough," Joe said. If he stood there long enough, someone would have to stumble upon them. Someone would have to get hurt for nothing. "Let's go where we can talk—your place."

Little Vinnie looked Joe up and down. Didn't Joe think it would attract attention, Vinnie asked, walking into the hotel with him dressed like that? His wrinkled nose said more about Joe's smell.

"There's gotta be a back way in," Joe replied.

"It don't matter. There's still people around."

"Okay," Joe said. "Come with me." With his pistol held inside his raggedy jacket pocket, Joe pushed Little Vinnie ahead of him. They walked the sixteen blocks to the fleabag place where Joe had his rented room. When they saw Little Vinnie, dressed as he was, accompanying Joe up the stairs, all anyone would think was that he was a young fag that got off on dirty old men. Fuck them, Joe thought. Let them think what they wanted to. They couldn't hurt him. No one could, anymore.

Once inside his room, Joe relaxed. He flopped down on his bed, back against the tinny headboard, gun out, watching Little Vinnie stand uncomfortably in the middle of the room.

"Roaches don't bite," Joe said. "Sit down, Vinnie. Relax."

"You gonna kill me?"

"If I do, then it won't matter about the cockroaches. Go on, sit in that chair." He pointed to a metal folding chair by the wall.

Little Vinnie pulled the chair into the center of the room, lifted it, shook it, looked underneath. Finally he wiped the seat with a shirt Joe had lying on the bed and sat down.

"Well, you gonna kill me?"

Joe sighed. He was tired. Tired of the dirt. Tired of the killing. Tired of suffering so.

"Vinnie, if I was going to kill you, you'd be gone already."

"Then what is it you want from me?"

Joe thought about that for a moment, then answered, "I don't know. Someone to talk to, I guess; someone who loved Chrissy too." Tears filled his eyes. "You know, I haven't talked to anyone in so long . . . so long." His lips hurt where they had crusted and split.

Joe Augusta and Little Vinnie talked into the night, about old times—about Chrissy.

"Remember how you used to break her balls when you were little?" Joe asked. "Always with a pinch, or a yank on her hair, or just teasing her?"

Little Vinnie's face drooped. "That was only 'cause I never really knew how to tell her how much I liked her."

"Boys never do," Joe answered. "Neither do men . . . I don't think they're supposed to. It's in our genes." That is, until they become fathers, Joe thought, feeling the tears well again.

They reminisced about Christmases, about ponies and Lionel trains. They laughed about summer vacations and cried when they spoke of Chrissy's smile.

What surprised Joe was Little Vinnie's acceptance of him having murdered his father.

"I knew all about the shit he pulled," Little Vinnie said. "I heard him, from upstairs, talking to you and Buster in the basement, about how he started that whole war, got all those guys whacked for nothing." His face twisted with anger. "I heard him talk about Mickey Boy being his son, then, too."

"You know, your father gave the order to whack that Irish kid, Skinny, that got my baby killed," Joe said, gauging Little Vinnie's response. "Even though I begged him not to."

Little Vinnie's eyes widened. He appeared fearful, then seeming to recover, said, "Joe, I swear, if my father did that, then he deserved to die. In fact, if I knew that, I woulda killed him myself."

Joe doubted that. He knew Little Vinnie had been a schmuck all his life, and probably couldn't kill a rubber duck, but he was sure the sentiments were sincere. Little Vinnie may not have been cut out to be a tough guy, Joe told himself, but he wasn't really a bad boy.

"You know," Joe replied. "I believe that. You've been the closest thing I ever had to a son, Vinnie. You were almost like Chrissy's brother."

Feeling as if thousands of pounds had been lifted off him

now that he could share his grief, Joe confided in Little Vinnie that he'd recently murdered both Georgie the Hammer and Buster.

"I heard about that . . . read it in the papers," Little Vinnie replied. "I don't have no contact with anybody anymore," he said. "That other fuck, Mickey Boy, had me chased out of the country. He's playing big boss of the whole family, an' me, I gotta live in Sicily—far enough away where he don't have to worry about me taking him down."

"Then why are you here?"

"Business . . . very special and very private business," Little Vinnie said. "And nobody, outside of you, of course, knows I'm around. In and out," he added.

"Yes," Joe said, feeling his throat constrict and his eyes hurt. "Me too . . . in and out. Forever."

"I could help," Little Vinnie said suddenly, his eyes glowing. "I could help you get everybody . . . Mickey Boy . . . the whole goddamn crew. Let me help you avenge Chrissy's death. Please, I beg you."

Joe mulled over Little Vinnie's suggestion. If past record was anything to go by, Little Vinnie was as useless as a third tit. He could be company, though; someone to talk to instead of crying into a pillow all the time. He could also serve as a driver and an extra set of eyes and ears. Yes, God had truly been kind to him now, sending him an assistant for his vendetta, which he was sure now was blessed by Him.

"You want Mickey Boy first?" Little Vinnie asked. "I know where he lives, what his car looks like, the whole—"

"No," Joe replied. Killing Don Vincenze's family was as wrong as that scum killing Chrissy. If he didn't take a moral stance, Joe asked himself, where would he go from there? Would he kill the don's two surviving daughters? Their children? No, some limits definitely had to be drawn.

"Why?" Little Vinnie asked.

"Mickey Boy was in jail when Chrissy went to Heaven," Joe said. "Besides, I need him to get me to Richie DeLuca, if he gets out of jail. With Mickey Boy gone, it would only be that much harder to find the real one I want."

"But Mickey Boy gives the orders. He'll have everybody come after you with everything they've got . . . . it'll be like

World War Three. At least, with him gone, I could talk to whoever is in charge. They'll understand. And Richie'll always be around, somewhere, to be found.

Idiot that the don always said he was, Little Vinnie had a point, Joe told himself. "I'll think about it," he said. "But for now, what I'm sure of is that I've gotta get that kid, Butch whatever his name is, and Richie DeLuca . . . also, if there's anybody else who took part . . . maybe that Irish kid, that the whole beef was all about, for your money. You know who he is."

"Yeah," Little Vinnie said with a nervous edge. "Skinny Malone."

"Why, does the Irish kid mean something to you?"

"No, I don't even think he's around anymore. I heard he was into the wind right after it happened," Little Vinnie replied. "It's just that I'm sick that I didn't kill him way before, when I had the beef with him originally. Maybe none of this shit would have happened."

"Don't blame yourself," Joe said. If anyone deserved blame, he thought, it was he himself. Hadn't he carried the order from Don Vincenze to Buster, for the Irishman's murder? Wasn't his own last name on the list of people who had to die, for poor Chrissy's early departure from Earth?

"Okay," Joe said with renewed enthusiasm. "You could work with me. But you gotta listen, and you gotta keep your mouth shut."

"No problem," Little Vinnie replied. He looked around the room, grimacing. "But you don't wanna stay here. Why don't you clean up . . . find a better place? Just keep the beard, and don't dress like a wiseguy. Nobody'll recognize you. Look at me," he said. "I can't tell you how close I come to people who should recognize me but didn't, because of the clothes and the moustache. Trust me."

Being clean did seem tempting, Joe thought. After all, he hadn't joined a monastic order of filth, for salvation. The homeless look had served its purpose this far; maybe it was time to assume a different role the rest of the way.

"You got any clean stuff in there?" Little Vinnie asked, pointing at the pile of clothes.

"Yeah, sure. Wrinkled, maybe . . ."

"Good," Little Vinnie said. "Why don't you get dressed, so you don't look too bad walking into my hotel with me. You could shower there. Got any money?"

"Some."

"If you need more, I could lend you some . . . get you some clothes, like at the Gap or something, where nobody'll look twice at you."

Joe shucked his filthy rags while silently thanking Chrissy and God for sending Little Vinnie to him now.

This boy is truly like my own son.

50

June 13: Upper East Side, Manhattan

THE PHONE RANG THREE TIMES BEFORE IT WAS PICKED UP. "Focacceria," the voice on the other end said.

Mickey Boy hesitated, looked at the receiver in his hand, then replaced it on the pay phone's hook. He'd done that a half-dozen times in the last two days. The first time, he'd gotten Rosalie, and had hung up immediately. After that he'd made up his mind that if she answered, he would speak. The other times someone else answered.

Did he really want to do that? Mickey Boy asked himself, still holding onto the receiver on its hook. Sure, Rosalie's name had been on his mind for days, though if he admitted the truth, he couldn't really picture her clearly. She was more an idea, a temporary escape, a brick in the wall to gird him for whatever happened with Laurel.

Could he get caught? Not if he was careful, he convinced himself. With his lifestyle, always out of the house, the percentage of Laurel finding out was way down. Besides, didn't just about every wiseguy he knew have at least one girl on the side? Was he supposed to be a saint? Was he supposed to be left like a sucker if Laurel decided to up and go to Florida without him?

Mickey Boy dialed the focacceria again. This time, however, when a male voice answered, Mickey Boy asked for Rosalie. He bit his upper lip, waiting for her to pick up. His chest felt tight and his palms felt uncharacteristically damp. He smiled, though, realizing his dick was hard.

"Hello . . . ?" Rosalie answered on the other end.

Mickey Boy hung up again. God, how was he going to talk to her on a phone that was most assuredly tapped? Goddamn FBI guys would like nothing better than to play a tape like that for Laurel; really turn his life upside down.

He looked over at Vito the Head, standing by the entrance to the restaurant's dining area, then looked at his watch. Freddie would be wondering what was taking him so long. He'd said he was just going to check up on Laurel and the baby, and had, in fact, called home, just to cover his bases. How would Freddie feel if he told him the truth? That he wanted to be in touch with Rosalie? After all, Freddie was his man and would have to help if so ordered. He just didn't want to do that. He loved Freddie and didn't want to have to see disappointment in his eyes.

When he dialed the phone again, Rosalie picked up.

"Listen," Mickey Boy said, his heart thumping in his throat. "This is the guy who couldn't fix a leaky valve the other day, remember?"

"Sure. Go to plumbing school since then?"

"Wanna meet me for a drink?"

Rosalie replied that she had to work through dinner and wouldn't be free until eight.

"That's okay."

"I'll look like hell."

"That's impossible," Mickey Boy said.

"If you give me till nine, I could go upstairs and change."

"Leave work a little early," Mickey Boy replied. Later would be pushing it. He'd have to get home later than what Laurel might normally expect—though he could make excuses, blame everyone else.

"I'm supposed to have a date later."

Mickey Boy's patience felt thin. His nerves felt shot. "Break it," he said.

"It sounds urgent," Rosalie teased.

"No, just a couple of drinks. There's something I wanted to talk to you about."

Mickey Boy felt lame. He hadn't spoken to a girl like this in a couple of years, since he and Laurel had first gone together. He expected Rosalie to laugh out loud over the phone.

"Okay," she said. "I can get out of here at seven, change, and be on my way by seven-thirty."

Mickey Boy looked at his watch. Six-ten. "Leave at seven," he said. "This way, I'll wait for you to have dinner with me."

"Where should I meet you?"

"Feel like Chinks?"

"Peking duck."

"Shun Lee Palace."

Still humming Sinatra's lyrics, "You're so right for what's wrong with my life," Mickey Boy slipped into his house after two A.M. He moved quickly and quietly to punch in the code on the wall alarm panel. Fumbling, he almost hit a six instead of a five, but finally hit the correct combination and saw the light turn green.

Thank you, God.

Mickey Boy walked slowly across the downstairs, stopping every few steps to listen for the sound of Laurel, awake.

Nothing.

. . . Through the darkness of night, you're my one shining light . . . You're so right . . .

After gulping some milk directly from the container, he climbed the stairs and set the upstairs panel for the alarm. His first stop was a quick check on Hope, whose head he patted gently. This was truly the love of his life, the being of his body that he would protect and set on a path for a good life.

From there he tiptoed into his own room, tentatively at first, until he was a hundred percent certain Laurel was asleep. At least he'd been smart enough to shower at the motel, after fucking Rosalie, eliminating that disturbance at home.

While undressing he thought about his adventure, picturing Rosalie's full breasts swinging as she undulated over him, her legs high over her head when he was on top. Yes, it had been a relief from the tension, and exciting for its illicit nature, but with it he now realized came a new tension: the fear of discovery.

With all the problems he had, including Richie's trial, scheduled to begin in just a few days, the last thing he needed was something to occupy another section of his mind. In spite of it all, he smiled, feeling like a kid who'd ditched school and not been caught.

Yet, anyway.

In bed, Mickey Boy looked down at Laurel's sleeping face, so peaceful and so pretty. Boy, did he love her, he told himself. If anything, he felt his time with Rosalie, nice as she was, made him realize how much in love with Laurel he really was.

Please, God, don't make her go away.

He began to stroke her hair back from her forehead, much as he had with Hope. When he bent and placed a kiss on her cheek, Laurel stirred.

"What?" she mumbled, her eyes half open.

"Nothing," Mickey Boy replied, and kissed her again. "I just want you to know I love you."

Laurel smiled. Her eyes seemed to sparkle in the glow from the television. "Come here," she said, and wrapped her arms around his neck.

Mickey Boy snuggled in close, hugging Laurel, and silently apologizing to her for his infidelity.

Soon Laurel's hand roamed down between his legs, and hers opened, making her satin nightgown ride up to her hips. Her eyes smiled in challenge, testing him, he knew, after coming home so late.

Mickey Boy smiled his own smile, with satisfaction, as his erection once again grew full. As he pushed Laurel's legs wider and entered her, all that went through his mind was, Thank God I'm still young.

51

June 14: Corinth, New York

SIX FUCKIN' HOURS DRIVING TO GET TO THIS GODDAMN LITTLE village in the asshole of the earth, Little Vinnie thought as he drove along a bumpy two-lane road. The sky turned violet, pink, and silver before him, silhouetting the uneven peaks of the Adirondacks. Joe Augusta sat alongside him in the passenger seat, seemingly mesmerized by the grass and foliage.

But for Little Vinnie, any inconvenience was worth it to appease the lunatic next to him. Vascillating between relative coherence and inane babbling, Joe had scared the shit out of him four nights ago, after he'd first accosted him near the hotel. It had gone on like that for hours, with Joe reminiscing about bittersweet times they'd spent as near-family, then speaking to Chrissy as if she were sitting there with them, telling her about murders and suicide as if he were discussing different flavored jellybeans. Boy, was this guy ever fuckin' nuts!

But dangerous.

Little Vinnie felt like he was working with plastique explosives—perfect for accomplishing his goals, but they could detonate in his hands at any moment.

That's why Butch Scicli had to go.

Joe had been operating in an ever-increasing insane mode since that first night. On the outside he looked one thousand percent better; clean and woodsy in boots, jeans, a plaid shirt, and, of course, his salt and pepper beard. Inside, though, he seemed to be bursting at the seams; carrying on about how he was wasting precious hours by not avenging Chrissy's murder in some way.

Little Vinnie had been afraid that if he kept Joe under wraps too long, Joe would turn on him, maybe see a goddamn face on him of someone else. Mickey Boy had been his first choice. He had practically begged Joe to kill Mickey Boy, but Joe had refused. Asshole!

When Joe mentioned Butch's name, Little Vinnie had shit a brick. He could guarantee that if Joe did find Butch, hidden away at his uncle's place outside of Corinth, the stool-pigeon bastard would give him up in a minute; blurt out that Little Vinnie had actually fired the shots that killed Chrissy, that he'd only driven the getaway car.

Imagine trying to explain to Joe that it had been an accident? Little Vinnie thought. It wouldn't have mattered a rat's ass that he'd mistaken her for Skinny Malone, that the stupid bitch had been sitting in Georgie's car with Skinny's hat on. Either he would have had to kill Joe, and lose his tool to get away clean on a Mickey Boy hit, or Joe would have skinned him alive. Shuddering, he made the decision to sacrifice Butch, keeping his mouth shut forever and appeasing Joe's hunger for bloodletting at the same time.

Little Vinnie stopped at a fork in the road, deciding whether to go right or left. The last time he'd been here was after Chrissy had been killed, and then he rarely left Butch's uncle's house.

"You sure you know where it is we're going?" Joe Augusta asked. His tone reminded Little Vinnie of the old Joe, a cool, demanding underboss of the Calabra clan.

"Well, we're in the right area," Little Vinnie replied. "There can't be that many people live here."

A beat-up red pickup truck rumbled past them.

Joe said, "We can't sit here forever. We'll get noticed. Go any way, but move."

Little Vinnie veered to the left, following a narrow offshoot of the road that looked vaguely familiar. He hoped he hadn't dreamed it, like a déjà vu thing.

Dusk turned to darkness as Little Vinnie reversed course, went back to the fork, then shot right. About a half mile later he jammed on the brakes, backed up about twenty feet, then turned right again, into a narrower, almost hidden path he was positive took them to Butch's uncle's house. Sure enough, a few feet ahead the foliage cleared and the house shone in the light of the moon and a zillion stars.

"Let's pull the car off here," Little Vinnie said. "We'll go on foot to the back of the house, where Butch's door to the basement is."

Crouching low and running along the perimeter of the surrounding forest, Little Vinnie and Joe Augusta made their way to the back of the newly sided and shingled colonial house. Unfortunately, there was no light in the finished basement where Butch slept.

"He's probably in the front, having dinner now," Little Vinnie said.

"How many in the house?"

"Just Butch, his uncle, and his aunt. Unless they got guests over."

Joe smiled. "No guests. Right, Chrissy?" he asked, looking upward. He kissed the air as if it would carry to the Heavens.

What a fuckin' bedbug, Little Vinnie thought. What the fuck did he intend doing, killing everyone in the house? Getting Butch out of the way was one thing, but a goddamn bloodbath was something Vinnie didn't think he could stomach.

"Follow me," Joe said, breaking into a crouched run toward the house.

Little Vinnie sucked in a deep breath, then followed. His skin felt soaked, and a chill sliced through him. He relaxed a little when Joe ran to the rear basement door instead of the front of the house. Goddamn crickets screamed all over the place.

Joe fumbled with a tool he'd had in his pocket, then picked the lock and let them both into Butch's room. Little Vinnie had to stand still for a couple of seconds to get his bearing in the dark. A dull sliver of light crept under the inside door that led to the main part of the house.

"We're gonna take this guy out of here," Joe said. "This one's going to go slowly . . . know why he's dying."

Oh, fuck! Little Vinnie thought. That's all he needed was for Butch to spill the beans.

"He's gonna scream," Little Vinnie said. "How're you gonna get him out?"

"Then you hold him here. I'll go tie up the uncle and aunt. Then I'll take care of him. Don't worry."

"Joe, please," Little Vinnie said. "Those people up there got nothing to do with this."

"I know. We won't hurt them. Right, Chrissy?"

Little Vinnie moved closer to Joe so he could whisper. "How about we go out now, then I come back and get Butch to come outside? This way, we could get him in the car without anybody knowing what's happening."

Joe looked at Little Vinnie, his eyes shiny spots in the dark room. He stayed silent for a while, staring but not speaking, then said, "Okay, let's go," and darted through the outer door.

"Thank you, God," Little Vinnie muttered on his way out.

Once outside, Little Vinnie told Joe to go to the car, that he would wait by the house until Butch came down. When Joe agreed and left, Little Vinnie sighed and collapsed against the white-sided wall. Fuck dealing with a maniac. It was just too draining.

Now Little Vinnie had to come up with a plan. There was no way he could let Butch and Joe meet. He fingered the revolver in his pocket. If he had to use it to kill Joe, he would, he told himself. At least a shot in the perimeter of the woods would give him time to take off before anyone responded. But if he shot Joe, then he might have to kill Butch too. His stomach knotted and his mind reviewed films he could remember. Maybe there was some scene he could pull that would show a scheme he might use?

"Fuck it," Little Vinnie said, just as the light went on in Butch's room.

Little Vinnie's heart raced. His mouth puckered from dryness and his hand felt like he'd just pulled it out of a sink full of water. The perspiration that ran down his temple felt icy. He knocked softly on Butch's door.

Butch opened the door tentatively, his fat head framed in the room's light.

". . . Vinnie?"

"Shhh," Little Vinnie said, lifting a finger to his lips. "I got something, a score, but I don't want anybody to know."

"Vinnie, I ain't—"

"Butch," Little Vinnie said, "this ain't a score I wanna do, it's one I already did." He told Butch that he had taken off a jewelry salesman in a nearby area and wanted to leave two suitcases full of stuff with Butch for a day or two. When he sold it, he said, he would give Butch ten percent.

Butch Scicli, never a genius, jumped at the offer. He shut the door silently and followed Little Vinnie toward the end of the clearing, where Joe Augusta waited by the car.

They spotted Joe Augusta as they neared.

"Who's that?"

"Joe Augusta," Little Vinnie said. "He wants to kill you." With that, Little Vinnie whispered, "Run," and gave Butch a shove forward.

Butch Scicli stumbled as he tried to reverse course. But not fast enough for Joe Augusta, who had already drawn his gun and aimed.

Little Vinnie hit the ground just as Joe fired off two rounds. He watched blood burst through Butch's chest, sending him lunging forward.

Little Vinnie rose so quickly that his head spun. Despite the dizziness and nausea he felt, he jumped behind the steering wheel, turned the ignition, and sped onto the road without putting his lights on. No point checking on Butch, he thought. When Joe Augusta hit a target, it was dead center.

"Jesus Christ, he made you!" Little Vinnie shouted at Joe, trying to use the offensive to keep Joe from reading the truth in his face.

As they hit the main road and turned toward the highway, Joe alternated between berating Little Vinnie for not following his initial plan, thereby denying him the pleasure of imposing a slow death on Butch, and thanking him for helping him avenge Chrissy's death. Between addressing Little Vinnie, Joe spoke to Chrissy, telling her that it would all be over soon.

Little Vinnie's heart raced faster than his automobile as he finally hit I-87 south. In his mind, however, he smiled— broadly and jubilantly. Butch Scicli would never be able to rat him out to Joe, and Joe would still be around to take care of Mickey Boy.

Who could say I ain't as good as my fuckin' father was, now? . . . If not fuckin' better?

52

June 16: Todt Hill, Staten Island

"ALL RIGHT, C'MON, MOVE," THE BEARDED DETECTIVE SAID, shoving Mickey Boy from behind. "Go out and meet your public."

Mickey Boy squinted at the flash of sunlight that blinded him, caught a lungful of the morning's humid air, then ducked his head down, foiling news cameramen who popped shot after shot.

"Come on, look this way!" they shouted. "Give us a big smile."

Mickey Boy saw the scuffle as police struggled to keep newspeople at bay as he hurried, head bent and hands cuffed, toward the waiting car. An officer pushed his head down with his hand, so it wouldn't smash against the side of the roof of the car upon entering. Mickey Boy flopped sideways onto the rear vinyl seat. With the cuffs on, he struggled to right himself. When the car lurched out and spun left at the corner, he toppled over again.

"Ain't exactly like riding in a Mercedes, huh?" the cop who rode shotgun called back through the wire grating that separated the front and rear seats.

Rage at law enforcement, which had been pumped into Mickey Boy on Brooklyn's streets of concrete and broken glass, filled him now. Cops were once again the enemy: faceless shields of authority that had disrupted his home;

dragged him out like a serial killer, with no other reason than to embarrass him and his family in front of his neighbors; called the press to ensure that embarrassment would be more widespread.

"Ain't talking today, don?" the cop in front asked.

Mickey Boy refused to speak. Silently, however, he wished the cop a slow, brutally painful death—then cleared his mind to think of Rosalie.

Today was supposed to be one of pleasure for them, one of pure energy-releasing sex. Since going with Rosalie for the first time just four days earlier, Mickey Boy had been with her every day. Fucking her was an animal mating ritual that left him drained of all tension and wanting even more sex.

He thought of Rosalie, so lush and inviting, a thin pad of fat over her entire body making her appear more soft and yielding. In time that layer would thicken, he knew, and she would take on the obesity of an old housewife; those tits, so full and milky, would sag with the years and make the front of her dress look like it was pumped up with helium; the bright red lips and dark mascara would turn her into a caricature of herself: a fat old broad with too much makeup, waiting for a guy in the neighborhood bar to get drunk enough to do her.

But for now Rosalie suited him just fine. For now her lust for him made up for everything the future might hold, because, in fact, he knew he had no future with her. Laurel was his wife and his first love, and would be there with him until whenever the end of his life came. In the meantime, though, there was nothing that pleasured him as much as Rosalie's sexual hunger for him. There was nothing about her that came out of a sex manual; nothing practiced or deliberate—or intimidating. When she fucked, she just wrapped her solid legs around him and humped away; she sucked his dick like she wanted to devour it. Rosalie was a whore, and Mickey Boy happily accepted anything she did within that context; she was not his wife, no excuses were needed. More important—for the moment at least, Mickey Boy thought—she was his whore.

With his erection at full capacity, Mickey Boy cursed the

detectives silently once more, this time for messing up his day with Rosalie.

Reporters already waited in front of Bath Avenue's Sixty-second Precinct when Mickey Boy arrived. Once again they pushed forward and scuffled with police to get a photograph of him. One reporter threw himself on the ground, trying to snap a picture of Mickey Boy's downturned face. Mickey Boy kicked out, catching the reporter's back as he rolled away.

"Look this way!" they shouted. "Pull his head up!"

Once inside the old station house the scene quieted down considerably. Other than a group of uniformed cops who guarded the door against intruders, the station seemed relatively quiet, with a low-key buzz of steady police work being done: papers being carried from one office to another, a desk officer speaking on the phone, a civilian worker typing up forms.

Ira J. Golden jumped up from a bench seat. "What the hell is going on?" he asked the detectives as they hurried Mickey Boy up the stairs. "You know my client is always available on call. Why roust him like he was Son of Sam? Bucking for promotions?"

The detectives ignored Golden all the way up. They shoved Mickey Boy into their operating room—old, cluttered desks, a cell against one wall.

Mickey Boy glared at the bearded cop as he opened the handcuffs. It took all his restraint not to clip him one right on the temple.

"Well, what are the charges?" Golden asked, his fat face heated and red.

"Questioning," the lead detective, a red-haired block of concrete with a military cut, replied. In his late twenties, he looked like an ex–Notre Dame fullback. "We got a homicide last night, another one of your client's goombahs: Frank Anthony Scarpucci, better known as Frankie Green Eyes. Ring a bell?"

The news stunned Mickey Boy. Once again, another of his men had been murdered and he had known nothing about it. He felt helpless, and frightened by the feeling of there being no control, no seeming order to his world.

Pulling thoughts through emotions, Mickey Boy was certain that Frankie Green Eyes's murder had to be a retaliatory move by the old-timers. With Patsy Luciano dead, it had to be either Bobby Rimini or Benny Donuts, or one of the other caporegimes left over from Don Vincenze's rule who had ordered the hit. Mickey Boy saw all his plans of pulling his family together as a legitimate business entity going down the drain. Once again, as with Frank Costello and Paul Castellano, the lower, more violent element of the crew would rule. Only in this case, he thought, they wouldn't rule him. He'd fuckin' ream their asses. If it was an animal they needed to respect, then that's what the hell he would give them—and they'd be goddamn sorry for it.

"And we got another report of another guy associated with your crew getting himself killed upstate . . . some young kid, Joseph Scicli . . . you called him Butch?"

"I didn't call him anything," Golden replied. "I didn't know him. And neither my client nor myself has a crew . . . that is, unless you're talking about a sweater."

Still reeling from the news of Frankie Green Eyes's murder and its ramifications, Mickey Boy was jolted by the news of Butch's demise.

Just then another pair of detectives entered, with Freddie Falcone in cuffs. Freddie held his hands up to show Mickey Boy, and smiled. "Tiffany's. Like 'em?"

"Yeah," Mickey Boy replied, happy to have Freddie's support. "I had a matching pair."

"Musta been a fire sale," Freddie said. "These cheap-skates don't get anything any other way." He turned to the detective nearest him and stuck out his wrists. "I would tell you that stickin' the key in the hole is something like sex, but I'm afraid you wouldn't identify with it."

"Fuckin' comedian," the detective grumbled, and opened the cuffs. Mickey Boy was sure that if Ira Golden wasn't present, the cop would have given Freddie a good shot to the balls, or somewhere else on his body where a mark wouldn't show.

"Okay, boys," Golden said. "Ask your few questions, which my clients will probably not answer, then let them go on their way."

"No reason to get nasty, counselor," the red-haired cop, whose desk sign read Terrance Kelly, said.

"No reason? My clients have always behaved like and treated you people like gentlemen. For some reason, you have decided to forget all that and go for the trash." Golden picked up his papers. "Now, do your goddamn job, and let us get the hell out of here. I can't wait to tell the newspeople outside how competent you people really are."

"Listen," Kelly said, "there's no reason to get bent out of shape. We got a call to roust your boys and bring them in. That's what we did." He turned to Mickey Boy and Freddie. "Now, are you fellas prepared to answer some questions?"

Mickey Boy refused to answer. He looked at Golden, who said, "Mr. Messina has nothing to say."

Freddie said, "I'll take the Fifth."

Kelly told him that he couldn't cite that constitutional privilege unless he was in court and under oath.

"Well, then, I'll take the quart," Freddie replied. "By the way, I got a question for you guys . . . what the fuck is this all about?"

Everyone in the room laughed.

"Listen, you guys," Kelly said. "For all I care, you could kill yourselves. As a matter of fact, considering the budget crunch we're in, I think it's probably the best thing that could happen. You have my full support."

The red-haired Kelly went on to say, however, that he didn't want what appeared to be in intrafamily struggle to affect the community at large.

"The first time an innocent bystander gets so much as a hair on their head mussed, I'm going to be all over you guys like stink on shit. My job is to protect the decent, law-abiding public, and that's exactly what I intend to do. Get it?"

Golden said, "I think you made your point, Detective Kelly, but my clients are completely legitimate business-men, and have no knowledge of the recent murders you mentioned."

"Yeah, sure," Kelly said. "You do your job, I'll do mine." He turned to Mickey Boy and Freddie. "Go on, get out. Consider yourselves rousted."

53

June 16: Downtown Brooklyn

SMILING, FRANCIS HALLORAN HUNG THE PHONE RECEIVER BACK on its base. Great to have friends . . . and lodge brothers, he thought.

"Now, let's see if that guinea FBI man could interfere in a good old-fashioned Irish network," he said, pleasantly talking to himself.

It had begun with it still dark out, when a phone call had wakened him.

"Red Kelly here," the voice had said. "Davey O'Brien, over at the prosecutor's office, told me to give you a call if I heard anything about a client of yours, Mickey Boy Messina. Since he put your home number, I figured it was important enough for you to get a jump on."

"Yes, sure," Halloran had said, shaking his mind awake. "What is it?"

Red Kelly, who identified himself as a city detective, and a proposed member for O'Brien's and Halloran's Shannon Lodge, said that a man associated with the crime family run by Messina had been found in his trunk—beaten, strangled, shot. "Not a pretty sight, even for a mob rubout."

"Shit!" Halloran cursed, shaking the cobwebs totally clear and remembering Paul Trantino's interference in the handling to the Messina matter.

"Problem?"

"Nah, just can't drop a paper on him because of politics . . . really can't talk about it."

"Anything I can do?"

Frank Halloran had been about to answer in the negative,

236

when he caught himself. "Yeah, sure," he said, with a broad grin. "Roust his guinea ass . . . him and his bodyguard, Falcone. Shake them up and upside down. Any problem with that? You know, politics-wise?"

"Well, we have a sort of standing order to notify his attorney if we need Messina for anything." Kelly had paused, then added, "But for a future lodge brother, anything!"

"Press too?"

"No problem."

This was the way law enforcement was supposed to work, Halloran thought while pouring himself a cup of coffee. This was the way it was back in the old days, when his father, Francis, Sr., had worked as a New York City cop, going from patrolman to personal assistant to Commissioner Lewis Valentine. He'd heard all those stories and more from his father and from his two uncles, one a U.S. Marshal and the other, his mother's brother, an assistant warden at Lewisburg prison.

At least four generations of Hallorans and Coreys, that Frank was aware of, had protected the people of the United States as officers of the law in the good old days. Those were the days when law enforcement personnel were clearly the good guys, with clear-cut goals and procedures that worked. One hand washed the other then, with their network of second- and third-generation law enforcers reaching out over city, state, and federal boundaries to put the goddamn crooks where they belonged.

Now it gave Frank Halloran a deep sense of comfort to know that on some level it still did.

If Milquetoast liberals had decided that a good crack on the noggin with a nightstick was police brutality, and violating a known criminal on his parole for spitting on the sidewalk was unfair, and the interests of some FBI hack getting his act together was more important than cleaning up the streets and protecting the public, then he would get things done in his own way.

The phone ringing made Frank Halloran smile. He would bet money on who it was.

"Halloran here."

"Yeah, Halloran—"

"*Mister* Halloran."

"Yeah, Mr. Halloran. This is Mr. Messina. I had a little run-in with the law, an' I know I got to report it to you."

Halloran's smile widened. "What was it?"

"Just a roust. Questioning about something I didn't know about. The Bath Avenue precinct."

"No problem. You can fill it in on your monthly report form when you come in."

"Gee, thanks," Mickey said. "Oh, and *Mister* Halloran, don't worry about a thing. In case you forget I reported the incident, I got it on tape."

Frank Halloran began to laugh, and hung up the phone.

54

June 16: Todt Hill, Staten Island

MICKEY BOY DROPPED THE RECEIVER BACK ON THE HOOK, PICKED up, and dialed Freddie's number. He had just tried Rosalie's number, something he had made it a practice not to do from his own home, but as luck would have it, Laurel had come down the stairs just at that moment with Hope.

"Say hello to Daddy," Laurel said, pushing Hope toward Mickey Boy's face. Hope cooed and called Dada a couple of times. Mickey Boy sucked on her nose.

"Bellevue Psychiatric," Freddie answered. "Chief nut here."

Mickey Boy kissed Hope again, then said, "Fred, what the hell is taking you so long? I'm almost ready to go."

"On my way," Freddie said. "Anxious for a day in the park?" he asked, referring to the Park Lane Hotel, where Mickey Boy and Rosalie were to spend a couple of hours.

"Yeah, please, call that party and move our appointment back from one to three."

"No problem."

Mickey Boy felt relieved. He'd almost slipped and called Rosalie from his phone, which he knew was tapped. That would have been like giving the feds a confession of adultery for them to hold over his head; to threaten to play for Laurel. Especially since he'd seen how two agents had used information—gathered tapes from the Paul Castellano bug —about his affair with a housekeeper to write a book. Mickey Boy feared them taking personal conversations a bit further and using them as blackmail.

But he'd almost taken that risk, and now he cursed himself for the near carelessness. Being wound up like a top didn't cut it; that was no goddamned excuse, not when your life depended on it. He'd been rushing to get to Rosalie, to release the tension that felt like it would paralyze him, sure. But there was more. Now he had a full-fledged war to deal with; had to take the reins and try to control a wagon that seemed headed off a cliff. Pretty soon there would be no more Rosalie, or, more important, Laurel or Hope. Life would be a guerrilla-type existence, moving quickly from sit-down to sit-down, shooting to shooting, away from the ones he loved so as not to endanger them.

Laurel pushed Hope in Mickey Boy's face again. This time he kissed her on the head and hurried off to finish dressing. Might as well harden himself to not seeing his family too much for a while—maybe never, if the shooters got to him first.

Mickey Boy threw a tie around his neck, but let it hang open. He put on his beige suit jacket and went to his bathroom mirror to spritz himself with Eternity. He stared in the mirror, troubled by yet another thought, one he couldn't quite grasp; something about Butch Scicli's murder that didn't fit into the scheme of things, as they seemed to appear. Then there was Richie, whose trial was scheduled to begin in just two days.

Suddenly, Mickey Boy leaned forward and bowed his head, overwhelmed by the problems that tore his heart and mind apart. Fuck everybody, and fuck all the answers! he thought, then turned and ran down the stairs. He found Laurel and Hope playing on the floor.

Plopping himself on the couch, Mickey Boy told Laurel, "C'mon, bring the baby here; sit with me. Let me hug my two favorite girls while I can."

55

June 16: Chelsea, Manhattan

LITTLE VINNIE FELT LIKE SMASHING THE CANDY DISH AGAINST the brick wall.

He looked at the clock: 9:38 P.M.

Fuckin' whore! he thought. Goddamn Rosalie, bitch, was nearly an hour late. For three days she'd tried to make excuses not to show up. The first two days he'd let her off the hook, but not yesterday. Last night he wouldn't take no for an answer, had insisted she show up at the apartment or he would come down and make her suck his cock on Mulberry Street, right in front of the focacceria.

Rosalie had shown up, reluctant though she might have been—and late—and Little Vinnie had punished her for it. He'd slammed and pummeled her, fucked her like a beast, humiliated her by letting Tempest and Hale into the bedroom to watch the abuse. If she hadn't walked into the apartment feeling like the biggest cunt in the world, he'd certainly sent her home with that impression. Now let her go cheat and fuck somebody else, he'd thought with satisfaction as he chased her out amid insults and threats.

Little Vinnie clenched his fist. He would have thought she'd learned her lesson and showed up on time tonight. If she had, he would have been willing to forgive and forget, and would have taken her out for a nice dinner at one of the places no one who knew him would go, like Café des Artistes or Pig Heaven; maybe even a few drinks afterward.

"Vincent, what is the trouble tonight?" Tempest asked, coming in from the kitchen area with a cup of tea. "Your little Italian fishwife got your goat?" Tempest, dressed in a black leather miniskirt and red satin blouse, sat on a chair across from Little Vinnie. "Anything I can do? Cup of tea?"

"Nah, nothing," Little Vinnie replied, then said, "Yeah, maybe a drink . . . real dry martini would do it for me now."

Tempest immediately went behind the white padded leather bar and began to pour vermouth. "So dry, it will pucker your mouth going in and your dick coming out."

"Thanks, just what I needed."

As promised, the martini tasted perfectly dry. Little Vinnie lay back on the sofa, trying to let the tension ebb from his body. He thought of Laurel, so hot and ready, as he'd seen her just a day earlier, when he followed her to the Macy's mall on Staten Island. Too bad she'd had that asshole bodyguard next to her every second, or he would have stepped in close enough to cop a feel or two; to give her a thrill, as well as himself. God, did she get him hot!

"Anything else?" Tempest asked.

"Don't be so nice," Little Vinnie said. "I don't wanna get spoiled."

"You bet your ass you'd be spoiled. No bitch out there is even in my league when it comes to pleasing a man."

That's 'cause you ain't seen Laurel, Little Vinnie thought. He chuckled, beginning to feel relaxed from the drink. "Another, if you don't mind." When Tempest went to mix the refill, Little Vinnie called, "Just don't get no delusions, Temp, honey. We could only be friends."

Tempest delivered the drink, then stood in front of Little Vinnie, hands on hips. "Why, don't I look great? Tell the truth."

Little Vinnie was tempted to say no, that Tempest had put weight on, just to see the reaction, but said, "Yeah, you're okay, but you know the deal—it's your balls that don't look so good to me. You know, guys could only be pals, that's all."

"I'm not a guy!" Tempest opened the satin blouse, exposing a set of conical breasts. "Does this look like a guy's?" Tempest asked. "Forget what you don't see, and think about what you're looking at. Come on, look at these tits. Do you think that fat cow you've been fucking has better tits than these?"

Little Vinnie stared at the pair of breasts. Even the nipples looked swollen and female. He gulped the martini to distract him from the erection that began to form between his legs. How the fuck did Tempest keep from getting a hard-on? he wondered.

"And look at these legs, Vincent," Tempest continued, hiking the skirt up just a couple of inches more to show amazingly firm thighs and legs, stretched taut by black spike heels. Tempest's blouse remained open. "Well? I saw the thighs on that baby horse, Rosalie. She'd die for these."

Little Vinnie had to admit that in body parts, Tempest had it all over Rosalie—except for one. He crossed his legs to hide his erection.

Tempest uncrossed Little Vinnie's leg and dropped to the floor between both knees, placing a hand on each thigh. The two exposed breasts dangled over Little Vinnie's crotch. "Touch one, Vincent," Tempest whispered. "You'll see, it feels like any other tit."

"C'mon, Temp, you know that ain't my game."

"What is your game? Is your hard-on make-believe?" Tempest took Little Vinnie's free hand and filled it with a breast. "Close your eyes and tell me what it feels like."

Despite the embarrassment Little Vinnie felt, he agreed to play the game, and closed his eyes. Picturing Laurel naked, he squeezed the breast and pinched the nipple. It amused him to think that he was probably turning Tempest on.

"Well, doesn't it feel like any girl's tit should feel?" Tempest asked in a low, throaty voice. "And my legs feel just as good."

Little Vinnie felt Tempest's feathery touch on his cock, but didn't say anything. Instead he imagined Laurel's fingers rubbing his shaft.

"And if you keep your eyes closed, my mouth and tongue feel like any other mouth and tongue."

Little Vinnie remained silent when he felt his fly being

unzipped and his erection hitting the air. Tempest was right, a tongue felt like any other tongue, a mouth like any other, a throat . . . goddamn, the inside of a throat . . .

Little Vinnie's body tensed as he felt his semen rise, and pictured Laurel's face at the end of his dick.

56

June 17: City Hall, Manhattan

MICKEY BOY HEARD THE TRAIN PULL IN, CAUGHT THE WAVE FROM the workman, then bounded down the IRT's Brooklyn Bridge station stairs two at a time. Freddie Falcone's heels clicked in time behind him.

When they reached the bottom, two young button men of Mickey Boy's, who he knew were part of the younger faction of his crew, stepped in to join the two bodyguards he'd brought. Together they formed a human chain that would keep anyone from following. The Transit Authority workman fell in with Mickey Boy and Freddie, leading them into a car of the southbound Lexington Avenue local train that was empty except for another pair of Calabra Family made men, who were also aligned with the young turks.

Mickey Boy's heart raced and his temples throbbed. He sucked in deep breaths, trying to steady his body. "Damn, I'm outta shape," he said, in an attempt to ease the tension. The two men, who were technically his, just smiled nervously and nodded their heads.

In spite of his own anxiety, Mickey Boy felt like laughing. It took real balls, or stupidity, to take sides against a family boss. Tomorrow, all beefs might be settled, and these two would have to depend on him for everything from promotions to settling problems with other crews. He knew it, and he knew they did too. The comedy came from them trying to walk the tightrope—committed to their faction, but not enough to offend him personally.

Responding to Mickey Boy's complaint of his own physical condition, Freddie said, "Have another bowl of gnocchi," then puffed his cheeks out to mimic a fat face.

Everyone, including Mickey Boy laughed.

Almost immediately, the train pulled into another station. When it slowed to a halt, Mickey Boy and his entourage jumped out onto an abandoned station platform. The doors instantly rolled shut and the train continued, screeching, grinding, and rumbling into a severe horseshoe turn that would send it back in the direction it had come from.

Mickey Boy looked around at the most unusual subway station he had ever seen. Not that he'd been on a train in more than two decades, but he certainly remembered the sights and smells of waiting on the Court Street platform to go to Coney Island or lower Manhattan as a kid. And this was like nothing he could even vaguely recall. Cream and brown tile walls, darkened by more years of service than he could imagine, looked even dimmer in the light of low-wattage incandescent bulbs in chandeliers.

"How old is this place?" he asked the workman, sniffing in stagnant air. He tasted steel dust on his tongue.

"Built in 1904. Did fancy work then, huh?" the workman replied.

Mickey Boy agreed, while looking all about. He imagined people dressed in turn-of-the-century clothing boarding and alighting from antiquated trains. No graffiti, no muggings; ladies in long dresses, gentlemen in vested suits and bowlers; parasols, spats. That's when he should have been around, he thought—when being boss really meant something.

"Now it's shut; just use it for turnarounds," the workman continued, as they walked. When the group reached the middle of the platform, the workman stopped and, with an outstretched arm, pointed Mickey Boy and Freddie toward five steps that led to a landing, out of sight of any passing trains, which became a dead end at the closed-off old entrance.

"We ain't gonna insult youse, an' feel for guns," one of the two button men who had been on the train said.

"I should hope not," Mickey Boy said, sternly enough to

remind them where their future lay—that was, if the meeting wasn't a setup, and he survived to have a future.

Up the stairs, Philly "Red" D'Alberto and Joe "Bus" Buselli, two of the younger Calabra captains, waited. Both were in their late twenties to early thirties; both wore expensive jogging suits and an abundance of gold jewelry; both had had their black hair professionally blown out and lacquered.

Mickey Boy and Freddie hugged and kissed them.

"Like the quarters?" Joe Bus asked. "I asked my cousin, Tommy—the T.A. guy—to get us a room, like where they keep the electrical stuff, between stations, but he thought this would be cleaner."

Mickey Boy unconsciously looked down at the pearl-gray suit he wore.

"Just no chairs," Philly Red added. "We gotta have a standing meeting."

"Maybe we could jog in place," Freddie said. "Lose a couple of pounds while we talk."

Mickey Boy began to lean against a wall, then remembered his light-colored suit and stood straight. "Nobody's losing nothing here," he said. "Not weight, not pride, not nothing." He kept his facial muscles rigid and his ears honed for the slightest off sound. Not that he could do much if they'd decided to kill him.

Another train roared through the station and around the loop.

"They come through every three minutes," Joe Bus said.

Mickey Boy shrugged. Perfect time to fire shots, he thought.

The discussion itself got off to a fast start; more direct, Mickey Boy quickly realized, than a conference with old-timers would have. Philly Red, the smarter of the two men, and a second-generation wiseguy, said that although there was no love lost between them and what he termed the "old farts," they had never done anything to deserve Frankie Green Eyes getting killed. He ranted on about revenge, saying that they were younger, stronger, and had more heart than "those faded old rags ever had."

The one thing he hadn't mentioned, Mickey Boy noted, was brains. If he, as boss, stepped out and let both sides go at each other, he would bet that neither Philly Red nor Joe Bus would live through the summer.

Freddie seemed to have a lot more patience with Philly and Joe, stopping them before their heated rhetoric became out of order, and agreeing with them occasionally.

To Mickey Boy, they were both jerkoffs, and epitomized what was wrong with their centuries-old thing, *la cosa nostra.* Once again, he thought that he'd been born too late.

"Don't you think they had a right to be pissed after the old man, Patsy, got whacked?" Mickey Boy finally asked, just as another train roared into the station.

"What?" Philly Red asked.

Mickey Boy repeated his question.

"We told youse," Joe Bus said, "we had nothing to do with that."

"Of course we believe you," Mickey Boy said dryly. "You're men of honor, right?" He remained blank-faced, as he'd seen the old-timers do when they'd cut people to pieces with double meanings.

"Yeah, we swear," Philly said. "We took an oath that we live an' die by."

"Well, what about the old guys? Didn't they take an oath too?"

Philly and Joe looked at each other, lost for words.

Freddie just smiled.

For the first time in a long time, Mickey Boy felt entitled to be boss. He leaned back against the wall, then cursed when he realized he'd dirtied his suit jacket.

"Well?" Mickey Boy asked again. "What do you think, they'd lie?"

"No, but we know they did it," Philly said. "These guys got lost right after Frankie got whacked. If we did Patsy, Frankie wouldn'ta been around to get suckered."

"They're right on that," Freddie said.

Mickey Boy agreed. "But just think how it looked to them, Patsy getting clipped after you guys have a few words." He waited a moment, hoping they knew how to think at all, then said, "What would youse do if Frankie had been hit first? Wouldn't youse have gone off on a tear?"

"We woulda ripped 'em a new ass; probably clipped a half

a dozen of 'em before it got light the next day," Joe Bus said. He added, "An' that's exactly what we wanna do now."

"You can't," Mickey Boy said.

Philly rolled his eyes upward. "I can't believe you're taking their side."

Mickey Boy waited for another train to go through, then said, "There ain't no sides. We're all supposed to be part of the same family, remember? Or you forgot that part of the oath?"

"Well, we didn't start it."

"Somebody did."

"Yeah, probably them," Joe Bus said. "Cocksuckers probably whacked Patsy themselves to get his cash. They're all stuffed up to their ears in *fazooles,* an' don't part with a cent."

Mickey Boy burned inside. He would have liked to throw Philly Red and Joe Bus in front of the next train that made the turn. Instead he feigned a genuine lack of understanding and asked, "Oh, so you mean that's what this is all about? That these guys got too much cash?" He nodded. "You're right, let's go whack 'em all for having more than we got."

"Nah, he didn't mean it that way," Freddie said. "Right, Joe?"

Fortunately, Joe wasn't bright enough to realize how angry Mickey Boy really was. He agreed with Freddie, explaining that money had nothing to do with it. They were never supposed to kill for money, right?

Fuckin' oath again, Mickey Boy thought.

After listening to all his younger group's complaints, many of them having nothing to do with the problem with the older faction, the meeting was adjourned. Mickey Boy promised to get to the bottom of what was going on, and vowed that if the old men were indeed at fault, he personally would take care of them.

"None of us want to see one of those twenty-year wars among ourselves, do we?" Mickey Boy asked, remembering stories about the internal Profaci and Bonnano wars of the sixties and seventies.

Both men agreed. They also agreed to go to a meeting that

Freddie would arrange, and to honor a truce at least until then.

"Tommy'll flag a train to pick youse up," Joe Bus said. "He coulda let you out of this door . . . before they sealed it," he said. "But even if we could, we wouldn't want nobody to see youse come out in the middle of City Hall Park, dressed all pretty like that." He laughed. "They might take youse for politicians, an' attack youse."

Mickey Boy laughed along, though getting out of there was all that would make him genuinely happy.

Mickey Boy and Freddie left the Brooklyn Bridge station by the stairs that led to the Municipal Building on Centre Street, a stone's throw from One Police Plaza. Though their men had been instructed to meet them by the Broadway line's City Hall station, the two leaders of the Calabra Family had decided to walk alone to Chinatown, and, as Freddie had said, "Eat the dirtiest, sloppiest food we could find."

"You know, I never felt more like I wanted out," Mickey Boy said as they walked. Even the humid, carbon-monoxide-filled air felt fresh after spending time in that abandoned subway station. "This thing ain't what it's cracked up to be," he added. "It ain't like the old days."

Freddie laughed. "What makes you think the old days were what they were cracked up to be?" he asked. "Because they told you so?"

Freddie had been in his twenties, and had known that life for at least ten of those, when Mickey Boy had just been a sperm. "I learned about all the bullshit from the bottom up," Freddie said. "You got fucked. You heard all the myths these guys told you, then shot right to the top, never getting a chance to see how full of shit they were."

Freddie gave an example of how he had uncovered one of the layers of lies. "When I was a young guy," he said, "if I had a beef, like any guy who wasn't straightened out, I'd go to a sit-down with my man, who was Vito the Bug. Right?"

"Yeah, sure."

"An' each time we'd get there, Vito an' whoever was representing the guy I had the beef with would excuse themselves an' go outside or in another room to talk. Right?"

Mickey nodded.

"That was the procedure; the code. Then, once the two wiseguys finished their private discussion, we were allowed to sit in."

"I know all about it," Mickey Boy said. "I been through it a dozen times myself."

"Then, one day, after the Bug had that first heart attack, he asked me to go represent him at a meeting with one of Benny Favara's guys," Freddie continued. "Naturally, I was thrilled."

Freddie went on to say that when he arrived at the meeting, and had, as a nobody, asked and been granted permission to represent Vito the Bug, the opposing wiseguy asked him to come outside for a moment.

"I was going nuts," Freddie said. "Here I was, finally gonna find out what these guys said, and I wasn't prepared. What if there was a password? Or something else I hadda say to prove who I was? Vito, that fuck, never told me nothing. I was sure he sent me down there to make a fool of myself, just as an excuse to keep me down."

Mickey Boy laughed at Freddie's animated delivery; waving his arms and biting his fist.

"An' guess what he said?"

"I don't know."

"Guess. 'Cause I know you missed all the steps that woulda showed you that. Go on, guess."

"I ain't got a clue."

Freddie stopped and grabbed Mickey Boy by the sleeve. "You know what he said, that dead mother's ass? He told me that I should tell my guy he hadda pay the debt, and he would tell his guy that he couldn't collect, an' we would cut up the money."

"What'd you do?"

"What the fuck do you think I did? I told this motherless cocksucker that I don't sell people out, an' went inside."

After that, Freddie said, he fought like crazy at the sit-down, and won the point decidedly. A month later, when Vito was feeling better, he said the issue was brought up again, and this time the decisions went the way the wiseguy had originally wanted. Vito and the wiseguy sold out both their guys and cut up the money.

"And me, like the jerkoff that I am, wound up with nothing."

"Don't say that," Mickey Boy replied, dragging Freddie around the corner to Canal Street. "You wound up with honor."

Freddie shook his head. "You really are ready to retire," he said, "to your dream of the 'good old days.'"

"Yeah. Right after we eat, an' I see Rosalie for an hour or two."

"I said retire, not commit suicide."

57

June 17: Downtown Manhattan

PAUL TRANTINO SHIFTED THROUGH THE MESS OF PAPERWORK ON his desk. He picked up a file, checked inside to see if there was any material pertinent to what he was working on, then, not finding a clear spot on top of the desk, tossed it on the carpet behind him. One day, he vowed, he'd have a secretary to put things in order. And no, he told himself, he would not be lost with all his stuff neatly arranged. He hated when slobs like himself said, "Please, don't move anything. Then I won't know where anything is."

Bullshit!

Paul checked through official reports from field agents that monitored just about every move Mickey Boy Messina made. Not too bright, with all that surveillance, to begin fooling around with some bimbo now. He was sure Mickey Boy was aware that he was being followed. Must be one of those self-destructive assholes, Paul thought. Too bad. He made a note to do a backup check on the girl.

From written reports, Paul turned to some unofficial tapes he still hadn't listened to; tapes that would never be allowed in court, but were invaluable for the information they contained. A mobster inadvertently tipping off a meeting could lead to intelligence gathering on how a family's politics were shaping up. A name could lead to another, more careless criminal, who might justify a tap warrant and allow the Bureau to work backward to the original source—legally. Tomorrow he would hear what went on in the closed subway station where Mickey Boy was presently having a meeting. Amazing what technology could do. They'd even be able to filter out most of the train noise that he knew would show up on the tape every three minutes. Thank God the bad guys hadn't come up into the space age and made his job more difficult, he thought.

Paul jotted down a note in his appointment book to see Jim Favioto, a Special Agent under his command, to check on what he'd picked up from the shotgun mike Jim homed in on Mickey Boy's private outdoor conversations, or on windows of any room Mickey Boy was in, to pick up the vibrations off the glass.

Poor bastard, Paul thought, chuckling to himself that he meant it in more ways than one. What a sonofabitch that old man, Don Vincenze Calabra, was. Paul had no idea how his own father could have been friends with that man at any time, even if it was only in their youth. Maybe that's why his father had given up the streets, after World War II, to go to law school and become a Suffolk County district attorney. His father could never have had the cunning—or downright meanness—to survive in the street life. Tough old bird, he thought affectionately, but not miserable enough.

More important, Paul felt sorry for Mickey Boy for being in way over his head. He really did seem like a decent sort, at least judging from all the hours of tapes he had listened to. The guy really was making an effort to bring those knuckleheaded guineas around him into the twenty-first century. Paul would have laid three-to-one odds against that happening. How do you start with inner city Italians who grow up with no idea who Supreme Court Justice Anthony Scalia is, but would canonize people like Don Peppino Palermo or Mickey Boy Messina? Thank goodness he'd had the good sense to keep his own kids out in suburban Long Island, away from the guidos and *cuginos*.

Paul flipped through a bunch of photos of Mickey Boy with various members of his crew: Freddie Falcone, the late Patsy Luciano, Bobby Rimini, and some broken-nose too new to have a name on yet. He held the photo of Mickey Boy with Patsy Luciano. Enough for a parole violation, in the hands of that asshole Frank Halloran.

Paul shuffled the photo back into the file, then lifted the last folder he would put into his briefcase to bring home tonight. He flipped it open and looked with annoyance at the photo of Frank Halloran with Red Kelly, the local detective who had rousted Mickey Boy Messina from his home; that, after Paul had asked Halloran to lay back and mind his own business for a while. So much for goddamn respect.

On his way out of the office, Paul Trantino thought that Frank Halloran was one guy he would eventually use all his influence to have transferred to Siberia—or better yet, if the occasion arose, just give a hell of a shiner.

58

June 21: Downtown Brooklyn

"I DON'T LIKE FUCKIN' WEST INDIANS," RICHIE WHISPERED TO Ira J. Golden.

"No, black guys are good," Golden replied.

"Not West Indians. When they're good, they're goddamn self-righteous, and would convict their own mothers. Get him off the jury."

Golden argued that they'd already used seventeen of their twenty preemptory challenges the previous day, wiping out prospective jurors without reason, and with four jurors left to seat—three and an alternate—he didn't want to get stuck with someone worse.

"Can't you get him out any other way?"

"Not unless there is some reason, some prejudice that I can show, that will make the judge disqualify him. So far, that hasn't happened," Golden said. "Trust me. Take this guy, he won't hurt."

Richie stared at the black man who sat as potential juror number nine. Neat; too neat, Richie thought. Probably a churchgoing, upstanding member of the community who couldn't wait to send a child murderer, like the lily-white Richie DeLuca, to jail. Richie felt embarrassed just to be sitting there on that charge of killing Chrissy Augusta. He would have rather been there for a major payroll theft, or swindling a bank out of millions—or something he'd really done, like gambling or shylocking.

"Okay, but if I get convicted, remember I didn't want him."

"This guy's not a leader, he won't sway anyone if he votes guilty, and he's not strong enough to hold out by himself," Golden said. "Just worry about the other eleven. If we can convince them of your innocence, he won't matter at all."

"Yeah, like my glass is half full instead of half empty."

"It's all a matter of perspective," Golden replied. He okayed the West Indian for the jury, and went on to the next possible juror, a female insurance broker.

God, Richie thought, how I hate insurance brokers; so much to the letter. She'll probably vote to kill me.

The female broker stayed.

"The good side is, I like broads, and they usually like me."

As did a waiter.

"He's great. I always tipped waitresses and waiters real good."

And a television studio employee.

"I don't know. Okay, I guess."

Golden passed on a teacher, not wanting someone who worked with kids to sit on a teen murder case. Richie insisted Golden throw out a construction worker.

"This guy is probably pissed that he's losing work time from his short season, and'll want to crucify me."

Golden laughed, but went along.

The alternate they sat was a retired postal worker. Good, Richie thought; postal workers were all crazy.

After lunch, opening arguments began.

The prosecutor, Assistant District Attorney Roland V. Flowers, spoke at length. Droning on in a lackluster monotone, he said he would present pieces of a puzzle to the jury, which, if they could see in their entire perspective, would give them enough of a picture of what happened on the night Christina Augusta was killed to convict Richard DeLuca of murder in the first degree, and send him away where he couldn't hurt any member of society for the rest of his life. He said they would be hearing from average people who had seen Richard DeLuca trying to flee the scene of the crime, as well as Detective Peter Tsakalis, who had shot DeLuca to keep him from escaping.

"Don't believe the wizardry of my colleague, Mr. Golden," Flowers said, "who would have the bits of evidence fly around in the air and never coalesce into a vision of Richard DeLuca's participation in that night's brutal murder of a sixteen-year-old girl. A poor, unfortunate victim of a mob rubout gone awry."

Flowers hammered away at Richie for another hour and a half, repeating adjectives that vividly illustrated the bloody execution of Chrissy Augusta.

"It will be difficult to bear, and I sincerely apologize for having to show them to you, but you will see photographs of Christina Augusta, that poor child, with her brains blown out . . . of her eyeball pasted to the dashboard by a bullet . . . of her Catholic school uniform covered in blood."

In fact, the longer Flowers spoke, the more he left Richie's name out, concentrating instead on the kind of brutal visual imagery that would disgust and inflame the jury.

By the time Roland V. Flowers had finished, Richie felt as though he would vote himself guilty if given the chance.

Golden countered with a reminder to the jury that guilty meant guilty "beyond a reasonable doubt." He hammered that home over and over again.

Was Richie DeLuca there? Yes. Did he murder Chrissy Augusta?

Reasonable doubt.

Was the murder weapon recovered? No.

Reasonable doubt.

The burden of proof was on the State; not on the defendant to prove his innocence.

Reasonable doubt.

Reasonable doubt . . .

Reasonable doubt . . .

"Be every bit as concerned," Golden cautioned near the conclusion of his opening statement, "about what you *do not* see and hear, as you are about what is presented to you. Remember . . ."

Reasonable doubt.

The slightly uplifting feeling Richie got from Golden's booming oration ended with a recess for the rest of the day. If Richie had any reasonable doubt on his way back to his cell at the House of Detention, it was that he would walk away from the proceedings as a free man.

Reasonable doubt, my ass.

New York State Supreme Court Justice Heather Jacobson banged court into session the next day with her gavel. Richie already felt worn out from the trips back and forth he'd made, stripping, being locked down, sleeping on metal slabs, getting banged around in a paddy wagon, eating goddamn cheap bologna sandwiches. Last night he hadn't gotten back to his cell until nearly nine P.M. Dinner had been long gone, so he filled up on the six hard-boiled eggs his contract, Blood, had left him, and half a bag of Chips Ahoy.

The first witness for the prosecution was an old lady, Margaret Mangiapani, who lived on the block where Chrissy had been murdered. Margaret testified, under careful questioning by Roland V. Flowers, that she'd been on her way out to visit a friend across the street when she heard shots fired behind her. She had turned, she said, only to have a young man come running by. That man, she was sure, was Richard DeLuca, the man sitting at the defense table.

Richie shifted uncomfortably. He looked over his shoulder at the two officers who stood behind him. If he even stood up, they would step in to push him back into his seat. He felt lost and, in spite of having Golden next to him and Mickey Boy there in spirit and financial support, totally alone.

Ira J. Golden walked slowly to the witness box to cross examine.

GOLDEN:	Mrs. Mangiapani . . . or is it Miss?
MANGIAPANI:	Mrs., but I'm a widow. Mr. Mangiapani passed on just last year.
GOLDEN:	I'm sorry. Mrs. Mangiapani, you saw Richie DeLuca run past you on the night of the murder, correct?
MANGIAPANI:	Yes.
GOLDEN:	Did he bump into you? Knock you down?
MANGIAPANI:	No, he ran by me, maybe four, five feet away.
GOLDEN:	Did he have a pistol?
MANGIAPANI:	Yes.
GOLDEN:	You're sure?
MANGIAPANI:	Yes.
GOLDEN:	Absolutely?
MANGIAPANI:	Yes.
GOLDEN:	No doubt?
MANGIAPANI:	I could see it clear as day. Well, you know, even though it was at night, the front was pretty well lit up by the bar's neon sign and the bagel shop next door.
GOLDEN:	So you saw everything clearly?
MANGIAPANI:	Yes.
GOLDEN:	What kind of pants was he wearing?
MANGIAPANI:	Well, I don't know . . . dark, maybe black . . . or jeans. You know, all these young people wear are jeans . . . we used to call them dungarees.
GOLDEN:	You're sure?
MANGIAPANI:	Well, it all happened so fast . . . I mean, I . . .
GOLDEN:	And the shirt?

MANGIAPANI:	Yellow? Or white, maybe?
GOLDEN:	Mrs. Mangiapani, this isn't a quiz show.
MANGIAPANI:	White. I'm sure it was a white T-shirt.

Golden offered as evidence the clothes Richie had been wearing the night of the murder. The sight of them tightened Richie's shoulder blades into a knot. Though stained nearly black by the blood that had soaked them after Richie had been shot, it was clear that the slacks were originally a medium gray, and the Italian knit shirt a burgundy and gray stripe.

GOLDEN:	Mrs. Mangiapani, did you see Richard DeLuca actually fire bullets into the car where Christine Augusta sat?
MANGIAPANI:	No. I turned around after I heard the shots.
GOLDEN:	So you couldn't be sure that Mr. DeLuca didn't run because he was frightened by the shots? That he had just happened to be in the wrong place at the wrong time, and ran for his life?
MANGIAPANI:	Well, I told you, it all happened so fast.
GOLDEN:	But you're sure it was a pistol Mr. DeLuca had in his hand?
MANGIAPANI:	Yes, I'm sure.
GOLDEN:	Not a bagel? Or a camera? Or a shoe?
MANGIAPANI:	I know a gun when I see one.
GOLDEN:	Just like you know colors. Thank you. No further questions.

On redirect examination, Roland Flowers had Mrs. Mangiapani say that once she saw the pistol in Richard DeLuca's hand, that had been all she focused on, understandably making her recollection of the colors of his clothes somewhat foggy.

Four more neighborhood witnesses were brought to the stand, mostly to repeat testimony that Mrs. Mangiapani had already given. All of them identified Richie as having run from the scene. Two said they saw a pistol. Two said they weren't sure.

Throughout the questioning, Richie concentrated on watching the faces of the jurors. The worst part was Flowers showing blown-up photographs of the murder scene. Each time they saw them, the faces of the jurors twisted, as they cringed from the sight of the Corvette with its windows blown out and Chrissy lying with her bloody head against the auto's dashboard. Earlier close-ups of Chrissy's body had made the jury cringe, their faces appearing ready to convict. The constant tension and anticipation of every word and nuance made Richie feel like he'd been beaten up.

By the time they had gone through the witnesses and argued points with the jury excused, it was past noon. Judge Jacobson recessed the trial for one hour, sending Richie back to the bullpen in the rear of the courtroom for another pair of bologna sandwiches and a cup of Kool-Aid.

The afternoon session was for pros, whom they'd had some difficulty in scheduling because of their availability. Detectives who arrived on the scene of the crime testified, having little to say about Richie other than finding him shot and damaged from a car having run over his hand. More photos of Chrissy. More times the jury looked as though it could kill.

Fuck me, Richie repeatedly thought. I ain't got a Chinaman's chance here. He scraped the skin off his lip with his teeth; his foot wiggled frantically beneath the table. He scribbled RIPs on tombstone drawings he made for himself.

One detective testified that the shots that killed Chrissy had come from the passenger side, slightly to the rear of the front seat. He described how many shots had hit Chrissy in the back of the head, even down to the detail about her eye bursting onto the dashboard.

Tears welled in Richie's eyes as the descriptions continued. He tried to wipe the corners without letting anyone see, but he caught the eye of a woman on the jury, who seemed to smile. Was it a smile of understanding? he wondered. Or a smile of vindictive righteousness for what she would do in finding him guilty? Was it a smile at all?

The detective went on to testify about the bullets that hit Georgie the Hammer as he'd emerged from the bar and grill.

Yes, they had come from the same gun as the one that killed Christina Augusta. He presented a ballistic report, which was entered into evidence as "Exhibit H."

Ira Golden asked perfunctory questions of the officer, but made no points and enlightened no one. The only good thing Richie saw in his questioning was that it was brief.

Richie went back to the jail on Atlantic Avenue that night wondering how he would stand having to spend the rest of his life in prison.

The last witness for the prosecution was Peter Tsakalis, the off-duty patrolman who had come upon the scene and shot Richie as he escaped. Tsakalis had since been promoted to detective, and looked heavier than when Richie had last seen him. The detective had also grown a beard, which Richie guessed was for undercover work.

Under Roland Flowers's questioning, Detective Tsakalis testified that he had been off duty that night and driving on McDonald Avenue, approaching Avenue X, when he heard what had appeared to be gunshots coming from the east side of Avenue X. He swung his vehicle onto Avenue X and came upon the scene of the shooting. When he jumped out of his car, he said, he saw two men, Richard DeLuca and a dark-haired male, near the Corvette, with what appeared to be pistols in their hands. When both men took off in opposite directions, he made the choice to follow the one that had turned out to be the defendant, DeLuca.

As the chase progressed, Detective Tsakalis testified, he had been looking for an opportunity to fire at the escaping suspect, DeLuca, but there were too many people on the street. It had been only when DeLuca ran out into the gutter, seeming to chase a slowly moving brown Buick, that he was able to fire. Tsakalis described how he fired multiple shots from left to right, cutting down the defendant with two of them, then how the rear wheels of the Buick ran over the defendant's hand as he fell to the ground. The other suspect, he said, had escaped. Tsakalis went on to say that when he came upon the injured DeLuca, he found no pistol anywhere in the area.

For what seemed an eternity to Richie, Tsakalis testified

about the incident, using the name DeLuca repeatedly, each time sending another nail into Richie's heart.

Finally, Flowers turned the witness over to Ira J. Golden.

GOLDEN: Detective Tsakalis, when you came upon the scene of the crime, where was Mr. DeLuca standing?

TSAKALIS: He wasn't standing. He was moving.

GOLDEN: But where was it that you first saw him? Was he on the sidewalk? Maybe hidden by the black Corvette?

TSAKALIS: He was in the gutter . . . the street.

GOLDEN: Doing what?

TSAKALIS: He looked straight at me, then ran back to the sidewalk.

GOLDEN: You say he went "back" to the sidewalk. Did you ever see him on the sidewalk?

TSAKALIS: After?

GOLDEN: No, before.

TSAKALIS: Well, I may not have—

GOLDEN: This requires a yes or no, Detective.

TSAKALIS: Well, no . . . I can't really say I saw him on the sidewalk.

GOLDEN: So, then, Detective, Mr. DeLuca may very well have never been on the sidewalk. Is that true?

Roland Flowers objected, on the grounds that it called for speculation, but Judge Jacobson overruled him.

GOLDEN: Well, Detective?

TSAKALIS: No.

GOLDEN: No, what?

TSAKALIS: No, I have no way of knowing where he was before I arrived.

GOLDEN: So, then, your statement that he ran "back" to the sidewalk was in error.

FLOWERS: Objection!

JUDGE: Overruled. He has stated that it was an error by admitting he had no knowledge. Continue.

GOLDEN: So, then, Detective, isn't it a fact that if Mr. DeLuca had never been on the sidewalk, he could not have possibly shot the victim, Ms. Augusta?

FLOWERS: Objection!

JUDGE: You're pushing it, Mr. Golden. Sustained.

GOLDEN: No further questions.

To Richie, the point made had been a small one. Sure, he knew he had never been on the sidewalk, or shot Chrissy, but he wouldn't be testifying.

Not that he wouldn't have liked to have stood up and screamed his innocence for the entire world to hear. To do that, however, would open too many areas that could hurt him. One would be his alleged association with organized crime figures. The other would be about the identity of the man who actually had shot Christina Augusta—Little Vinnie Calabra. No way he could be a stool pigeon, Richie thought. And no way he could defend himself on the stand by claiming he didn't know. He didn't feel nearly smart enough to try that one.

For the defense's case, Golden submitted a statement he'd obtained from Georgie the Hammer before his death, saying that he knew Richie DeLuca, and that the man who had shot him the night of Chrissy's murder, as he ran out of the bar, was not Richie.

After a lengthy discussion between the judge and two lawyers in the judge's chambers, the statement was left out. Richie burned, knowing that that paper could mean the difference between his getting convicted or not. Shit, he thought; everything could be that difference.

Golden then said he had only one witness to call: the homicide detective who had been in charge of the case, and who had already testified for the prosecution. Detective Albert Grimes had been made aware of his required presence, and was available to take the stand again.

GOLDEN: Detective Grimes, we already know your position on this case, as chief investigating officer, and we're aware of the testimony you gave earlier, for the prosecution. I'm

not going to go over any part of that testimony. I just have two new questions for
you.

GRIMES: No problem.

GOLDEN: Good. Now, then, Detective Grimes, in
looking over all the reports, and evidence,
and what we sometimes call *mishagoss,* I
find no copy of a paraffin test.

GRIMES: What?

GOLDEN: A paraffin test. You know what that is.

GRIMES: Yeah, sure.

Ira Golden made a big show of shuffling through discovery material given to him by the prosecution.

GOLDEN: Well, then, just point me in the direction to
find it.

Detective Grimes shifted uncomfortably in his seat.
Golden waited, saying nothing. He looked toward the jury,
gave a slight shrug, then continued.

GOLDEN: Detective Grimes, would you please explain
to the jury, for me, what a paraffin test is.

GRIMES: A paraffin test is done on a suspect who is
believed to have recently fired a gun.

GOLDEN: And how is that accomplished?

GRIMES: A soft wax cast of the suspect's fingers are
made, which is later tested with chemicals
to detect traces of cordite and nitro on the
fingers.

Ira Golden moved near Detective Grimes. He leaned
against the wood railing alongside the witness seat and
spoke in the same casual manner, acting as though he were
just spinning wheels, asking questions to justify his fee.

GOLDEN: And, tell me, where is the paraffin test done
on Richard DeLuca?

GRIMES: I, er, uh . . . there is none.

GOLDEN: (mugging for the jury) Did you say there is none?

GRIMES: Yes.

GOLDEN: Would you please explain, Detective Grimes, why on a Murder-One case, where the defendant can go away for the rest of his life—

FLOWERS: Objection!

JUDGE: Sustained.

GOLDEN: . . . Why, on a Murder-One case, where there was no gun found, that a paraffin test wasn't done? Just to make sure that the suspect in custody had at least fired a weapon?

GRIMES: (stammering) The suspect was badly wounded at the time.

GOLDEN: Were his fingers somewhere else?

GRIMES: No, it's just that between the confusion and getting him to a hospital, it kind of got overlooked.

GOLDEN: Kind of got overlooked?

Ira J. Golden took a long pause, during which he strolled over to the jury box. When he spoke again, he bellowed.

GOLDEN: Let me ask you this, Detective Grimes. If you had done a paraffin test, and, for argument's sake, you found no traces of cordite or nitro, could you have charged Mr. DeLuca with murder?

GRIMES: No. We probably would have—

GOLDEN: I didn't ask what strategy you might have used to lock up any suspect, to look good—

FLOWERS: Objection!

JUDGE: Sustained.

GOLDEN: All I asked, Detective Grimes, is whether or not you could have charged Richard DeLuca with the charge he is being held on today, if he had tested negative in a paraffin test. Yes or no?

GRIMES: No.

Golden waited for the answer to sink in to the jurors' minds, then walked toward the jury box. Standing near the jurors, he bellowed to Detective Grimes.

GOLDEN: My second question, now, Detective, is if you had not been able to arrest Mr. DeLuca, how would you have handled his being shot by Officer Tsakalis?

Detective Grimes wiggled in his seat, obviously aware he'd been hooked.

GRIMES: How do you mean, "handled"?

GOLDEN: Well, would you have given him a medal?

FLOWERS: Objection!

JUDGE: Sustained.

GOLDEN: Would you have arrested Officer Tsakalis, for shooting an innocent bystander?

FLOWERS: Objection!

JUDGE: Overruled. I'll permit that as a legitimate question, as to procedure.

GOLDEN: Well, Detective Grimes, would you have arrested Detective Tsakalis?

GRIMES: No.

GOLDEN: Would you have given him a departmental hearing?

GRIMES: I wouldn't have . . . I mean, not me personally, but yes, he would have been given a hearing.

GOLDEN: And, if it were determined that he had acted, let's say, to be kind, hastily, would he have been given some type of punishment?

GRIMES: Yes.

GOLDEN: Such as?

GRIMES: I couldn't speculate.

GOLDEN: Can't, or won't?

FLOWERS: Objection!

JUDGE: Sustained.

GOLDEN: But it is fair to say, is it not, that Richard

DeLuca's being charged with the murder of Christina Augusta eliminated that problem for Officer Tsakalis?

GRIMES: I guess so.

GOLDEN: No further questions.

Richie felt jubilant for the first time. He wanted to jump up and hug Golden. If there was an issue that clouded the certainty of his guilt, it was this. Now all he needed was for the jury to feel the same way.

On his cross-examination, Roland V. Flowers had Detective Grimes state that the same way Richard DeLuca could have tested negative on the paraffin, he very well might have tested positive; that it was just an error committed in the heat of battle, and that no result at all could be read into the State's failure to submit the defendant to the test.

Summations were brilliant on both sides.

Roland V. Flowers scared the shit out of Richie when he spoke, hitting emotional highs on each salient point that dramatically contrasted with his normal droning way of speaking. He was almost fanatical in his description of how Chrissy died, of the chase Detective Tsakalis made, of the witnesses who all identified the defendant as being there and having a gun. At the end of his speech, Richie once more felt as though he would have convicted himself if he had a vote.

Ira J. Golden countered with one point that he hammered home repeatedly:

Reasonable doubt . . .

Reasonable doubt . . .

Reasonable doubt.

There was no burden on the defendant, Richard DeLuca, to prove his innocence, Ira Golden restated, and that no inference should be drawn from the fact that he did not take the stand in his own defense. That was his right, to exercise as he saw fit.

Golden also reminded the jury of every point he'd made with all the witnesses: that no one had seen Richie DeLuca fire a pistol; that no one had seen Richie DeLuca on the side of the car that the shots had been fired from; that the witnesses who claimed he had a gun couldn't identify other things about him, like his clothing; that he could just as easily have been someone in the wrong place at the wrong time who panicked and ran. Above all, he drove home the point that no paraffin test was given to determine if Richie DeLuca had indeed fired a gun at all that night. He submitted to the jury that the test may have purposely been omitted, because of fear that if it were negative, they could not arrest Richie DeLuca for the murder and solve their case in one night.

"Not only that," Golden shouted, "but without Richard DeLuca arrested as a murderer, one of the department's own officers, Peter Tsakalis, would have been brought up on charges before a review board. That is exactly why there is no paraffin test . . . it is what you *did not* get to see."

Golden lowered his tone as he implored the jury, "Each of you, just imagine this: you have just witnessed a shooting, only a few feet from you . . . the gunfire, the screams, the shattered glass . . . so you start to run—"

When Golden suddenly paused, the courtroom was as silent as any place Richie had ever been.

Ira J. Golden looked from juror to juror, then said, "And you see a guy pointing a gun at you! What do you do?" he shouted. "Stand there and say, 'Hi, how are you? *Who* are you?' No. If you have any sense at all, you get the hell out of there as fast as you can."

Golden pointed at Richie. ". . . And Richard DeLuca tried to get out of there as fast as he could. Only he got shot, and run over by a passing automobile . . . and arrested. Why? Because the good-old-boy network in the police department needed someone to take one of their own off the hook. 'John Q. Citizen . . . *unarmed* John Q. Citizen, got shot by one of ours. What do we do?'" Golden said in a raised voice. ". . . Arrest him!" That, he said, solved all their problems.

But in the end, taking all they'd seen and heard and all they hadn't seen or heard into account, Ira Golden said, it boiled down to one thing, and one thing only: reasonable doubt.

Roland Flowers, in his rebuttal, said, "This suggestion of my colleague's, of why no paraffin test was done on Mr. DeLuca, is preposterous. To think that the police department of the great city of New York would arrest an innocent bystander to cover up for an officer, who was, in reality, carrying out his duty above and beyond the call, is not only ludicrous, but an insult to the very force that protects and serves all New Yorkers, including yourselves, and to all of us who are part of the criminal justice system."

He said the omission of residue testing was an oversight caused by the confusion of the night, and when viewing the entire picture of Richard DeLuca's actions during that period, and the resulting murder of Chrissy Augusta, that any reasonable person would assume he was guilty, and convict.

As a final reminder to the jury, Roland Flowers flashed one of the photographs previously admitted as evidence, of the mutilated corpse of Christina Augusta.

"For this lovely child, whose life and beauty was so brutally cut short," Flowers said. ". . . For Christina Augusta, there is no doubt, reasonable or otherwise. She is dead."

They roused Richie from a troubled but deep sleep on a metal slab in the bullpen. He felt crippled as he tried to stand, then unrolled the suit jacket he'd used for a pillow and put it on. He staggered out of the cell, wiping the drool of a dead sleep from the corner of his mouth. This was the way he was to face the future of his entire life, he thought, with some black amusement.

Inside the courtroom he sat next to Ira J. Golden, whose stony expression gave him little hope. It gave Richie a small bit of comfort to see that Assistant District Attorney Roland V. Flowers seemed no more upbeat in his mood than Golden. And, when Judge Jacobson entered, her expression was just as solemn. Richie's heart beat in his throat.

The jury filed in, looking like they'd spent the last three and a half hours thinking of ways to torture the killer of Christina Augusta. Richie's palms became slippery and wet, and his foot shook at a rapid pace.

"Jury Foreman, have you reached a verdict in the case of the People of the State of New York versus Richard Anthony DeLuca?"

"We have, Your Honor."

"May I have that written verdict?"

The jury foreman, a squat man in an ugly brown plaid

sport jacket, handed the ballot results to the court clerk, who, in turn, handed it to the judge.

The judge then said, "Will the defendant please rise."

Richie stood, his heart beating more loudly and rapidly.

"Would you now read your verdict out loud."

The jury foreman then said, "We, the jury, find the defendant . . ."

Each word seemed like an eternity.

". . . Richard Anthony DeLuca . . ."

God, please help me . . . don't let me lose the rest of my life.

". . . not guilty."

Ira J. Golden let out a whooping cry and jumped into the air. The rest of the courtroom burst into a loud cacophony of voices, each fighting to be heard over others.

Richie DeLuca just collapsed in his seat, the emotional release bringing a flood of tears down over his cheeks. Golden's assistant and secretary both came to Richie to congratulate him, while Golden himself rushed over to speak to the jurors. When he returned, Golden told Richie that the first vote had been eleven to one for acquittal, but that the jurors had to spend the balance of the time swinging the one vote their way.

"Want to know who wanted to fry you if they could?"

"Who cares?"

"Well, I'll tell you anyway," Golden said with a broad smile. "The West Indian."

After completing paperwork formalities that were required by the court, Richie was released inside the Supreme Court building.

Ira J. Golden grabbed him by the arm and led him down a staircase to a rear door. By the door, two men waited in the shadows.

"What the fuck?" Richie said, turning to Golden, who rapidly backed away. Was this his choice all along? To be convicted or die?

Suddenly, one of the men stepped forward into the light.

"Sonofabitch!" Richie shouted, and jumped on him. "Mickey Boy, you fuck! You scared the piss out of me!"

Both men hugged and cried over each other; brothers in victory at the end of a long and painful road.

"Go on," Mickey Boy said. "I want you to get out of here now." He pointed to the other man. "Nicolo Fonte, here, is the only guy I trust to get you to someplace where nobody'll bother you."

"Nobody in the goddamn world could bother me now!" Richie said. "Not after what I've been through. Everything else is bullshit!"

"No it's not," Mickey Boy solemnly replied. "There's press, more cops, and who knows what else. Just take a vacation. You deserve it." He pointed to Fonte. "He's got tickets, I don't even know to where, and don't wanna know to where. He'll see you're hooked up with somebody there who'll take care of whatever you need, moneywise, broads, whatever."

"How long I gotta stay away?"

"At least three or four weeks," Mickey Boy said. "At least till I see where everything falls after the verdict. Now go on, get the fuck out of here, and have a good time."

Richie left the court building excited, but also fearful that he was being set up to be murdered.

59

June 25: Bayside, Queens

MICKEY BOY DREW SMALL RECTANGLES ON THE PINK LINEN tablecloth. In one he printed Georgie the Hammer's initials.

Buster's went into another.

Patsy Luciano's into a third.

Then Frankie Green Eyes's and Butch Scicli's.

He tried to rearrange them by redrawing the boxes in common groups:

Buster and Patsy were old-line wiseguys from his crew, and went one over the other.

He put Frankie Green Eyes, a young made guy in the Calabra Family, alone, then made a new group made up of all three of the wiseguys.

Butch Scicli, an associate of his crew, and a nephew of Buster's, went by himself.

He did another grouping, with all four men, as they had all been part of his family.

Then came Georgie the Hammer. Had nothing to do with the Calabra Family. Bothered with junk. Had been shot once before, when Chrissy Augusta had been killed. If he removed Georgie's name, everything else had at least a small link. Maybe Georgie had nothing to do with the others, and was just throwing him off track? he wondered.

"I do not believe da Vinci began this way," Nicolo Fonte said. "Not even Picasso."

"I'm sorry," Mickey Boy said, covering up his doodling with a napkin. He had purposely chosen Café on the Green for his dinner with Nicolo Fonte because it represented the legitimate goals he had undertaken. After all, both cousins' meetings had taken place upstairs. "I just got these things on my mind. Ever have something that you think you know, but you don't know?"

"I have lived most of my life that way."

"No, I mean, like you know it somewhere down deep, but you can't bring it up to the front of your brain? That you got the answer to something, but you can't put your finger on it?"

"It happens all the time," Fonte replied. "I just do not remember it happening as frequently when I was a younger man."

"Great," Mickey Boy said. "That means it's gonna get worse?"

"Life is not easy."

Nicolo Fonte suggested that they not discuss problems during dinner. "Food is digested much more easily when the stomach is not twisted with tension."

Mickey Boy agreed, but remained wound up anyway. Fonte was not responsible for at least four people who had been killed, Mickey Boy thought. *He* was.

Butch Scicli bothered him most. Why kill some failed

wannabe living in the boondocks? Because he'd been Buster's nephew? Why Buster at all? If the younger captains of his were telling the truth, Mickey Boy reasoned while swallowing a variety of macaroni shapes and mixed seafood, they had never whacked out Buster. Forget Patsy Luciano, he told himself through sips of Orvieto. Patsy had just been a reaction. No, Frankie Green Eyes had been the reaction. Then what was the link between Buster and Patsy?

After dinner, over fresh berries and zabaglione, Mickey Boy shifted mental gears, to discuss his proposed plan for pasta houses with Fonte.

"Do you want the truth?" Fonte asked.

"Of course," Mickey Boy replied, not sure he really did.

"Right now is not the time for you to attempt this project. And, if I am totally honest, I would suggest that there may never be a proper time."

"No, I can't believe that."

"Then do not."

"These guys ain't as bad as they seem," Mickey Boy said. "They just need somebody to show them the way."

Fonte asked, "Do you go to the theater often?"

"Only when my wife makes me. Otherwise, I ain't got time to do anything often."

"Have you ever seen *Fiddler on the Roof?*"

"No."

"In that play," Fonte said, "they ask Tevye how he sits on a pitched roof. His answer is, tradition."

"I don't understand."

"What is your tradition? The tradition of those you would transform into purveyors of pasta?"

Mickey Boy answered that *la cosa nostra*'s roots went back centuries, in Sicily; that they had been freedom fighters, and the only true source of honor and justice for the average Sicilian when their country, as always, was occupied by invaders.

"I am well aware of Sicilian history," Nicolo Fonte said. "But that tradition does not really reach down to you. For example, what was the date the Sicilians rose up to drive the French out, at the ringing of the vesper bells?"

"I don't know."

"March thirtieth, 1282. And what was the name of the French sergeant who precipitated that uprising by murdering a Sicilian bride on her wedding day?"

Mickey Boy sat silently, unable to even begin to form a response.

"Pierre Drouet." Nicolo Fonte stopped to sip his espresso. "Do you see, now? That tradition of Sicilian history, even of the Mafia, does not affect you and your American-born people at all. I would wager that you cannot name two famous mafiosi from Sicily's past. Correct?"

Mickey Boy shrugged.

The tradition the American-born mobsters, Nicolo Fonte went on to explain, went back no further than the early part of the twentieth century.

"Who is the oldest person you know of?" Fonte asked.

"George Burns?"

"Your tradition, of American *la cosa nostra,* as far as you and your people know it, is not as old as George Burns. Is he a tradition?"

What did all that have to do with his pasta houses? Mickey Boy wanted to know.

Fonte said that the American *la cosa nostra* tradition was not one of honor and respect, but one of crime.

"Who is the oldest American *uomo rispettato* . . . man of respect, of your own *borgata,* living or dead, who you remember anything about?" Fonte asked. "Even a name alone will do."

"Lupo the Wolf?"

"What do you know of him, other than that he butchered bodies in a Harlem stable? That the screams of the victims could be heard for blocks?"

"Lucky Luciano? Vito Genovese?" Mickey Boy said, reaching back to find historical mob figures of enormous renown.

"Luciano allowed Meyer Lansky's brother to turn over evidence about Waxey Gordon to the Internal Revenue Service, to get Gordon sent to prison. Luciano made a deal to get himself out of prison, but left his codefendant, Davey Betillo, to serve about thirty years. Luciano went to prison for overseeing a prostitution ring, and in Italy trafficked in narcotics."

Fonte sipped some more, then told Mickey Boy that Vito Genovese had thrown the husband of a girl he loved off a roof, so he could marry her.

"How the fuck you know all that?"

"I read. I remember," Fonte said. "More important is that that is the tradition these people of yours have. This is the tradition they admire and aspire to mold themselves into. You, and the more intelligent of your people, are, and always have been, lost."

Fonte pointed out how Frank Costello had been shot at Genovese's order, and had retired rather than fight back; how Paul Castellano had been killed because he was a lamb trying to control lions.

"If you persist in trying to make the lowest level become what it is not, you too will die."

"But not all these guys are the same," Mickey Boy argued. "Some of them do what they do only because they don't know nothing else."

"And assume you successfully put them in business. What will they do when the other few begin to extort money from them? Will they revert to gangsters and fight? Will they become *pentiti* and seek help from the authorities? Tell me, how will they survive in the face of an attack from those who remain thugs?"

Nicolo Fonte looked down sadly into his cup. "I know. I have experience in dealing with matters like that. When your father, Don Vincenze, ordered me to cast you out into the street, I did not fight back and I did not turn to the authorities for help. I ran away." He looked up at Mickey Boy. "Are you and all your decent people prepared to run away?"

Though Mickey Boy hated to admit it, everything Fonte said had been slowly becoming apparent. He'd thought that perserverance would overcome all odds, but now realized that success, especially where others' lives were concerned, took more than mere human will. At least in this day and age. Despite Nicolo Fonte's assessment of the "good old days" not having been all that good, Mickey Boy still felt that they were a far sight better, at least in the respect that mob bosses' edicts were more strictly adhered to, than the present.

Mickey Boy told Fonte that he would shelve his idea of opening pasta houses for the time being, but would consider it again once he'd straightened out the mess he presently had to deal with in his crew.

In response to Nicolo Fonte's general, polite questions about his problems, Mickey Boy gave Fonte a detailed account of the recent rash of murders within his family. He hated to involve Fonte in mob stuff, but needed a fresh point of view; a sounding board; an objective insight into what answer gnawed at his gut, but remained too elusive to understand.

Fonte moved the napkin Mickey Boy had placed on the table and examined the pattern of rectangles and names.

"Were any of these people involved in business with each other?" Fonte asked.

Not that Mickey Boy knew of. Buster and Patsy, of course, were old-line members of the Calabra Family, and might have done some kind of business, legal or otherwise, with each other in the past. Buster and Butch, he said, were related.

Mickey Boy knew that Butch Scicli had driven the getaway car when Chrissy Augusta had been murdered, but did not want to mention that at all to Nicolo Fonte. He did tell him, however, that Georgie the Hammer had been shot the night that Chrissy had been killed.

Suddenly the connection dawned on Mickey Boy. Georgie and Butch had in some way been tied to Chrissy's death. Buster, he knew, had sent the order down to kill Skinny Malone, which turned into the mistaken shooting of Chrissy. All three could be tied to that one incident. Patsy Luciano? Maybe, in some way, but he couldn't be sure. Frankie Green Eyes? Same thing. The only ones who could have possibly answered those questions, Don Vincenze and Buster, were now dead.

Mickey Boy stared at the names he'd written as if in a dream. His face felt swollen and throbbing. His hands felt numb. His heart thumped loudly.

When Mickey Boy finally moved his lips, ever so slightly, only two words came through: Joe Augusta.

60

June 30: Hell's Kitchen, Manhattan

SCREAMING, JOE AUGUSTA GRABBED LITTLE VINNIE BY THE lapels. "I can't keep waiting! Don't you understand?" he shouted, lifting Little Vinnie off his feet.

"No, please," Little Vinnie said, not wanting to incite Joe any more than he already was. "I understand, and I'll help," he added. "Just let me go. I'm on your side, remember?"

Joe Augusta shoved Little Vinnie onto the motel's bed, then turned away and stepped to the dresser. He leaned forward on his knuckles, resting the top of his head against the mirror.

"Don't you understand?" Joe moaned. "I can't keep this up forever. I gotta get it done and over with. There's only so much I can take."

Fuck this maniac, Little Vinnie thought. If not for the fact that Joe Augusta was the perfect pawn for his plot to get rid of Mickey Boy, Little Vinnie would have stayed miles away from him.

Fuckin' maniac.

Sometimes, though, Joe Augusta was bearable. In those moments he reverted to his old self, which was at a higher intelligence level than most street guys. Having gone to college, Joe would make sense about topics from world hunger, to the social ramifications of television programming, to theories of life on other planets.

If only Joe would kill Mickey Boy, then himself, Little Vinnie thought, all his problems would be over at once. Except that if Joe had decided to murder one offspring of Don Vincenze's, as some sort of revenge against the blood-

275

line, he, Little Vinnie, might also be included as a victim. No way, José, he'd told himself.

But now things had changed. With Richie DeLuca's court victory a few days ago, Joe had become absolutely driven.

First, they'd missed Richie when he'd left the courthouse that night. Bastard must have sneaked out a back way while they waited in the front.

Then Joe had dragged Little Vinnie out for nearly seventy-two hours straight, trying to find some clue of where Richie might be. They'd parked up the hill from Mickey Boy's house at various times, looking in the windows with high-powered binoculars. All they'd seen was Mickey Boy in the morning, then Laurel by herself or with bodyguards during the day. Freddie Falcone had shown up; also some fat guy with a moustache.

Joe had gotten disgusted.

Little Vinnie had had a good time watching Laurel.

They'd followed Mickey Boy too, hoping he would hook up with Richie somewhere. But nothing. Once again, Freddie Falcone and the tubby old guy were always around.

Little Vinnie had wanted to call DoDo, maybe have him find out where Richie could be located, but he thought about it too long, wondering whether or not he wanted the greaser to know he had a murderous tool like Joe at his disposal. When Mickey Boy finally did get his due, Little Vinnie wanted DoDo to be able to report that he, Little Vinnie, had done it.

During that time, Joe had become disgusted, and made a phone call to someone who seemed to be helping him here in the city. Had to be another nut job, Little Vinnie thought, but the contact had come up with information on the spot: Richie had left town, having been dispatched secretly by Mickey Boy.

Where?

No one knew.

For how long?

No one knew.

Now Joe seemed to be really going off the deep end, needing some kind of movement toward his goal, or he might turn into one of those guys who just started killing everyone in sight, Little Vinnie thought. Being the closest one to Joe, Little Vinnie figured he'd better defuse him quickly or become his next victim.

"Listen," Little Vinnie said. "Just relax—"

"Don't tell me to relax!"

"No, no, I just mean that I got an idea, an' I wanna see what I could do."

"What is it?"

"I don't wanna say, unless I could do it. You know, like jinx it."

Joe glared at him.

"All I need is a little time, an' I'll try to get Richie for you. Just give me a little time."

"How much time?"

"I don't know. Nine, ten days . . ." When Little Vinnie saw Joe's features harden, he said, "Okay, a week; that's all. Just give me a week."

"Half that." Joe checked an automatic, releasing a bullet into the chamber, then went to the dresser, wrote the exact time on a pad, then stuck the top sheet into the mirror. "Seventy-two hours," he said. "I can't stand no more."

61

July 3: Todt Hill, Staten Island

BRILLIANT SUNSHINE WASHED AND WARMED LAUREL'S SKIN. SHE soaked up the rays, conscious of the fact that her midriff and legs could have used a little more color before she decided to wear her new shorts and halter set. She felt free, though, and as if she were blossoming in the sun's glow. If anyone didn't like the shade of her stomach and legs, they didn't have to look.

Laurel stepped lively, tossed her bag into the Mercedes, then slid in quickly, before anyone showed up to tell her she couldn't go anywhere unescorted. Despite her haste to get off for a bit of free time, she paused to look at herself in the visor's mirror, pushing away permed strands of golden brown hair that had fallen out of the knot she'd piled on her head. She tugged at the curly tendrils that framed her face, adjusted the yellow hair ribbon that coordinated with her flowery outfit, then pulled out of the driveway.

"Alone at last," she mumbled as she headed down the hill. Everything about the day seemed enhanced by her freedom. Normally lush lawns in that exclusive residential area took on a more verdant beauty, the sky looked more blue, children with their parents more alive.

A quiet excitement, bordering on the sexual, filled Laurel. She unconsciously squeezed her bare thighs together, indulging herself in the sensations that shot from her crotch to her navel. How silly, she thought, for a grown woman to be so affected by a simple trip from the house to a mall. It saddened her briefly to realize how caged she really was, but she shook it off to allow the full pleasure of the day to permeate her.

Things would improve soon, Laurel told herself, entering Richmond Road. Richie winning his trial had been like a sign that all things gloomy would indeed brighten. She was also encouraged by Mickey's dogged determination to get his people into legitimate business, no matter how resistant to change some of them were.

Though she didn't like the whole idea of mobs and mob families—especially when they interfered with her own family's existence—Laurel admired her husband for his willingness to sacrifice of himself for the obligation he felt to others. My God, he spent enough evenings out lately, away from her and Hope, meeting with Nicolo Fonte, he said, to get the pasta houses off to a fast start. It was as though his burden was a demanding mistress, tugging him away from a serene life to drain him of his energy. Leave early in the morning; fall into bed exhausted in the middle of the night. Some routine for a young man—and his wife.

Laurel wondered when he would have another cousins' meeting at Café on the Green, to go over whatever progress they'd made. Those two get-togethers were the most socializing she did, and she looked forward to them. She made a mental note to call her cousin Tammy and see what was going on.

Laurel fumbled with the list she'd compiled of stuff she still needed for the Fourth of July celebration they planned. Connie would be down from Boston to help with the cooking—and to take over some of the babysitting chores from Laurel's mother, Anne, who was watching Hope at that moment and overseeing the new Polish cleaning girl's first day. Skimming over the list of food items they still needed for the planned party for almost three dozen, Laurel thanked God one more time—for mothers in general.

Mushrooms for the shish kebab; Fourth of July napkins and paper dishes; fifteen pounds of jumbo shrimp; an extra garbage pail. Laurel made a mental note to also get some vitamin E, for those who would inevitably burn themselves while setting off the storeload of fireworks Mickey Boy had stashed in the garage. But first, she thought, a new bathing suit and maybe a new negligee, stark and sexy. Better yet, she'd browse the Barnes & Noble, see if any new sex manuals had come in. Some author had to have the key to waking up Mickey Boy.

She smiled, acknowledging and understanding why girls called their husbands their "old men." Especially her old man, she thought, as old-fashioned as her grandmother's underwear. Mickey Boy just couldn't seem to realize that sexual activity was an intimate sharing of something special between partners; fun that excluded the rest of the world. To him, sex was a necessary release of pressure, or better yet, like the last couple of weeks, an effort to make another baby.

Laurel pulled off the main drag and into the parking lot of the huge Staten Island Mall. She parked a few rows away from the building's entrance, set the Club on her steering wheel, flicked on the alarm, and left the Mercedes, determined to find a book or video to stimulate her sex life with her husband; there had to be some button of his that could be pushed to make him experiment and have more fun in bed. The way it was now, he considered anything other than the missionary position daring.

As Laurel reached the next open row between parked cars,

a beat-up gray car stopped in front of her, blocking her way, and a long-legged brunette in hot pants and a silk blouse got out.

Goddamn bitch, Laurel thought. She stopped, waiting for the car to move, but instead the girl stepped toward her, smiling, and punched her in the stomach.

62

July 3: Upper East Side, Manhattan

MICKEY BOY FASTENED HIS BELT, THEN CHECKED HIMSELF IN THE mirror. No marks—bites, hickies, lipstick. Great.

He turned, walked to the bed, and sat down next to Rosalie, who remained snuggled under the sheets.

"Tired?" he asked, brushing away fallen black wisps from her forehead.

"Mmmm."

"Need anything, before I go?" The answer, of course, would be no. One of the things he liked most about Rosalie was that she was independent, working in her father's restaurant, and wanted nothing from him other than time and affection. His time, of course, being married, was limited. His affection, though, was endless.

"What are you doing for the Fourth?" he asked.

"Just hanging around at home. Watch the fireworks at night."

"You want more fireworks? Anything?"

Rosalie pulled him to her and kissed him on the lips. "I'm fine, really," she said. "You know, I almost wish I was your daughter."

"Making fun of my age?"

Rosalie ran a finger over his face, stopping by the sides of his eyes. The sheet dropped, exposing her breasts. "Yes," she said. "Look, wrinkles."

While Mickey Boy bent and kissed first one nipple, then the other, Rosalie reached down and grabbed his erection. "Not too old to get it up, though," she said.

Mickey Boy moved to peck her on the face. "Not yet, anyway," he said, then stood up. "Gotta go."

"So, I guess I won't see you tomorrow?" Rosalie asked, not accusingly, just matter-of-factly.

"No," he replied. "Gotta do the right thing. See you the day after. Freddie'll call and tell you where."

"Meenkya, I feel like I'm driving for an escort service," Freddie said when Mickey Boy entered his Mercedes.

"Now you wanna call me a whore?"

"No, whoremaster. In fact, I think we should change your name to D'Artagnon L'Amour."

"C'mon, I ain't that bad," Mickey Boy said. "Guys I know got dozens. I just got this one I gotta get out of my system, then I'll be like an old man again. Besides, who the fuck is that guy, L'Amour?"

They toyed some more, bantering and chiding each other before getting down to business. Freddie reported that he'd met again with Joe Bus and Philly Red.

"I'm getting tired of that goddamn cave they like to meet at. Between the dust and the noise, I'm coughing and banging my ears for an hour after I leave. And those dim lights," he went on. "You gotta be a fuckin' bat to see anything down there."

After airing his list of complaints, Freddie reported that the younger faction's mood had changed after he'd blamed the murders on Joe Augusta.

"Whether he did it or not don't even matter," Freddie said. "Blaming him was brilliant. Gave these guys the excuse to throw down their guns an' save face at the same time."

"It's no joke," Mickey Boy said. "Believe me, Joe A.'s gotta be around, and whacking people like he's got a license."

Freddie confessed that Mickey Boy's conclusion sounded

a bit farfetched, but certainly possible. "It's so hard for me to imagine how I would react if something woulda happened to a kid of mine, like happened to him . . . that is, if I ever had any kids."

"Well, I got a kid," Mickey Boy said, "and if anything ever happened to Hope, God forbid, man, I'd want to kill anybody involved with my bare hands."

He remembered the feeling in the delivery room, at the moment Hope was about ready to come out. Worry had filled him; questions about whether his child would be born all right, if at all. He'd glared at the doctor, ready to pounce on him and beat him half to death if he came up with a child that didn't cry. Later, when he told Laurel how he'd felt, she called it irrational. Of course she was right, he answered, but that hadn't changed the animalistic way he'd felt. Seeing people he loved get hurt automatically opened his nose and filled his eyes with blood.

"To tell you the truth," Freddie replied, "I wish you're right, an' it is Joe. At least then we'll know what we're dealing with. 'Cause I'll tell you," he continued, "there's absolutely no defense for treachery and deceit."

They entered the building where Bobby Rimini had his office cleaning company, on Woodhaven Boulevard, through a gated parking area. After being admitted through the gate by a voice that questioned their identity over an intercom, they had to be buzzed into the building, go through a metal detector, and sign in. The security guard directed them to the elevator that would take them to suite 303.

Bobby Rimini greeted Mickey Boy and Freddie in the front office, hugging and kissing them, then introducing them to his secretary and two men Mickey Boy had seen around but paid little attention to. As a captain, Mickey Boy thought, Bobby should have had made men around him, but with the problem going on between factions, probably felt safer with men who were further removed from the politics of mob life. Mickey Boy didn't blame him at all for that, and in fact admired him for using his head.

Bobby led them into the back, to his private office. Done in mauve and dove-gray carpets and sofas, with a marble desk and silver track lighting, it reminded Mickey Boy of something that belonged in a Manhattan penthouse.

"Meenkya," Freddie exclaimed. "This is a fuckin' palace. You're lucky Mickey Boy's old man ain't still around. He woulda taxed you to death."

"Don Vincenze was here many times," Bobby replied. "Want coffee? Espresso? Cappuccino?"

Mickey Boy and Freddie both okayed espresso.

Bobby poured and served while speaking. "Yeah, the old man came here plenty," he repeated. "But I'll tell you, this guy was the greatest. Not a jealous bone in his body. I did the right thing with him, an' he never questioned it. One of the only bosses I ever knew that was happy to see his men earn."

At least someone had something good to say about his father, Mickey Boy thought. Probably only because he was dead, he told himself. He could imagine Bobby cursing Don Vincenze for taking too big a bite of his income when the old man was alive. He then wondered how much Bobby had cut the figure he'd given Don Vincenze when he began kicking it in to a new set of bosses, namely himself and Freddie. It was all he could do to keep from laughing.

Bobby went through an elaborate ceremony of taking anisette toast and pignoli cookies from a cabinet and setting them out on a plate in front of Mickey Boy and Freddie. Now Mickey Boy understood why Bobby weighed in at a good 250 pounds.

Once the cookies were in place, Bobby opened an attaché case on his desk. He lifted an antenna and switched on a couple of knobs, then picked up the open case and walked around the perimeter of the room. Finally satisfied, he shut the case.

"Now we could talk," Bobby said. "Can't be too careful."

Mickey Boy began the conversation, centering on the internal battle that had so far claimed at least three lives. He told Bobby that Philly Red and Joe Bus had sworn up and down that they'd had nothing to do with either Buster's or Patsy Luciano's murder, then he asked, point-blank, if Bobby could make the same claim about the demise of Frankie Green Eyes.

"If you know anything about me at all," Bobby said, "you'll know I have a reputation for being honest. If I fuck up, I say I fucked up, and take my medicine."

"That ain't an answer," Mickey Boy said.

Bobby nodded his head. "Yeah, it came from over here," he said, referring to his older faction of the Calabra Family. "Who, I'd rather not say. But it was done, and there was nothing I coulda done to stop it. Now what?"

Mickey Boy turned to Freddie. "Now what?"

"It's good to hear you didn't have nothing to do with it," Freddie said to Bobby. "It looks like all you guys have been victims, an' we know for sure who's been causing the trouble: Joe Augusta."

Freddie's passing over Bobby's confession startled Mickey Boy at first, but he, as well as Bobby, recovered quickly to go along with it. That move by Freddie had signaled the end of the murder discussion, never to be mentioned again. Mickey Boy's only concern was that Bobby might feel that Freddie was covering up for the younger faction as well, and might seek further revenge. In fact, Mickey Boy wondered if Freddie was doing just that to him too.

Sly old fox, Mickey Boy thought with admiration.

They spent the rest of the time discussing the fine points of setting up a meeting between Bobby Rimini and either Philly Red or Joe Bus. The meeting would be in a public place, and the hatchet would be buried for all time. At least, Mickey Boy thought, until the next beef occurred.

Once outside, Mickey Boy questioned Freddie concerning Bobby's perception of what went on with the younger guys.

"It don't matter whether he believes it or not," Freddie said. "Acting like he believes it gives him a chance to save face; to bow out of a battle he got no stomach for, without losing any honor."

"But what do you believe?" Mickey Boy asked.

Freddie said he was sure that the younger crew had nothing to do with either Buster's or Patsy Luciano's murder. He wasn't, however, certain that Joe Augusta was to blame.

"Maybe with the kid, Georgie, I could see it," Freddie said. "Buster? I don't know; iffy. Buster's nephew, upstate?

Yeah, maybe that too. Patsy? Not in a million years. Frankie Green Eyes? Well, we know who did that one for sure."

Freddie said that he had discussed the problem with Nicolo Fonte, who offered to reach out for some of the foreign mafiosi here. Fonte believed that anything of importance that went on was known by that group, and Freddie said he was inclined to go along with him.

Much as Mickey Boy didn't like the idea of Fonte getting involved in mob business, he agreed.

63

July 3: Chelsea, Manhattan

COMPLETE DARKNESS WAS ALL LAUREL WAS AWARE OF WHEN SHE woke up. So dark, in fact, that at first she actually thought she was dead. It was only after a brief reasoning process that she realized it was a blindfold that had her in a blackened void. Her mouth felt filmy and ugly, her stomach ached where she'd been punched, and she had to pee. When she moved to get up off the bed, she realized her hands were bound above her head. The spot on her arm, where the needle had been shoved in while she'd been held on the floor of the automobile, stung, and her head throbbed where it had banged on the car as the girl who had hit her and an accomplice shoved her in.

Her clothes were still on, but her cork-and-rope wedgies were gone. She wiggled her feet, which were free, to try to find the shoes, but felt only satin bedding. The urge to scream out came to Laurel, but she had the strength only to whimper and sob. Why would anyone do this to her? Why her, God? What had she done besides want a little free time to live?

"Awake, poor thing?" a husky female voice asked. "I thought you'd sleep until you got old, like in one of those movies where they freeze people, then bring them back."

Laurel felt the bed move, as the bearer of the female voice sat down next to her. Still crying, Laurel turned her head and body away from the voice.

"Come on," the female voice said. "You'll be all right. No one's going to hurt you, darling, and you'll be back home again before you know it."

"Why? What do you want?" Laurel sobbed.

"Don't ask me. I'm just doing a friend a favor."

Suddenly unafraid of being hurt, Laurel turned back toward the female voice, shouting, "A favor? You idiot! Do you know who my husband is? He'll have you ground up like sausage meat!"

"Your husband isn't a cop, is he?"

Laurel began to panic. Myriad thoughts ran through her head at the same time. What if they really didn't know who Mickey Boy was, and would kill her out of fear when they found out? What if these were FBI people, who wanted her to admit who he was? What if? What if?

Panic also sounded in the female voice, "Tell me, is he a cop?"

"No," Laurel said. "He's not a cop."

When the female voice kept up, asking who Laurel's husband was, Laurel answered that he was a businessman, who just happened to be a very tough guy. The voice persisted, sounding frightened, but Laurel stuck to her story: Michael was opening a pasta restaurant, one which he hoped to build into a national franchise chain.

"He's not a mafioso, I hope."

Laurel determined that if they had kidnapped her as a random choice, she might have a chance to come out of this alive. She repeated, "No," then offered a large sum of money if they would just let her go.

The female voice replied that she was not the one to talk to. "Listen, honey, I really don't like this whole idea. In the meantime, though, we're both stuck with it. So let's make the best of it. Let me help you be as comfy cozy as possible. Hungry?"

Crying again, Laurel shook her head no.

"Thirsty? That sedative they gave you must have left you with flannel mouth."

Laurel just cried.

Laurel's captor left the bed, then returned and sat down in the same spot. Lifting Laurel's head with one hand, she moved a straw between Laurel's lips. Laurel sucked at the straw, letting ice-cold cola cut through the foul coating in her mouth. She sucked at it until crude slurping noises of an empty container were all that was left.

"I'll get you some more a little later," the female voice said. "Too much gas all at once. Don't want to give you a tummyache."

The voice finally got around to asking Laurel if she had to go to the bathroom, which Laurel confirmed. The bathroom, however, was to be a bedpan, which the female voice fetched and set down next to Laurel.

"I'm going to untie one hand," the captor said. "Please be a good girl and don't give me a hard time."

Afraid to sound unconvincing, Laurel just shook her head. She felt clothed breasts brush against her face as the female captor reached over her to release her left hand's bond.

Dizzy as she sat up, Laurel allowed her captor to help swing her legs off the bed. Needles tingled inside her feet. The girl helped her pull her shorts and panties down, and slid the cold metal bedpan under her. Laurel felt glad she had a blindfold on and didn't have to face the woman who had peeled her down naked. She urinated as if she'd held it for a week, the stream splashing upward in the bedpan to wet her bottom.

"Here," the female voice said when Laurel had finished. She handed Laurel a wad of bathroom tissue.

Embarrassed to have to clean her vagina in front of the girl, even with a blindfold for protection, Laurel wiped herself dry, then tugged her panties and shorts back up.

When her captor bent into her to bind her hand again, Laurel pulled her down and rolled over onto her. She ripped away the blindfold.

Caught off balance, her captor remained entangled with her as Laurel scratched and bit. The brunette who had assaulted Laurel in the parking lot struggled to get up.

Laurel wrapped her leg around the brunette to hold her and pulled at her hair—which came off in her hand.

"Stop that shit, you bitch!" a black man with dreadlocks screamed as he charged into the room. He pulled Laurel off and smacked her full in the face, sending her reeling back on the bed.

Laurel kicked out helplessly as the black man straddled her and tied her free left hand to the bedpost again. Crying hysterically, she spit and cursed while he fastened the blindfold again. He tugged it extra tight, pinching her hair in the knot. She screamed out for help.

Still straddling her, the black man slapped her again. "Shut up, you silly bitch!" he said. "No one can hear you." He began to laugh, then suddenly grabbed one of Laurel's breasts. "Keep it up, and I'll show you how to scream for real." He squeezed the breast hard.

"Hey, enough!" another male voice shouted. "Get off her! I told you before to leave her alone!"

"Man, this motherfuckin' bitch is just making some uproar. Had to shut her motherfuckin' mouth," the black man replied, but got off her anyway.

Laurel sucked in deep breaths between sobs.

"Listen, I'm sorry," the other male voice said, coming close to her. He sat down next to her and stroked her forehead. "You just gotta cooperate, an' I'll see to it that you ain't hurt in any way."

He touched a place on her head that made her jump. "Nasty bump," he said. "If you want, I could put some ice on it."

Laurel snapped her head away to face the other direction.

"Okay," he said, stroking her hair again. "But if you need anything, just tell the girl, an' she'll tell me. If your husband loves you enough, you'll be back in your own bed in no time. I know I'd do anything to get you back."

As the man got off the bed he said, "Give her another shot. Make her rest for a while."

Laurel kicked, screamed, and spit, but the needle jabbed her arm anyway. She continued to struggle even after it was done—until consciousness left her.

64

July 3: Todt Hill, Staten Island

LAUREL?" CONNIE CALLED AS MICKEY BOY ENTERED THE HALL-way of his home. "Laurel, where have you been?"

"No, it's only me," Mickey Boy answered. He checked his watch. It was 8:37 P.M.

Connie came to him, carrying Hope in her arms, and kissed him. "I got in at five-thirty," she said. "Took a cab here from Port Authority, after waiting until after six. I sent Laurel's mother home, and took over watching my baby girl," she continued, kissing and hugging Hope, who cooed back her affection.

It felt good to see his mother there. Mickey Boy wished she would spend time with him and Laurel more often; better yet, move in permanently. Alley and his family did fine in Boston, moving among the upper class and living a typical Cleaver family life. They didn't need her around as much as he did. Besides, he knew that kind of existence couldn't possibly make his mother happy. The only reason she could be up there that much, he reasoned, was to try to escape her memories.

To Mickey Boy, the catch phrase "Get a life" should have been coined specifically for his mother. As he'd found out after his natural father, Don Vincenze, had been murdered, she'd spent over thirty years pining for him while claiming to Mickey Boy that his natural father had died. Her second stab at happiness, marrying Al Messina, Alley's father, had ended prematurely when he'd died of a heart attack behind the wheel of his cab. After that, Mickey Boy couldn't ever remember Connie with a man in her life, even for one day.

That Laurel should be more like Connie, satisfied to stay home and make her life around her family, crossed Mickey Boy's mind as he took Hope from his mother's arms and nuzzled her babyfat neck. She smelled deliciously of lotion.

"Where'd she go?" Mickey Boy asked.

"I don't know. Anne said she went shopping. When she left, I sent your friends away too. They waited around for Laurel all afternoon."

"What!" Mickey Boy screamed. "She's doing that again?"

Hope, startled by his shouting, began to cry. Mickey Boy handed her back to his mother.

"What the hell is wrong with that girl?" he asked. "For a teacher, she's so goddamned stupid sometimes! I try to tell her how dangerous it is . . ." He rushed toward the phone, then realizing there was no one to call who would know Laurel's whereabouts, turned back to face Connie.

"I swear to you, I'm gonna kill her," he said quietly, then stormed off into the den.

By ten o'clock Mickey Boy began to panic. He dialed Freddie's beeper number, and when Freddie returned the call, ordered him to come get him. His next call was to Nicolo Fonte, who he also told to come to the house. He started to dial Billy Sneakers and Vito the Head, but changed his mind. If it turned out to be nothing, and Laurel traipsed home in a little while, at least he wouldn't have to be embarrassed in front of them. Freddie and Fonte were different. They were probably the two closest people to him, and with them Mickey Boy didn't mind looking foolish or airing his personal problems.

Freddie and Nicolo Fonte arrived together, Fonte having paged Freddie after having spoken to Mickey Boy.

Still no Laurel.

Without explaining, Mickey Boy rushed to Freddie's car. "C'mon, let's go," he said.

On the way down the hill, he explained that once again Laurel had snuck out on the bodyguards he'd provided, and still hadn't come home or called. All he could think of was to cover as much of Staten Island's territory as was humanly possible, looking for her car.

Though he cursed her, saying he'd tear her apart when he found her, Mickey Boy's stomach tightened with fear. Somehow, deep in the recesses of his consciousness, he knew Laurel wouldn't be found.

65

July 3: Chelsea, Manhattan

LITTLE VINNIE SLAMMED ROSALIE DOWN ONTO THE FLOOR, CLAW-ing at her panties even as the two of them fell. Once he had them off, he entered her immediately. He fucked her as brutally as he could, smashing himself between her spread legs like his efforts were being graded by ringside judges. And when he came, it was with a burst that left his heart pounding.

Rosalie lay there afterward with her clothes still on and her legs splayed, his semen dripping down onto the fleabag hotel's seedy gray carpet; her mouth open and gasping for air, even as tears trickled down toward her ears. He'd checked in here, at the cheapest hourly-rate hotel he could find, because he couldn't have Rosalie at Tempest's apart-ment, and he certainly couldn't bring her to the room he shared with that other nut job, Joe Augusta.

For once Little Vinnie rose not feeling guilty for the punishment he regularly dished out to Rosalie. She deserved it, bitch that she was, he reasoned. Always making like it was an ordeal for her to come see him. Always trying to get out of it to go fuck whoever else she had going for her. Goddman cunt. She was cheap, and made him feel that way every time he fucked her.

If not for his having become so aroused after seeing Laurel tied up in the bed, he would have never called Rosalie in the first place. Now, he told himself, he wouldn't bother with her at all anymore. He had better plans.

Little Vinnie felt proud of himself as he drove back to his own room on West Fifty-seventh Street. Not only had he engineered Laurel's kidnapping, but he'd taken the first step toward having her really want him, and he'd chased that douchebag, Rosalie.

Timing had been in his favor, Little Vinnie thought, catching that fuckin' nigger, Hale, as he'd begun to feel up Laurel. He'd seen red rats when he'd seen that black hand crushing Laurel's breast, and had pulled Hale off yelling loud enough for his championing her to register in Laurel's mind.

Spending time in Sicily had brought him in contact with a couple of ex–Red Brigaders who had outgrown their idealism and were now Mafia operatives under Don Genco's control. Hours of war stories, traded back and forth, had yielded information about how they used to turn around the victims they'd kidnapped so often in the sixties and seventies, so that they identified with their captors rather than the friends and families they'd left behind. After the initial shock came terror for the victims, then came unexpected gentleness, then rewards, until their minds viewed everything in relative terms, rather than in absolutes.

When he finally did get to fuck Laurel, it would be because she wanted him to, maybe even begged him for it. The only difficulty he saw for himself, in the future, would be parting with her.

Joe Augusta sat on the edge of his bed, praying, when Little Vinnie entered, after rapping their agreed-upon signal on the door, of course. If not, Joe would have been pressed against one of the side walls, for sure, with a pistol pointed at the door.

Joe, his eyes glazed over as if in pain, looked up at Little Vinnie, then bowed his head again to continue muttering his offerings to God and whoever else. Little Vinnie wouldn't have been surprised if Joe prayed to goats and chimps. The room already smelled like a zoo, with the goddamn guy never leaving to air out his skin.

When Joe finished, he fell back on the bed, letting out a groan of exhaustion.

"I got good news for you," Little Vinnie said. "But you look too weak to handle it."

"Don't be a smartass," Joe said, dour as usual. He sat up on the bed.

Little Vinnie turned Laurel's bag upside down, dumping all its contents onto Joe's bed. Papers, a wallet, makeup, and more bounced and scattered on the spread.

Joe just looked up questioningly, then lifted the wallet. He looked inside, pulled out a driver's license. "Messina?" he asked. "Mickey Boy's wife?"

"Yup, got her all under wraps," Little Vinnie said proudly.

"I don't understand."

"I snatched her today. Got her wrapped up an' on ice."

Joe shot at Little Vinnie as if he'd been launched, grabbing Little Vinnie by the throat and toppling over with him.

"You kidnapped a girl?" Joe Augusta asked, climbing on Little Vinnie's chest. "You piece of shit!"

"I'm sorry . . . I don't know . . . what's wrong?" Little Vinnie cried in rapid succession. When the words were out, he gasped, trying to refill his lungs with Joe Augusta on his chest.

"A girl? A goddamn innocent defenseless girl? What are you, a fuckin' homo . . . a girl yourself?"

"No, please," Little Vinnie managed between sucking in air. "I tried to help you!"

Joe Augusta slapped Little Vinnie in the face, then got off him and dragged him up by the shirt. "That girl is somebody's daughter!" he said, then shoved Little Vinnie on the bed.

"I was only trying to help . . ."

Joe Augusta paced back and forth, fists clenched, working out his anger silently.

"It was for you . . . man, you know what pressure you been under . . . you know how bad you look?"

"But a girl . . . a daughter?"

When Joe took a step toward him, Little Vinnie backed up around the bed.

"I hadda do something to help you, and the girl will never get hurt. She's just the best thing we could use to trade for Richie, that scumbag," Little Vinnie said, continuing his speech in rapid fire. He felt as wet as if he'd just stepped out of the shower.

"Mickey Boy'll definitely give up Richie for her; he has to. Then she'll go right home," Little Vinnie said, silently swearing that she wouldn't. "It was the only way I could think of to get you—us—the satisfaction we gotta get. It was for Chrissy . . . for Christ's sake, Joe, I did it for her."

As Joe Augusta's frenetic pacing slowed, Little Vinnie began to relax. What a fuckin' bedbug, he thought. If he had any sense, Vinnie told himself, he would pump a couple into Joe's head and be everyone's hero. But then, what would he do about Mickey Boy?

Joe finally stopped. "Come on," he said. "I want to go see her."

"N-No, you can't—"

"I can't what?" Joe shouted. "If you've got this girl, I want to make sure she's all right. I want to see her for myself."

"Joe, listen, buddy," Little Vinnie said, as careful about his tone as he was about not mentioning Tempest's real gender. "Just think a minute. You want the girl who's watching her to be able to identify you later? I mean, who knows how things work out or turn around?"

At least he didn't have to worry about Joe seeing Hale, Little Vinnie thought, having chased Hale out of the apartment after having caught him touching Laurel's breast. He'd used the sizable fee he'd promised Hale as leverage to insist he not stay at the loft while Laurel was there.

"Please, just think," Little Vinnie implored. "I'm only trying to protect you."

"Then get her out before we get there," Joe replied to Little Vinnie's argument about him being seen by Tempest. "Or lock her in a closet. I don't care. I want to see this girl and make sure she's okay."

Tempest was already gone by the time Little Vinnie and Joe Augusta arrived at the Chelsea apartment. Little Vinnie had called ahead and ordered a petulant Tempest out, eventually promising to buy her a new dress, partially to appease Tempest's complaints about having to sit alone and partially to assure Joe that it was indeed a female watching Laurel. Only God knew what Joe would do if he found out that Tempest had a workable male organ between her legs.

When Joe looked through the hidden spyhole and saw Laurel tied to the bed, he grabbed Little Vinnie by the shirt. "You tied her, like a fuckin' rump roast. What are we, animals?"

Little Vinnie argued that Laurel had fought with the girl watching her, and that tying her Laurel was the only way to subdue her and avoid trouble.

"You rather we gotta hurt her if she attacks the girl who's feeding her?" Little Vinnie asked. "Come on, Joe, man, gimme a break. I'm trying to do the best I could."

"Will we wake her up if we go in?" Joe asked.

"I doubt it. We gave her a shot to put her to sleep." Controlling his tone so as not to appear too sarcastic, Little Vinnie asked, "Why? An' if she did wake up, then what? She can't see you, or nothing, with the blindfold."

Little Vinnie led Joe into the bedroom. Joe walked slowly to the bed and inspected Laurel. "Why's she got a bump on her head?" he whispered.

"She hit her head getting in the car."

When Joe gave him a disbelieving look, Little Vinnie said, "I swear to you, nobody hit her . . . it was the car."

Laurel lay still throughout their conversation, looking peacefully asleep. With her arms tied over her head, her breast bulged out of the side of her halter. Her legs pulled up sideways as if yearning for the fetal position.

"If a hair on this girl's head is touched," Joe said, "I will personally skin you alive."

Little Vinnie nodded and turned quickly away so that Joe wouldn't notice the bulge in his pants.

66

July 4: New Springville, Staten Island

2:12 A.M.

I'm never gonna find her, Mickey Boy thought, wanting to scream out the words, but holding them because of Freddie and Fonte being with him in the car.

So far, with Freddie driving, they'd searched streets from Todt Hill to New Dorp, then around to South Beach, looking for one car among thousands. They'd slowed by every restaurant, bar, or diner they passed, skimming in and out of parking lots to see if she'd hidden her Mercedes behind one of the buildings.

The worst part had been, at Freddie's suggestion, checking the parking area of the Holiday Inn.

Could she really be out fucking some guy, while he himself was crazy with fear? Mickey Boy wondered. Why not? he told himself. Hadn't he been in the sack with Rosalie only hours earlier? Could she have worn herself out so, with sex, that she'd fallen asleep in her lover's arms, not realizing night had fallen?

As Freddie turned the car from Victory Boulevard onto Richmond Avenue, Mickey Boy began not to see. His eyes still focused on the road, but he pictured Laurel, naked and bent over, her tits hanging while she sucked off some strange guy, maybe getting banged from behind as she did. Her and her goddamn sex; always wanting to experiment—fuckin' handcuffs and nipple clamps; always reading those goddamn sex manuals as if they were Bibles.

Maybe he hadn't really known her all along. Or maybe he had, and just hadn't wanted to face the truth. He hammered a fist on the armrest.

"What is it?" Freddie asked. "You see something?"

"No, nothing."

Nicolo Fonte leaned forward in the backseat and gave Mickey Boy a sympathetic pat on the shoulder.

Mickey Boy's anger quickly turned to guilt. Laurel could be hurt, or even dead, somewhere. If that was the case, it had to be God punishing him for past sins:

For having pissed on religion . . .

For crimes he'd committed on his way up the mob ladder . . .

For Rosalie.

What am I, fuckin' crazy? he thought. Maybe Laurel was already home. He'd had Freddie driving him around all night only because he couldn't sit home doing nothing. Too late to call and ask his mother, who was watching Hope, and find out.

"Let's start for home," Mickey Boy said. "She may—"

Suddenly, Freddie cut the wheel sharply to the left, throwing Mickey Boy toward him. Freddie gunned the car into the entrance of the Macy's mall, then sped across it till he stopped with a screech—alongside Laurel's car.

Outside, as Mickey Boy looked through the bedroom window, rockets and sparklers lit up the night with hot pinks, whites, and yellows. Each explosion matched a beat in Mickey Boy's forehead. He turned away to face once again everyone in the room.

Laurel's mother, Anne, sat on the edge of his and Laurel's bed, hunched over and sobbing, her husband Jack's consoling arm draped over her shoulder. Freddie leaned against the white enamel chest, his arms folded in front of him. Tammy sat at the edge of the room's single chair, hands crossed in her lap.

Staring at Mickey Boy, Connie shook her head slightly. "I'll go look in on the baby," she said. On her way out, she added, "I'll put some tea up too."

"What am I going to do? My baby . . . my baby . . ." Laurel's mother wailed.

Tears seem to run backward into Mickey Boy instead of out.

"Shouldn't we call the police?" Tammy asked.

"No," Mickey Boy replied. "I already explained to them before you got here. Till we hear from somebody, I don't think it's safe to bring anybody in. It might scare whoever's got her . . ."

"They killed her," Anne cried. "My baby's dead!"

"No! She's not!" Laurel's father replied. "Stop that talk! I don't want to hear it anymore. Laurel's safe, and will come home soon. God will protect her."

"I know it's hard," Mickey Boy said, "but you guys gotta trust me. We'll find out who it is and get her back. But you can't put her in any danger by calling the cops . . . they're bunglers, and'll only make things worse."

Tammy said, "But the FBI——"

"I don't want to hear it," Mickey Boy said. "Just, please, listen to me, and don't mention a word of this to nobody. Not to a friend, and especially not on a phone."

"I don't want to argue with you," Jack said. "And I'm aware of how, with your lifestyle, going to the FBI compromises you, but this is my daughter's life we're talking about here."

"Jack, believe me, I swear to you, on my own life, that if that was all I was worried about, I would've called the FBI long ago. It's just that I really don't wanna spook whoever's got her."

Jack Bianco stammered, as if afraid to voice his mind, then asked if they shouldn't have heard from the kidnapper already, if it was ransom they wanted.

"We don't know that," Mickey Boy said. "We don't know what whoever it is wants, or who they are. Just, please, go along with me, and don't undermine whatever I try to do to get Laurel back. I got your words?"

Anne cried harder; Jack nodded. Tammy said, "What about everyone outside, at the party? What explanation will you give them when they wonder where Laurel is?"

"She's at a sick cousin's, or something . . . anything."

"Wouldn't I be there too? After all, I am part of the family."

"Come on, Tammy!" Mickey Boy shouted, and a moment later was disgusted with himself for losing control. He softened his tone, adding, "It could be on Jack's side, anything. The truth is, as long as they got free food and fireworks, they couldn't care less who's here or not, including me."

"Okay," Tammy replied. "I'll go along with whatever you think is right."

"No," Mickey Boy said. "What I *know* is right."

"I don't fuckin' know what's right, or even which side is up," Mickey Boy told Freddie after the relatives had left, to slip out and go home. Outside, the other people he'd invited before Laurel's disappearance continued to eat, drink, and set off fireworks.

"What's right is what you're doing," Freddie replied. "We gotta sit tight till we find out where the hell this is coming from."

Who, that they knew, would possibly do something so horrible? Mickey Boy asked. Mob guys classically didn't bother women and children; they went directly after their targets. Even Joe Augusta, if he were really behind the other killings, had too much of a code of honor to do something like that. Why didn't they just come after him?

"You said it before," Freddie said. "'Cause we don't know who it is, or what they want . . ." His voice trailed off, ". . . if they even want anything at all . . ."

Mickey Boy's heart sank at the thought that Freddie might be right; that all whoever-it-was wanted had been Laurel. If she were dead or injured, he was positive it was him God was punishing, and he was doubly sure of why—Rosalie.

"If we put out the word," Mickey Boy said, "somebody, just one of our people, gotta come up with something."

Freddie came alongside Mickey Boy and took hold of both his arms. "Listen, you know I love you an' Laurel like my own blood," he said. "An' anything I tell you, I tell you what I would tell myself."

"I know."

"Well, you can't put the word out. You can't let whoever it is, if it's one of our people, have that upper hand." He let go of one of Mickey Boy's arms to point a finger. "And more important, you can't let everybody else know you're in trouble an' can't straighten it out. It's gotta be you, me, an' the greaseball downstairs, until we get a clue . . . till somebody reaches out for us."

"And how long do we wait, before we do something?"

"As long as it takes."

"God, I hope she's all right!" Mickey Boy howled.

"Don't worry," Freddie said, hugging Mickey Boy. "She'll be just fine."

67

July 6: Chelsea, Manhattan

LAUREL DIDN'T KNOW HOW LONG SHE'D BEEN THERE. SHE ONLY knew she slept, then awoke, then slept again. The sedatives barely wore off when she was awake, making her groggy and move in a dreamlike state. Now, when her brunette captor freed her from the handcuffs they'd taken to using to bind her to the bed, and cuffed her behind her back to walk her to the bathroom, Laurel let her without putting up a struggle. And she didn't make a fuss or try to pull her blindfold off when the brunette then cuffed one hand to the sink pipe, leaving her other hand free to wipe herself clean.

Cooperating had its rewards too. Though they fed her during those times she awoke, mostly sandwiches or burgers she could hold in her one free hand, the meals were obviously too infrequent to keep her stomach from churning. Fighting, she learned at the beginning, had made her miss even those scheduled feedings. To top it off, the brunette had given her a soapy washcloth to clean herself while she was cuffed on the toilet, and had powdered her down afterward. At least her own smell didn't offend her anymore.

Now, lying there on the bed, almost completely conscious,

Laurel's thoughts were interrupted by the familiar male voice.

"You okay?" he asked.

Laurel didn't answer. She felt the mattress sink a bit when he sat down next to her.

"I hope they're taking good care of you," he said. "If there's anything you need, please, let me know."

She still refused to answer, struggling instead to try to place that voice. She knew she'd heard it before. It was no stranger that had kidnapped her, that was for sure. She just couldn't remember who it was.

Laurel felt a hand stroke her cheek, gently, moving down under her chin, then grazing her cheek on the other side. Still cuffed to the headboard, she tried to move her face away, but his hand followed her movements, stroking ever so lightly.

"You know, I can't understand why your husband wouldn't answer us right away. I would be going nuts if you were my wife." His finger drifted down the side of her neck and ran across her collarbone, tickling and frightening her at the same time.

Laurel gritted her teeth. She felt his fingers toying with the bow that knotted in the center of her halter top. "No, please," she whimpered.

"I just don't think he appreciates you," the voice said. "I don't think he really understands how beautiful . . ." He opened the bow. ". . . and attractive . . ." He popped the first of two buttons that kept the halter together. ". . . and sexy, you really are."

"No, please," Laurel cried. "Please don't . . ." She felt the second button open and the cloth fall away from her breasts. Crying, she thrashed her head from side to side.

"Come on, don't cry," the voice said. He tried to wipe her tears, but she kept moving her head away from his hand. He stopped touching her until she lay still again, her breasts exposed.

"They're magnificent," he said after a time.

"Why? Why are you doing this to me?" Laurel cried.

The man sitting next to her went back to touching her cheek. "I'm sorry," he said. "You just wound up in the middle of something your husband could have avoided." He repeated his tickling of her neck and collarbone, then ran his finger down between her breasts. She felt him move the diamond and gold crucifix Mickey Boy had given her for Christmas from its position hanging off the side of her neck to flat on her chest.

Laurel trembled as his finger circled over and underneath one breast, then did the same thing with the other. His feathery touch sent tremors down her stomach and chills through her spine. She felt goose bumps rise all over her exposed skin.

Laurel tensed as the man touched her, then relaxed when he stopped, only to tense again when he touched her breasts again. "Oh, God," she whimpered. "Please, please . . . leave me alone . . . let me go home."

"You will, I promise," the voice said. Suddenly he bent and sucked one of her nipples into his mouth.

Laurel gasped. With her nipple still between his teeth, she began to kick and scream. His sucking, however, was uninterrupted by her movements.

"Stop, you fucking bastard!" Laurel screamed. "Stop!"

"No, your husband's the bastard," the voice said, then took her other nipple in his mouth. He squeezed her breast as he sucked, heightening a sensation she didn't want to feel. She continued to kick her legs without success.

One hand moved to her stomach and pressed downward toward her navel, making her feel like she had to urinate.

"Oh, God, no," Laurel cried out as his fingers slipped under the waistband of her shorts and touched the top of her pubic mound. Why hadn't she worn jeans and a sweater? she asked herself silently, cursing herself for dressing as she had; blaming herself for attracting a nut by dressing to attract.

Despite her kicking, Laurel's male captor removed her shorts and panties with ease. She lay totally naked and vulnerable. Instead of kicking, she now tightened her legs shut to try to keep her vagina from view.

"You are more beautiful than I even imagined," the voice said. His tongue began to follow the trail his fingers had just explored, from her breasts down her stomach and under her navel.

Laurel bit her lower lip and squeezed her legs together more tightly. Each time she squeezed, however, sensation in her vagina increased, adding to the sensitivity the licking caused. Her body thrilled while her brain hated.

"I beg you, please," she cried. "Please, don't . . ."

Her captor's response was to grab her thighs and firmly pull them apart. Holding them in place, so she couldn't kick, he began to lick between her legs.

"Oh, my God," Laurel gasped, unable to control the response of her body.

Laurel's sobs turned to groans. The licking and nipping over and in her vagina made her arch her pelvis upward. The male's grip loosened on her thighs and moved underneath to lift her. His squeezing of her ass intensified her feeling as she felt herself moving toward a crest. Her breasts heaved and she felt as though she were expanding and burning at the same time. Her vagina began to pulsate . . .

Then he stopped, dropping her to the bed and getting off.

Laurel's chest heaved even more. She squirmed and wiggled, unable to satisfy the raw nerve endings that screamed for release. "My God, my God," she cried, feeling as though she were going insane.

Then she heard him laughing and felt him drop his entire weight between her legs. Laurel screamed as he quickly spread her legs and began to force his way into her. Defying her will, the walls of her vagina stretched outward to accommodate his entry.

Laurel bucked and fought as best she could, the handcuffs that held her arms over her head cutting into her wrists, curses and saliva spewing from her mouth, but the motions only seemed to encourage him. He grabbed her legs and lifted them back toward her shoulders, immobilizing her. His testicles slapped against her bottom as he repeatedly rammed his penis up into her.

Though blindfolded, Laurel squeezed her eyes tight and called up her only available defense—she fantasized that it was her husband, the love of her life and father of her child, Mickey Boy Messina, whose warm semen she felt spurting inside her body.

68

July 7: Little Italy, Manhattan

Anything else?" Rosalie asked, coyly brushing against Mickey Boy as she set down a tray of coffee and pastry for the assembled group of Calabra Family executives.

Mickey Boy ignored her, looking away toward Freddie, who shook his head slowly. Mickey Boy knew Freddie understood how close he was to going over the edge; to exploding and causing a disaster.

After two more brushes against Mickey Boy were ignored, Rosalie left the room—with a major attitude.

Mickey Boy remained silent while Freddie conducted the business at hand: bringing both factions of their intrafamily dispute together for the first time since the rash of murders. He knew it didn't look good, him not taking charge of such an important event, but he didn't care. If he'd had to participate, he was sure he would have lost control, probably beat the shit out of each and every one of them until he found out what had happened to his wife.

Someone in the room had to know.

Which one of them had been close with Joe Augusta in the past? he wondered.

He stayed silent, though, heeding Freddie's advice about not mentioning Laurel's disappearance, for fear that one of the men present was involved.

Mickey Boy looked from face to face—Bobby Rimini, Benny Donuts, Syl the Hat, Sally Stabile. Which one? he wondered. Could it be Bobby Rimini, who he knew for sure had been a part of the Frankie Green Eyes murder? Look at the phony bastard, he thought, talking about being brothers when he'd shed Calabra Family blood. Had Joe Augusta been involved with Bobby in some past business deal? Both men were known to be more interested in making legitimate money than in traditional mob operations like gambling, thievery, or extortion.

Was Joe Augusta even invovled in what had been going on? Mickey Boy asked himself again. Was it just coincidence that some of the murdered men were in some way connected to Chrissy's death? Was it just his own imagination run wild?

Once again, Mickey Boy assured himself that he was right on target, that Joe Augusta was indeed back, and with a bloody vengeance. Richie, then, would have to remain hidden where Fonte had stashed him, until Joe was found. The only question that Mickey Boy couldn't form a positive answer to was whether Joe Augusta was also involved in Laurel's sudden disappearance.

No, that don't make sense, he thought. I ain't even making sense anymore.

Mickey Boy excused himself and left the small living room above the focacceria to go to a bathroom in the hallway. Rosalie waited for him by the top of the stairs.

"Are you all right?" she asked.

"Yeah, fine," Mickey Boy said.

"Then it's me?"

"What?"

"You haven't called in what, four, five days? And in there, it's like I have something catching?" Rosalie said. "Tell me what's going on. Is it something I did?"

Looking at Rosalie increased Mickey Boy's pain. He was afraid that even by talking to her he would be offending some god or spirit, hurting Laurel even more.

"Nothing. It's not you," he said. "I just can't see you no more. That's it."

Rosalie's face flushed. "That's it? Wham, bam, thank you, ma'am?"

"Yeah." He pushed past Rosalie and entered the bathroom. Seconds later he heard her stomping down the stairs. If only chasing Rosalie away would help bring Laurel back.

If only he could believe that.

In his mind he could hear Frank Sinatra singing, . . . *It's over, nobody wins.*

Mickey Boy splashed water over his face, then, feeling more in control of himself, went back to the meeting. He sat there, in the DeStefanos' upstairs parlor, unsmiling, through the bullshit "You know I'd die for you's" and the deceitful hugs and kisses of his men.

Afterward he accepted hugs and kisses in his sullen mood.

"You know, you scared the shit out of them," Freddie said as they left the building. "I know it's hard to act normal, with what's going on, but the worst thing you could do is scare guys like this."

"Fuck 'em."

"Don't say that. Scared guys are the most dangerous. If they're real tough guys, you're okay, 'cause they'll be cocky too. But if they're cowards, they'll clip you in a heartbeat."

"Fuck 'em. Let 'em try," Mickey Boy snapped. "Maybe they'll put me out of my fuckin' misery."

Freddie put an arm around Mickey Boy's shoulders as they walked. Mickey Boy saw the shared pain in his eyes, and loved him for holding things together when he couldn't.

"You know, they all know about Bobby's whacking Frankie," Freddie said as they reached the car. "He's gotta go for there to be peace."

"I don't wanna know," Mickey Boy said. "Do whatever the fuck you want."

Strong operatic singing wafted out of Nicolo Fonte's brownstone apartment as Mickey Boy and Freddie approached the second-floor landing.

Freddie shook his head and knocked on the door. When Fonte opened it, Freddie stepped back for Mickey Boy to enter first, then followed. "I didn't know you listened to this shit," he said.

"Di quell'amore, di quell'amore ch'e palpito," the tenor voice bellowed from Fonte's CD player.

"Ah, 'tis with love that palpitates," Nicolo Fonte said, turning off the music. *"La Traviata.* All Italians listen to opera, and all Italians listen to Verdi."

Freddie did a comic double take, which he'd identified to Mickey Boy as a "skull," then said, "I'm Italian, and I don't listen to opera."

"You are not Italian," Fonte countered. "You are American. One who just happens to have ancestors that were born in Italy. To you, Frank Sinatra is classical music."

"Don't talk about Sinatra," Mickey Boy said. He dropped into a kitchen chair.

Nicolo Fonte began pouring espresso from an old-fashioned maganette, one aluminum pot that dripped coffee through a sieve into a spouted pot below.

"The man I met now for the second time, on your behalf, from the old country, played *La Traviata* throughout both discussions," Fonte said. "It became infectious, and I have been listening to it constantly ever since."

Mickey Boy sipped the black coffee. The last thing he cared about was opera, or who listened to what. "Well?" he asked. "What did your friend say?"

"Please, an acquaintance is not a friend," Nicolo Fonte said. "He is merely someone recommended by a real friend, who I called overseas for advice."

Fonte claimed that the man in America was supposed to be reliable, and had loyalties that were so firmly entrenched in Sicily that they transcended American mob politics.

"I thought it was positive that, after my first discussion with him, in which I had asked for some personal insight into the problems within your *borgata,* he called on me for a second meeting."

"I don't like the sound of the 'you thought' part," Freddie said.

"You should not," Fonte replied.

"What?" Mickey Boy said, stepping forward. What the fuck else was going on that he wasn't aware of? What other thing he hadn't counted on was going to stab him in the back?

"Please, calm down." Fonte claimed that nothing terrible had transpired. "It is just that little was said at our meeting that would be of any value to you, except two things."

Mickey Boy's body tensed as if he were preparing for a blow.

"One was a message that our friends from the old country want nothing to do with the problems of the Calabra Family," Fonte said.

"Come on," Freddie said. "Stop dragging this shit out."

"The second was a suggestion that I, or whoever my interested party is, contact the one man who might shed some light on what goes on."

"And?" Mickey Boy asked.

Nicolo Fonte half smiled, and said, "Don Peppino Palermo."

69

July 12: Upper West Side, Manhattan

"YOU SURE SHE'S OKAY?" JOE AUGUSTA ASKED, HIS MOUTH churning moo goo gai pan while he spoke.

Little Vinnie chewed on hot, spicy kung pao beef. "Of course, I'm sure," he answered. He tossed more food in his mouth to relieve the peppery fire on his tongue. "I got the girl taking care of her as if it was her own sister, an' I go up an' make sure she's getting everything she needs." It was all he could do to keep from laughing at that one.

For the last week or so, Little Vinnie had been having sex with Laurel every day; sometimes twice a day. To him it was more like making love. He really did love the sight and scent of Laurel, and took pains to be as gentle as possible. She was everything he'd hoped for in bed, and more. She was so easy to ignite.

At first he knew Laurel's resistance and tears had been due to fear and guilt, but once liberated from that, he was equally sure she would come to really enjoy it—and him.

That first day, after he'd fucked her, Little Vinnie offered her food, but she'd declined. However, she'd cryingly accepted his offer of a sedative shot. After she passed out from the medication, he left a box of Godiva chocolates near her, and uncuffed one of her hands. His orders to Tempest were to leave Laurel with one hand free as long as she didn't fight, but to cuff her again before he came to see her. She could see Tempest, he reasoned, with no harm done, but was not ready to recognize him yet. After Mickey Boy was dead, she'd be too grateful and loving toward him to identify him for authorities. He'd also ordered her dressed, in case Joe Augusta decided to look in on her on the spur of the moment.

Little Vinnie had been pleased to see that Laurel ate half of the candy when he returned the second day. Once again he carefully undressed her and made passionate love to her. Of course, she resisted again, but he sensed her heart wasn't in it. All part of that same guilt trip, he'd reasoned. That day, he left fried shrimps. Tempest had later reported that Laurel ate all of them.

Each time he'd had sex with Laurel since, he rewarded her with a sedative and some delicacy. The last time, he left her a small sample bottle of cologne, which, at Tempest's urging, she'd used. For next time, he'd left a lacy white negligee, which he told Tempest that Laurel must slip into herself. She had to want to look nice for him.

The other part of drawing her to him, and the one that he enjoyed most, was constantly questioning why her husband would ignore messages sent to him, and leave her with them.

"I still don't like what we're doing," Joe Augusta continued, both speaking and eating at the same time. "We have to send a message to Mickey Boy . . . tell him what I want."

"No, it's still too soon," Little Vinnie replied. "You know how much heat there must be around there?"

"I don't think he would have gone to the cops."

Little Vinnie shook his head. "Joe, think clear. We don't know that. An' even if he didn't, he's gonna be blood mad, with all his assholes running every which way. One of them is bound to run into us."

Once again, as he had since they captured Laurel, Little Vinnie begged Joe to wait before trying to reach Mickey Boy for the first time. There was no way he was ready to give up Laurel yet.

Joe hesitated, real pain over their operation apparent in

his eyes. "I don't know . . . I never was wrong like this. This isn't part of our code."

"Joe, please. I'm risking everything for you . . . and for Chrissy," he said. "All I ask is that you don't move too quick and mess things up. That's all."

The mention of Chrissy hurt Joe a little more, enough to get him to agree to wait awhile longer. He would do anything, he said, code of honor or no code of honor, to avenge his poor, sainted daughter—and he appreciated Little Vinnie's sincerity and help.

"You know, you are a good boy," Joe said. "I'm glad I didn't move too fast and clip you when I found you."

"It was fate," Little Vinnie replied. "You running into me like that was like a sign from the gods for me to help you."

"No. No gods. I found you because somebody gave you up."

Little Vinnie's head jolted back. "Nobody knew I was here."

"Not nobody," Joe said. "At least one guy knew, who's been helping me. An' he almost never leaves his house, so you know somebody else had to tell him."

"Who?"

"How could I tell you that?"

Little Vinnie struggled to look hurt. "How could you *not* tell me that?" he asked. "Here I am, putting my life on the line to help you do the right thing for Chrissy, and you don't even trust me enough to tell me who else is on our side? I wouldn't bother him or nothing for giving me up, or try to find out how he knew."

Little Vinnie shrugged, then let his shoulders drop. "Ah, what's the difference, never mind," he said, looking down. "It don't matter."

Joe leaned forward over dishes of chow fun and eaten-clean spare-rib bones. "You're right," Joe said in a low voice. "But I want you to understand that this man was not wrong in what he did. You gotta respect him for wanting to help me get revenge for Chrissy."

"Of course," Little Vinnie replied.

Still leaning toward Little Vinnie, Joe whispered, "Don Peppino."

* * *

Little Vinnie couldn't understand how the man always smelled like a pizza. Strong oregano odor even permeated the room after he'd left. Didn't he ever bathe?

DoDo sat across from Little Vinnie in the small Cuban café in Washington Heights, giving him a message from Don Genco, in Sicily. Don Genco, DoDo said, was becoming concerned about why Little Vinnie had to stay in America so long. The don had sent word that not only did he miss Little Vinnie, but that Ninfa did too.

The mention of Ninfa stung Little Vinnie with both pleasure and pain. Though he knew he had a fine future ahead in Acireale, as Ninfa's husband and a nephew and heir of Don Genco, he now had something to pull him here too—Laurel. What a feather she would be to add to the cap he could wear as head of the Calabra Family once Mickey Boy was dead.

"Tell Don Genco that I am very close to accomplishing my goal," Little Vinnie said. "I would have finished long ago, but there was a complication."

"Qui fa?"

"Complication . . . something happened that changed things." He had purposely never mentioned Joe Augusta to DoDo, to cover for him using Joe to kill Mickey Boy for him. "People here knew I came back."

"No one should know that," DoDo said.

"But they do. One sent a guy after me, who wanted to whack me," Little Vinnie said. He proudly added, "But I turned him around. I'm using him to set up what I have to do. Then he's gone."

"Who is this man?"

Little Vinnie didn't say it was the man who'd killed his father, for fear of offending DoDo and Don Genco. Those zips were all so goddamn touchy, he thought, and said it was some guy he'd had a beef with long ago. The last thing he needed was for them to tell him to kill Joe too.

"Who is it, then, who informed on you?"

"Some old fuck . . . I don't think you know him."

"His name?"

"Don Peppino," Little Vinnie said. "But that's no big deal. I could fuck him up later."

DoDo smiled slightly, but did not say a word.

70

July 13: Todt Hill, Staten Island

DESPITE BEING AWAKENED FROM AN UNEASY YET INTERMITTENTLY deep sleep, Mickey Boy could recognize the figure shown on his den's monitor as a lawman. Even though his consciousness had not yet fully caught up to his opened eyes, he jumped from the leather couch and staggered toward the front door. No need to have this bastard wake Connie and Hope.

"Who are you? What do you want? And why are you here in the middle of the night?" Mickey Boy rapid-fire-questioned through the intercom. He prayed it wasn't a messenger saying they'd found Laurel's body.

"FBI," the intercom answered back. "But I'm here as a friend. You can see I'm alone." He held his open wallet, with the badge showing, up to the camera.

Friend? Mickey Boy wondered. Since when was the FBI, whose initials he swore stood for "Forever Bothering Italians," ever there to be his friend?

Connie came halfway down the stairs, clutching her robe closed. "What is it?" she asked.

"Nothing, go back upstairs."

Rather than banter through the door and wake Hope also, Mickey Boy unlocked and opened it. He kept one hand in the pocket of his windbreaker, his index finger secure on the trigger of a .38.

"Always sleep in your clothes?" the FBI man asked, stepping over the threshold, onto the marble hall floor.

Mickey Boy had taken to sleeping dressed and armed, in the den instead of his bedroom; prepared to run out to help Laurel, if he could, at a moment's notice.

"Is it a crime?"

"Yeah, slobbery in the first degree."

The FBI man held up a printed index card in Mickey Boy's face. Mickey Boy squinted, trying to read through the sleep still in his eyes. Neatly printed letters read:

DON'T TALK!
THIS PLACE IS BUGGED
OUTSIDE OR UPSTAIRS IS OKAY

Mickey Boy followed the FBI man into the kitchen. The agent sat himself on a chair as if he owned it. "Tea will be fine," he said. "No decaf, if you can," he added, pointing toward the rear entrance to the backyard.

Mickey Boy nodded in agreement. He looked across at his digital clock: 5:11 A.M. Caffeine would do him also, he thought, and put up a pot of water. His heart beat rapidly. If this asshole had some information about Laurel, he wished he would just tell him and stop playing this supercool game.

"Listen, this ain't the Colonnade Diner," Mickey Boy said. "Nobody recommended my house for coffee in the middle of the night."

"Tea."

Mickey Boy poured tea for the FBI agent, coffee for himself, grabbed a box of Entenmann's chocolate doughnuts from the refrigerator, then led the way out to the rear patio.

As soon as he and the FBI man had seated themselves across the patio table from each other, Mickey Boy asked, "Now, what is it you got on your mind? Should I call my lawyer or what?"

"I told you I was here as a friend."

"I got no friends who are cops . . . or FBI men. My name's Messina, remember, not Gravano. I don't even eat cheese."

"My name is Paul Trantino, and I was a good friend of your father's."

"What the fuck is that supposed to mean?"

"Just what I said. Your father and my father grew up together. In fact, they were crime partners until the war . . . World War Two, that is. Afterward, your old man went back to the streets, mine went to law school, became a D.A. in Suffolk County."

"What does that make us?" This was the most original pitch Mickey Boy had ever heard. He bet with himself that Paul Trantino would shortly give him a deal for cooperating with the FBI. His heart fell at the realization that Paul hadn't come with information about Laurel. He didn't know if that was good or bad.

"I told you, friends," Paul said in answer to Mickey Boy's question about what relationship Paul thought they had in common. "My father only kept in touch with your father through greeting cards at Christmas and birthdays, but I saw your father on various occasions. We talked."

Mickey Boy jumped up. "Get a warrant or get out!" he said. "I got enough problems without your bullshit at five in the morning."

Paul sipped his tea as if Mickey Boy hadn't said a word, then said, "I figured you wouldn't believe me, so I brought this." He reached into his jacket and pulled out a small tape player. He shoved it across the table toward Mickey Boy. "Go on," he said. "Play it."

Mickey Boy stared at small black machine, then up at a calm-looking Paul Trantino.

"Afraid?" Paul asked.

Mickey Boy bent over and pushed the play button. After a few seconds he heard Paul Trantino's voice giving the date as January tenth, the time as six-seventeen A.M., and that the subject, Vincenze Calabra, had just arrived.

"Good morning, Vince," Paul Trantino went on to say. *"I ordered it for you when I saw you fly in. And a belated Happy New Year."*

Mickey Boy assumed it was coffee Paul Trantino had ordered that dawn, and from that concluded he was in a diner somewhere.

Don Vincenze's unmistakable voice answered, *"Thanks. A Happy New Year to you an' your family too."*

Big fuckin' deal, Mickey Boy thought. So the FBI man had a cup of coffee with his father. So what? So why, at six o'clock in the morning? He strained to listen, to hear if the voice of Don Vincenze wasn't just a good imitation.

"How's your father?" Don Vincenze's voice asked. *"You sent him my regards?"*

"Pop's fine," Paul Trantino's voice said from the tape player. *"I sent him your regards after we spoke last time, and he said to send you his love. But naturally, since you and I don't see each other too often . . ."*

Paul's face remained stony; no smug look of satisfaction, as Mickey Boy would have expected.

"Why don't you fast forward it a little," Paul suggested over Don Vincenze's taped voice. "Unless you want to hear all the bullshit formalities."

Mickey Boy remained still, listening closely, wanting to catch the little glitch in the voice that would give the Don Vincenze impersonator away—if it was an impersonator at all.

". . . I knew that for you to want to meet, it had to be important," Paul's voice continued on the tape.

"Well, you understand how tough it is for me to get away without either your people or mine watching me," Don Vincenze's voice replied. *"My trip to Atlantic City was the only time there'd be enough confusion to sneak away."*

After a pause, Don Vincenze's voice continued, *"As a matter of fact, if we could take care of business quickly, I could probably be back at Harrah's before my friends wake up an' start panicking."*

"I can understand how they feel," Paul said, laughing. *"I wouldn't want to be the poor schnook who let his boss get kidnapped or killed. That could mean suddenly looking like a slab of Swiss cheese."*

"Now, now, Paolo, you guys must be getting your ideas from television again."

That sarcasm convinced Mickey Boy that the voice on the tape player was indeed Don Vincenze's. His stomach churned and he bit his lower lip, anticipating something— what, he wasn't sure—that he knew couldn't be good.

"Yeah, like the seven o'clock news," Paul's voice replied. *"Your friends are dropping like flies. A nasty little dispute they've got going for themselves."*

"There are a few minor problems in every business. The key is to keep them from getting out of hand. That's why I

called you. I'm gonna give you an opportunity to end that problem you been seeing on TV, an' make you score some more brownie points in Washington besides."

Mickey Boy reached over to shut the tape player, but Paul moved faster and grabbed his wrist.

"Listen a little more," Paul said.

"Why is it, Vince, that every time you've offered me help during these last eight years or so—since I helped you with the Messina kid's case—I feel like I'm walking into a revolving door in front of you and coming out in back?"

Now Paul released Mickey Boy's hand to shut the tape player.

"He ate cheese," Paul said.

Mickey Boy's jaws rippled and his face flushed. Finally he said, "Get the fuck out!"

"I told you," Paul said. "I'm here as a friend, to help you find your wife."

Too much to think about at once. Mickey Boy shook his head to clear it. Sure, he'd jumped from the bottom of the barrel to the top of the heap in one leap, without uncovering myths, as Freddie had said, but this was more than just learning new street knowledge. This was turning everything he'd always believed in upside down, and making him feel as though he'd been raped. How much had they heard from his house? How long? What had he ever said?

"My wife is fine," Mickey Boy replied.

"I hope so . . . wherever she is." Paul downed the last of his tea, then said, "I told you your place is bugged. I've heard every recent conversation between you, Falcone, Fonte, and whoever else you spoke to."

"For how long?"

"Don't worry, there's no case coming out of anything you said." Paul smiled. "The bugs aren't court-ordered."

"Ain't that illegal?"

"Ill-eagle is a sick bird," Paul said. "Unlawful? If you can prove who put it in. But then again, you don't eat cheese, right?"

"What do you want?"

Paul insisted that he only wanted to help Mickey Boy find Laurel. If some harm had come to her, whether kidnapping or worse, no one would be able to uncover it better than the

FBI, he said, arguing that they had resources that Mickey Boy could not even imagine.

"I've got a wife too, and if this happened to her, God forbid, there would be no stone I'd leave unturned, even if it meant going to you guys for help." He leaned forward and added, "You owe it to her."

"I need more coffee," Mickey Boy said, and went inside to refill his and Paul's cups. He needed time to think, alone. But clear thoughts wouldn't come. When he went back outside, he felt as lost as before.

"What did you mean when you said you helped my old man with my case, and what did he give up?"

Paul Trantino explained that when Mickey Boy had first been indicted, the U.S. Attorney's Office had been adamant about seeking a maximum sentence for him. They had an airtight case, and wanted to build up the figures of how many total years they'd handed out. It was then that Don Vincenze sent a message to him, setting up a meeting. Without having disclosed to him that Mickey Boy was his son, Paul said, Don Vincenze had asked for Paul's assistance in getting Mickey Boy a lighter sentence.

"All he'd ever said was that you were someone he had an interest in. I didn't find out you were his son until later, after he'd been killed."

"Through more bugs?"

"And informants."

"What did he give you in return?" Mickey Boy asked, praying silently that Paul Trantino would say, "Nothing."

Paul said that if he told Mickey Boy everything, Mickey Boy would never believe him. For a clear example, however, he said, while fast-forwarding the tape, Mickey Boy should just listen.

After a few stops and starts, until Paul found the spot on the tape he was looking for, Don Vincenze's voice said, *"In a couple of weeks you'll probably get a call telling you a time an' place. Now, if I was a betting man, I'd lay odds that if your guys happened to lay a couple of bugs in that place before the time that's mentioned, you might hear a certain Mr. Rossellini an' his friends planning a couple of murders."*

Each decible of recognizable sound jolted Mickey Boy as though it had punched him square in the chest. Years that

317

had seemed so painful, never knowing who his father was, now seemed a blessing.

After a whistling sound, Paul Trantino's voice said, *"Boy, there's a big fish on my plate this time."*

"And if you raided the place after you got some good tapes, you might get lucky an' find a whole shitload of guns there."

"What happened, is Ross too hot to handle, or are you just a closet Vallo fan?" Paul Trantino's voice asked.

"I'm sure your father taught you—"

Mickey Boy stopped the tape player. It had been a painful internal struggle, but he'd managed to swallow the fact that his father had manipulated him into the streets by having Nicolo Fonte chase him from his law practice, and that he fomented a mob war that left orphans in three of the five mob families. He'd hated the old man for it, and had been so afraid that those same deceitful, vicious genes would emerge in him, that he'd fought to even the score; use his influence to benefit those he'd been forced to rule over. Somehow, Mickey Boy had rationalized Don Vincenze's faults as lessons that balanced him, Mickey Boy, and had forgiven him somewhat. Being a stool pigeon, however, was something different.

"Look, I can guess how you feel," Paul said. "But he wasn't all bad. He felt a great responsibility for you, and, I imagine, loved you in his own way."

Mickey Boy sat silently, unable to control the tears that filled his eyes. Emotionally vulnerable from his worry over Laurel and guilt over his affair with Rosalie, he now felt completely destroyed inside, dramatically equating himself to a doomed genetic failure.

Paul Trantino fast-forwarded the machine again.

"Please," Mickey Boy said. "I heard enough."

"Just this one thing," Paul said while fidgeting with the tape player.

Paul's voice finally said, *"Messina must be very special for you to do what you did. Usually the only time we've ever been able to work with guys in your position was when they wanted to deal for either themselves or their sons. This case is highly unusual. I just hope the kid is worth it . . . and stays out of trouble."*

"He'll be just fine," Don Vincenze's voice replied. *"He's a*

good boy, with good blood in him . . . like you." There was a pause, then the don's voice added, *"And please, Paolo, don't forget Joe Augusta. It's important."*

More important than the old man had ever imagined, Mickey Boy thought. He was smart enough to know what was ahead, but was either too blind or too courageous to let it keep him out of reach of the mentally broken man who would eventually kill him. Mickey Boy felt too weary to move.

Paul Trantino stuffed the tape player back inside his jacket. "I know this is a lot of shit to swallow, especially with what you're going through with your wife." He paused, then added, "I'm sorry. I just felt I had to shock you to reach you. I just want to help."

Mickey Boy stood up. His eyes, swollen and burning, stayed half closed, as if the lids were too heavy to lift. "Come on," he said wearily. "Let me show you out."

Paul pursed his lips and shook his head. "I'm sorry you feel that way," he said, then pulled a card out of his pocket and dropped it on the table. "If you change your mind, please, call me. I wrote my home number on there, so you could call any time, day or night."

Mickey Boy left the card and shuffled off toward the front door. Shredded inside by worry, pain, disappointment, anger, and most of all, indecision, he walked like a zombie. When he let Paul Trantino out, he looked away from him, but remained in the doorway as the FBI man walked to his car.

Suddenly Mickey Boy called out, "Wait!" He lumbered over to where Paul had stopped. "Thanks," he said.

Paul nodded, obviously affected by Mickey Boy's pain. He nodded, then turned.

Mickey Boy grabbed his arm, turning him back.

"Joe Augusta," he said. "And it really is important."

71

July 16: Chelsea, Manhattan

"I WANT TO LET YOU LOOSE," LITTLE VINNIE SAID. "COULD I trust you not to create a problem if I do?"

Laurel, lying blindfolded and cuffed to the headboard, nodded. Her legs moved sinuously, pressing closed at the thighs, then parting, while her hips shifted as if there were no comfortable spot for her.

So ready, Little Vinnie thought. It was almost like training a dog. He undressed and lay down beside her.

"Soon," he said, then began his ritual of removing the negligee she wore and kissing his way from her neck to her knees. To his satisfaction, Laurel moaned and squirmed under his caresses immediately. He inserted one finger into her vagina, happy to feel her soaked.

Holding the keys to her cuffs in one hand, Little Vinnie placed himself between Laurel's legs. She opened them wider to accommodate his entry.

Once impaled inside her, with her legs wrapped around him, he leaned forward and opened one of her handcuffs. Laurel's hand dropped, and lay there, as if she couldn't believe it was free. He stroked inside her a couple of times, then opened the other lock. Laurel still did not remove her blindfold.

Little Vinnie bent and kissed her on the mouth, hesitantly at first, in case she decided to bite him. When she didn't, he kissed her face, her ear, then her mouth again, letting his tongue slip between her lips.

When he touched her blindfold, to remove it, Laurel said, "No," and pulled his hand away. She undulated her hips under him and brought her fingers to the back of his head.

Little Vinnie's head felt like it would burst. He kissed Laurel with an uncontrollable passion as he came inside her. When he finally collapsed, she did too, opening her arms and legs wide.

"Can I go to sleep now?" she asked. "I'm so tired."

Little Vinnie couldn't have been in more pain if Laurel had kicked him in the balls. Naked, he stormed out of the room. "When did you give her a shot?" he asked Tempest.

"A few hours ago. I figured she wouldn't be as feisty for you."

Little Vinnie rushed back into the room, furious at Tempest for having interfered with his procedure. Laurel was only to be given a sedative *after* he left, but was to be wide awake for him. He lifted Laurel off the bed and carried her into the shower. The first burst of water was colder than he could stand, so he warmed it up to a medium cool. Shivering, Laurel clung to him for warmth. He hugged her too, standing under the steady shower with her, letting the cold water run over both their heads.

When Laurel's trembling wouldn't stop, Little Vinnie upped the water's temperature. He felt all of Laurel's muscles relax as her naked body pressed full against his.

"You okay?" he asked.

Laurel just shook her head, fighting to become fully awake. Her movements became more alive.

Little Vinnie pushed her gently against the shower wall, then lifted her and impaled her with his erection. Once inside her, he reached up and pulled the soaking blindfold from her eyes.

"Open them," he said. "I want you to see me."

Eyes still closed, Laurel buried her face in his shoulder. "No," she moaned.

"Yes." Little Vinnie slipped out of Laurel's body and stood in front of her. She leaned toward him to try to bury her face again. "Stop," he said, holding her gently by the face. "I want you to look at me. I want you to know." He paused, then added, "Because I love you."

72

July 17: Gravesend, Brooklyn

"THINGS LIKE THIS ALWAYS PAIN ME," DON PEPPINO SAID, WITH an emotional frown that made Mickey Boy sick. From the look on Freddie's face, he felt the same way.

Upon the suggestion of Nicolo Fonte's Sicilian contact, Mickey Boy had met with Don Peppino a week earlier. He had told Don Peppino of the problems within his own ranks, and had confided that Laurel had been abducted or killed.

Don Peppino listened more than talked, and, as usual, had acted as though he was solidly in Mickey Boy's corner. He had proposed intervening with both sides himself, not to diminish Mickey Boy's power, of course, he'd said, but to show the others how much he supported Mickey Boy, and how concerned he was about the well-being of the Calabra Family. He also promised to use all his power to try to discover what had happened to Laurel. Mickey Boy, however, had walked away from that meeting feeling more than ever that he couldn't trust the old don.

Now, Don Peppino acted so sincere that, had he not known better, Mickey Boy told himself, he might have believed him.

"What has happened to your wife is an *infame* . . . it is terrible and tragic," the don went on.

"Do you know something?"

"Unfortunately, yes." Don Peppino leaned forward in the La-Z-Boy throne. "After I made some inquiries as to your wife's disappearance, I was contacted by someone——"

"Joe Augusta?"

Don Peppino looked startled. He hesitated, as if deciding

what to say next, then replied, "Yes. But how did you know?"

Mickey Boy stared into Don Peppino's eyes. "Because I'm not as stupid as many people, not you of course, take me for." He wanted to jump at the old man and beat the entire truth out of him, make the don tell him exactly what he knew. The only real thing that stopped him, however, was fear that Don Peppino would die during his interrogation and take his secret to the grave with him.

"Please," Mickey Boy said. "Tell me what you know."

"Your wife is well. She awaits her return to you and the rest of her family."

"When?"

"Do the authorities know? The FBI?"

"No," Mickey Boy snapped. "You shouldn't even ask me that."

Don Peppino shrugged. "I did not mean to suggest that you would ever violate our code and go to the authorities. But, who knows? They could have found out on their own, or through someone who—"

"Just tell me, when am I gonna get her back?" Mickey Boy asked, his patience for Don Peppino's flowery language worn thin.

Don Peppino stared at him coldly, then sat back. "I want you to know that I am not a part of this, and I do not support it. I believe it is a disgrace, and a dishonor to *la cosa nostra.*" He went on to say that if it were a lesser situation, he would not have become involved. There was, he said, always the danger that the messenger got the worst end of the deal.

While secretly swearing revenge on Don Peppino once Laurel was safe at home, Mickey Boy assured him that would not be the case.

Throughout the discussion Freddie Falcone remained mute. He and Mickey Boy had agreed that since the issue was so personal, Mickey Boy should do all the talking. Besides, Freddie had said, if he kept his mouth shut, he'd be able to listen better and remember more of the conversation's nuances to discuss with him afterward.

"I was told," Don Peppino went on, "that you can have

your wife back as soon as you would like. All you must do is deliver something Guiseppe Augusta wants."

"And what is that?"

"DeLuca."

"Fuck this old man, get all my skippers together! I want every single inch of this goddamned city searched till they find my wife!" Mickey Boy banged a fist on the dashboard. "And God help them if they don't!"

Looking out through the windshield, Mickey Boy saw the Ocean Parkway entrance to the Belt disappear behind him.

"What the fuck you doin'?" he snapped at Freddie, who just smiled.

Their car passed under the railroad trestle at Brighton Beach Avenue and curved around to the right. On the right, high-rise project buildings stepped in to block out the rest of the city; on their left, beachfront: boardwalk, bikinis, handball courts, blue-green water that opened outward as far as Europe.

For the first time that day Mickey Boy noticed how brilliant the sunshine was, and it annoyed him. Ahead of him, Coney Island's skyline, its Ferris wheel and parachute jump stretching up into the air, looked like a giant pop-up card.

"C'mon, don't play fuckin' games. Where are we going?"

"When was the last time you had a good hot dog?"

Shabby open-front game booths—spin a wheel, burst a balloon, roll a ball into a ring—lined both sides of the street. One had been converted to display used furniture. Freddie made a left and pulled up diagonally to a meter set in the middle of Schweikerts Walk, a street leading directly to the boardwalk and sign-posted by huge signs covering the building that housed Nathan's Famous, possibly the most well-known frankfurter stand in the world.

Despite Mickey Boy's protests, Freddie loaded them down with burnt hot dogs and crinkle-cut fries, then led the way up Schweikerts Walk to the ocean. The people seemed browner than Mickey Boy remembered, the streets dirtier, the bikinis smaller. He and Freddie leaned against a rail on the boardwalk, looking out over the beach to the water.

"You know, I feel guilty as shit, standing here, holding a

hot dog, watching all these tits and asses, when Laurel is . . ." Mickey Boy closed his eyes.

"Laurel's gonna be okay," Freddie said. "But you gotta stop the guilt nonsense. It don't help, it can't change things, it drains your fuckin' energy. What you gotta do is focus on the problem, think more clear than you ever did, an' when the time comes that you gotta make a move, and it will, do it quick and with strength."

"That's why I want everybody out on the streets, banging down doors if they gotta—"

"See, that's what I mean about thinking clear."

Mickey Boy took a bite of one of the two hot dogs he held in one hand, only because he didn't know what else to do to quiet his anxiety. They really were the best, he thought as salty frankfurter juices ran around his mouth. When he felt mustard on his mouth, he realized that between the french fries and hot dogs, he had no open hand to wipe it.

"How the fuck you expect me to eat this like this?"

"I could see you never worked as a waiter," Freddie said, pushing his sleeve back and lining the paper dishes up his arm. "Go ahead, wipe your mouth so I could finish what I was telling you."

Mickey Boy smiled, ready for Freddie's compliments about his order to get his men mobilized to search for Laurel.

"See, about thinking clear . . ." Freddie said, ". . . you ain't."

"What the fuck are you talking about? I'll get our people to rip every inch of this fuckin' city apart till they find her."

"Alive?"

"What . . .?"

"Well, if you scare whoever it is enough, they just might dump her an' run," Freddie said. "But that ain't even the worst part."

"There can't be a worse part."

Oh, but there certainly was, Freddie said. Getting Laurel killed was only one third of getting both of them murdered also. "Who of our guys could you swear—on our lives, all of ours—ain't involved?"

"No . . . nobody with us would—"

"Stop!" Freddie said, his color rising.

Mickey Boy was taken aback by Freddie's vehemence, so contrasting to his normally flip nature.

"Guys around us would sell out their own fuckin' mothers if they could get ahead!"

"No! I can't believe that!" Mickey Boy shouted back. There was no way, he told Freddie, that he would ever believe that every one of their people was no good.

"Exactly," Freddie countered. "Which ones are and which ones ain't?" He paused, then added, "Remember, your choices mean your life, my life, and Laurel's life. Which ones?"

Mickey Boy stood there saying nothing, unable to formulate a sensible answer to Freddie's question. He threw his food down toward the sand, getting a flash of déjà vu—seeing himself leading Sandy Monafo under the boardwalk when he was fifteen. In an instant he saw her naked breasts, felt her tongue . . . saw Rosalie . . . felt guilt overcome him again.

"Well?" Freddie asked. "The buzzer's gonna go off soon if you don't answer . . . and it could be attached to a .38 shell."

"I don't know."

"Good," Freddie said. "At least you're being honest with yourself." He handed Mickey Boy one of his hot dogs. "Here. And don't throw it away. It's a sin to waste God's food . . . or Nathan's." He laughed. "Remember when they used to tell you people were starving in Europe, so you'd eat shit you couldn't stand?"

"So, who do we talk to?" Mickey Boy asked.

"Nobody. We can't let anybody around us know what's going on, at least until we see if any of them comes up front as being involved, like that old scumbag Peppino did. Also, we can't let 'anybody,' period, know that you got a problem like this and can't straighten it out. It's a confidence thing."

"But we gotta do something," Mickey Boy said.

"Yeah, we'll do something," Freddie replied, shoving a french fried potato in his mouth.' ". . . Wait."

73

July 18: Hell's Kitchen, Manhattan

"YOU'VE BEEN AWAY A LONG TIME," THERESA SAID, her voice sounding tinny through the pay phone's receiver.

Joe Augusta wiped perspiration from his brow. Having always lived an air-conditioned life, he'd never realized how stinking hot New York could be in the summer.

"My business is almost done," Joe replied.

At first Joe Augusta had been in a hurry to exact his revenge against everyone involved in his daughter's murder. He'd gotten off to a fast start, killing Buster, Georgie the Hammer, and Butch Scicli. There had been one obstacle, though: Richie DeLuca. The time spent waiting for a shot at Richie, through his incarceration, trial, and disappearance, had been agonizing. That's why, despite Little Vinnie's caution about setting up a Laurel-Richie trade, Joe had decided to call Don Peppino and get him to move things along more quickly. As expected, the old don had reported that his message had been delivered and something would be worked out.

As his task got closer to completion, however, Joe felt himself emotionally torn. Yes, he'd tried to convince himself, he still had to seek revenge for Chrissy's murder; he was bound by honor, oath, and love to kill Richie DeLuca, then himself. But with his initial bloody drive somewhat satisfied, and time between murders giving him time to reflect, Joe had begun to doubt his strength to carry on.

"You know, Elizabeth's been sick," Theresa said, bringing him up to date on the two weeks since he'd last dialed collect. "I had to take her to the doctor for her throat . . . that French doctor, with the long name."

327

"Lepeletier."

"That's him."

"Did he take a culture?" Joe asked.

"Yes. He's very good; says her tonsils should come out."

Joe hung his head, fighting back tears. He missed being with his family, as it used to be, and prematurely missed the near future, when he knew he'd be gone. Completing his circle of vengeance wouldn't mean the beginning of a new life, but of the end.

"Joe? Joe, are you okay?" Theresa asked when Joe remained silent for a while.

"No, not really," Joe said. "But I will be." He spoke to Theresa a bit more, and then a few minutes with Elizabeth, who, over the phone, sounded amazingly to him like Chrissy. Fighting to keep his voice even, he told her he loved her, then hung up. He realized that to be able to fulfill his mission, he could not call his wife again until it was over.

His heart heavy, and with tears dribbling down his cheeks, Joe Augusta headed for the Church of the Sacred Heart.

74

July 20: Todt Hill, Staten Island

"MEMORIES OF YOU."

Like so many of the songs Frank Sinatra had sung, this one too brought vivid but painful memories to Mickey Boy, as the words wafted sinuously to his ears. Each one of them—"These Foolish Things"; "I'll See You Again"; "Where Are You"; "Baby Won't You Please Come Home" —had something special to say about Laurel, something that seemed written especially for his situation and that tore at his heart. His eyes remained shut and, despite the fact that he lay back on his sofa, his muscles stayed tense and ready to bound for the door if she should arrive. Sinatra's words and music continued to nudge his memory.

He could see her so clearly, walking through the front door, as she'd done so often. Smiling. Loaded down with packages. Carrying Hope in her arms.

". . . Your face beams, in my dreams, 'spite of all I do."

God, how he wished he could have her back, safe and sound in his home and in his arms. As he had so often since Laurel had been abducted, almost a month ago, he prayed for her return and begged forgiveness for every little thing he'd ever done to hurt her—especially having had an affair with Rosalie. He silently swore to be faithful to Laurel for the rest of his life, if only she would be returned to him unharmed.

"Everything . . . seems to bring . . . memories . . . of . . . you."

All he had to do was wait. Wait for a time and place to get her, and hope that she would be there; that Don Peppino, that old fuck, wasn't full of shit. Chances were he wasn't. Even the Sicilian Mafia contact Nicolo Fonte met with had assured them that Don Peppino would set up Laurel's return. "He never produces less than promised," the mafioso had told Fonte. And with a subtly bitter edge, as Fonte had reported, the man had added, "More sometimes, but never less."

Mickey Boy heard footsteps on the stairs and opened his eyes. Before tossing the newspaper he had in his lap onto the table, he looked at the photograph of Bobby Rimini again, lying in a pool of blood in a KFC parking lot. Stood to reason that the 250-plus–pound captain would get caught going for food. He flipped the paper away, not wanting to think about whether Freddie had been involved in the killing or not. Right now, he had only one thing on his mind—Laurel.

Connie entered the room, looking as weary as he felt.

"Want anything?" she asked. "Hot milk, chocolate, anything?"

"No," he replied, wanting only a few stiff drinks, but resisting. If and when he got news about Laurel, he wanted to be at optimum alertness; jump right into activity and make every effort to rescue her. He would never be able to live with himself if he messed up his chance to get her back because his brain was cloudy.

Connie dropped into a soft armchair near the sofa. She stared at him for a long while, then said, "You know, I'm sorry for everything."

"You? For what?"

"Everything," she said. "When I think back over my life, I see how so many decisions, maybe wrong decisions, brought you to where you are right now. I can't help but blame myself, in part, for all of this."

Over Mickey Boy's objections, Connie went on to ruminate first about getting pregnant by Don Vincenze, who was married at the time, then keeping the don from Mickey Boy from then on. "Maybe if I had let you grow under his influence, a lot of things never would have happened. Maybe he would have kept you out of jail . . . or taught you things that could have avoided what has happened now, to Laurel."

"Mom, oh Mom," Mickey Boy said. "If we all had crystal balls, life would be a snap. But somehow I don't think it's supposed to work out that way. I think, if there's a God, He needs some kind of amusement . . . and that's us." Mickey Boy threw his head back, looking up at the ceiling to keep tears from rolling down his face. "He must be having a helluva good time with us now," he said.

Connie, moved to tears herself, came to where Mickey Boy sat, kissed him on his forehead, and shuffled out of the room.

The phone ringing woke Mickey Boy. "Yeah, what is it?" he mumbled. His neck hurt from having slept with his head slung back on the sofa's top.

"Come, open zee door," Freddie said with an energetic snap. "I'm turning the corner to your house."

Mickey Boy darted to the door, watching Freddie pull up, then swung the door wide open.

Richie came through first, hugging Mickey Boy. The two of them swung each other in circles.

"Sonofabitch, look at you," Mickey Boy said. "You look like a blonde *tootsoone.*"

"Shit, mon," Richie replied. "I learn de reggae too, on the island where de Fonte send me."

With contradictory feelings of kinship and sorrow tearing him apart inside, Mickey Boy hugged Richie again.

Nicolo Fonte and Freddie Falcone came inside too. Freddie shut the door. "Sure, no fuckin' greeting for us—" He covered his mouth when he saw Connie coming down the stairs. "Oops!"

"Don't worry," Connie said. "I think I've heard one or two swear words in my life. And more than a few of them from you."

Nicolo Fonte took Connie's hand and kissed it. *"Signora, che bella,"* he said. *"Buona sera."*

"Good evening to you too, Mr. Fonte."

"Nicolo. Nicolo, please, *signora.*"

Richie hugged and kissed Connie.

"C'mon," Mickey Boy finally said. "Let's go out back and talk." On his way toward the door to the backyard, he wondered if it were safe to talk even out there. What if Trantino had pulled him out to make him believe it was safe? If Paul Trantino had taped Don Vincenze's conversations, why should he believe his were off limits? Mickey Boy wondered.

Before they got to the patio, Freddie pulled Mickey Boy aside. "Listen, about fatso," he began, speaking about the recently murdered Bobby Rimini.

"I told you I don't wanna know . . . good or bad," Mickey Boy replied, and hurried outside. "Whatever happened, happened, and he brought it on himself. I'm out of it."

Mickey Boy strolled away from the patio, out over the grass toward the tall bushes that separated the rear end of his property from the estate next door. If there was a bug outside, it would definitely not be that far from where everyone was expected to sit, he reasoned. He would come in close, or reenter the house only to discuss information he wanted to be sure got through to Paul Trantino.

Right now, though, he had private and very special business to take care of.

When they reached the farthest corner of his land, Mickey Boy pulled a key from his pocket and opened a shed where the gardener stored his equipment and supplies. Cartons, sacks, tools, and dirt were everywhere. A hose leaked a puddle of water on the floor. Dusty, humid air plugged Mickey Boy's nostrils.

Mickey yanked a chain in the middle of the room to light a single incandescent bulb.

Freddie shut the door behind them.

"Pretty, huh?" Mickey Boy asked. "But private . . . and right now, that's all that counts."

Richie, Fonte, and Freddie nodded solemnly. Perspiration on their faces shone brownish-yellow in the barely adequate light.

Mickey Boy lifted a paper grocery bag and set it on top of two piled-up boxes of outdoor Christmas decorations.

"They told you the deal?" Mickey Boy asked Richie.

"Yeah, he told me," Richie said, pointing a thumb at Nicolo Fonte. "He told me everything on the phone. I'm sorry."

"No, it's me who's sorry. You know, I didn't want to call you. It was a horror for me to try to decide what to do."

Having a choice of sacrificing one of the people he loved had tortured Mickey Boy for days. Of course he loved Laurel, and wanted her out of danger, but he was a boss too. Besides being one of his wards, Richie felt like as much a relative to him as his wife.

Richie said he was glad Mickey Boy had let him know about Laurel's kidnapping and Joe Augusta's demand for his head on a platter. He said he would never have forgiven himself if he'd let harm come to Laurel because he'd stayed away.

"I want you to know one thing before we start," Mickey Boy said. "I ain't giving you up. I'm getting you both out of there when we go to trade, or, pal, you an' me are dying together."

"Please," Freddie interrupted. "Let's not fit anybody out for toe tags yet. We're gonna kick ass when they give us a time an' place." He pointed to the bag. "Now, how about we get this show on the road?"

Mickey Boy opened the paper bag and lifted a box. From it he took a gun, a knife, and a picture of a saint.

"We're gonna face death together," Mickey Boy told Richie. "And when we do, I want you wearing the same shoes I do. I want you to be part of me. Do you want that?"

"Yes."

"You were already proposed and cleared before you got pinched," Mickey Boy went on. "So there's no problem. Tonight I am going to finish what Buster and my father started, and make you one of us."

To Nicolo Fonte, Mickey Boy said, "I want to make you one of us because you are one of the most honorable men I know, and I want us to really be a part of that seven-hundred-year tradition of honor and respect you told me about. Do you want that too?"

Nicolo Fonte shifted uncomfortably. "Though I am deeply moved by what you propose, and know the honor you intended, I do not feel that I should be . . . that I belong . . ."

"Of course you belong," Mickey Boy said. "You're one of us anyway." Aware of Nicolo Fonte's distaste for American mob guys, Mickey Boy braced for his refusal and prepared to press him further.

"One of who? You?" Fonte asked. "Frederico? Yes, I would be proud. The others?" He shrugged. "If it was years ago, maybe, yes."

"If it was in Italy?" Mickey Boy asked.

"Possibly. The tradition there is different. Men from all walks of life, all parts of society—"

"Well, I ask you to help me fix things here too," Mickey Boy said. If need be, he'd play on Fonte's guilt by bringing up the past; anything to make him feel as if he were truly upgrading the declining tradition he'd inherited.

Freddie said, "Nicolo, listen. Even here we've brought in gentlemen . . . just not enough. I know of at least one doctor Don Peppino straightened out, and there's a famous guy you would never believe that got made too. You wouldn't be alone, and you wouldn't be helping by running away.

Bringing in more honorable men, like yourself, is the only way we could hope to see this thing turn around for the better."

"Please, Nicolo," Mickey Boy said. "Do this for me . . . for all the people we care about."

Nicolo Fonte hesitated, each moment for Mickey Boy seeming multiplied by dozens. Finally Fonte said, "Yes. I would be proud to become your brother."

Mickey Boy nodded, satisfied. The shed's dimness made him feel like he'd stepped back in time, almost before electricity, before America, to a farmhouse somewhere in Sicily.

"Do you both realize that once you swear this oath, the only way you could leave is dead?"

Richie DeLuca and Nicolo Fonte both nodded.

"Good." Mickey Boy turned to Freddie, signaling him with a nod of his head to take over.

Freddie picked up the picture of the saint, crumpled it, and placed it in Richie's cupped hands. Striking a wooden match on its box, he said, "Repeat after me . . ."

75

July 25: Chelsea, Manhattan

"YOU LOOK PRETTY," LITTLE VINNIE SAID. HE WATCHED LAUREL primping in the mirror, fixing her lipstick, then stroking her hair with a brush. The gaunt look she'd developed over the first ten days of captivity was gone, leaving her with normally full features and a healthy blush. Instead of his eyes having been drawn constantly to notice her ribs showing, as she'd lain there in bed, her hands bound above her head, now he was able to concentrate on the lushness of her breasts as they swelled over the bras and panties he liked to see her in. The room smelled of the Paris perfume he'd given her.

When Laurel didn't respond to his compliment, Little Vinnie turned off the Sinatra tape she'd asked for and played repeatedly.

"Did you hear me?" he asked once the music had stopped. "You look pretty today."

"Thank you," Laurel said. "Would you be a doll and put Sinatra back on, please?" She rose from the dressing table, took off the diamond and gold cross she refused to wear when they had sex, and walked toward the bed, her legs stretched and narrowed by the high-heeled mules he'd bought. Unlike the religious pendant, the gold bracelet he'd given her dangled from her wrist.

With no expression on her face, Laurel unclipped the front of her bra, then removed her panties. His heart quickened watching her slide into the bed, waiting for him to make love to her.

"I brought us duck for dinner," he said. "With black cherry sauce. Sound good?"

"Yes," Laurel answered dryly. "You brought my medicine?"

"Listen, I don't think you should keep taking that shit," Little Vinnie replied, referring to the sedatives that Hale supplied.

Laurel flared. "I need that to sleep!" she said. Catching herself, she said, "Please, Vinnie, just to sleep."

Though the sedatives had served their purpose in the beginning, Little Vinnie now felt their time had passed. Laurel had obviously become too dependent on them, he told himself. Besides, he wanted them stopped. He wanted her thinking cleared. When she was with him, he needed her to want to be there.

"Vinnie, please," Laurel repeated, rising from the bed and coming to him. Still naked, she put her arms around his neck. "You wouldn't deny me peaceful sleep, would you?"

"I just don't want you hooked on that shit."

"I'm not," Laurel replied. "It's only to sleep . . . please." She kissed him on the ear and down his neck. "Come on," she said, leading him to the bed by his hand. "Let me take good care of you . . . then you take care of me."

Little Vinnie could hardly breathe. It was the first time she had ever come on to him. "I—I . . ." he muttered.

Saying, "I'll make you happy, then you'll give me my medicine, right?" Laurel stripped Little Vinnie's clothes off and placed herself between his knees. As she bent toward his erection, his heart stopped.

To that point Little Vinnie had never given Laurel the opportunity to give him oral sex, afraid that she'd bite his cock off. He clenched his fists as Laurel's mouth slipped over the top of his penis. Oh God, don't let her . . . he thought. It was only after she'd stroked it with her tongue a few times that he let himself relax.

Exuberant at the sight of Laurel's head bobbing up and down over his penis, Little Vinnie thought he might just cut down her dosage of sedative gradually, instead of eliminating it altogether.

Laurel sat up and prepared to mount Little Vinnie while he lay on his back. "Do I get my medicine?" she asked.

"Yes . . . anything you want."

76

August 1: Little Italy, Manhattan

THIS TIME WHEN MICKEY BOY TRAVELED TO MEET HIS CAPTAINS IN the apartment above the focacceria, he brought Nicolo Fonte too. Even though Fonte had been initiated into their *borgata* for his, Mickey Boy's, personal satisfaction rather than performance in street life, Mickey Boy had an obligation to introduce him around for him to get the respect due him as a made man. Fonte was reluctant, but agreed, smarting at the first taste of the demands that went along with the centuries-old honor.

Richie, of course, though requiring the same introduction

ceremony, would still have to remain hidden for his own protection.

Bad enough he'd jumped a few steps to get Fonte and Richie in, Mickey Boy had thought before leaving for Manhattan. He was sure, however, that with the internal war settled—not to mention his having leaked out word in the street about Laurel's kidnapping—he would have enough support from his men for inducting O.J. Simpson, if that were what he wanted. And putting out word of the kidnapping, after having fruitlessly waited for a traitor to identify himself after the meeting with Don Peppino, would help mobilize his troops to help him find his wife.

Knowing Paul Trantino was on his side—at least thinking so, he told himself—gave Mickey Boy even more confidence. Now he could go to the meeting without worrying about being grabbed for consorting or violating parole. Then again, Mickey Boy thought, how sure could he be that his parole officer, Frank Halloran, didn't know what was going on, or would cooperate if he did?

Shrugging his fear off as something he had to deal with, Mickey Boy and his two men entered the focacceria's private entrance, which led upstairs.

In the apartment's living room, Mickey Boy found most of his captains, from both the younger and older factions, at ease and socializing. It amazed him how it took the sacrifice of human life to give them excuses to compromise on their arguments. Without Bobby Rimini having been murdered as an offer of peace, he thought, these morons would have killed each other into their next generation. He just shook his head, then took to the task of greeting each of his people with a hug and a kiss.

Freddie brought the meeting to order by congratulating them all on having settled their "little disagreement." Now, once again, they would behave like brothers in the same family.

Mickey Boy then introduced Nicolo Fonte as a new made member of their *borgata*. He apologized for jumping steps, like informing them first, then waiting to see if there were any objections to Fonte's membership and checking Nicolo Fonte's family tree all the way back to Italy. He said Nicolo had given him a complete family breakdown, which assured him that his lineage on his father's side was indeed Italian, and that Fonte's word was good enough for him. If a problem should ever come up, Mickey Boy said, he would accept full responsibility, which, in fact, meant the possibility of being killed. So strong, he told them, was his faith in Nicolo Fonte.

Richie DeLuca was another matter, Mickey Boy said. He vouched for Richie too, having known him for almost fifteen years, and explained that Richie had to stay away from their meeting because of Joe Augusta being back and gunning for him.

Freddie took over, explaining formally to the men about Laurel. Though word had been sent to them a few days before, this was the first high-level, face-to-face meeting between family brass since then, and protocol had to be followed.

Freddie said that Joe had abducted her to bargain with for Richie's head. He assured them that Mickey Boy, as a man of honor and respect, had not contacted the authorities, and, as the boss of their family, would not consider sacrificing Richie, a brother of theirs, for his wife.

The men seemed seized the opportunity for a dramatic show of support. One by one they offered sympathy and help as they stepped forward to hug and kiss him again, and to whisper a personal vow of vengeance into his ear.

Each of them had family of their own, Mickey Boy thought, and could identify with his predicament. Nevertheless, their sincerity, which he felt more than saw, filled him with strength and pride. For all their faults, he thought, they were men, real men, and they looked up to him.

Freddie went on to say that they should use all their influence to find out any bit of information that could lead them closer to Joe Augusta.

The response was unanimous and overwhelming. Every human being under control of the Calabra Family, they swore, would be utilized in their boss's behalf.

One captain, Vinnie Lobsters, offered to keep an eye on Joe's brother-in-law, Nunzio D'Amato. "I'll keep one of my guys on him, and if Joe does make contact, we'll be on him in a fuckin' flash."

"No, just get to me right away," Mickey Boy said.

"You're the boss."

Mickey Boy sighed. "Yeah," he said.

With the meeting still under way, Mickey Boy picked himself up and left the room. The pity in his men's eyes, staring at him and, he knew, trying to picture themselves in his place, made his skin crawl.

Rosalie stood in the kitchen, cutting replacement chunks of sopresata salami and provolone cheese to bring to the living room. When Mickey Boy saw her, he turned to go back where he had come from.

"Mickey, please," Rosalie said.

Just what he needed, he thought, a sob story about being dumped—and having to face his guilt for more punishment. Deciding he deserved whatever punishment he got, he turned back to Rosalie. "Yeah, what is it?" he asked.

Rosalie nervously tapped the knife on top of the cheese. "I heard, yesterday, about your wife," she said, barely audible. "And I'm sorry." Rosalie paused, then said, "I'm sorry for a lot of things."

"Listen, Rosalie, please. There's no need to go through this."

"I just want you to know that I understand. I didn't at first. I thought you thought I wasn't good enough—"

"Rosalie, stop! I don't want to hear that."

"It's true."

"I said stop!"

"Well, anyway, I do now . . . understand. And I want you to know that I'm sorry for her too." Tears rolled down Rosalie's cheeks. "I'm sorry I ever wished her bad. I was such a jealous bitch, and cursed her for—"

Mickey Boy stepped over to Rosalie, who convulsed with sobs, and put his arms around her. Tears filled his eyes too while she shook in his arms. If he lived twice, he thought, he'd never understand women; never be sure of their desires; never comprehend their insecurities.

"It's all right," Mickey Boy said. "It's not your fault." He wanted to add that it was his, but knowing his guilt had to include her, he said, "It's nobody's . . . it just happened." Recovering, he mumbled, "But we're gonna get her back, I swear."

When Rosalie's crying subsided, she pushed back away

from him. Wiping her eyes and motioning toward the living room with her head, she said, "They won't understand."

Mickey Boy stepped forward and kissed Rosalie on the forehead.

"You're gonna pray to get her back, right?" he asked. "And celebrate when I do?"

"With magnums of champagne."

"And no feeling guilty, no more," he said. "'Cause it's not your fault. Curses or not, you had nothing to do with it."

"Neither did you."

Mickey Boy shrugged, then managed to form a weak smile for Rosalie's sake. "Friends?" he asked.

"Always."

77

August 1: Little Italy, Manhattan

FRANK HALLORAN NORMALLY HATED RAIN, BUT TODAY HE DIDN'T care if spikes fell from the sky. True, the rain annoyed the shit out of him, soaking his legs below his khaki slicker as he crouched behind the roof's end wall, but thank God, it managed to stay light enough to photograph through. So far he'd snapped at least three known felons entering the guinea restaurant across the street. More important, he'd also captured a picture of Mickey Boy Messina going in too. He'd hang around awhile longer, though, hoping to catch Messina coming out with one of the other ex-felons, so his evidence would be airtight instead of circumstantial. FBI agent or no FBI agent, he was taking Mickey Boy down for a violation.

What had really pissed off Frank Halloran had been that someone had reached out to Red Kelly and two other locals he'd called to break Messina's balls after the latest mob casualty, Bobby Rimini, had been found. Today, it seemed, more law enforcement guys were interested in their own careers rather than the obligation their jobs carried: get the goddamn criminals off the street. What they needed was more old-fashioned cops like his father and uncles, who would split a nightstick over a guy like Messina's head, instead of protecting him. At least he, Frank Halloran, knew his duty, and would make sure everyone knew it—including Paul Trantino and his adopted goombah, Mickey Boy Messina.

Halloran cursed as the sky darkened and dumped more water on him. Who knew if he would catch a decent photo now? he wondered. If he didn't know better, Halloran told himself, he would believe Trantino had reached God too.

"Don't move," a voice said from behind. Halloran felt the barrel of a gun push against his head.

Without moving a muscle, Halloran said, "Take it easy, I'm a federal officer." It dawned on him that that wasn't exactly what he should have said. What if they were junkies, who would off a federal officer faster than anyone?

"Put your hands behind your back and lay on the floor."

These had to be cops, Halloran thought. He began to turn. "Hey, I said I'm with the—" A foot shoved him sideways, dumping him head first into a puddle. "Hey, what the fuck—"

One of the three huge men, in raincoats and hats, rolled Halloran on his stomach and quickly cuffed him behind his back. The man lifted him straight up. Halloran's pants stuck to his body, and rain ran down his face and neck, as the hood had slid off his head.

"Hey, I'm a federal parole officer," Halloran said. It had to be a misunderstanding. "Check my wallet, in my back pocket." He stuck his hip out toward the man who had cuffed him.

The man, who had FBI written all over him, lifted Halloran's wallet and, without looking at it, tossed it over the side of the roof. "Now, where did you say your ID is?" he asked.

"What the fuck's going on here!" Halloran screamed. "Is this Trantino's doing? You'll be up to your tongues in shit when I report this!"

"Who's going to listen to you?" Paul Trantino asked, walking out from the stairwell. "A vagrant? No ID? Stalking people from the roof? Maybe a child killer?"

"I'll have your fuckin' job for this!" Halloran screamed.

"Be thankful you have your own when I get through with you." Trantino turned to his men. "Where am I now?"

"Newark, as far as we know," one answered.

"Newark it is." Trantino stepped closer to Halloran. "It's not nice to fuck around with Big Brother."

"Fuck you!"

Halloran screamed, catching a mouthful of rain as Paul Trantino's knee smashed into his balls.

78

August 3: Upper West Side, Manhattan

"HOLD PLEASE," THE LONG DISTANCE OPERATOR SAID. "WE'VE got some difficulty on the circuits."

Little Vinnie wrinkled his nose. The dreariness of DoDo's Hell's Kitchen railroad flat was bad enough; the smell was almost intolerable.

"Why don't you hang odor eaters all over yourself?" Little Vinnie asked DoDo, who sat across the table from him, cutting chunks of salami and provolone cheese and shoving them into his mouth.

"Wha? *Qui fa?*" DoDo asked. "Wha's is, this 'hodor'?"

"Odor, not 'hodor.' Fuckin' Hodor sells kitchen sets," Little Vinnie replied, laughing. "Odor . . . odor, like the fuckin' smell of oregano."

DoDo waved a dismissing hand, saying, *"Tu si pazzo,"* you're crazy, then went on eating his cheese. "Oregano, itsa smell good."

"Yeah, if you're a fuckin' pizza."

Suddenly, the familiar old voice crackled in the receiver. "Vincenze, Vincenze, *come sta?*" How do you feel? It was Don Genco, from his villa in Acireale.

"Good . . . I'm okay," Little Vinnie replied. "And you, you're okay?"

"As always. But it is you I worry about. That is why I had DoDo ask you to phone me."

After some small talk, about the weather, Don Genco's arthritis, and Ninfa—in that order—Don Genco got down to the real matter at hand. "What takes you so long?" he asked in flowery Sicilian dialect. "This task of yours should have been completed weeks ago. You know, I have given you a lot of support, an' am now beginning to feel embarrassed . . . for you, of course. What is the problem?"

"No problem . . . just takes time here . . . things are different than over there—"

"I know very well the differences!" Don Genco snapped. "But time is time, and duty is duty . . . everywhere."

Little Vinnie's foot shook wildly under the table. His fingers drummed steadily on the yellowed white tabletop. Why couldn't this old bastard just fall off during the night; die quietly in bed? He was certainly old enough, Little Vinnie thought. Much as he cared for Don Genco, he told himself, he could use the easing of pressure that Genco's passing on would bring.

"I promise, it won't be long now," Little Vinnie said. "I just want to make sure everything is done right . . . that I don't make things worse."

"Worse than what? How much worse could they be?"

Little Vinnie could almost feel Don Genco's smug little sneer, his gold tooth winking in his oversalivating mouth. "Worse could mean me being in jail instead of courting Ninfa."

"If I give my permission."

The smell of raw garlic wafted across the table as DoDo began chewing a couple of peeled cloves. Little Vinnie fanned the air. "But I know you will," he said into the phone.

No reply.

"Right?" Little Vinnie asked nervously. His stomach knotted up. On one hand, he would have liked to tell the old man to go fuck himself, and stay with Laurel. On the other hand, he knew where his future lay. "You'll say okay, right?"

"Maybe," Don Genco replied. "The longer you take to complete your business, the less I feel good about you marrying my niece."

"It'll be soon. I swear."

"Good," Don Genco said. He changed his tone and asked if Little Vinnie thought Joe Augusta had really found him because of Don Peppino's advice, as Joe had claimed, or by coincidence. Did Vinnie believe what Joe said, or was the man just crazy?

"Yeah, he's nuts," Little Vinnie replied. "But not out-of-it nuts, where he don't know what's going on, and he don't lie, 'cause he's too much of a maniac to care what anybody thinks."

Don Genco said Little Vinnie's language had lost him, and made him repeat his assessment of Joe Augusta, in Sicilian.

"But don't worry about him," Little Vinnie went on. "One of his guys probably spotted me, and he probably said it to Joe offhand. I'm just glad he didn't say nothing to that other bastard," he said, not wanting to even mouth Mickey Boy's name.

"It might have been better if he had," Don Genco said, with an accompanying chuckle. "Maybe he would force you to do what you are supposed to . . . or maybe he would end it another way."

"Don't worry, I'll do what I gotta!" Little Vinnie said.

The phone clicked off on the other end.

Little Vinnie walked into the Greek doughnut shop, happy to smell cinnamon and chocolate after an hour and a half with DoDo. Joe Augusta sat at a small table in the rear, dunking a cruller into a paper cup of coffee.

"Good news," Joe said, looking up as Little Vinnie walked up to his table. "I sent word out to Mickey Boy, my own way, through my own contact. Now we'll have this thing over and done with in a few days, as soon as my guy can cover himself."

Little Vinnie felt as though he'd been stabbed in the chest. "But shouldn't we wait till—"

"Till nothing!" Joe snapped. "You got me waiting for things to cool down, till the weather changes, till your balls get big enough to do what we gotta do. A month I put up with that bullshit. Enough is enough. Now we're moving."

Little Vinnie's breathing quickened and his fists balled beneath the table.

"Besides," Joe continued, "I hate keeping that girl from her family . . . from her kid. It ain't right, what we're doing. I want her back there already."

Yeah, in a pig's ass, Little Vinnie thought, determined not to lose Laurel this quickly. He still needed time with her, still had work to do to win her over completely. So far, he'd been able to keep stalling. Now he was in a corner. Please, God, he begged silently. Please let me find a way to keep her a little longer.

Beneath the table Little Vinnie squeezed his finger, pulling on the trigger of an imaginary gun he wished were real and pointed at Joe.

79

August 4: Elizabeth, New Jersey

MICKEY BOY DROVE OFF THE GOETHALS BRIDGE AND ALONG Bayway Avenue. He was surprised to find that at four-thirty in the morning his wasn't the only vehicle on the move. No traffic jam, but a few trucks and one or two cars. Hopefully no one he knew.

Dressed in jeans, an old blue sweatshirt, and one of Laurel's New York Yankee caps, he felt like a goddamned *mammaluke.* Certainly not the kind of look that would get him recognized. He'd heard that each person had an almost exact double walking around somewhere. He wondered if his double looked like he did at that moment, or was some tattooed gorilla riding with a motorcycle gang.

A few blocks farther Mickey Boy made a right into the Bayway Diner's parking lot. Once again trucks on their way to early deliveries were most represented. None of their drivers to worry about recognizing him, he thought while getting out of his car, unless they were hijackers stopping for coffee before going on to Staten Island or Brooklyn.

Once inside the diner, Mickey Boy immediately spotted Paul Trantino in a booth to his far right. In contrast to his own appearance, Paul wore a tan sport jacket with a brown Italian knit shirt underneath. A tiger-eye ring adorned his pinky.

"You look like a shylock waiting to collect from a shmuck customer," Mickey Boy said. "One who looks like me."

Paul laughed and stood to shake Mickey Boy's hand. "You have no idea how many times I turned down offers to go undercover with you guys."

"Thank God you didn't."

"Not that it's not a useful and necessary procedure many times," Paul said. "Just not for me. I couldn't become intimate with someone, then hang them. I'd rather establish clear lines of battle, and do my job straight up—with honor."

After ordering breakfasts of sausages, eggs, and buttered rolls, Mickey Boy asked Paul if he was taping him, like he'd done to Don Vincenze. Paul replied that if he were, they would be like Nixon's tapes, which should have been burned. If their meeting were recorded, he added, it would probably cost him his job rather than make him a hero.

While Mickey Boy felt an affinity for the burly FBI man, he still didn't fully trust his motives. Paul had started an investigation into Laurel's disappearance, which he said was strictly off the record. Who knew? The only thing Mickey Boy was sure of was that, as far as he knew, no street gossip had reached his or Freddie's ears of his having gone to the authorities for help.

"I told you I'd bring you up-to-date with anything I found," Paul said. "That's why I wanted to see you."

Paul told Mickey Boy that they'd finally received their

first break in their search for Joe Augusta. "We stuck a tap on Nunzio D'Amato's phone . . . you know who he is?"

"Yeah, Joe's brother-in-law." Mickey Boy wondered if the FBI had seen his men keeping an eye on Nunzio. Thinking both that he couldn't leave one of his men in the spotlight that way and that if the FBI had Nunzio covered it was enough, he made a mental note to have Freddie call off whoever they had on that job.

"Right, Theresa's brother," Paul said. "Anyway, yesterday Theresa called, complaining about Joe being gone and her having her daughter, Elizabeth, sick——"

"Not serious?" Mickey Boy asked.

"Chronic tonsillitis . . . had it myself as a kid; my daughter, Kim, suffers with it too. Anyway, they were on the phone long enough for us to 'trap' it, that is, trace it back to its point of origin."

Paul went on to say that he'd contacted the Canadian police and had sent one of his men up to work with them. "Obviously, if she's calling, looking for him, then he's not there. He will, however, eventually show up . . . that is, if we don't get him first."

"What about Little Vinnie?"

"Nothing yet," Paul replied. "We'll locate him, though I can't guarantee protection overseas."

"Another curse my old man left behind," Mickey Boy said, shaking his head.

Paul laughed. "I think if you would have talked to him, he would have seen it differently."

"How?"

Paul told Mickey Boy to think about all the mob fathers who had been murdered because of their offsprings' transgressions.

"I know a half dozen: Sally Burns, Jimmy Ip——"

"Your own father."

Mickey Boy nodded. Nothing more to say. Who else could matter more?

Now, Paul asked, how many reverse situations did he know of?

Mickey Boy thought for a moment, then replied, "None that I know of."

"If your old man were sitting here right now," Paul said,

"I could hear him saying . . ." He imitated Don Vincenze's slow, deliberate speech, as he continued, ". . . 'We give them the blood of our fathers, and you know what they give us back in return? Death. We die for the sins of our sons.'"

"He'd be full of shit."

"It wouldn't be the first time. But I think he'd really believe that . . . and he might not have been entirely wrong." Paul shrugged. "Anyway, I'll keep plugging away till I find Joe Augusta . . . and I will."

Mickey Boy thanked Paul for his concern and help. "I know you guys give away ice in the winter, but you never asked me for nothing," he said. "I just want you to know I can't trade off information about other guys, or—"

Paul raised a hand to stop Mickey Boy. "I haven't asked you for anything, and I won't. I'm helping because I want to."

"Thanks, but—"

"No buts," Paul said. "When I look at you, I see me . . . what I could have been, if not for my old man deciding to do the right thing after the war." Paul shook his head. "I don't envy you. Since this started, I look at my two girls in bed and silently thank my dad, over and over, for doing what he did."

Mickey Boy felt touched by Paul's obvious sincerity.

"I was lucky my father was born before me."

"Me, I'm not so sure," Mickey Boy said, trying to imagine how his life could have been different if Don Vincenze had been a different man.

"I don't know, you may be right. All I know is that my father loved your father, and felt sorry for him too. Told me stories about your father's uncle, Nino—a real mafioso tyrant; how he used to abuse the shit out of your father; leave him and your grandmother like paupers, while he rode around in a big Cadillac and spent fortunes on wine, women, and song."

Paul said that, according to his father, Vincenze Calabra had always been driven by poverty in back of him and the example of his uncle as a success in front.

"The man never really had a chance," Paul said. He paused, then added, "But from the few meetings I had with him, I saw that he felt guilty for what he'd done to you, and tried to make up for it. Just think of what it meant to a man like him, with his upbringing, to work with the FBI . . . to be a snitch."

Mickey Boy tensed at the reference to Don Vincenze in that way.

"I'm sorry, you can play semantics with it, but that's basically what he did. It may sting to think of it that way, but think about how much love he had for you to make him do it."

Paul claimed that because he knew of Don Vincenze's reputation for treachery, it had taken him a while to trust his motives. "That's why I taped all our meetings. The man was just so goddamn slick, I was afraid I'd wind up on the short end of the stick, and had to protect myself."

As usual, any discussion of his father made Mickey Boy's stomach and throat knot up. "Anything else you found?" he asked quickly, while glancing around the room to avoid eye contact with Paul. "Any little clue you mighta forgot?"

"Nothing, really," Paul replied. "Dropped a bug on the old man, Palermo's phone . . ."

Would he ever love to listen to every sneaky, double-banging word Don Peppino said on the phone, Mickey Boy thought. Would he love to ask Paul to turn the tapes over . . .

"The minute he gets a call from Augusta, I'll be on the horn to you," Paul went on. "I know how frustrated you must feel."

"Nobody knows how I feel."

Paul shrugged, then told Mickey Boy about Halloran; how he'd found him on the roof, stripped him of his ID, then had him pulled in.

Though pleased, Mickey Boy felt too weary and troubled to laugh.

"This Halloran just never learned how to play modern politics in the system," Paul said. "It isn't the old days, when it was a father and son club. Too many outsiders in power. Can't step on their cocks."

"Like yours."

"Like mine," Paul said, chuckling. "In your business, the guys who mess up the politics wind up in a trunk. In mine, they wind up in the asshole of the earth, either getting cabin fever in the winter and eaten alive in the summer, or in the jungle, getting sniped at by every crack addict who manages to get his hands on a Saturday night special."

"Which did Halloran get?"

"Don't know, and don't care," Paul replied. "All I know is that when you report again, you'll be assigned a new guy."

Once more Mickey Boy thanked Paul Trantino. And once more he brought the discussion back to Laurel's abduction. "We're gonna hear real soon, huh?"

Paul nodded. "I expect Augusta is going nuts to get his hands on DeLuca. There'll be an exchange offer soon."

"You're all set, the way we planned?"

"Like a Cecil B. DeMille production," Paul answered. "I even spoke to your wife's cousin, the doctor, personally. Sweet girl."

"Yeah, Tammy's great."

Mickey Boy had had enough. He remembered the words that he'd told Richie and Nicolo just a short while ago: "Do you both realize that once you swear this oath, the only way you could leave is dead?" If he couldn't throw in the towel and walk away from mob life, he would have to sneak away.

Working with both Paul Trantino and Tammy, Mickey Boy had devised a plan: When an exchange was attempted between Laurel and Richie, a barrage of gunshots would be fired. Mickey Boy would hit the deck. Paul would pronounce him shot and rush him to the hospital, where Tammy would keep him under wraps, both literally and figuratively. The word would go out that Mickey Boy had barely survived, had sustained permanent damage, and would be unable to continue with any kind of active life, let alone mob life.

As a known cripple, Mickey would be able to retire to Florida, with Laurel and Hope, and spend his remaining days in quiet obscurity. All he needed was to get Laurel back unharmed.

"Just make sure any word you get about your wife is said where we can monitor it," Paul said. "Once we get a time and place, we'll be there in a flash." He reached across the table and grabbed Mickey Boy's hand. "We're gonna beat this," he said. "You and Laurel are getting out of this in one piece."

"Richie too."

"Him too."

"When this is over, I guess I won't be seeing you no more," Mickey Boy said.

"I'll know where you are. We can still send Christmas and birthday cards, like our fathers did all these years."

"I guess we're more like them than we think sometimes," Mickey Boy said, feeling doomed by the thought.

Paul smiled. "And less."

80

August 7: Chelsea, Manhattan

LITTLE VINNIE DIPPED INTO THE BENTO BOX TO LIFT A SHRIMP tempura. He bent over the snack table, biting at the seafood at the end of his chopsticks.

"Mmmm, good," he mumbled with his mouth full, then told Laurel, "Go ahead, taste it. Just make sure you don't burn your mouth."

He watched Laurel lift a cucumber from the sunamono and set it in her mouth. Just seeing the tip of her tongue dart out to accept the morsel of food made him so goddamn hot. He could have sucked on her tongue all day, he thought. Just lay alongside her, hold her, and kiss her till neither one of them could breathe.

When Laurel looked up at him, he caught the pensive stare that, according to a conversation related to him by Tempest, marked her recognition of something of her husband in Vinnie. Looking down at his food, he gnashed his teeth and felt what he'd already eaten stuck in his chest. Why did that Mickey Boy bastard have to be born? he asked himself. Why did he have to cast a shadow over his entire life, from his lack of relationship with his father to his love for Laurel?

As Little Vinnie looked up over his chopsticks again, he

felt, more than saw, a glimmer of a smile from Laurel. Suddenly his anger ebbed and he felt warmth and sexual excitement. For the time being, he decided, once again, he'd take whatever Laurel had to give, for whatever reason. If the reminder of Mickey Boy moved her now, in time she'd remember no one but Vincent Calabra.

But when?

Though time had worked on his side so far, Little Vinnie knew it would become his enemy soon. Through a system of rewards, constant reminders that Mickey Boy didn't care about her, and real caring on his part, he'd managed to turn Laurel from a bound prisoner to an accepting, free lover. It had begun that day when she made love to him because she'd wanted more sedatives.

Little Vinnie, however, considered himself no dope. He'd promised her the sedatives, but had been gradually diminishing the dosage she received. Laurel became markedly nervous, sleeping for shorter periods of time, but more alert and more actively sexual in seeking whatever doses of sedatives he dispensed. Her depression would end soon, he told himself, when she was totally weaned from the medicine.

He'd also assured her that he found out that Mickey Boy's mother was on permanent babysitting duty, and he offered to snatch the child and bring her, which stopped Laurel from constantly worrying about her daughter. Laurel never mentioned Hope to him again. In his heart, however, Little Vinnie felt there was a better than even chance that when release time did roll around, Laurel would choose to stay with him—especially if Mickey Boy was dead.

"Can we change the Sinatra tape for a while?" Little Vinnie asked. "I love the guy too, but this is—"

"No," Laurel said, staring off vacantly past him.

"Okay, okay," he quickly replied, smiling and lifting his hands in defense. "Relax," he said. "You know my job is to please." It amazed him that even though he loved to see her happy, he enjoyed angering her, then bringing her to smile even more. He gazed down at the cleavage showing through the gaping front of the Japanese-style kimono he'd bought her.

"You know, you look great in red," he said.

"Better without it, right?"

"Absolutely." Little Vinnie's erection sprang to life instantly. "But is there something wrong with that?"

Laurel began to answer, stammered, then remained silent.

"You should be proud of the way you look naked . . . and how great you are in bed," Little Vinnie added.

Laurel looked up at him. Her expression appeared strangely inquisitive.

"When two people care about each other, like I do about you, sex is the greatest thing in the world. You could shit on my chest, an' I'd love it," he teased. "I only wish there were more places on your body I could make love to."

"Can I have my medicine now?" Laurel asked, her mood suddenly morose.

"Wait awhile . . . a little later."

Laurel let her silk kimono fall completely open. Her breasts glistened like porcelain. Her nipples bloomed into stiff buds.

"Please, now," she asked.

Little Vinnie moved the snack table aside, then stepped in front of Laurel. He gently took her head in his hands, running them down behind her ears to massage her neck.

Laurel responded exactly as he hoped she would, unzipping his pants to let his erection free. He stepped closer to the bed so that his penis could slip between her breasts, their delicate blue veins becoming more vivid behind the pure white skin as she pushed them in from either side. The feel of warm flesh against his felt so good. Through half-closed eyes, he watched her head bow . . . when the doorbell rang.

"Fuck!" he shouted. He moved closer, massaging Laurel's neck and shoulders as she pressed her breasts in on his pelvis.

The doorbell rang again.

"Maybe you should answer it," Laurel said, massaging his erection with her breasts.

"Fuck 'em."

The doorbell rang a third time.

"Maybe it's important. Go, we'll finish when they leave."

Angrily, Little Vinnie stuffed his penis into his trousers

and stormed off, zipping himself up as he went. When he got to the bedroom door, he turned to Laurel. "Do I have to lock you in?"

Laurel shook her head. "Just hurry," she said.

Muttering, "I know . . . and bring your fuckin' medicine," he went to the front door and peeped through the hole.

The bell rang again.

"What the fuck do you want?" Little Vinnie said, pulling the door to the apartment open a small amount.

"I wanted to talk to you," Rosalie said. "Just for a minute."

"I ain't got a minute."

"Please, Vinnie, I just want to apologize for the way I've been. You know, late, moody, not wanting to come see you."

"What happened?" Little Vinnie asked. "The other guy dump you?"

"Vinnie, please, I didn't come here to fight."

Little Vinnie looked at Rosalie's face for several seconds, studying her strong features. This one could be a real bitch, he told himself. The last thing he needed was her blabbing that he was in the city, just to spite him. He opened the door a bit wider and stepped outside.

For the next five minutes he tried to convince Rosalie that he couldn't let her in because he had a business associate there, and it was very private. She, of course, challenged him, saying that she believed he had another woman there, but that it was all right.

"What could I expect, after the way I acted, like I didn't want to be with you?" she asked.

"Listen, how about I promise I'll call you tomorrow, an' we'll get together?" he said. "A drink, maybe dinner. Okay?"

"Yes," Rosalie replied. "That's good. You and me."

Little Vinnie opened the door to step back inside. "Okay, I'll see you tomorrow," he said.

Rosalie stared at him strangely, then turned and stepped to the elevator.

Puzzled, Little Vinnie turned to see the door to the bedroom closing. It took a couple of seconds to realize that

Rosalie had probably seen Laurel—too many seconds. He darted at the elevator, but it was already on its way down. He pounded his fist on the door, then started for the stairs. When he realized he'd be leaving Laurel alone, with all the doors open and access to a phone, he changed direction and stormed back into the apartment.

He rushed into the bedroom, where Laurel lay on the bed, totally naked.

"What the fuck did you do?" he screamed.

"Nothing," Laurel said. "I just opened the door a crack to see if you were coming back, that's all."

"She saw you."

"No, Vinnie. No one saw me. The door was barely open enough for me to look for you."

Little Vinnie stared at Laurel, trying to read her eyes, then looked back at the door, then back to Laurel.

"Come on," she said, lifting her arms to welcome him. His eyes roved down her body to the thatch of golden brown hair. Her legs parted slightly. "Come, relax."

Calculating how much time he had to get her the hell out and into another place, Little Vinnie stripped off his clothes and headed toward Laurel's outstretched arms.

81

August 7: Gravesend, Brooklyn

SOFIA PALERMO LOOKED FIRST AT THE EMPTY SPOT NEXT TO HER on the bed, then at the gold provincial clock on her nightstand. 12:32.

What is wrong with that man? Sofia wondered, slipping out of bed and into the robe she kept nearby. If her husband, Peppino, didn't have a mind that constantly demonstrated how young and agile it remained, she would have worried about senility lately. But she knew that if her Peppino seemed preoccupied, it was with matters dealing with his other life. Lately, he seemed more and more disappointed in the way things were going.

A quiet and dutiful wife, raised in the old Castellamarese tradition, she said little but heard a lot; understood even more. It was time, she hoped, that Peppino would decide that the younger generations didn't deserve his help, though Lord knew they needed it. With God's help, she would finally get him to come up with the idea for them to spend the rest of their time together in their Long Island home, in retirement. Maybe she could even manipulate him into deciding they should spend a few months in Sicily.

On the way down the stairs, Sofia took pride in how well women like her managed to get what they wanted out of life. Not like the women of today, whose demands were unreasonable for a healthy, strong-minded man to meet. Even her own daughters had spoken at times of divorce.

Sofia sniffed the air as she approached the den. Oregano, she identified to herself, something a woman who had been cooking for over sixty years could do easily. Was that *sfatcheem* of hers eating pizza that late at night? Didn't he know how fragile his digestive system had become? What did he think, he was twenty years old again, when he would *shcaff* up cold meatballs and pasta in the middle of the night, when he'd come in from wherever he'd been? Or whoever he'd been with? She smiled, satisfied that she'd outlasted the few bimbos that had come into her beloved husband's life.

When she swung the door open and entered the room, the pizza smell became stronger. Whoever had baked that one could take a lesson in cooking, Sofia thought.

"Peppino, dove sono tu?" Sofia called, in a low voice. Where are you? She walked slowly toward the recliner, which her husband had facing the stereo. Luciano Pavarotti, singing "La Donna e Mobile," came softly through the stereo speakers.

"Peppino," Sofia said again as she stepped around the La-Z-Boy.

No Peppino.

For some reason, Sofia's eyes were drawn downward and to her left, where her husband's body lay, his mouth gaping open and blood pouring out onto the carpet from where his tongue used to be.

82

August 8: Todt Hill, Staten Island

"WHAT THE HELL ARE YOU DOING HERE?" MICKEY BOY ASKED, shaking his head to clear it of cobwebs. The dawn sun, peeking over neighborhood rooftops, glared in his eyes.

"I'm sorry," Rosalie said. "I had to come . . ." Her entire body seemed in motion, as if she were about ready to take off on a race, or holding her urine. "I have to talk to you."

Mickey Boy looked into the house, then out at Rosalie. "Okay, come in."

Rosalie rushed past him, but stopped before leaving the foyer for the living room. She looked Mickey Boy up and down, wrinkling her nose at how rumpled he looked from sleeping in his clothes.

"Gotta be ready to go at any time," he said. "How did you know where I live?" Seeing Rosalie again, especially in his home, brought overwhelming feelings of guilt to him.

"I found out right after you were married . . . passed by more times than you can imagine." Rosalie grabbed him by the sleeve. "But that's not why I came here now," she said, looking more nervous than he'd ever seen her.

Mickey Boy led her into the living room. "Wanna drink or something?"

"No."

Though Rosalie had obviously come to tell him something of importance to her, it appeared difficult for her to begin. Whatever it was, Mickey Boy thought, he wished she would blurt it out—tell him how much she missed him or how sorry she was about Laurel—then leave.

Rosalie instead began to confess about an affair she'd had over a period of time beginning before she'd started seeing him.

God, no. Don't let her tell me she's got AIDS.

Rosalie went on, saying that when she began sleeping with Mickey Boy she tried to cut it off with the other guy, but he'd threatened her and scared her into continuing to see him.

If she needed help with getting some guy off her back, Mickey Boy wished she would get to the point, then leave him alone.

"I need a cup of coffee," he said, stepping toward the kitchen. "You want any?"

"It was Little Vinnie."

Mickey Boy spun around. "What?"

"Little Vinnie . . . your brother. He's the one I was seeing." Rosalie hung her head.

When did that little prick get back? Mickey Boy wondered. And why hadn't anyone told him before this? If Rosalie had been seeing Little Vinnie first, he had to be in New York for at least three or four months. So much for a boss knowing everything that was going on in his territory. He made a quick mental note to have some of his men look for Little Vinnie and either put him under wraps or boot him out of the country again, at least till Joe Augusta was taken care of.

Mickey Boy glared at Rosalie, feeling betrayed. Goddamn cunt, he thought. How the hell could he have ever been so stupid as to cheat on Laurel with a slut like her?

"So you confessed," he said. "What now?"

Speaking with her head still hung, Rosalie said, "I stopped seeing him when he stopped bothering me, a few weeks ago. I figured he must've found somebody else . . . that he was another guy who felt I wasn't worth more than a couple of humps."

Mickey Boy's patience thinned even more. "I told you before, I don't wanna hear you rippin' yourself down." He sighed, then asked, "That it?"

"I'm so ashamed to tell you this," Rosalie went on, "but

yesterday I felt really lonely, and, jerk that I am, instead of looking for some straight-up schmuck, I went up to his apartment to try to make up with him."

"Listen, Rosalie, I ain't a fuckin' priest. Just tell me where he is."

Rosalie looked up. "When I went there, he had a woman inside. I saw her through the open door . . . but just for a second."

"And she was a nigger . . . hopefully over three hundred pounds."

"No, I think she was your wife."

Mickey Boy sped as quickly as he dared through the Brooklyn Battery Tunnel and out onto West Street. The last thing in the world he wanted was to be stopped by some doofus traffic cop, and take a chance of him finding the .38 revolver he had stuck under the armrest.

He'd taken the address from Rosalie and shot out of his garage, without even having tried to reach Freddie or any of his other men. If Rosalie had been bright enough to come to him immediately, the previous evening, he might have proceeded differently. But she claimed she hadn't been sure that it was Laurel, and had debated with herself all night whether to come to him at all, and now he didn't have any time to waste.

Mickey Boy cautioned himself against getting too excited. If Joe Augusta really had Laurel, then chances are Rosalie had been mistaken. It was inconceivable that Joe would be working with the person who had blown his daughter's brains out.

That goddamn Little Vinnie remained a curse his father had left him, Mickey Boy told himself. If only that scumbag wasn't his brother . . . if only his own sense of honor would let him overlook that bond.

Mickey Boy found a parking spot, facing south toward the tunnel and bridges, around the corner from the address Rosalie had given him. Getting away was as important as accomplishing whatever it was he wanted to once he saw what he faced.

He half walked, half ran the distance to the warehouse

building where Rosalie said Little Vinnie was. As he passed a doorway a few numbers ahead, two men stepped out, seized him by both arms and dragged him in.

"What the fuck!" he yelled, then had a hand slapped over his mouth to silence him.

"Relax, we're waiting here for Trantino," one of the men said. "He's on his way from the Island; be here in a little while."

It took Mickey Boy a few seconds more to pull the danger signals his brain had sent out and stop struggling.

Without speaking to the men, Mickey Boy followed them to a parked van. He waited inside for about twenty minutes till Paul Trantino arrived, dressed as Mickey Boy hadn't previously seen him, in jeans, a navy Polo shirt, and a mangled blue fishing hat. He ordered the other men to take up positions on the street, checking it for anything unusual, then to follow him into the building.

When the FBI men had left, Paul told Mickey Boy, "We're going in, and hope she's there. Just hang on here till we—"

"No fuckin' way!" Mickey Boy said. "I'm going with youse, or I'm going myself. It's my wife and my brother we're talking about here."

"That's why you shouldn't. You're too close to it."

"I don't give a fuck! I'm going," Mickey Boy insisted. "Besides, don't we have something planned, just in case?"

"I don't know . . . maybe we can find another way."

"I thought we had a deal?" Mickey Boy said, glaring at Paul. "Me and Laurel outta here, with no questions and no heat?"

Paul Trantino thought for a moment, then said, "Yeah, I guess you're right. I haven't reached Tammy yet, but that's no problem. I could get her on her beeper and have her at the hospital to cover for you in no time."

Paul opened a built-in floor locker, then grabbed a bullet-proof vest and a heavy sweatshirt.

"Here," he said, handing them to Mickey Boy. "Just to show you I intended to keep my promise. I had this shirt set up just like in the movies. Press those lumps you feel, and you'll be spurting the nastiest-looking blood you can imagine."

"What about the vest?"

"You must wear that," Paul said. "Just flip it open when the action stops and fall down. I'll get to you and cover you right away."

The one thing Paul insisted on was that Mickey Boy leave his gun behind. No criminal charge, he said, and he would return it if this turned out to be a false alarm.

Paul read off a list of instructions as they walked toward the building. Mickey Boy was to follow them in, diving for the ground and rolling as far as he could to his right.

Upstairs, the FBI men paired off on either side of the door. All wore vests, like Mickey Boy and Paul Trantino, that had stenciled on the back FBI in big white letters. One of the men stuffed the apartment's lock with something Mickey Boy couldn't make out too well from his position behind Paul.

"Open up, FBI," Paul Trantino whispered. "I guess they refused," he said instantly, nodding to his man, who lit whatever he had stuffed in the keyhole.

When Mickey Boy saw the FBI men cover their ears, he followed suit.

A couple of seconds later the lock exploded with a roar that pierced Mickey Boy's hands and rocked his eardrums. Almost at the same time, the FBI men, guns drawn, charged through. Mickey Boy ran behind them in a crouch, then felt Paul Trantino push him hard to the right. He slammed into a wall, but rebounded to try to follow through the second door the men smashed through. This time he saw someone in bed pointing a pistol at them and firing. A bullet whizzed past his head as he dove for cover without Paul's help, feeling things pop on his chest as he hit the floor. Two more shots blasted from his right.

Then it was quiet.

When Mickey Boy pulled himself to his knees, he saw a splash of blood over the wall behind the bed and a lifeless half-naked woman's body, her head hanging back off the bed. Blood ran down her neck, through her dark hair, and onto the white carpet.

Mickey Boy took deep breaths and hung his head, trying to regain his balance while the FBI men searched the house. The front of his shirt was soaked red with whatever Paul had used as blood.

"Sorry," Paul Trantino finally said. "No one here but her." He stuck one finger into the corpse's waistband and lifted it to peek inside. "I mean him," he added.

Mickey Boy felt like he would throw up, as the tension and excitement he'd felt at the thought of recovering Laurel went plummeting down. Trembling, he leaned on the dresser for support—and saw the diamond and gold cross he'd given Laurel for Christmas.

83

August 10: Morningside Heights, Manhattan

"I DON'T CARE HOW YOU DO IT, JUST GODDAMN DO IT!" JOE Augusta said through gritted teeth. He looked around at the other, mostly black patrons in the beat-up coffee shop, to make sure they hadn't heard. "We waited too long. That's why this happened."

After Rosalie had left, Little Vinnie made love to Laurel, then panicked. On the spur of the moment, he'd packed her up quickly and spirited her off to Hale's apartment, which he shared with a common-law wife, not far from the Columbia University campus. Hale protested Little Vinnie's bringing Laurel there, but Vinnie convinced him that a huge ransom for Laurel was imminent and that he would get a bigger chunk of it. That settled, he then posted Hale outside the bedroom door and slept with Laurel overnight for the first time.

Waking up next to her had been one of the most pleasurable experiences in Little Vinnie's life. He stayed next to her, studying every movement of her mouth, every flutter of her eyelids, until she too awakened. Despite a weak protest from her, he convinced her to shower with him, then shared a breakfast of eggs and turkey sausage that Hale's wife had prepared.

It was only later, when he had tried to call Tempest, that his day began to change. Afraid to show up in person, Little Vinnie had called intermittently all day—until he read that evening's *Daily News,* and saw that Tempest, whose name he found out was Ernest Holzen, had been found murdered in his apartment. The paper said that police thought it might be a sex-related crime.

In a pig's ass, Little Vinnie had thought, with both anger and sadness, knowing for sure Rosalie had ratted him out to Mickey Boy.

The previous day's newspaper carried a headline story that Don Peppino had been murdered at home.

Now, Little Vinnie argued with Joe Augusta that they should wait even longer before contacting Mickey Boy, but faced a brick wall. Joe, having been told by Little Vinnie that Mickey Boy had murdered the girl who had been watching Laurel, and shaken by the fact that Don Peppino had been killed, unwaveringly insisted that Little Vinnie reach out for Mickey Boy directly, visiting him at home if need be.

"All right, all right," Little Vinnie said. "I think I got a way to reach him, without fucking us up. All we gotta do is take some time to find a place, and then—"

"I have a place," Joe said. "And no arguments. Good or bad, we're going with it." He paused and stared with an intensity that tightened Little Vinnie's bowels.

When Joe Augusta spoke again, it was in a soft, even, frighteningly final tone. "Either that, my friend," he said, "or I am going to kill you myself . . . as originally planned."

84

August 18: Todt Hill, Staten Island

"COULD YOU MEET ME RIGHT NOW?" ROSALIE ASKED THROUGH the phone's receiver. "It's important."

"Where are you?"

"Near your house . . . at the bottom of the hill by the flower place." Rosalie sounded breathless and urgent.

"What is it?" Mickey Boy asked. "Tell me."

"Not on the phone," Rosalie insisted, and hung up.

Mickey Boy cursed to himself. When he needed information passed to the FBI, everyone around him suddenly became smart. Had it been the other way around, where incriminating evidence he needed hidden was to be passed, he was sure Rosalie would have blurted it out.

"What is it?" Freddie asked. He looked up from his task of applying pink circles of calomine lotion to mosquito bites on his legs. Richie lounged across from him, on a club chair in the air-conditioned den, reading the *Daily News* that had been left on their doorstep earlier. He read by lamplight, even in that sunny morning hour, since all blinds remained shut while he was a house guest.

"Rosalie called. I gotta meet her."

"Not without me," Freddie said, pulling down the legs of his white jogging suit.

"Or me," Richie said.

Mickey Boy told Richie to stay where he was, that it could be a setup, just to get him out of the house and in view of Joe Augusta's gun.

"Remember how he killed my old man?" Mickey Boy asked. "With a rifle, from a roof?"

Richie offered to lay on the floor in back of the car. This

way, he said, if something really were up and they had to go get Laurel, they'd be one step ahead.

"Good idea," Freddie quickly said.

Mickey Boy wanted Richie in the house, to be able to contact him there and discuss plans, if there were any. Outside, there was no way for him to get a message to Paul Trantino, whereas any phone call he made to the house would be overheard. His two men's arguments were so correct, though, that he had no choice but to agree.

After Freddie dispensed weapons, three Smith & Wesson Bodyguard Airweight revolvers he'd brought—light, small, with shrouded hammers that wouldn't accidentally get snagged on their clothing—they entered the garage from the house. While Freddie placed himself behind the wheel and Mickey Boy sat next to him, on the passenger side, Richie crawled onto the carpet between the front and back seats. Mickey Boy took a deep breath, then pressed the automatic door opener.

Rosalie ran to the sidewalk as soon as she saw the car, then stopped, waiting for Mickey Boy to come to her.

"Fuck," he cursed under his breath as he left the car, realizing that Trantino had never told him if the FBI had managed to put a bug in it.

Mickey Boy noticed the discoloration on the side of Rosalie's face immediately. Her top lip looked like it had taken a collagen injection.

"What happened?" he asked.

"Little Vinnie, that shit, knew I ratted out his place. He said you croaked his friend," she replied. "That should teach me to stop fucking street guys . . . but that's not important." She handed Mickey Boy a folded slip of paper.

He opened it so quickly, he ripped it along one crease. On it, scrawled in print:

> BOHACK SQUARE
> BACK PLATFORM
> ALONE—JUST YOU 2

"You know where this is?" he asked.
"Never heard of it."

Mickey Boy dashed to the car and bent inside. He showed the note to Freddie and Richie. "Youse know exactly where this is?"

Freddie recognized the proposed exchange spot for Laurel and Richie immediately. "Metropolitan Avenue, Queens," he said. "It's a whole complex they used to distribute to supermarkets from. It's been abandoned for years."

Mickey Boy returned to Rosalie. "Got it. We're gonna take off right now."

Rosalie said, "Vinnie says that he could spot anybody else who's with you, for blocks, that if—"

"Yeah, I know," Mickey Boy said, trying at once to figure out how he'd approach the spot and how he'd let Trantino know where it was. He finally handed Rosalie the note and his keys. "Go wait in my house. My mother went to get a birthday present for my daughter. When she gets back, tell her where I'm going . . . that I went to get the baby her mother for her birthday . . . that we're gonna have a party."

"Me, in your house?"

Mickey Boy kissed her quickly on the cheek. "Why, you ain't good enough to be in my house?"

"Yeah, but—"

"You're just a friend," he said. "Make sure you *tell* her where I'm going." He hesitated, then took the note back from Rosalie. Better safe than sorry. "You remember where it is, right?"

"Yeah . . . Bohack Square."

"Queens. Metropolitan Avenue."

"Yeah, all right."

"Say it."

"Metropolitan Avenue, Queens."

"Good, then just make sure you tell her that." At least now he'd be sure Rosalie wouldn't just hand Connie the note, never giving Paul Trantino a clue to where the exchange was to take place.

Mickey Boy ran back to the car and jumped in. "Let's go," he said, hoping for the first time in his life that his car was bugged. "They're waiting for us there, with Laurel."

Freddie peeled out and headed for the Verrazano Bridge. Suddenly, he spun around to head back in the direction he'd come from.

"What the fuck?" Mickey Boy asked.

"A fuckin' tail," Freddie replied. "Don't worry, I'll lose them."

Gee, thanks, Mickey Boy thought, and cursed his luck again.

Freddie made a series of sharp rights and lefts, then pulled into the open garage of a commercial Italian bread bakery. "Wait here," he said, and trotted into a small office in the warehouse. Two minutes later he ran out.

"Come on," Freddie said. He got behind the wheel of a white step-up van with a long brown Italian bread painted on its side. Mickey Boy and Richie piled in.

Freddie swelled with pride and excitement as he pulled out of the garage and headed for the bridge out of Staten Island. "This way if they followed us by helicopter or waited by the bridge," he said, "they'll be fucked . . . by old Frederico."

Mickey Boy dropped back against his seat and closed his eyes. *And so will we.*

Mickey Boy and Richie stepped tentatively along the filthy yard of Bohack Square. What once had been a distribution center for the popular old supermarket chain had become decrepit after years of abandonment and neglect. Old newsprint, crushed beer cans, and broken glass littered the cement, cracked and dipping itself in spots. Brightly colored graffiti highlighted the ugliness of the bare brick walls.

Freddie Falcone, looking all around and up at the rooftops, brought up the rear. If Joe Augusta wanted Richie as bad as Mickey Boy thought he did, chances were that he would overlook Freddie's presence. Without FBI aid, Mickey Boy gambled in order to get whatever edge he could.

Mickey Boy's skin crawled, thinking of how many rodents and insects must be in the old warehouse buildings. Inside his jacket pocket he tightened his grip on the lightweight revolver Freddie had given him.

Near the rear of the yard Mickey Boy slowly made his way up a few steps to the chest-high platform. Perspiration soaked his entire body.

Mickey Boy stopped, listening for any sounds of movement, swallowed, though his mouth had no moisture, then proceeded to the first door he saw. He tried to pull it by its rusted handle, but it remained locked. He looked at Richie, shook his head, and slowly moved to the next door.

The third door he tried opened.

Musty air, damp and pungent with disuse, filled Mickey Boy's nostrils. Dust scratched his lungs. He motioned Richie to wait in the shadows, and waved Freddie to come forward and accompany him inside. They left the door partly open to light the once-refrigerated warehouse's interior. Mickey Boy was sure some rodent scurried by right in front of him.

He stopped and waited until his eyes adjusted to the darkness. He could see that inside there was another small platform in the back of an enormous warehouse room. Strips of thick plastic curtain still hung on one side, separating what used to be the cold area from the sorting and loading part.

"Don't follow orders well, do you?" Joe Augusta's voice echoed throughout the open space. Mickey Boy stopped. His hand felt clammy on the pistol he held dangling by his thigh.

"Where's DeLuca?" Joe called.

Mickey Boy's heart felt like it would burst. His temples pounded. "He's here," he answered. "Is my wife here?"

Suddenly, on the right side of the rear platform, about fifty feet from where he stood, Little Vinnie stepped forward holding Laurel in front of him.

Mickey Boy gasped, seeing her there, leaning against Little Vinnie as if she were either drunk or in love. His breathing came in deep but unsatisfying drags.

On the left of the platform, Joe Augusta stepped forward so Mickey Boy could see him. In the semidarkness Mickey Boy couldn't see his features too well, but could make out what seemed to be a bulletproof vest. Mickey suddenly became aware of his own vulnerability. He prayed Paul Trantino and his group were nearby, that Tammy had been alerted to spirit him and Laurel away—that he and Laurel would live through this at all.

Joe held an automatic weapon pointed at him, and a smaller gun pointed at Little Vinnie and Laurel. Aware of

Joe's reputation as an expert marksman, Mickey Boy stood in place, without moving. Hearing no sound directly behind him, he knew Freddie had stopped too.

"I want DeLuca," Joe bellowed. "Bring him out."

"Why? What do you want with him?" Mickey Boy asked.

"Stop stalling!" Joe yelled. "I want that cocksucker who killed my baby! I want him now!"

"Joe, I swear, Richie never shot Chrissy. That's why the jury sent him home."

"I told you he would say that!" Little Vinnie screamed.

Joe said, "You mean they couldn't prove he was a child killer. Bring him out, or your wife dies!"

Where was the line that he would have to step over, Mickey Boy wondered, where he would have to sacrifice either Laurel or Richie? He felt dangerously close, as sweat soaked him and his heart threatened to burst out of his chest.

"Joe, I swear, on my baby daughter—an' you gotta know how much I love her—like you did your daughter . . . that Richie didn't do it."

"Why don't you tell him that that piece of shit Vinnie did it?" Freddie yelled from behind. "You didn't tell him that, did you, scumbag?" Freddie shouted to Little Vinnie.

"I told you, Joe. Didn't I tell you what they'd try to do?" Little Vinnie screamed. "They're full of shit!"

Mickey Boy heard the click of Joe's gun being readied to fire. "My baby's dead," Joe said. "My poor innocent baby. I have to end this now . . . no more time . . . no more tricks . . . no more pain." Joe remained silent for a moment, then said, "By the power vested in me, by the Almighty and by the Angel, Christina Marie Augusta, beloved child of Joseph and Theresa, and loving sister of Elizabeth, I now sentence her killer to death . . . or, as a temporary replacement, the children of the devil, Vincenze Calabra . . . and the whore that would bear their offspring."

"Joe, you fuck," Freddie screamed. "I swear to you, on the sacred oath we took, that Little Vinnie shot Chrissy . . . it was an accident, he didn't know it was her."

"Joe, no," Little Vinnie cried. "I swear, it was Richie."

"Shut up! All of you!" Joe screamed. "Vinnie, did you do it? Did you kill my baby?"

"No, Joe, I swear—"

"DeLuca? Richie, where are you?"

Mickey Boy heard footsteps behind him. "Joe, it's me," Richie said. "I'm here, but I never shot her, Joe. Please, let Laurel go."

"Come closer, Richie," Joe said. "I can't see you."

"Joe, let her go, please," Richie begged. "I didn't kill Chrissy, but I'll come closer and let you do what you want, if only you let her go."

"Joe, he's lying! He did it!" Little Vinnie cried.

"Stop! Stop!" Joe screamed. "You'll both die . . . all of you! Richie, come here or the girl dies by three. One . . ."

While Freddie, Richie, and Little Vinnie all pleaded with Joe Augusta, Mickey Boy remained silent. He inched forward, holding his breath, trying to get close enough to get off accurate shots.

". . . two . . ."

Suddenly, Little Vinnie shoved Laurel toward the front of the platform. Mickey Boy saw her go over the edge and began to run toward her, firing his pistol at Joe Augusta at the same time. Shots blasted all around, in front and in back, deafening Mickey Boy as he ran. His heart seemed to pound in stereo as his body moved in slow motion.

Joe fired in two directions at once, flame pointing at Little Vinnie and the charging Mickey Boy. Shots kept coming from behind.

Mickey Boy saw Little Vinnie thrown backward, blood exploding from his back. A sharp jolt hit Mickey Boy in the chest, searing him inside and momentarily stopping his forward movement. He got hit again, this time in the stomach. Churning his legs in Laurel's direction, like a fullback hitting a line, he moved forward for a few steps until his legs turned rubbery and collapsed under him. Ear-shattering gunfire continued as Mickey Boy hit the concrete floor face first, his pistol scattering across the floor and pain bursting in his head.

Mickey Boy stretched one arm toward Laurel. He tried to call her, but couldn't bring up any sound. Numbness below the waist and agony above it overcame his attempt to crawl. He lay there, face smashed against the murky wet floor, silently begging forgiveness from Laurel and telling her he loved her.

Iciness inside him moved from his feet up toward his chest.

Breath wouldn't come . . .

Then, nothing.

Epilogue

May 22: Clearwater, Florida

MICKEY LOOKED OUT AT THE PINKS, PURPLES, AND GOLDS THAT ushered out the day, reflecting off the shimmery Gulf waters. He breathed in the humid air with respect. That he might not have been breathing at all never stayed far from his thoughts, and he felt lucky despite the daily pain of healed wounds he lived with. Living was enough.

Across the deck of his waterfront home, Laurel slept on a chaise longue, her face crunched with an intense suffering Mickey hoped would eventually leave. So far, private therapy with Dr. Williams had brought her from not speaking to anyone at all to carrying on neutral conversations. She still became seized occasionally by bouts of crying, but they came less frequently now and lasted for shorter periods of time. One day, Dr. Williams promised, the demons of Laurel's past experiences would be almost totally under control. Never one hundred percent, but enough for her to appreciate tomorrow more than bleed over yesterday.

Mickey shifted in his chair, feeling stabs of pain where bullets had torn muscle and bone. One rib had been totally removed; only one lung operated at full strength; his stomach had been pared down to eliminate a damaged area. At least it had helped him lose the weight he'd been unable to shed before, he'd joked recently, over the phone with Tammy. Now, he'd said, his heart would last longer from less baggage it had to pump for.

Mickey looked at the painkillers on the patio snack table, but decided to bear his discomfort for a while longer. Addiction scared him more than pain.

Connie, Mickey's mother, stepped out onto the patio. In her arms, Hope wiggled and reached out for Mickey. She gave Hope to Mickey, careful to place the baby on his good side and not directly on his wounded area, then looked toward where Laurel slept. In a low voice she said, "I told Maria to go home early. Is that okay?"

"Yeah, fine." He felt more private and normal without the combination nurse and housekeeper around anyway.

"The baby is all bathed and in bed."

"Good," Mickey said. Albert Frederico Messina, born just two months before, had become the first of Connie's grandchildren to be born male. Mickey had been saddened by the fact that it was a boy.

Despite Laurel's refusal to discuss her captivity, the feeling that she might have been sexually assaulted by Little Vinnie gnawed at him. He would never forget how she'd clung to Little Vinnie before the fireworks began, or how Vinnie had saved her life and sacrificed his own by pushing her away from him.

If that were the case, if Laurel had indeed had sex with Little Vinnie, it would be virtually impossible to distinguish who actually was the father, since both he and Little Vinnie shared a common father and were similar enough in appearance that Mickey Boy had been sentenced to prison for crimes Little Vinnie had committed.

Thinking that the child was cursed to be a boy and carry Calabra blood, Mickey had named him Albert, after his stepfather and Connie's only husband, the late Albert Messina. Al Messina had been one of the most decent, honest human beings Mickey had ever known. Maybe that small symbolic naming would help counter the criminal genes the baby carried. That, and a lot of prayers.

The fact that Albert could be his was enough to allow

Mickey to show him affection at all; the chance that he wasn't limited that affection.

Mickey hugged Hope, as if to compensate for the dark spot in his heart for Albert. Hope snuggled her head under his chin, the heat emanating from her head telling him she was ready to sleep herself.

"Come on," Connie said, reaching for Hope. "Say good night to Dada."

When Hope pulled away from her, Mickey told his mother to leave her alone. He could put Hope in her crib after she fell asleep. He kissed Hope's damp hair.

"I'm going to get ready, then. Nicolo is coming to take me to dinner."

Mickey smiled. At least Connie had a companion now, he thought. She certainly deserved it. And who was a better companion than Nicolo Fonte? As Connie rushed off, Mickey chuckled to himself, wondering if his mother and Fonte were lovers too.

Nicolo Fonte had been the last of the caravan that Mickey had led down to Florida. A bachelor, Fonte insisted he was free and wanted to assist Mickey for at least the first few months of his recuperation. As time passed, however, Fonte settled in nearby, and he'd revived Mickey's interest in opening a pasta house. No worries now about having to fight their own people to provide them a better future. No one to worry about but themselves. Next week they would be signing a lease for a store in a brand-new strip mall.

No, Fonte was there for good, God bless him, and mob life was gone forever. An occasional call from Freddie, still full of jokes and wisecracks, was the closest Mickey came to the life he'd shed. And then nothing other than how Mickey and his family were doing, or that Freddie and Richie were physically well, was ever discussed. The less he knew about what was going on in New York, the better.

Now, as he looked out at the horizon fading into night, Mickey felt happier and more at peace with himself than he'd ever been. The road had been rough, but now he saw a future as calm as the water. No bumps, no falls, no nights spent anywhere but in his own bed, no one knocking at his door to drag him off to jail.

The only lawman Mickey ever heard from was Paul

Trantino, and that was only via holiday cards, like the one he'd recently received for Easter. Paul had certainly lived up to his word on that one, keeping law enforcement off his back. One day, Paul had written in the card, when he traveled to Florida to visit his father, he would like to stop by and say hello in person, maybe fish a little in the Gulf. He never mentioned the agony Mickey knew he felt at not having been able to capture Joe Augusta, who'd doubly outfoxed the authorities by having snatched his wife and daughter from under their noses, in Canada, and disappeared again.

Despite all that Joe had done, Mickey could understand the pain that had motivated him. God forbid anyone ever harmed his darling daughter, Hope. In a strange way, he wished Joe well, wherever he was—as long as it was far away from the Messina household. He felt sure, though, that he had nothing to fear from Joe Augusta; that Joe's quest for revenge had been finally satisfied with Little Vinnie's death. Not that worrying about the alternative would do him any good anyway.

Closing his eyes, Mickey could hear Frank Sinatra singing to him personally, in his mind. *The record shows, I took the blows . . . and did it my way.*

Then, with Hope clutched tightly in his arms, Mickey drifted off into sleep.

Read about the
SHOCKING and
BIZARRE
Crimes of our Times from Pocket Books